# The Van Helsing Incursion

## Evelyn Chartres
*(Nom de Plume)*

### 2020

Ottawa, Ontario

# ABOUT

During the Roaring Twenties, Clara Grey hunted things that went bump in the night. On her last mission, she paid the ultimate price to rid the world of a powerful foe. As a reward, she ascended to Heaven and joined its ranks as an angel.

Ninety years after her death, Clara fell to Earth, intent on saving a soul. While successful, killing an old god in self-defence barred her from returning to Heaven. Lost in the modern world, Clara was forced to seek unlikely allies to navigate through these uncertain times.

Four months later, Clara has settled in with Elizabeth, a young woman she saved shortly after descending to Earth. For a gal who had sworn off anything that hinted at normalcy, Clara learns that being average takes more effort than she suspected.

Alas, repercussions from choices made on that fateful mission have not been idle. Her enemies trigger a chain of events that forces our fated femme fatale to act. Is Clara prepared to deal with the fallout? Will her allies come to her aid? Or must she stand on her own?

Before reading on, be sure to consider: Hunting things that go bump in the night is child's play when compared to juggling relationships.

# CONTENTS

# ACKNOWLEDGEMENTS

I wish to thank everyone who helped make this novel a reality. Namely, those who were integral to the process.

Thank you to K.C. Bloom for her insights on the mechanics of certain scenes. She is not only a great author, but also lends her expertise to those within the writing community. What more could a gal ask for?

Thank you to Pamela Belyea, for her diligence in scouring my manuscript for all manner of faults. She is proof positive that no amount of self-revision can successfully purge all flaws. While there will always be something, I am certain that the most glaring offenders have come to light.

Lastly, I wish to thank A.V. Kott, Kayla Ray Tidwell, Simon Hillman, and those who indulged in my Saturday Scenes submissions, several brave souls who read through my work during their early incarnations. These are my beacons in the night, proof that I am not navigating these waters alone.

Evelyn Chartres (*Nom de plume*)
theportraitofawoman@gmail.com
http://evelynchartres.com

# CHAPTER 1

## *THEY'RE MAGICALLY DELICIOUS*

Clara had been lying flat against the snow-covered ground since the witching hour. The sky was taking on red hues, and the moon would soon secede its dominion over the celestial plain.

She maintained a low heart rate while her movements were kept to an absolute minimum. Freshly fallen snow had accumulated during the night, all of which helped to conceal her position.

In truth, Clara was toasty warm since her ghillie suit was both warm and waterproof; the perfect balance of modern and natural materials. Not only did it help her to blend in, but it also imbued the wearer with the ability to endure long periods outside in the cold without freezing to death.

Up ahead, there was a black cauldron, about the size of her head, which overflowed with gold. Logic dictated that it should have been covered by the falling snow, but the precious metal continued to glisten in the crepuscular light.

That was expected, since Clara had sensed something was wrong the moment she entered the clearing. There was a darkness to this place, unearthly and impure. Hunters from the Tower, a secret order that preyed on monsters of myth, would have known to steer clear. That or raze the place to the ground, and salt the earth for good measure.

"Six deaths in the last month, and all of them centred on this area," Clara voiced silently to herself as a way to busy her mind.

All of these deaths had been classified as freak accidents, each so noteworthy that the news of those deaths had spread throughout the world like wildfire. Not because of the hilarity, although a few heartless souls would certainly think so, but due to the improbable series of unfortunate events needed to make such a death possible.

A recent macabre article mentioned how a man narrowly avoided a runaway parked car, only to slip on some ice and fall on his ass. While he counted his blessings, a mysterious funnel cloud formed in the area channelling cold air from the upper atmosphere into the troposphere, flesh freezing some hapless raven in mid-flap. Before the funnel dissipated, the *birdcicle* was sent hurtling towards the unsuspecting victim with enough force to tear through his chest.

If not for nearby traffic and security footage, investigators would have not been able to piece together what happened. As it stood, no one questioned why the victim was found without his gold watch, chain, and fillings.

"Vermin," Clara added in silence as her eyes narrowed to focus on faint movement in the distance.

Of course, the other goldbergian-style deaths only served as a catalyst for the conspiracy theorists. Who could blame them? Clara had been just as drawn in by the suspicious nature of these *accidents*, not to mention their proximity to one another. The difference was, Clara had a good idea about the threat she faced.

Clara held a white crossbow that blended in perfectly with the snow, except for the draw string, cables and cams. Fortunately, the snow had built up over those components, along with the spring-loaded prongs that defined the bolt's tip.

Now that this creature had broken through the opposing treeline, the movements ahead were more overt. Despite the twilight, Clara made out what she was up against. There it was. About the size of a cat, but standing upright, it was dressed in green with elfin ears and fiery red hair.

"Bastard," Clara mouthed before adopting a smile that went ear to ear because she was right.

Dead ahead, the leprechaun stared at the gold Clara left behind as bait. It left no traces of its passing in the snow, a detail they missed during her lectures back at the Tower. How odd? Although, it did much to explain how such creatures remained undetected for so long.

Even with the growing sense of anticipation, Clara remained perfectly still. She kept an eye open for any surprises, even as a snowflake reached her iris. Despite the discomfort, Clara kept her eyes on this creature because she only had one shot at this.

It moved very much like a bird, the motions quick and jarring. Clara watched and anticipated a pattern to evolve, but found none. The moves appeared to be random, but sometimes such observations were nothing more than a matter of perspective.

On a hunch, Clara focused until the snowfall was nearly arrested. The ability to manipulate her interaction with time, increased strength, and enhanced healing made up the bulk of an angel's arsenal. Unfortunately, running in an accelerated state was, ironically, time limited.

In this state, she noticed that the creature phased out of existence, only to reappear in another location a split second later. Prior to every move, the leprechaun scanned its surroundings, conscious of there being a rival. Who else marked their territory by leaving behind a large quantity of gold? Well, other than this femme fatale who was hell bent on its eradication.

"That's it," Clara said to herself once she understood what was going on.

With the creature in range, she slowed down time even more, enough to identify every phase of its movements in detail. When the leprechaun completed its look-around, it would appear to be in two places at once.

Next, Clara took in two deep breaths which was followed by a long exhale. As the precursor became visible, she focused on that spot, depressed the trigger, and let loose a bolt.

To reduce her agonising wait, Clara returned to normal speed just in time to hear the loud thwack of the string coming home, followed by the blur of the bolt. Just as quickly, the leprechaun wildly changed direction and bounced across the snow-covered ground. Eventually, the bolt struck a tree, and stopped cold, leaving a trail of golden blood behind.

The snow fell off in clumps as Clara stood. She stretched out her back and neck while her wings unfurled to their full size.

"Hmmm, that feels nice," Clara said with a smile.

Casually, she sauntered towards the tree and kept an eye out for any other potential threats. That's when she noticed how eerily quiet it was. Her attack had shifted the balance in this cursed grove and curiously, caused the wind and snow to die down.

The uneasy silence may have left her feeling leery, but that changed once she approached the tree. A high-pitched squeal reached her ears, sounding more like a wounded rodent than a legitimate threat. It was fortunate for Clara that she knew better.

The golden colour of its blood took on the colour of rust. Just like it did when she bled… or any old god for that matter. For any other hunter, such details meant nothing because they were never meant to know about gods and goddesses.

Her interactions with Hecate had opened her eyes to the old gods and goddesses who still cursed this world. While she still knew very little about them, Clara did know they could bleed and be killed. So, she guessed that this was either a minion, or a construct of an old god. *Just how bored are those golden-blooded bastards to create such pests? How bored were they to create something like me?*

From where she stood, Clara had a great view of the leprechaun. It was exactly what she imagined it would look like, what with the red hair, small tailored green suit, and bulbous hat. She was even tempted to giggle but knew better than to give away her state of mind. Given the theme, she settled on naming it Sean.

"Curse you!" Sean exclaimed in Gaelic upon seeing the fallen angel.

Clara grinned widely before replying, "I've already been banished from the Kingdom of Heaven. I doubt there is enough left in you to do worse than that."

The shaft was embedded into Sean's shoulder which left the rest of the bolt intact. The blood trail had originated from lesions on its head and bare hands which made sense given the rough ride. Even now, despite this creature's magical properties, the wounds were bleeding with no sign of healing.

"I'll get—" Sean tried to say.

"Get me?" Clara asked. "My, my, don't we have a temper."

Clara reached down into the snow and picked up a metallic line, the one that led all the way to a pile located near her crossbow and terminated at the knock of the bolt. She yanked on the line and pulled the creature closer to her, just like a fisherman reeling in her fish.

"Stop!" Sean yelled.

"Why?" Clara asked with a grin.

For a moment there was silence. Clara could not catch any stray sounds or heartbeats in the area, other than their own. Still, a light breeze picked up from behind, one that carried forth the scent of wet dog.

"Oddly familiar," Clara muttered, unable to place the odour.

"Gold," Sean said.

"Gold?" Clara asked. "You really think that I'm some biscuit who hangs on to the arm of any man who flashes their money clip?"

Sean looked at her suspiciously. These types of bargains had been going on for millennia. The act of surrendering their ill-gotten goods nearly always worked in their favour. Chiefly, it helped that their gold was cursed, damning the victor to a fate worse than death.

"Either way," Clara added. "The illusion that conceals the true nature of this place will end once you die."

"No! Anything," Sean said.

"So, what do you have for little ole me?" Clara prodded.

"A path to your realm…" Sean said.

"My realm?" Clara asked.

The leprechaun did not elaborate. However, its eyes were darting from one corner of the woods to the other in fear. Clara guessed that Sean was worried that too much had been said.

"You mean Heaven?" Clara confirmed.

Once more, the smell of wet dog wafted in her general direction. She froze time for a fraction of a second and took the opportunity to look behind her. Again, there was nothing out of place, nor any sign of a threat.

"Curiouser and curiouser," Clara mumbled.

Sean merely nodded but did not reply. That left her to wonder if the mere mention of the name triggered an undesirable reaction.

"You can't say it," Clara said. "Can you?"

Sean could only nod, and Clara left it at that. Of course, there was a tactical advantage to finding new ways in and out the place from which she was banished. Still, she doubted they had forgiven her for killing an old god who suffered from a serious case of multiple personalities. They had deemed it a case of interference in their internal affairs.

"Where is it then?" Clara asked holding the line taut to make this interrogation more interesting.

"H-H-Here!" Sean stuttered.

"How?" Clara asked.

Sean focused those hate filled eyes on the angel. If looks could kill, Clara would have died then and there. Fortunately, once had been more than enough.

"How?" Clara repeated sternly, this time twisting her hand to reel Sean in.

"Blood sacrifice… on … gateway…" Sean managed to say.

"Destinations can be controlled?" Clara asked.

"For… your kind?" Sean said before a sickly grin came across its lips. "Never!"

Clara caught the sound of the arrow's tip falling off. So, she pulled out a pen-sized device with a red button affixed at the top from of her pocket. Without hesitation, she flipped off the protective cover and pressed the button three times in quick succession. As her thumb rammed the button home for the last time, the arrow blew apart. *Odd, it sounded just like a firecracker going off.*

The explosion originated from within the bolt's shaft, and tore through Sean's torso. The look of surprise on what was left of this thing's face was priceless.

"Horsefeathers," Clara swore, knowing that she might have been able to gain more intel. However, that would have required her to be vigilant and ensure that this thing had no recourse of escape.

"I'm getting rusty," Clara said.

On a hunch, she turned towards the centre of the clearing and found a tall mirror that resembled an oculus. Upon closer inspection, she discovered that the surface had the feel of cold steel but was non-reflective. Even in the light of the moon, two nights away from being full, and a peeking sun, the surface did not reflect anything.

With nothing to lose, Clara pulled on the wire to drag what was left of the corpse toward her. She smeared some of its blood onto the surface and watched the oculus flicker with what appeared to be a reflection. Alas, the reaction was too brief to catch more than a glimpse of the other side.

"It must need a fresh specimen," Clara murmured while mulling over the idea of using her own blood.

While the idea had merit, she had a sinking suspicion that there was truth to Sean's last words. Besides, testing a magical gateway in such an isolated area, without taking precautions, left her vulnerable.

Clara walked towards the edge of the clearing, specifically the spot where she had been waiting. She then took an additional five steps and pulled out a duffel bag from a snow drift.

She unzipped the bag and rummaged around for a bit until she came upon a series of sturdy resealable plastic baggies. Clara was not thrilled at the idea but could not leave the creature behind. She imagined what happen if a group of kids came across the remnants of a leprechaun.

"Time to clean up," Clara said while heading towards the bloody mess.

* * * *

After loading her gear out back, Clara hopped into the truck. She had ditched the ghillie suit in favour of a black greatcoat, toque and a pair of jeans. Being practical, she opted to wear the same boots. These featured a waterproof lining and were reinforced with steel shanks, which put what soldiers wore during the Great War to shame.

Fog billowed out from her mouth every time she exhaled, which brought forth memories of her brief childhood. For a moment, she hung on to the cherished memory of the buttoned nosed version of herself throwing snowballs at her sisters. Alas, she was soon reminded of the work that remained, all thanks to her phone.

"Yeah. Yeah," Clara said dryly.

She looked up at the vanity mirror to make sure there was no blood and saw those steel-grey eyes reflected back at her. Given the sharp facial features, pointed ears, and dark-brown shoulder length hair, this was a woman who had no trouble luring men, or women for that matter. The latter was a positive development from the social norms of her youth.

During the Roaring Twenties, female hunters were expected to manipulate people, especially men. Those in her line of work had to hide in plain sight, and there was nothing better to avoid getting noticed than posing as a couple in love. It provided them with a patsy and permitted their partner to lurk in the shadows. Such skills were also invaluable for information extraction and wealth redistribution, which Clara had been rather good at. No surprise, since the Tower had gone through a great deal of trouble to make sure she was.

"The ability to hook-up every day of the week but have no desire to follow through," Clara said.

When she turned the key in her ignition, the vehicle roared to life, and the ventilation blasted a jet of cool air into her face. Clara ignored the annoyance, knowing that the cabin would soon be toasty warm once the engine warmed up. *Besides, I have heated leather seats.*

While waiting for the engine to settle, Clara synched up her phone with the car and brought up mapping software to get a better prediction on the traffic conditions. It turned out that getting into the city would not be pleasant at this time of day which was a problem since she needed to get onto the island. Still, there were options, and there was enough time to make the ferry.

With an idea of the route and the vehicle beginning to warm up, Clara slipped out of her greatcoat and let her wings expand. She then wrapped them around her seat, buckled up, and put the vehicle in gear.

"Wonder if I'll get a tongue lashing today?" Clara asked before letting off a long and woeful sigh.

Since there was no way of avoiding her fate, Clara decided it was time for a distraction. With that in mind, she paused, grinned, and pressed down on the throttle. As the rear-wheels bit into the ice and snow, they sent rocks and ice flying behind her.

"May as well have some fun before I reach the main road," Clara said.

\* \* \* \*

Clara raced up the stairs, skipping every second step just because she could. When she arrived on the landing, a neighbour opened his door to take a peek at the one who dared make all that noise. When he caught sight of her in the greatcoat, the man shut his door as quietly as possible to avoid making eye contact.

"Good ole Eugene," Clara said remembering their last heart-to-heart talk, which effectively put the fear of God into him.

She made her way down to the end of the hall, and despite the weight in those boots, there was a spring in her step. In her hands, she held a set of keys, jiggling away as she focused on what was taking place on the other side of that door.

There was one person inside, someone with a heart rate low enough to assume they were either meditating or sleeping. With a bit more concentration, Clara discerned that the alarm was not going off, nor were there any other sounds associated with someone waking up.

"That gal loves to sleep," Clara said lightly and hoped that this storm would pass by without incident.

With her key, Clara unlocked the deadbolt before stepping inside. To her left there was a row of wall-mounted hooks, which she used to hang up her greatcoat. She always felt better knowing it was there, in case there was a need to make a quick exit.

Further out on her left, she walked into the kitchen and turned on the coffee machine. For now, it was quiet, but soon it would be burping and gurgling away to fill the carafe below.

She ignored the dirty dishes floating around in the sink, along with any other visible mess. This was one of the few disadvantages to living with Elizabeth, the woman she saved from a certain death last fall. That gal's ability to spread dust and dirt around the house was classifiable as a plague. *So what? I'm happy? Right?*

"Am I?" Clara asked absentmindedly, while pulling out some ingredients from the fridge.

* * * *

After a half an hour and five snooze alarms later, Elizabeth lumbered out of the bedroom. The tall woman of mixed Asian and European descent was half-naked, and due to her bust size, the bathrobe barely covered her breasts.

Clara permitted herself to slow down time for a moment, long enough to get a good view of her roommate without making it obvious. Despite the heavy bloodshot eyes, gaping mouth, and wild hair, she really was a betty. Clara's eyes ran over every detail of those long flowing legs, flat stomach, and ample chest before letting out a soft gasp.

"They say that winter is a time for hibernation," Clara said after noticing the five o'clock shadow around Elizabeth's berry patch and legs.

Elizabeth never said a word. She rarely did before getting in her first sip of coffee. Instead, she stumbled into the bathroom, and soon the water could be heard running.

"Either that or she's given up trying to impress me," Clara said to finish her thought.

* * * *

It took thirty minutes for Elizabeth to shower, get dressed, and come out a changed woman. A chrysalis of sorts, which shed away that grumpy caterpillar, and left a magnificent butterfly. Albeit, one suitably dressed to work as a social worker.

Clara smiled warmly as her friend entered the kitchen and poured herself a fresh cup of brew. This portion of the morning was sacred, as though communing with a god. She would wrap her hands around the ceramic mug, let the heat soak into her hands, and relish in the decadent aroma.

"Good morning," Elizabeth said with a deeply contented sigh.

"Morning," Clara said in a light tone while getting the plate ready.

"What's on the menu today?" Elizabeth asked.

Clara beamed a wide grin before replying, "A spinach and smoked gouda scramblet with a side of bacon and lightly buttered whole grain toast."

"A scramblet?" Elizabeth asked before picking up a plate, because Clara always let her choose.

Clara nodded before answering, "Well, it should have been an omelette, but I screwed up so…"

"Ah! I get it," Elizabeth replied. "That's cute."

The girls sat down at the table and began to eat in silence. Elizabeth invariably needed a few minutes to get acquainted with her breakfast before opening up. It was as though she was afraid that the food would spoil.

"You weren't here last night," Elizabeth said dryly.

To many, this could have been interpreted as a question, one that provided the recipient with an opportunity to come up with an excuse. Preferably, one delivered with enough eloquence to sway the hearts of a jury. However, Clara knew from the tone that this was an observation.

Clara wiped her lips and excused herself from the table. While heading to the sink, she picked up a baggy filled with something akin to a forgotten lunch that had been discovered in the depths of a backpack after months.

"No," Clara said calmly. "I had some hunting to do."

"You promised me that you'd be here at night," Elizabeth said anxiously.

Upon hearing those words, Clara quickly spotted the empty bottle of bourbon in the living room. That certainly explained the rough start to Elizabeth's morning, she concluded.

"We talked about this," Clara said before pouring the contents of the baggy into the sink.

After a quick splash of water, she turned on the garburator. The noise gave her a moment to prepare for the onslaught. Unfortunately, a green viscous liquid splattered against the backsplash. Clara grumbled and pulled out a rag to clean up the mess before it stained.

Elizabeth had been watching from the comfort of the table. She had no idea what was going on, and frankly, had no desire to find out… yet.

"You told me that you'd provide for my safety at night, until I—" Elizabeth began angrily.

"You were," Clara said while scrubbing the grout with a stiff bristled brush and an abrasive cleaner. "She—"

"She? You had *her* look out for my safety?" Elizabeth demanded.

That was the clincher. This particular *she* was the very same vampire who tried to kill Elizabeth. Without Clara's intervention, they would not be having this discussion nor have access to the financing and arsenal necessary to keep hunting in the modern world. Despite their alliance, Elizabeth was understandably distrustful, and with good reason. Although, Evelyn knew full well that there would be severe repercussions if Elizabeth's feelings ended up getting hurt.

"She promised—" Clara said but refused to face Elizabeth.

"She fucking tried to kill me!" Elizabeth yelled, loud enough that the words reverberated throughout the room.

"Pause… two… three…" Clara whispered.

Clara considered using the pretext of saving a life to guilt Elizabeth. While that might have been effective, it came at the cost of bulldozing over her friend's legitimate feelings.

Instead, Clara engaged the garburator after saying, "I'm sorry."

"You're sorry?" The wide-eyed Elizabeth said. "You break your promise in the worst way imaginable, and that's all you have to say?"

"You're right," Clara said while turning around, but remained behind the kitchen island. "I wasn't thinking."

Elizabeth scoffed and paused as her mind mulled over scenarios that would keep this fight going. Still, silence filled the room, suffocating them, but Clara was not about to speak out of turn.

"Did you get it?" Elizabeth finally asked to end the deafening silence.

"Get what?" Clara queried.

"The thing you were hunting for?" Elizabeth asked.

"Oh," Clara said meekly. "Yes, I did."

Elizabeth looked down at her food, or at least what was left of it. She was no longer feeling it, so it seemed like an opportune time to ask.

"What was it?" Elizabeth asked.

"A leprechaun," Clara replied.

"As in, they're magically delicious?" Elizabeth asked before mimicking some lines from that childhood jingle.

Clara had absolutely no clue what her friend was driving at. Instead of showing her ignorance on popular culture beyond the Twenties, she opted for a bit of humour.

"More like maniacally devious," Clara said in all seriousness. "At least, this bastard won't be bothering anyone anymore."

"Good," Elizabeth said but gagged once she realised what was in that baggy. "So, tonight?"

"Of course," Clara said with a smile.

They locked on to one another's eyes and kept on their best fake smiles. Deep down Clara knew this was not over since betrayal, even as a matter of appearance, was hard to soothe over.

Elizabeth finished off the last piece of bacon, wiped her mouth, and headed towards the door. Meanwhile, Clara turned back to the kitchen, determined to make Sean's remains disappear. A shame that she could not simply snap her fingers and make it vanish.

"I'm off!" Elizabeth shouted!

"Wha—" Clara said over the infernal racket.

The sound of the door's locking mechanism being engaged reached her just as the garbage disposal was flipped off. She stared at the door for a minute or two, sighed deeply, and returned to work.

"So, I have about an hour to clean up before a workout," Clara managed to say before another splotch of green spewed forth from the depths of the drain. "Awww nerts."

# CHAPTER 2

## *OF MONSTERS AND MEN*

The wind picked up as the sun peeked over the concrete horizon. Despite the winter chill, the sight of daylight brought a smile to Elizabeth's face. It meant that the world was a bit safer since she only needed to worry about thieves, muggers, murderers, and rapists.

A cab blew by, slammed its brakes, and narrowly avoided another. The squeal and the heated exchange of horns that followed sent a wave of pain travelling straight from her eardrums to the centre of her forehead. The throbbing was a painful reminder of last night's drinking binge. To feel functional, she popped some pills to dull the pain.

"Impact," Elizabeth said through her teeth.

She stopped near an empty bench long enough to bring up her coat's collar to cut the wind driving down her back. As a precaution, she scanned the area but found no trace of Clara. Was it even possible to be certain that her *friend* was not lurking about?

When the altercation between the cabbies grew worse, Elizabeth remembered there was somewhere she needed to be. Alas, she would have preferred to call in sick, but their exchange of heated words had driven her out of the house.

Elizabeth walked on in silence, nursing her hangover while contemplating her lot in life. Introspection was not necessarily a bad thing, seeing that it gave her an opportunity to delve into her life objectively. Like how she once considered humanity to be on top of the food chain.

She might still believe it if it were not for the ex-girlfriend's attempt on her life, all for looking into a friend's disappearance. Sure, she looked innocent, harmless, and sexy as fuck, but that did little to alter the fact that this was actually a four-hundred-year-old vampire.

The memory of Evelyn's last words never failed to send a chill down her spine. Fortunately, the sign denoting access to the subway station countered the effect. Elizabeth scurried into the bowels of the city and escaped the elements above.

"Impact," Elizabeth repeated.

Today might have goten off to a great start had she been able to get a good night's sleep. Clara may have been the one to save her from Evelyn's plan, but that did not let her off the hook for breaking a promise, one that would be fulfilled once things *settled*.

"Settled," Elizabeth scoffed.

A passer-by stared at her, confused. Elizabeth put on her best false smile and hurried on by while her cheeks radiated with heat.

"In a city this big, one would think that people would have stopped giving a shit by now," Elizabeth muttered.

How long would it take for her to accept that she might become a late-night snack for a vampire? Or end up fertilising the forest floor in the form of werewolf scat? This was not some run of the mill concern that could be brought up as casually as the weather. It could not be brought up with her workmates or within the confines of a support group. After all, people were committed for making such assertions.

The only person she could talk to about this new reality was Clara. Alas, Elizabeth was not convinced that her friend did not have demons of her own to contend with. How could she not after living through all that death and tragedy? How many were capable of maintaining a semblance of normalcy after decapitating their first childhood crush in a bid to save their own life?

*"She did have a reason for shirking her responsibilities," Elizabeth's internal voice said.*

At first, the voice was faint, drowned out by all of that anxiety and doubt swirling within. Still, with every reverberation, it gained clarity. Her friend had been talking about this mission for at least a week. Elizabeth was very much aware that Clara had briefed her about the alternate arrangements. Of course, Evelyn's name never came up during that exchange.

*"One night spent drinking away your fear, compared to saving countless lives,"* her voice added.

Elizabeth paused long enough for those words to sink in. Had her friend been bound to this promise, they would have caught news of more freak accidents. Could Clara live with the fact that an innocent died due to her inaction?

The thought left her cold and numb. Her musing had turned into a revelation, which was not what she hoped for. Still one rarely controlled the occurrence of such events.

"I have her on a leash," Elizabeth whispered.

Well not precisely, Clara was free to come and go as she pleased, all within reason. So why was this fallen angel sticking around? Sure, there were a lot of reasons initially, but she was a quick study. Heck, Clara understood the features on her phone better than she did.

"Duty—," Elizabeth said before running into someone

"Excuse me," a nondescript man said before circling around her.

"Sorry…" Elizabeth said in a milquetoast fashion.

Elizabeth watched as the man melted into the crowd. Only then did she realise that the mass of people was fast multiplying.

"I'm running late," Elizabeth said as she passed through the turnstiles.

There must have been more to Clara staying than honour and duty? Her friend had even gone out on a few dates, at Elizabeth's insistence, but always came back disappointed. Every date brought forth a new excuse, each more fantastical than the last. Was Clara hanging around for something? Someone?

"For me?" Elizabeth asked.

For the bulk of the morning, Elizabeth had been chilled to the bone but suddenly needed to loosen a few buttons now. Still, something was missing from the big picture, a tiny detail that continued to elude her.

"She wants me to take the lead?" Elizabeth asked in a whisper.

That question floated up to the forefront of her thoughts. Why would a woman like that not just take what she desired? It was clear they had chemistry, that was evident from the moment they met. God knows there had been many a night spent alone and frustrated. Toys were no help at all, not when the answer to all her frustrations slept on the couch outside her room.

As she approached the subway, a thought flashed through her mind, "Perhaps I should send her a message and apologise?"

When she reached into her purse, the voice from earlier asserted, "*Just remember that she had Evelyn make sure you weren't harmed.*"

With that thought, Elizabeth let the phone drop right back into her purse and zipped it up. As her jaw tensed, the developing picture in her mind's eye was marred by the emotional turmoil swirling within.

"I'll give her a bit more time to stew," Elizabeth said while boarding.

When the train lurched forward, Elizabeth darted her head from side to side, searching for something. Eventually, a look of confusion overtook her facial features. She could have sworn that someone had been giggling with glee when she got in.

* * * *

The curved steel blade cut off a series of buttons as it travelled over Clara's shirt. It was fortunate that her back had already been rounded towards the ground in an attempt to avoid the strike.

When the blade cleared the girls, Clara continued on her trajectory. She then used her arms as a pivot which sent her legs flying upwards. Near the apex, Clara's left boot made contact with her assailant's face which sent him looking straight up at the ceiling.

Her right boot followed and pushed against the assailant to get some distance. As he moved backwards in response, Clara sprung up and landed on her feet a couple of yards away. The two stood there in opposition, knowing that both had left their mark.

Clara sighed while looking down at the three missing buttons from her white shirt. Without much thought, she tore off the rest and let the shirt puddle to the ground. All that remained was her sports bra to maintain some modesty.

She held the shotgun in her hands, an old school breech loader with an over and under barrel. The weapon shone in the light, especially in areas used to block this swordsman's attack.

"You'll need to up your game if you want to see them," Clara said with a smirk. When the other said nothing in response, she added, "By the by, they *are* fabulous."

Clara watched her attacker run an arm across his face to wipe away most of the blood. That strike had broken the skin on his lower lip, nothing serious, but that would be a feather in her cap.

This man's physique was a work of art despite being no taller than the average woman these days. He was built like a strong man of old, powerful, but without the defined muscles exemplified by modern muscle builders.

Despite being a *still-living* member of the French monarchy, this man had distinctly Spanish traits. His dark chocolate eyes, sun kissed skin, and nearly black hair worked well in conjunction with a powerful jawline. Still, he looked good for a man *living* through his sixtieth decade.

Clara knew that his wound would soon heal over. A blessing, since she was not entirely sure how Evelyn would react if her beau ended up bloodied and bruised. When Marc shifted to the left, she followed suit. Her eyes never left him just to ensure he did not make a move.

Like always, Marc was sizing her up, looking for an opportunity to strike. Clara knew this game well, seeing how this was not her first sparring match. Sometimes she liked to lure him in, creating the illusion that she was nothing more than a flighty female, one who was easily distracted by those long and thick eyelashes.

This time, he was not taking the bait. Marc opted to maintain a defensive posture, meaning he would wait for her to make a move.

"When fighting a defensive war, one needs to win every battle," Clara said casually as her wings spread out to their full size.

Those majestic black wings flapped once which propelled her towards the high ceiling. After another flap, she tucked in her wings and adjusted her trajectory. Initially, she would have overflown her opponent but would now land at his feet.

On a hunch, she slowed down time long enough to observe her approach and noted that Marc's movements remained consistent. He had been waiting for her to make such a move, to commit herself to an attack that left her exposed.

Clara let gravity drive her down onto her knees. With a flick of the thumb, she broke the breech of the shotgun which caused two blank shells to eject. An inexperienced opponent may have been distracted. Alas, Marc was anything but. Still, it managed to mask her true intentions.

When Marc came down on her, she made sure that the breach of her weapon was lined-up with the blade. Once the sabre came into contact with the hinge, the motion naturally forced it shut, which locked his weapon into place. She only hoped that the hinge would hold under the strain.

Luck was on her side for now, but she doubted the weapon would function after that kind of abuse. Without hesitation, she slid on through between his legs and forced his sabre to follow her.

Marc attempted to disengage, but the handguard complicated matters. Knowing that he was committed, he let himself fall, hoping for a fast recovery.

Once clear of Marc, she pushed up with her knees and twisted around. That move appeared as a well-rehearsed dance move, and despite having to take a few extra steps to get some distance, she was ready for more.

In contrast, Marc's landing was less than graceful, impacting the dead centre of his back in a dull thump. Still, he pushed himself up from the floor without skipping a beat. Once he had solid footing, he swung the sabre in a long arc as he turned. Clara reacted by blocking with the barrel of her shotgun. This time, the weakened hinge gave out, leaving her with two separate pieces.

Clara's eyes widened as she backed away while holding the pieces. Because of that unexpected development, she stepped on the mat's edge and the change in balance caused her to fall backward.

On cue, Marc slashed with his sabre using the force of both arms, intent on cleaving his opponent in two. Clara responded by blocking the blade with her boots. While this was an unconventional manoeuvre, most fighters did not have her footwear.

The blade buried itself into the thickest part of the soles and came up against the reinforced steel shank. Clara grinned, winked, and twisted her legs in opposing directions.

Clara watched the blade flex and warp under tension until it snapped. Even in a space this size, the sound echoed. Clara used his bewilderment to regain her footing, although, the cool air that seeped in from her soles meant that gamble almost cost her.

"I just need to win once," Clara said.

Marc was not known for being emotional. In fact, Evelyn often said there was none to be had. Still, the sight of his blade sheared into two distinct pieces had a profound effect on the man. He grabbed her bare arm and held on with a tremendous grip, one powerful enough to worry her.

Before Clara could counter, his head came towards her in a blur. The impact snapped her head back, leaving her dazed, and for a moment, stunned. That's when things really got weird. Despite being in freefall, she never hit the floor. While the stars faded from her vision, giggling rang out through the room.

In response, she gave her head a shake to clear out the cobwebs. Clara then repositioned herself in an effort to relieve the pressure on her arm. Now that she was better able to focus, it was time to turn her attention to the most pressing problem.

Marc loomed over her as expected, however he was colourless and faded like an old discarded photograph. That was a telling detail for something frozen in time. What really caught her eye was how Marc was the only one affected. This time, the rest of the room was intact, which would have been a new twist for an old god she thought dead.

The giggling from the corner got louder and more pronounced. Clara took a chance and shifted the position of her thumb to reduce the overall size of her hand, and with a bit of effort, slipped out from his grip.

Free from constraints, she turned to face the source of all that giggling. Evelyn stood near the exit wearing a leather trench coat. Clara was familiar with that particular garment since it was a personal favourite for a gal who anticipated getting dirty.

Still, Clara gazed at those sharp facial features and green eyes to see something only she could perceive. Evelyn's soul was healing up nicely, so her selected victim had done her further good. This differed greatly from Marc, who appeared to have no soul at all. That truth did much to explain his overall lack of connection to human emotions.

So how was this possible? Hecate, the goddess she killed last fall, was nowhere to be found. To Clara's knowledge, only the old gods were capable of manipulating time to that extent. *Then... why is Marc frozen in time?*

"Bravo! Bravo!" Evelyn cried out. "That's quite the gambit you played, *ma chère.*"

Clara got back on her feet and joined the new arrival. Her hips swayed slightly from side to side as she approached Evelyn, all in an effort to distract. Although, there was little to be done to hide that her sire was essentially a statue.

"Glad you liked it," Clara said before pausing and curtseying for show. "Have you been watching us for long?"

"Not long. No," Evelyn replied then topped it all off with a suggestive smile.

Evelyn was a woman of immense beauty, and if motivated, could have dominated high fashion runways. Long smooth legs, a tight body, green eyes, and shoulder length black hair were all elements that left people weak kneed.

The fact that this woman was normally dressed to the nines was the proverbial cherry on top. Very few people today understood just how fashion could be used to further one's goals. Hence, Evelyn exploited that vacuum to her advantage.

Still, Clara had to wonder how recent trends had been formative for this woman's ideal of beauty. A girl like that during the reign of the Sun King would not have fit the generally accepted definition of beauty. Evelyn likely saw all of those traits as flaws, drilled into her mind by the French hierarchy. In fact, Clara believed that Marc had turned Evelyn in an act of compassion, not because he was enamoured by her radiant looks. *So, who is laughing now?*

"We've been at it well over an hour," Clara said with a grin. "I hope that I wasn't depriving you of his affections."

Evelyn would not play along, but giggled, since it was obvious that something was up. A true gentleman knew how to greet a lady.

"How long has he been like that?" Evelyn asked as her smile melted away for effect.

Clara did not step back nor react to this change in demeanour. The Tower had trained her to hide her emotions, to keep the illusion of being calm, cool, and collected even when she was anything but.

"Honestly? You tell me," Clara said. "I think I blacked out for a moment."

"I noticed," Evelyn said. "How is your head?"

Evelyn approached, and looked as though she would wipe the blood from Clara's face. At the last minute, reason rose to the surface and she pulled back.

Clara may have been a *fallen* angel, but there were consequences to direct contact for their kind, just like coming into contact with holy water, the particularly faithful, or certain religious artefacts. First, the skin of the undead would heat up, begin to smoke, and bubble. Those were the precursors to their bursting into flame.

That's why Clara had been caught off guard. Marc, even as powerful as he was, risked significant injury by pulling that stunt. Younger vampires would have simply stepped out of the way, unconsciously aware of the threat she posed.

Clara moved her jaw from side to side until the joints popped and said, "I'll live."

"What about Marc?" Evelyn asked.

Marc was Evelyn's sire, the elder vampire who almost never spoke but kept a watchful eye on his charge. Clara knew very little about their relationship, only that it was a bond few would ever experience in life. What she did know was that Marc had been a soldier, emotionless, and thirsted for combat. Despite his partner being a stunner, he never sought to make it a romantic relationship. That last part confused Clara, and she suspected that this baby vamp had mixed feelings about it as well.

Despite the obvious power Marc should have held over Evelyn, their dynamic was actually reversed. The elder behaved more like a protector and followed her lead through thick and thin. Evelyn effectively spoke for the both of them, and her humanity is what kept them grounded in the world. *What kind of a monster would Marc be without her?*

"I've seen this before," Clara replied. "He's fine, although I have no idea how that sheik of yours ended up like this."

"None at all?" Evelyn asked.

"Unless you see an old god in the room?" Clara asked.

"I do," Evelyn said with a giggle.

"Oh?" Clara inquired. "Do tell!"

"Are you sure?" Evelyn asked at nearly a whisper.

"Of course—" Clara said.

During that exchange, Evelyn had withdrawn a glove from her coat pocket and slapped Clara hard across the face. The snapping sound was loud and distinct, just like the stinging sensation that soon spread over her left cheek.

"What was—" Clara said before a thump rang out throughout the room.

"There we go," Evelyn said while Marc recovered from his unplanned fall. "One can never trust those pesky old gods."

"Me?" Clara asked, dubious of that statement.

"*Et qui d'autre?*" Evelyn asked.

"How?" Clara asked, and realised that further thought on this revelation would only give her a headache.

"Gods move in mysterious ways," Evelyn said before breaking away.

The younger vampire walked casually over to Marc, looked right into his eyes then wiped away some of the blood from his face. Clara kept her distance, sensing that any involvement on her part was both unnecessary and unwelcome.

After a silent exchange, Marc backed away, picked up the pieces to his sabre, and walked out of the room. While Clara had seen this behaviour before, she had no idea what was going on between them. *Does he even know?*

"You broke his favourite blade," Evelyn said with a giggle. "He's fine, although you did manage to get under his skin."

"So that's actually possible?" Clara asked.

Evelyn simply nodded, and without warning, proceeded to undo the buttons on her coat before letting it drop to the floor. Clara's eyes widened for the briefest moment for effect; it paid to play along with Evelyn's game.

It was normal for Evelyn to dress in the latest fashions, but tonight she wore something else altogether. Black and white striped stockings, a blue dress with puffy sleeves, and a white pinafore, a style of outfit that had a decidedly juvenile bent. Nonetheless, it evoked imagery of a sultry Alice from Alice in Wonderland.

If it wasn't for the droplets of blood covering the outfit, Clara might have wondered if this was some sort of come on. After all, Alice was one of her favourite fictional characters.

"Do you like it?" Evelyn asked with her trademark smile, the one that promised a lifelong pursuit of pleasure.

Clara bit her bottom lip and asked, "Who was this charmer?"

"A scrumptious older gentleman who had a thing for little girls," Evelyn responded before slipping out of her costume.

Under most circumstances for those blessed with a modern beauty like Evelyn, a dress like that could have a profound effect on any potential witnesses.

When the first couple of layers of her dress dropped to the floor, Clara noted that Evelyn had taken the time to wrap her chest with tensor bandages, just enough to hide the bulk of her chest and roll back the clock on her physical appearance. Clara had done the same during the Great War, only she had done it to pass off as a young man.

"Is this one going to make the news?" Clara asked.

"I'm not sure," Evelyn said while undoing the bandages.

Once Evelyn's breasts were freed from their tyrannical bond, she massaged them until they regained their original shape. All the while, she kept her eyes focused on Clara, for reasons that only this vampire was privy to.

While this one loved outfits and wielded them like weapons, there was nothing more freeing for her than creating in the nude. It was often argued that this was Evelyn's natural state. Clara was comfortable with it as well, but her hostess often took it to extremes.

"There are so many murders in this city. So, my art gets lost in the noise," Evelyn replied before adding a slight sigh for effect.

"So, what made this one special?" Clara asked.

Evelyn beamed a warm smile, overjoyed that someone cared enough to ask such a pertinent question. After all, this was not the type of conversation someone had while getting all dolled up at the hen coup. Even now, people called the cops when conversations drifted towards a kill.

"The details are not that important really," Evelyn said bluntly. "What matters is *how* I used his weapon against him."

Evelyn then proceeded to detail the whole sordid affair. How she lured him online, and how she let him make the first move. Finally, she described how he had been raped repeatedly with his own penis.

Clara was not sure what to say or do, so she stood there in silence, listening to all of it. The whole time, she was reminded that, yes, Evelyn was in fact a monster. For the moment, they happened to share common goals. The world would not miss a child predator, so chances were that no one would mount a rigorous investigation. *So, what happens when Evelyn runs out of predators?*

# CHAPTER 3

## *QUARRELS AND TRAUMA*

Elizabeth added some notes to her case file while fighting off a headache that was aggravated by the clickety-clack of her keyboard. She grimaced, paused, swallowed two more pills, and finished off the rest of her orange juice.

"It's days like these that are going to kill me," Elizabeth said out loud.

She could not afford to keep drinking like this. Although, if Clara had kept her promise, then her indulgence last night would have been far more muted. Before reality hit, Elizabeth indulged in a glass or two of wine every so often, but that got worse when Clara started bringing rare vintages to sweeten the deal. Still, polishing off a bottle of hard liquor to drown out her fears was not exactly social drinking.

"How are you doing, Lizzie?" Anna asked.

Elizabeth jumped a few inches and immediately clutched her chest. Her pulse shot up, which was followed by shallow breathing. To regain control, she closed her eyes and forced herself to calm down.

Anna's mouth gaped open, but did not intervene. Who would blame her for hesitating before approaching this giant ball of anxiety?

"Sorry," Elizabeth managed to say between deep breaths. "I guess I was in my own world for a moment."

"Ummm… okay," Anna said, hinting that she was not buying it.

"So, how can I help you, Anna?" Elizabeth said to move this along.

Neither wanted to delve into that particular trigger. Anna may be a force to be reckoned with, one who managed this office with an iron fist, but she was wholly unprepared to deal with Elizabeth's shit. Would anyone be able to go through the grinder like she had and turn up fine?

"Kim called in sick today," Anna said.

"Oh no!" Elizabeth exclaimed. "Is she okay?"

"Just a cold," Anna said. "I kind of feel bad for even asking…"

"So, you'd like me to stay late?" Elizabeth confirmed as the blood drained from her face.

Elizabeth knew that Anna was using this window of opportunity to interact and observe. One did not need to have the deductive powers of Sherlock Holmes to notice that Elizabeth had been avoiding late night shifts. Nor did it take much to realise that her drop in performance was tied to a particular weekend last fall.

"Is this going to be a problem?" Anna asked.

Elizabeth put on her best smile and replied, "None at all. I'll just have to let my roommate know about the change."

"Sounds great…" Anna said. "I thought you were married?"

"So did I," Elizabeth muttered. "No. It turns out that getting married in Vegas when flat out drunk is neither wise nor recommended."

Anna chuckled and said, "At least you didn't wake up with a face tattoo."

"True," Elizabeth said. "Now is there anything else you need? I have to finish up these notes before my next appointment shows—"

"No." Anna said. "Thanks for stepping up tonight. I'll forward you her appointments for this evening."

Elizabeth nodded before saying, "Please do!"

She returned her focus to the screen, reading over the last few lines of notes to reconnect with the flow of her prose. All the while, Anna lingered, taking in the scene before disappearing from sight.

"Finally," Elizabeth whispered, hoping that the Vegas comment would explain away most of her behavioural changes.

> Elizabeth: Can't get home until late tonight. 📷
>
> Elizabeth: I'll let you know when I'm leaving. Okay?

> Clara: Horsefeathers. ☹ Want me to come get you?

Before she began typing again, Elizabeth reached for her phone. She eyed the dark glassy surface for a bit before pressing on the home button to unlock.

She placed the telephone on her desk and got back to her notes. Fortunately, it did not take long to get a reply.

It took her some time to mull things over. Clara was being thoughtful, but it was time to start standing on her own two feet. Her reliance on her saviour was turning into an emotional crutch, an aspect that would sour their relationship as time moved on.

> Elizabeth: That's so sweet! Thank you. 😊 But I'm going to grab a cab and head straight home. Okay?

> Clara: Sounds good! I'll let the 🍷 breathe!

Elizabeth giggled, thinking about the progress her friend had made in regards to technology. Initially, she had to draught messages on Clara's behalf. Now this angel was not only texting without assistance, but also embedding the appropriate emoticons.

"What's next? GIFs that feature popular culture references or memes?" Elizabeth mused while returning the phone to her purse. "Right… right… notes."

\* \* \* \*

"Horsefeathers," Clara swore.

Evelyn looked up while retrieving her blood covered clothes. At this point, she was almost entirely naked except for a G-string that left very little to the imagination.

"Anything wrong, *ma chère*?" Evelyn asked.

Clara raised a lone finger to request a few moments of peace while focusing on her screen. Evelyn used the opportunity to carry her clothes to a laundry chute.

"Sorry," Clara said before another brief pause. "Elizabeth won't be home tonight."

"Oh no!" Evelyn said. "Nothing serious I hope?"

"No… just work," Clara said faintly.

Evelyn picked up on the change in demeanour. In response, she approached Clara while her hands were joined behind her back to make that chest pop out. However, Clara remained oblivious, to this overt attempt at getting noticed.

"How are things going between you two?" Evelyn asked after making a quick pout.

"What?" Clara snapped, before turning her head sharply towards Evelyn to focus on that disarming pout. "Oh… fine."

"Doesn't sound like it is," Evelyn said bluntly.

Again, Evelyn appeared tempted to touch Clara, to give her a great big hug, as though yearning to take on the role of the big sister. Still, there was only so much one could do under the threat of spontaneous human combustion.

"Come," Evelyn said while heading towards a door that led deeper into their living quarters.

"Why?" Clara asked, unsure of the wisdom in venturing deeper into a vampire's lair.

Evelyn giggled and blew Clara a kiss before saying, "Don't worry, I had no plans on taking you to the boudoir. My asbestos lingerie is still at the tailors."

"Oh!" Clara exclaimed. "Lead the way then."

Evelyn winked before venturing through the door which passed through their sitting room. Clara could have sworn that this furniture had been stolen from out of the Versailles palace. With the exception of two chairs located near an oversized fireplace, the room did not have a *lived-in* look.

After a series of twists and turns, Clara was brought into what appeared to be a kitchen, the very existence of which surprised Clara. Against the wall, there was an old-fashioned gas range and stove. Evelyn picked up a cast-iron kettle on her way to the range and filled it from the tub-style sink on the opposing wall.

"Tea?" Evelyn asked.

"Chai?" Clara asked in return.

Evelyn giggled, dropped the kettle on the range, and pressed a dial until a solid blue flame appeared. Without pause, she pulled out two packets from the cupboard.

"Great choice," Evelyn said with a warm smile. "Now sit."

There was a small table on Clara's left with two simple chairs. Everything in here clashed with what she had seen of their home, a term loosely applied to this place. She often wondered about the purpose of this complex prior to their moving in.

Clara headed towards the nearest chair, but the wear patterns on the seat were a clue as to Evelyn's preference. So, she chose the other and sat at the wooden table just as an idea floated into her mind.

"Weren't you supposed to be watching Elizabeth last night?" Clara asked.

Evelyn did not miss a beat. She pulled out two mugs, one of which was chipped, and dropped a tea bag in each one. Clearly, this manoeuvre afforded her the luxury of time.

"*Ma chère*," Evelyn said. "Marc and I agreed that she would not be harmed, not that we would personally ensure her safety."

"So—" Clara tried to ask.

"So, I had an acquaintance look over her last night." Evelyn added. "How do you think she'd react if I was the one standing guard over her?"

"How indeed," Clara said while cursing the fact that she did not think of that before. "A bit like asking the vixen to look after the hen house."

"*Exactement*," Evelyn said after removing the kettle from the flame and pouring hot water into the cups. When she placed the cups onto the table, she sat down and added, "Be honest. How are things between you two?"

* * * *

"I'll see you next week," Elizabeth said as her client left the office.

She was famished since she had been booked solid all morning. That, and she never picked up something on her way to work, all on account of being late.

Despite the hunger, she pushed those thoughts aside and took the opportunity to catch up on her Email. The gods were smiling down on her today; there were only a couple of messages addressed to her, and the rest were group wide notices.

"Fuck me," Elizabeth swore, while running a hand through her hair.

The last Email was from Anna, and as expected detailed her appointments for the evening. While there were only two, it was the late hour of the second appointment that got her. *Or is it early?*

"Fuck," Elizabeth repeated when she encountered a particularly painful knot in her hair. "I should have just calmed down, told Clara how I felt, and called in sick."

Just as the imagery of dragging Clara off to the bedroom materialised, that voice of *wisdom* from earlier resurfaced.

*"And let her off the hook so easily?" her inside voice asked.*

"Right," Elizabeth replied dryly before extracting her phone. "Is it possible for this day to get any worse?"

\* \* \* \*

Clara's back straightened when the phone vibrated from within her back pocket. As she reached back to check her notifications, Evelyn realised what was going on.

"Is everything alright?" Evelyn asked.

> Elizabeth: Fuck! My 💩 boss forgot to mention that I'd be stuck here past midnight! 😫

> Clara: What? How? 😧

> Elizabeth: Dunno. So, don't wait up for me…

Clara: Are you sure you don't want me to be there when you get off work? 😊

Elizabeth: Positive. Just be happy that you're not in the 🐕 🏠 tonight! Gotta get back to work. 🙀

"Oh… just peachy," Clara lied. "Why do you ask?"

That was when she noticed how Evelyn was staring at her in a peculiar way, as though she were committing every detail of Clara's face to memory.

"*Ma chère*," Evelyn started to say, "you've gone two shades paler since you picked up that phone."

"Really?" Clara asked at nearly a whisper.

Until now, Clara had not considered the effect Elizabeth was having on her state of mind. She had been trained since childhood to be a hunter, someone who held dominion over their mind and body. Emotions were a natural part of life for many, but for the most part, Clara wore an impenetrable mask.

"Do you love her?" Evelyn said before taking a sip from her tea. "*Merde!* Still too hot."

"Love?" Clara asked absentmindedly.

"Ever been in love?" Evelyn asked. "Sugar? Cream?"

Clara shook her head and cupped her tea. The warmth radiated into her hands and gave her a sliver of comfort. That was a good question. Had she?

There was Jack, that young acolyte two years ahead of her back at the Tower. She would have gladly given up her virtue for him, and yet she ended up severing his head. In that case, it was a matter of life and death. However, what attracted her had been nothing more than cheap charm and infatuation.

There was also Edith, a woman who had been her role-model for years. Clara knew how she looked at her when they changed clothing, and that Edith would have gone through hell and back just to be together. Still, Clara never looked back when their partnership dissolved. *How could I have been so callous?*

There had been a string of men in life, but they were a means to an end. To be honest, her time with Elizabeth, whatever this was, had been the longest stretch she had with anyone. *How telling is that?*

"Have you?" Clara replied in an attempt to deflect.

Evelyn smiled warmly prior to answering, "Love is a complicated affair. I have known the love of a woman and felt devotion so powerful for another that few today could relate."

To give herself a bit more time to think, Evelyn took a sip of her tea. Now that the temperature was just right, it left her entirely content with the world, she let out a soft sigh.

"Mind you, I've never experienced that with one person," Evelyn added with a giggle. "So… you haven't answered my question."

"Because, I'm not sure," Clara said.

Evelyn raised an eyebrow and locked onto Clara's eyes. The two were then caught up in an uncomfortable silence for what felt like an eternity.

"I don't want to be without her," Clara finally answered.

"Bravo!" Evelyn shouted. "Now we're getting somewhere."

"Wait. Why did Elizabeth arrange for me to go on blind dates then?" Clara asked.

At her friend's insistence, Clara had gone out on a series of utterly boring dates that ended up in spectacular disappointment. The men during the Roaring Twenties were different, or at least the memories of her exploits from that era left her with that impression.

Chivalry and gentleman-like behaviour were nothing more than moral guidelines. After all, these men had no trouble running an enemy through with their bayonets during the Great War. These were the type of men that treated every sexual encounter as a conquest, the kind of individual Clara loved to break.

In Clara's eyes, the *modern man* was disconnected from their baser instincts. Many had not tasted the bitterness of life, killed a fly, or experienced true terror. Sure, there were adrenaline junkies, but that was just treating the symptom. In her mind, these men were already broken, so what was a gal like her to do?

"Have you made a move?" Evelyn asked.

"No…" Clara queried.

"*Vraiment?*" Evelyn asked. "No wonder she's trying to find you some company."

"Really?" Clara asked.

"Shit or get off the pot!" Evelyn exclaimed before giggling. "You really expect that scrumptious dish to wait around until you figure this out?"

While Clara was not familiar with that particular expression, the vivid vernacular did wonders to explain it all. Was all of this tension and their fighting a result of her indecision?

Evelyn got up without warning and nearly pushed the chair over. The imp smirked, gulped down the rest of her tea, and turned to face the door.

"Well, we may as well make the best of this situation," Evelyn said. "Follow me."

"Where to?" Clara said, before noticing that her cup was still brimming with tea.

"My room." Before Clara could object, Evelyn added, "We are going to a masquerade party."

"We?" Clara asked.

"*Mais oui*! I've had no luck convincing certain council members to declare Elizabeth out of bounds," Evelyn added before turning to face Clara. "I think you'll do wonders to help them see reason."

"That sounds like fun," Clara said as a great big shit-eating grin covered her face.

"We shall see," Evelyn said. "Now, onwards!"

# CHAPTER 4

## *THE TRUTH IS ONLY SKIN DEEP*

C *utaneous porphyria?"* Elizabeth asked from the inside of Anna's office, while waiting for her phone to bring up the relevant wiki page.

Anna nodded, and her eyes turned towards the ceiling as though the definition was written on one of the panels. Despite the end effect, Elizabeth doubted that was how Anna's memory actually worked.

"Kim informed me that her skin reacts severely to direct sunlight," Anna said. "Some associate this condition with—"

"Vampirism," Elizabeth guessed.

While Elizabeth had not been thrilled before, the idea of staying late at night with just one security guard on duty made her cringe. Sure, it was probably just a coincidence, but the hairs on the back of her neck were nonetheless sticking straight out.

"Yeah," Anna said. "That's it."

Elizabeth quickly scanned through the wiki to find some of the relevant points. There were two variants of this condition, including one that had a negative effect on the skin.

"How long has she been seeing Kim?" Elizabeth asked, because she guessed this was a new patient.

"Early August of last year, I think," Anna said while scrolling through the file. "Yeah, that's when she was first brought to us as a runaway."

Unbeknownst to her conscious mind, Elizabeth had been waiting for that answer before taking in a breath. A great weight had been lifted from her shoulders since August was well before Clara got mixed up in her life and prior to Evelyn's attempted murder. So, this case had to be unrelated.

"I can see that," Elizabeth said. "Her affliction forces her to hide from the sun. With that kind of limitation, she must wear out her welcome quickly."

"I count three—no four homes in the last two years," Anna confirmed.

"Poor thing," Elizabeth said.

Even the act of being able to empathise with a patient, despite her fears, had a positive effect. Her compassion and professionalism were things she felt rooted in. The act of helping this child through a rough patch was the type of hurdle she excelled at.

"So, no trouble?" Anna asked.

"You know what?" Elizabeth said softly. "None at all."

* * * *

"Can you stop your heart?" Evelyn asked while applying some finishing touches to her costume as their limousine drove into the city.

Clara furrowed her brow at the question. All the while, she admired the spectacular work Evelyn had put into their costumes. Evelyn's costume featured porcelain skin, a white dress, and purple haired wig, all complemented by the adorned wings and halo.

Those elements may have made this costume seem unimaginative, but Evelyn had taken it to the next level. She also wore a latex bodysuit, one that fit her like a glove. Not only did it make her skin look like painted porcelain, but it also created the illusion that she was a living, breathing doll.

That look fell into place when the mask was fitted. This was a porcelain affair, with screens that covered her eyes and mouth, all to create the look of an angelic figurine with oversized eyes. Clara had seen that style of art before, but could not place the cultural origins.

"I've never tried," Clara said flatly. "I can tell you that I'm not particularly thrilled at the idea of stopping it at all."

"*Merde*," Evelyn swore. "So, we can't pass you off as a fledgling vampire."

"Wait," Clara said. "You can stop yours?"

That particular question just begged for an answer. If Evelyn could stop her heart at will, then why bother with a pulse at all? Clara assumed that maintaining such functions only increased her need to feed.

"I can," Evelyn said with a giggle. "But it makes me feel… ill."

Evelyn's face lit up when an idea came to her. She opened up a side compartment in the cab and pulled out a spiked collar and chain. Clearly Evelyn was the type of gal who prepared for every situation.

"Now, I do know that skilled hunters can adjust their heart rate," Evelyn said while approaching.

Clara let this *angel* advance, edging ever closer without fear. It was a new experience for her to be so close to someone like Evelyn. Still, they got a lot closer when the car hit a bump and sent the vampire flying straight into Clara's chest.

"*Ouff!*" Evelyn exclaimed after wrapping her arms around Clara.

Clara stiffened up considerably, half-expecting the need for a fire extinguisher. When nothing happened, she looked down at the angelic doll and smiled.

"It worked," Evelyn said with a giggle. "Now let's get this collar fitted."

Evelyn pulled away just enough to attach the collar around Clara's neck. Those latex covered fingers grazed over her bare flesh and sent a tingling straight down Clara's spine.

"Now, look at you," Evelyn said.

She had been rather creative when coming up with Clara's costume. In contrast to the porcelain angel before her, Clara had embraced her inner-demon.

Her red leather bustier was accompanied by a flouncy layered knee duster. The latter flourishes were used to accentuate her curvy figure while permitting a wide range of motion. Clara also appreciated the ability to conceal a few surprises underneath.

To accentuate the *look*, Evelyn fitted two long black horns atop Clara's head. Her ensemble was complemented by a red leather tail, black stockings, and red stilettos. The play on red and black worked beautifully with her wings, although she would need to leave them partially extended to make them look like cheap props.

Of course, the *pièce de résistance* was the functional steel trident. Clara was excited about the potential of putting it to good use, since she had not trained with one in nearly a century.

Evelyn smiled and said, "You look splendid, *ma chère*. I'll need you to keep your heart rate around fifty, slow down your breathing, and dilate your eyes."

Clara nodded and figured out where this was going. The collar and chain mixed with the appearance of being under the influence of drugs, the actual effect would have numbed her mind. That meant people would ignore her, making this deception truly ingenious.

To get down to the specifics, Clara asked, "So what role will I be playing? How will you address me?"

"You'll be posing as my blood doll," Evelyn said with a smile. "I'll address you as I see fit."

"Am I to remain silent?" Clara asked.

Evelyn nodded before replying, "You catch on fast."

"To be a fly on the wall at this party," Clara said with a woeful sigh. "Oh wait! I will."

\* \* \* \*

Elizabeth walked through the desolate office space. Every door was locked shut, all except for one. Normally, her steps were muffled by the carpeting, but when the place was essentially shuttered, every sound was crisp and clear.

She stopped at a heavy door and took a moment to centre herself before pulling down on the latch. When the door opened up onto the waiting area, Elizabeth assured a big smile.

Her eyes drifted first onto the office's fixture, the guard. Adam always worked nights and was often at his post before she left for the day. Tonight, this man was the reason why Elizabeth was not jumping at the sight of her own shadow.

She then scanned the room until she came across the only other occupant. The child was tall and scrawny, a girl who looked to be no more than twelve. Her pale skin, blue eyes, and strawberry blonde hair were clear enough to see, even with an oversized hoodie.

The girl appeared to be completely engrossed in whatever app she was using on her phone. Since Elizabeth was interested in getting home, it forced her to move things along.

"Grace?" Elizabeth said.

The child stopped tapping away on her phone before turning to face the doorway. Elizabeth maintained a smile while keeping an eye out for any tells that hinted at this child's state of mind.

"You're not Kim," Grace said bluntly.

"No," she said without missing a beat. "I'm Elizabeth."

"So… where is she?" Grace asked just as bluntly.

"Oh? Didn't they tell you?" Elizabeth asked. "Kim called in sick tonight."

Grace shrugged before answering, "Might have. Guess they let Jane know."

"Your foster mother?" Elizabeth asked, although she knew this to be true based on the files.

Grace adopted a sickly smile, one difficult to read. Her records indicated that she did not see eye to eye with her foster parents nor anyone else in a position of authority. Still, there was something about that stare which made her seem anything but childlike.

"Grace. Why don't you come to my office so we can talk?" Elizabeth said.

Grace stood up from the chair and slipped her phone within her hoodie's front pocket. Instead of walking with her hands exposed, she opted to keep them buried in the same oversized pocket before heading for the door.

"Would you like something to drink before we go?" Elizabeth asked.

"No. Thank you," Grace added belatedly.

Elizabeth smiled as she raised a brow. This session certainly promised to be a challenge.

* * * *

As Clara half-expected, the club they were going to looked like anything but. For one, the front of the building was made of glass and steel, a high-rise that towered over its neighbours, which was a definite indication of the wealth and power behind it. Secondly, to reach the entrance, their limousine had to drive into the building's underground parking and wind its way down to the lowest sublevel.

It seemed that vampires had no appetite for advertising where their kind congregated. Still, it created a series of similarities between where they were going and speakeasies from her time.

When they came to a stop, as expected, Clara was the second to leave the limo. Maintaining her heart rate at such a low level left her feeling weak. Fortunately, it gave her plenty of opportunity to stare.

Dead ahead, there were two glass sliding doors with a palooka standing tall on either side to keep an eye out for new arrivals. Since no one else was there, that meant they were either early or late. *I wonder how night and day plays out in vampire society?*

Clara focused on the bruisers who were named Marco and James based on Evelyn's briefing. She detected the absence of heartbeats in the area, which included Evelyn. That implied everyone was a vampire, a significant threat to any hapless human who dared show up unannounced. She supposed the pistols they were packing also worked as a powerful deterrent.

Since there was a void of sound just beyond that door, Clara figured the designer had gone through extraordinary lengths to conceal the truth. In turn, that meant Marco and James would be unaware of what was going on inside, unless they were notified by wireless.

"*Madame Chartres*," Marco said. "We were not expecting you."

How did Marco know who this *doll* standing before him was? He may have recognised their chauffeur. His unmasked presence would help on that front.

"Why would I need to be expected?" Evelyn said flatly.

There was something about the tone that was hard for Clara to explain. Most would claim Evelyn was being dismissive, but there was a subtle nuance to her wording that implied otherwise. Evelyn had a degree of power and authority, and the fact that her elder was standing right behind them only heightened the threat.

"But—" Marco said.

"Are we really going to play this game tonight?" Evelyn asked, her tone implying this was not a question.

Clara took in the totality of the scene and spotted a series of cameras mounted throughout the venue. This discovery was followed by sighting the earpiece in Marco's left ear, which he activated by pressing a button with his hand. *So, there are additional layers of security.*

After a series of successive nods, Marco opened his eyes and said, "No, Madame Chartres." After a casual glance at Clara, the man added, "You know the rules. No humans allowed."

Evelyn did not reply and instead opted to stare the bouncer down through her mask. The absence of any real facial cues had an effect all its own. Clara felt a smidgen of sympathy, but that soon faded. Since this so-called man was one of *them*. These two also lacked souls, leaving Clara to wonder if that was the norm.

For the second time, Marco brought up his hand to the earpiece. Once again, he nodded several times before turning to face the other bouncer.

"Check her," Marco said.

James reached for his holster under his suit jacket and withdrew the pistol. Clara recognised it instantly and knew it would get messy in here if this man had an itchy trigger finger.

As expected, Evelyn yanked on the chain and brought Clara forward several steps. She made sure that her reactions were delayed, disconnected from the events of the outside world. This one was thorough, checking for breathing, heart rate, and using a pen light to verify her pupil response rate.

Clara could control all of these facets; her training ensured as much. Still, it took a lot of conscious thought to have it all fit together. In reality, faking human behaviour itself was an art form, one they needed to practice all the time just to maintain an edge.

James circled Clara and said, "So how many ravens did you have to pluck to make those?"

Evelyn giggled and said, "None. It's easier to get an angel to fall from Heaven instead."

Both men chuckled, and Clara laughed several seconds afterwards. While her wings were impressive, real or not, she could not help but wonder what precisely he was looking for.

"I don't see any needle marks," James stated.

"I have my blood dolls inject themselves between the toes," Evelyn said. "Why mar that soft and supple flesh?"

James got in real close and hovered his hands over Clara's body. All the while, she remained unmoved by the attempt at contact. Her eyes remained vacant and unresponsive. *Wait! He's faking the pat down.*

This *man* was reacting adversely to Clara's proximity, subconsciously aware of just how dangerous she was. Faith was a potent weapon against the undead, and she had faith in kind.

"She's clean," James announced.

"Madame Chartres, I apologise for the delay," Marco said. "New directives from management."

The glass doors parted, revealing the inside of an elevator. With an opportunity to play it up a notch, Evelyn yanked on the chain which sent Clara tripping forward.

"He's cute," Clara said out of the blue, slurring the words to the point of being nearly incomprehensible.

The bouncers turned to each other and chuckled. In the end, all men, including those cursed by vampirism, liked to have their egos stroked.

# CHAPTER 5

## *THE TIDES OF WAR*

As expected, Grace turned out to be tight lipped and uncooperative. This girl's file was littered with references to her trust issues and her tendency to challenge authority. Elizabeth was sure that Kim calling in sick did not help matters. *So why didn't she cancel?*

Not to be defeated, Elizabeth tried various techniques to get this child to open up. Every attempt appeared to work, at least initially, but soon ended up in silence once Grace figured out what was going on. Clearly, this child had spent a great deal of time in the system, or at least enough to learn the playbook.

Still, this was the fourth time that Elizabeth got the silent treatment. To bide her time, she considered a few of the non-standard strategies while measuring the risk against potential rewards. Every attempt ended up in silence, forcing her to look into the eyes of a child who had no interest in cooperating tonight.

Since nature was calling, Elizabeth decided it was high time for a break. That left her with an opportunity to delay and observe this child's behaviour.

"If you'll excuse—" Elizabeth said.

"Don't go!" Grace said, latching on to the other's arm.

The reaction was so quick that Elizabeth's head snapped back. Sure, this type of behaviour would normally be better than silence, but this appeared to be a gross overreaction. Odd, since her docket made no mention of suffering from any phobias.

"Is there any particular reason—" Elizabeth tried to ask.

Grace turned to face the door at the end of the hallway. She then returned to her original position so quickly that, for a split second, it looked as though this child had two faces.

From experience, Elizabeth knew this was not a trick of the eye. Clara herself had put this on display when fighting her ex. Those two had fought at speeds that the human eye could not follow.

That was when it dawned on her that she was with one of *them*, as Clara loved to say. There was a vampire in this very room, which meant this meeting was anything but coincidental.

Her eyes widened and her mouth grew in size until it took on the perfect shape to unleash an earth-shattering scream. Grace was not about to tolerate this type of behaviour, so she muzzled Elizabeth's mouth to silence the scream but left her nose clear to breathe.

"Shhh," Grace said softly. "Scream, and we both die."

\* \* \* \*

The first thing Clara sensed when the doors slid open was the resonating in her bones. Oddly enough, this scene reminded her of a Roaring Twenties clip joint, given the mass of people along with the art deco revival. If the music and dancing had not differed greatly from her era, it might have dredged up memories of the wild parties from her time.

Dutifully playing her role, Clara waited for Evelyn to move forward, allowing herself to be drawn by the pull of that chain attached to her neck. Despite the elevator arriving on to the packed dance floor, people moved away from the pair, creating a disturbance that resembled a boat's wake.

Clara ascertained that this place was crawling with the likes of *them*. Evelyn may have been a woman of importance for this group, but they were reacting to her presence alone. As a hunter, this behaviour would have been her way of determining who were the proverbial wolves amongst the sheep. *Again, almost no one here has a visible soul.*

As an angel, the effect she had on the likes of *them* was exaggerated. The effect was so powerful that their kind actively avoided any contact with her. Clara could see it in their eyes. They feared being set aflame if they ventured too close to the source.

"These are all young ones," Clara thought while pushing past the crowds on the dance floor and onto an elevated platform.

This new area had a series of standing tables with white tablecloths, blue napkins, and a candle lit flower ensemble at the centre. Every time a patron left a table, one of the staff would swoop in to reset for the next group. This was nothing more than a gross display of decadence which was exactly what she expected from the likes of *them*.

From here, she had a better view of the club. The dance floor was expansive and packed. Speakers surrounded the crowd and thumped in conjunction with the beat. In the dead centre, she spotted an elevated platform that hosted the deejay. Most of the patrons were congregated around this point as though they were praying to a pagan god.

Along the far wall, there was a bar that ran nearly the entire length of it. Bartenders were busy pouring drinks, but most of them had a distinctly red tinge to them. It seemed that many did not possess Evelyn's ability to indulge in human food and drink.

"Does this mean those who order a normal drink are actually human?" Clara whispered.

While a great question, Evelyn tugged her along before she could think it over. Now was not the time to delve into the crowd's composition.

"You'll be able to have your fun in a minute, *ma chère*," Evelyn said once a server passed by.

Until then, Clara had not noticed that this club featured multiple levels. A large circular staircase flanked the bar which led patrons upstairs. This was precisely where Evelyn was headed with her blood doll in tow.

The second floor of the club was quieter, although the staff here were just as busy. Like the first level, there was a bar, and Clara noticed a series of swinging doors located on the opposite wall. As judged by the smell of food wafting from within, they featured a fully stocked kitchen. *There's decidedly more of a lounge feel here.*

On this deck, the tables were shorter and were accompanied by fancy metal chairs. Clearly, the decor here was meant to provide a relaxed atmosphere, one without the hustle and bustle of youth. *I could use an appetiser right now.*

Alas, they did not linger. Evelyn took them up to the next stairwell. This time the transition surprised Clara, since the deafening music from below was relegated to the background.

Unlike the lower levels, this one was nearly empty. As judged by what was visible, this floor would have served as a games room, but a pair of bouncers were keeping out uninvited guests. Evelyn paid them no mind and slid right past without uttering a word.

At the centre of this level, Clara noticed another bar surrounded by tables. There were five individuals that occupied the ones directly in their path. Everyone was in costume, but their masks had been removed. *Surprise. Surprise. Not a soul among the lot.*

*"This must be the council,"* Clara thought. *"Why else make such an overt display of power?"*

*"Mes amis!"* Evelyn exclaimed while waving.

None of the council members reciprocated Evelyn's enthusiasm nor acknowledged her. Not a surprise, considering this group was said to hold the balance of power in this city. So that made everyone else in the room, including Evelyn, part of the *little people.*

Evelyn would not be ignored. She pushed forward as if she owned the place. The group remained stoic, reminding her of a painting, and that left Clara to wonder if something was amiss. Still, this was not a hunter's domain, so Clara deferred to Evelyn to safely navigate these treacherous waters.

"What do you want?" Edwin said, a young man with a thick German accent and the sole occupant of the table.

According to Evelyn, this was a man who had risen to prominence through the German military during the rise of the Third Reich. In Clara's mind, anyone who worked for the Huns, in either war, deserved nothing more than contempt.

Evelyn held her hands parallel to her face to feign shock. Since the mask restricted her ability to emote, she used body language to do it for her.

"My, my," Evelyn said before resting her hands on her hips for added effect. "That's not a nice way to address a lady."

Some face stretcher scoffed from the table to the right of the Hun. Unlike Edwin, she was accompanied by another lady and appeared to be *quite* close. Clara guessed this was Kathryn, an eighteenth-century woman and the eldest of this particular group, one who slept her way up the social ladder until she found herself in the bed of a railroad tycoon. Not content with sharing the wealth, Kathryn subsequently murdered the man to gain control of his fortune.

"That's not an answer," Horace said.

Clara spotted the man with a weak chin and pegged him for the one they called Horace. A career bureaucrat in life and in death because everyone needed paper pushers to run their institutions. Although, smart people rarely left such people in charge of the shop. Like Kathryn, he had a silent partner on his left.

"Oh, I'm sorry," Evelyn said. "I didn't see you there."

Clara waited for the uncomfortable silence to permeate through the room before chuckling. She only stopped when Evelyn yanked on the chain for effect.

"What is that *thing* doing here?" Edwin demanded in an attempt to deflect how their show of force failed spectacularly.

"This sexy devil?" Evelyn asked while approaching Clara and planting a fake kiss on those warm lips. "That's my blood doll."

"You are not authorised—" Horace said.

"You like?" Evelyn asked without acknowledging the bureaucrat.

"Whore," Kathryn muttered while her partner chuckled in support.

"Looked in the mirror lately?" Evelyn said while resting her chin on a fist, mimicking the famous pose from *The Thinker.*

One did not need to be an expert of human behaviour to tell that this comment had goten under Kathryn's skin. The woman's eyes narrowed on Evelyn while blood drained from those thin lips. Filled with an intense desire to guffaw, Clara bit the inside of her cheek all to keep herself under control.

"She's lovely," Edwin said to set the tone for the rest of the council. "A tad old for my taste."

"I never took you for a man that preferred grape juice over a fine wine," Evelyn said.

Edwin raised a brow before a sickly smile overtook his features. Evelyn did not appear to be bothered by that particular development. In fact, she seemed to expect it.

"So, you brought us a peace offering?" Edwin confirmed.

Evelyn circled around Clara once while changing hands to avoid getting entangled. When positioned behind her doll, Evelyn ran her hands all the way down Clara's chest, skirt, and legs to showcase that stunning hourglass silhouette.

"One taste," Evelyn said while moving back to face the assembled council, "and you'll think that you've died and gone to heaven."

"Edwin—" Horace tried to interject.

"So, you decided to finally get on the winning side?" Edwin said.

"She's not—" Horace attempted to say but cringed once he caught sight of the annoyance in Edwin's eyes.

Evelyn interlocked her hands behind her back, a trick that pushed out her chest for show. Even in that body suit, her curves readily enticed. Before the question was asked again, she nodded slowly and giggled.

"As a show of good faith," Evelyn said, "I'll let you have the first bite."

The false angel shifted slightly to the side and pulled down hard on the chain to force Clara down on to her knees. She waved her arms like a game show hostess to frame the offering while sticking out her bum for that added pizazz.

"Wrists!" Evelyn barked.

Clara sat down properly on her feet and dropped the trident before presenting her bare wrists. This was sure to be an interesting experience... *for the both of us.*

For one, she had never experienced the ecstasy of being drained by a vampire. Some hunters were rumoured to have committed suicide using this method. Overall, it was a quick death, one that left them with a mind-blowing orgasm. *Wait! Am I in danger?*

Another great question that came without the blessing of a ready-made answer. Clara's blood would be like drinking vitriol, but how long would his grip on her mind last?

A hand cupped Clara's shoulder, a strong yet gentle grip that came from Evelyn. This false angel must have guessed that there was conflict growing within.

When Edwin got up, Clara did not make any attempt to move. As judged by the looks adopted by the rest of the council, this was a highly controversial move. Horace wore a face that was particularly dire, which left Clara to question if this bureaucrat knew more than he was permitted to divulge.

"You know, you'll need more than this... offering... to get on my good side." Edwin said. When Evelyn did not reply, he added, "Since you're a *whore*, I'm sure we can work something out."

Evelyn knelt on the floor before her head fell to a forty-five-degree angle. Clara saw Evelyn from out of her peripheral vision and maintained her vitals below normal. Once he looked at those dilated steel-grey eyes, his smirk expanded on the right side of his face.

He took her hand and brought her wrist right up to his fangs. In the distance, Horace shook his head and that meant they all knew who they were dealing with. So, by extension, the security team must have known as well.

By then, it was too late. His fangs penetrated the soft skin on her wrist. She gasped as the sensation reached her brain, and just like that, the world stood still.

\* \* \* \*

The sound of glass breaking was followed by dull, heavy thumps permeating through the walls. Elizabeth was not entirely sure what was going on, but the protruding fangs and wide-eyed stare hinted that this girl was concerned.

"Is the back door alarmed?" Grace whispered before removing her hand.

"Is—" Elizabeth said.

"Shhh," Grace whispered before flicking off the lights.

They heard several shots go off which were promptly followed by screams of agony. In response, both turned towards the wall to observe. Later on, Elizabeth wondered why they had done so, since neither possessed the ability to see through walls.

"Back door," Grace reminded her.

"It's alarmed," Elizabeth said.

"Audible?" Grace asked.

"Yes," Elizabeth said.

The girl growled, her face clearly moving over one item to the next in search of something. Elizabeth was not entirely sure what to make of this situation, but the fact that Adam's screams were waning forced her to reconsider her fear of vampires.

"There's a lighter—" Elizabeth tried to say before another shot was fired, followed by a howl. "Top drawer of my desk."

The girl blinked out of existence and re-appeared holding the lighter. She lit it, used a rubber band to hold down the trigger, and tossed it on a stack of paperwork piled up behind the desk.

When the flame took hold and spread, Grace said, "Head for the back door."

Without question, Elizabeth left her office and headed straight towards the back door as calmly as she could. At the far end of the hall, an office door was now open, and she was able to make out Grace's partially concealed face.

Despite a loud thump originating from the security door, Elizabeth never chanced looking behind her. Instead, she pushed herself to walk faster while praying that one of two things would happen: Firstly, that the fire would set off the sprinkler system and trigger the alarm. That would drown out the door's own klaxon and alert first responders. With a little luck, it might dissuade their attackers from making further attempts to breach the door. Lastly, all of this needed to happen before whatever that was on the other side broke through. A raging fire, smoke, and alarms were perfect distractions, but only if they made it out unnoticed. *Oh please! Let this half-cocked plan work!*

Fortunately, the timing worked in their favour. Water rained down from the ceiling which made Elizabeth's blouse turn translucent and worsened her urge to pee. Grace had already opened the door and was waiting for Elizabeth to catch up. Moments after the emergency escape door closed, the hinges from the security door were sheared clean off, sending the door hurtling down the empty hallway.

\* \* \* \*

Clara's eyes opened in a flutter, and she discovered that a few moments were needed before her surroundings came into focus. This was a place she knew well, one where she spent a great deal of time exploring this particular marketplace within a deserted version of Pompeii. This was a favoured place to think of schemes and pranks. It also served as a refuge when she needed a break from Tower life.

Despite the market being filled to the brim with exotic foods, none of it had any flavour. This location was anchored to a specific time and place. Her group had given up much for such a defence, one that made it near impossible to attack physically.

"Do you know where we are, Child?" The Reverend Mother asked.

Clara had no desire to ruin her memory of the Reverend Mother Augustine, the head of her order. Instead, she rummaged through the various stands filled with jewellery and trinkets, in awe of how real this illusion was.

"Child?" The Reverend Mother asked again.

"Pompeii, Reverend Mother," Clara said flatly. "A pocket in time designed to protect us against our enemies, like Drusilla. That traitorous bitch, I killed decades after this memory."

"Very good," Augustine said. "This confirms that your memories are intact."

*"So, what am I doing here?" Clara asked while trying on a silver bracelet. You have to love Pompeii, it's the only place where you can find jewellery that features a nymph barneymugging a satyr.*

While not a memory per se, the familiarity of the moment intermixed with a personality of great importance helped her come up with some theories.

"You don't know?" the Reverend Mother asked.

With no obvious way to bypass this mental construct, Clara decided to play along. After all, there were matters more pressing than dealing with programming.

"This is a failsafe of some sorts," Clara guessed. "All of this was triggered the moment one of *them* bit me."

"Go on," Augustine urged.

"Such a mechanism would present us with an opportunity to negate the effects their kind have when we are most vulnerable," Clara said. "Wait! This isn't the first time this program has been triggered, is it?"

Since there was no immediate response, Clara bit her lower lip and turned around to observe the matron. The Reverend Mother looked up towards the sun, lost in the moment, as though absorbing a great deal of information. Whatever *this* was, it clearly had access to Clara's memories and was designed to be interactive.

"Correct," the Reverend Mother said.

"Let me guess," Clara said. "I'm going to wake up with no memory of this. However, I'll be consumed by rage, and go on a killing spree?"

"Correct," the Reverend Mother repeated.

"Can this directive be overridden?" Clara asked.

There was no change in facial expression since this was just a pale copy of the real McCoy. Despite there being no exchange of words, she knew.

"My God," Clara said. "You really did turn me into a weapon."

# CHAPTER 6

## *CAT AND MOUSE*

E lizabeth had guessed that the journey down the emergency stairwell would be the stuff of nightmares. As water poured from out of the sprinklers, the diffused lighting gave everything an ethereal glow. Water rapidly pooled on the landings, turned the stairs into white water rapids, and waterfalls fell over the sides for effect.

The cold had no effect on her mind, to the point of remaining completely unaware that her nipples were protruding through her bra and blouse. Stress brought on by whatever was chasing them, along with her need to pee, was more than enough to distract her. The adrenaline coursing through her veins also helped to block out potential distractions.

Still, after six floors of pushing through this torrential downpour, her body began to slow down. It was enough for the chill to set in which made her wonder what would happen once they left the building. The nearer they got to the exit, the more difficult it was not to dwell on that cold winter air taking the wind out of her.

Grace appeared to be no worse for wear. When they came across floors where the emergency lighting had failed, she took Elizabeth by the hand and guided her down to the next level. As a precaution, the *young* vampire periodically took a moment to pause for a listen.

"What—" Elizabeth yelled the first time, and because of the ambient noise, her voice sounded as faint as a fart in a gale force wind.

Grace shushed her and returned to whatever she was doing. This girl was somehow able to filter out the deafening sound from all that rushing water. In contrast, Elizabeth was barely able to hear the fire alarm blaring. *Or am I imagining it?*

Upon reaching the exit floor, Elizabeth spotted the red exit sign flashing on and off. Once more, Grace stopped to confirm, but this time, she grabbed Elizabeth by the arm, hard enough that it felt like it would be torn from its socket.

Elizabeth was led down another flight to the basement level. Here, the water was a good three feet deep. Grace waded in and pulled Elizabeth along until they were under the landing. The worried girl then pointed above and slipped below the surface.

Under normal circumstances, this would have been sheer nonsense. However, this went well beyond attention seeking behaviour. Elizabeth paused for a moment to calm down and took a deep breath. When Grace tugged on her sleeve, she dunked her head beneath the water.

The sounds that had been hurting her ears turned into a muted roar. It brought up memories of her childhood when she used to dunk her head underwater while the tub filled up. *Wow that's amazing—scary!*

While that thought materialised into her head, she felt ripples through the water. Someone or something was above them, and it was large enough to send vibrations straight through the steel and into the water.

To lend some comfort, Grace grabbed Elizabeth by the hand. Even in this frigid water, Elizabeth could not believe how cold this child's hands were. However, that thought soon slipped from her mind as the threat loomed above and her lungs began to burn. The urgent need to breathe worsened with every passing moment, causing anxiety to flood her mind. *What the fuck is that thing waiting for?*

Without being prompted, Grace moved in close and pushed Elizabeth against the wall. She then covered the other's nose, while pushing against the chest. Given Elizabeth's need to breathe, this added pressure forced air past her lips. By then, Elizabeth was close to a full-blown panic attack, but the girl's iron grip prevented her from struggling.

Before outright panic set in, Grace's cold lips pressed against hers. Elizabeth was not sure what was going on until she felt air rush in. She took in a breath which tasted foul and compared it with trudging through a sewer. Still, it tempered the burning in her lungs. Unfortunately, this distraction also caused her to relieve her bladder. *God dammit!*

This exchange happened two more times, and before a third was needed, the vibrations grew faint and ceased. It was Grace who first broke through the water's surface, and without direction, Elizabeth followed suit.

She gasped, taking in the fresh air. Her eyes even teared up from relief. Her mind was far too preoccupied with breathing normally again to register the scent of wet dogs.

Certain that they were not out of the woods yet, Grace did not wait around. She dragged her partner out of the water and exited this nightmare through the door.

"Cold!" Elizabeth yelped.

She watched as a fog escaped her breath, and their comparatively warm waterlogged outfits steamed up. It would not take long before the cold numbed her mind which would lead to incoherence.

"Over there," someone said in the distance.

Elizabeth turned to find a group of firefighters circling the building. Despite the excitement, her knees turned to jelly before they got near. Out cold on the frozen ground, Grace was left to play the part of the concerned daughter.

"Mom?" Grace croaked. "Mom!"

\* \* \* \*

"I'm a weapon," Clara whispered as memories from that triggered failsafe consolidated with her conscious thoughts.

Directly in front of her, Edwin had just punctured the first few layers of her epidermis and was about to draw blood. Upon hearing those words, he looked right up into Clara's eyes. These were no longer the steel-grey eyes of some doped-up doll, but those of a hunter with an icy detachment.

Clara cocked her head to the side, grinned, and punched Edwin right between the eyes. The shock caused him to jerk back.

"Bank's closed," Clara said

Intent on maintaining the upper-hand, Clara lunged forward and grabbed his lower jaw from that gaping mouth. She then pressed down hard enough to force him on to his knees. Still, she kept on pushing down until the jaw gave out, disconnecting from the skull, and tore it from the soft tissue.

The sound was sickening, but Clara's mind had put up a firewall. Her vision was also affected, and she became hyper aware of anything that moved or posed a threat. In that moment, there was no beauty nor depth to the world.

"Clara?" Evelyn asked, her voice filled with concern.

Clara held on firmly to this ass' jawbone and jabbed Edwin a couple of times for good measure. Without missing a beat, her free hand reached for the trident, and she focused on slowing time down.

In this state, Clara could see that a number of threats were taking root around her. What remained of the council reminded her of a badly drawn portrait, like silhouettes against the background. Several were unsurprisingly in shock, although one in particular was enjoying the show. Either way, they were not an immediate threat.

From out of the corner of her eyes, Clara caught movement. Her head turned towards the danger, and she noticed that the guards had their weapons drawn.

On instinct, she tossed the bloody jawbone, hurtling it towards Kathryn to create a distraction. Meanwhile, she brought the trident to her shoulder and used those wings to get back on her feet.

Clara took three full steps and launched the trident with everything she had towards the closest guard. Sensing she would not have time for another attack before there was gunfire, Clara reached for the only thing with a heartbeat. Running on autopilot, she enveloped Evelyn with her wings.

After returning to normal time, there was a loud thunk. The trident managed to skewer a guard before it buried itself into the wall behind him. Given the trauma to his chest, he was effectively out of the game.

Kathryn reacted wildly when that jawbone struck her left breast. She looked down, realised what was between her legs, and shrieked. It was a horrific scream, one that sounded like the tinkling of glass when struck.

"Clara?" Evelyn asked, her voice quivering and unsteady.

Clara felt every round strike, but they had no effect. As long as no one brought out a heavy machine gun or a tactical shotgun to this party, she would be fine.

Without thinking, her hands reached for the skirt and tore away at the material. There were now two pistols visible with three additional clips each. There were four unmarked canisters held by their pins. She tugged at the first canister which yanked out the pin and sent the spoon flying. As the piece of metal travelled in a long arc through the air, the shots kept on coming.

"One," Clara said calmly.

"Cla—," Evelyn said.

"Two," Clara said, hitting the timing perfectly.

"Stay down," Clara ordered instead of counting off three.

Once again, time was slowed to give her an opportunity to plan her next move. When the last round impacted her wings, Clara stood up tall. Using her dominant hand, she threw the canister towards the remaining guard.

Before returning to normal time, she scanned the room. The council were rousing themselves from their stupor. So, to make things interesting, Clara tore away another canister and let her spoon fly off before ramming it down Edwin's throat.

Since he was too close to the steady heartbeat, Clara kicked him hard. The sound of the sternum cracking echoed through the room. The last she saw of Edwin was his body flipping over the railing before dropping out of sight.

When Clara returned to normal time, the remaining guard collapsed. There was a red glow within his chest which was followed by molten metal pouring out of his rib cage. The high temperatures of the reaction disintegrated everything that came in contact with it.

"Four," Clara said.

The thermite set the hardwood flooring, paint, and drapery ablaze. While unintentional, the fire effectively isolated them from the rest of the club. This gave Clara all the time in the world to clean house.

To finish off the skewered guard, she withdrew her pistol and fired several hollow-point rounds into the base of his skull. As the head rolled off his shoulders, she casually grabbed the trident and headed back towards the council.

On a hunch, she slowed down time just a smidgen. While the bureaucrat was nowhere to be found, the women and Horace's assistant were now active threats. Clara even spotted Kathryn's partner bare her fangs, upping the ante just enough to make this entertaining.

The woman's fingertips were now black talons, and she moved so fast that it looked as though she had been captured on a long exposure photograph. Clara held her ground, gripping that trident with both hands.

When Evelyn looked up, all she saw was the arterial spray as the neck was severed. Clara's strength was significantly enhanced and the soft tissue surrounding the neck was vulnerable to a precisely timed attack. This time, Evelyn did not make a sound, deeming it unwise to draw Clara's ire.

Kathryn screeched in response to her partner's death. Clara looked up, smiled, and threw the trident at her. As expected, her target moved out of the way just enough to impact Horace's assistant in the abdomen.

The music from below stopped cold, and soon screams of panic filled the air. The thermite grenade had gone off inside Edwin and set everything aflame, including the electrical wiring beneath the dance floor.

Unconcerned about the events below, Clara used her wings for a boost of speed and raced towards Kathryn. The vampire was first to draw blood, striking Clara across the face with a wine bottle. Due to the force of impact, the glass shattered, sending shrapnel and wine everywhere.

Clara stopped dead in her tracks and rubbed her jaw before she spat out the blood from her mouth. The golden liquid flew out of those lips and made contact with Kathryn's exposed face. While there was no response initially, the skin soon began to bubble and smoke.

Once more, this creature shrieked loud enough to drown out the chaos below. Without hesitation, Clara fired off three more rounds, ending this fight just like she had with the shish kabobbed guard.

With all further threats on this floor neutralised, Clara tore the trident from its unwilling host and made her way to the railing. Prior to taking the plunge, she turned around to focus on the heartbeat. Clara's eyes were glassy and unresponsive, devoid of that spark associated with consciousness.

"Stay here," Clara said.

Without confirming that her order was followed, Clara looked down and lept from the railing. As soon as she was out of sight, Evelyn ran over to the railing to witness the ensuing carnage.

"Well, that turned out better than expected," Evelyn said with a giggle. "Now where is that snivelling bastard?"

\* \* \* \*

Elizabeth vaguely remembered being lifted onto a stretcher and taken to an ambulance. Despite the freezing cold, bright lights, and the incessant cacophony generated by the emergency response crews, she slipped out of consciousness.

"Hang in there, Mom," Grace said while holding Elizabeth's hand.

No one questioned how a soaking wet girl, wearing nothing but a hoodie, showed no signs of being cold. Nor did they wonder how this child was Elizabeth's. Despite the mother being of mixed race, this child was decidedly not.

All of these contradictions, the child continued to hold her *mother* by the hand. However, the cold seeped into Elizabeth's mind, forcing her awake. She opened her eyes and found the vampiric child smiling down on her warmly.

"How are you feeling, Mom?" Grace asked.

"Mom—" Elizabeth whispered.

Grace squeezed Elizabeth's hand hard using more than enough strength to distract without leaving any bruises. All the while, the girl looked up towards a paramedic who was busy taking vital signs.

"They told me you're going to be just fine," Grace said.

Memories of Elizabeth's most recent shit-storm left her torn between screaming for help or thanking some deity for her good fortune. Despite being safe, a part of her knew this was not over.

"You're lucky," The paramedic said. "She helped you—what the fuck!"

A loud crash cut through all of that hustle and bustle. While Elizabeth was still too disoriented to know what was going on, Grace had no trouble ascertaining what was taking place beyond the ambulance doors.

One of the glass doors had been reduced to shrapnel, sending a shower of glass everywhere. At the centre of the explosion, there was the distinctive shape and colouring of a firefighter. Either they had leapt out of the building to save their own hide, or something with immense strength *encouraged* them to take this shortcut.

"Did you see—" The paramedic said before ending up face first into a snowbank.

The rear doors slammed shut followed by the passenger-side door. The driver-side door was next, followed by the hurried footsteps of the driver. The driver's complexion was ashen, and the man never looked back as he ran off. A beat cop found him the next day, penniless and face down on the gutter. Fortunately, that uniform managed to save him from spending the rest of the morning in the drunk tank.

Despite being in the centre of all this chaos, Elizabeth had no clue what was going on.

"You better hold on. It's going to get bumpy," Grace said before they jumped the curb to avoid a parked police cruiser blocking the way.

* * * *

Clara yanked on the chain, forcing the individual links to dig into her victim's neck. Had this been a living and breathing human, their veins and eyes would have bulged. However, this one was essentially dead, so choking alone would not be enough.

To compensate, she planted a foot in the centre of this vampire's back and pushed him away with all of her strength. The chain worked like a saw, biting deeper into the flesh with every shift. Once the neck broke, she loosened all tension.

Tired of wearing that infernal collar, Clara reached around to unfasten it, and casually tossed it away with the bloodied chain. Only then did she become aware that this place was quiet.

The repetitive dance music had ceased, along with the stampeding mass of people and their screams. It was the complete absence of these sounds that snapped her out of her fugue. Despite the flawless execution of that program, Clara still remembered being triggered and the attack that followed.

She closed her eyes, opened her mouth, and focused. All told, she counted fourteen hearts beating around her, a number that did not include her own.

"Wait! One of the heartbeats is faltering?" Clara asked.

To figure out what was going on, Clara turned to face the bar. While Clara had the intention of tending to the wounded, something unexpected threw her off course. At the bar, surrounded by mounds of deanimated corpses, stood an indigenous woman.

This was not their first meeting. The long raven black hair, black eyes, and flowing white dress were all distinctly familiar. Sure, the memory of their encounter was hazy, but she did recall being warned about this apparition shortly before dying.

"Get away from him," Clara said as her wings opened up to their full size.

Eleanor was not intimidated, far from it. She reached over the counter and grabbed a bottle of vodka along with two glasses. As she filled the tumblers, the world dimmed, lost saturation, and took on decidedly sepia tones. The world looked like an aged photograph, all except Clara and this dark-haired woman.

"You must think me a monster," Eleanor said.

Clara realised that this woman possessed the ability to freeze time, very much like the goddess Hecate could. Since time was stopped, Clara had ample opportunity to gain valuable intelligence.

Before responding, Clara counted the piles of corpses, shrugged and said, "I can't cast the first stone on that account."

Eleanor giggled and pointed towards the adjacent stool. Clara furrowed her brow and thought it over before joining the woman at the bar.

"I'm Clara—" She began.

"Grey. I know. I go by Eleanor," she said. "You were on my list back in the Twenties. Which makes you the one that got away."

"I died that night," Clara said bluntly.

"You ascended," Eleanor corrected. "Technically, you never died. They brought you up for a higher purpose."

"Is that what happened to you?" Clara asked while eyeing the coffin varnish.

When Clara lifted the glass, Eleanor did the same. They both smiled and pounded back their shots.

"I was never a mortal," Eleanor said.

"Does it help?" Clara asked, looking toward the bar to find a white-haired man clutching his chest with a furrowed brow, bulging jaw muscles, and prominent neck veins.

"Try spending millennia helping souls reach their final destination," Eleanor said. "Eventually some of their humanity *will* rub off on you."

Clara noticed a distant stare in those dark eyes. Their conversation must have dredged up memories buried deep in her subconscious. Clearly, the dead were capable of haunting more than the living.

"Is there anything I can do to save him?" Clara asked.

Eleanor filled up the tumblers and shook her head. Clara guessed that even if the time and place of death were not predestined, the human body could only take so much.

"Do you ever tyre of this?" Clara asked to change the subject.

Eleanor turned to raise her glass, and when Clara mirrored the motion, they slammed back their drinks and immediately refilled. Alas, these shots were pretty much just for show. When one considered their metabolisms, it would take these women a *lot* more than that to even take the edge off. Still, there was a bond between them, namely that both needed a diversion.

"What else am I going to do?" Eleanor said. "I was created from nothing, specifically to serve this purpose."

"I sometimes feel the same way," Clara said.

Eleanor chuckled and replied, "I can see why. You were not the first nor the last hunter to cross my path."

"Were they all as fucked up?" Clara asked.

Eleanor cocked a brow before giving Clara a good once over. The latter simply stared back since they were in no hurry to return to this chaotic world.

"Some went mad, others chose to embrace the sins your order taught them to fight against. Some greeted death as though it were an old friend, and a few still haunt the living." Eleanor said.

"So?" Clara asked.

"You are—*were* human, knew the hardships, and still chose the bitter taste of life over a continued existence in *paradise*," Eleanor added.

None of this was newsworthy for Clara. But there was something about hearing it from another that helped her to digest it. The Tower fashioned her into a weapon that hunted things that went bump in the night. Ironically, that made them monsters in turn, but it was her humanity that gave her strength to fight on.

"So did a lot of hunters ascend?" Clara asked.

"You, and you alone," Eleanor said. "The one who accepted her fate and chose to make the best of it."

"The one who gave up the chance at living a normal life to end a living nightmare," Clara said.

"Would you have crossed paths with Elizabeth otherwise?" Eleanor asked. When Clara's eyes narrowed, she added, "Relax, she's not on my list *tonight*."

"Tonight?" Clara queried.

"Everyone dies," Eleanor said flatly.

"So how did you know her name?" Clara asked.

Eleanor grinned and replied, "I know a lot. Still, I am little more than a bystander."

"What do you mean?" Clara asked to gain clarity.

"Imagine yourself gazing at the portrait of a woman hanging in some museum. You can visualise that moment in time, and even get a feel for the emotions going through the model's mind. Still, you have no insight on the artist's mental state, nor can you truly know what they thought."

"Like looking at the world through a series of photographs?" Clara confirmed.

Eleanor poured two more glasses to finish off the bottle. They smiled and gulped the contents in silence.

"In a way," Eleanor said. "I've risked a lot to interact with a few souls in an attempt to... comfort..."

"I take it that those *interactions* didn't go well?" Clara asked.

"No," Eleanor said as though she was far away. Once she snapped out of it, she added, "I will try again when it feels right."

"Why?" Clara asked.

"Do I need a reason? Do you need a reason to quit being afraid and allow someone else to see how vulnerable you really are?" Eleanor interrogated.

"What—how?" Clara asked.

Eleanor smiled before answering, "You have taken blind leaps of faith before."

"You are not going to make this easy for me, are you?" Clara asked.

"Never," Eleanor said as she moved away from the bar. "Well… It has been nice."

"Next time the drinks are on me," Clara said with a smile.

"Deal," Eleanor replied as everything in the room was bathed in a bright white light.

A staircase opened up from out of the wall behind the bar. Until that moment, Clara had not noticed there was a soul standing tall before the array of alcoholic drinks. So, this had all been a distraction? A way to keep Clara from doing something to prevent this man's death? So why did Clara not feel robbed?

"There's always work to be done," Clara said just as time resumed.

* * * *

For five whole minutes, Elizabeth was at peace. The ambulance sped through quiet streets with the lights off, all in an effort to avoid being reported. Elizabeth, the only one who looked old enough to drive the vehicle, sat in the passenger seat wrapped in a wool blanket. All the while, she kept a wary vigil for any signs of pursuit.

"What was that back there?" Elizabeth asked.

The heat was slowly returning to her body, and she was thankful for her fingertips being warm. The blanket was doing a great job of warming her up, as well as the hot air blasting from the vents. Elizabeth was fortunate that Grace did not show any concern about summoning the fires of Hades to warm up the inside of this ambulance.

"You don't know?" Grace asked while keeping her eyes on the road.

"No," Elizabeth said. "Should I?"

"Now, that was a *mild* infestation of werewolves," Grace said.

Without warning, Grace changed lanes to avoid a cluster of vehicles in their way. For someone who did not look old enough to drive, this girl displayed a mastery that rivalled professional race car drivers.

"Werewolves?" Elizabeth questioned in voice that came in at an octave higher.

"Yeah," Grace said. "A bit odd, since they rarely venture this far into the city."

Elizabeth remembered talking to Clara about these creatures. Werewolves were nomadic, social outcasts who had been nearly hunted to extinction centuries ago by the sustained efforts of vampires and hunters. These creatures were powerful, dangerous, and feral which was a lethal combination.

Clara did have a run in with them when she first fell to Earth, one that unfortunately resulted in the death of their alpha. At least, that was the version Clara had given her. But what really happened? Since the fabric of space and time had been shattered, who really had a firm grasp on what was real anymore?

"Why were they after you?" Elizabeth asked.

"Me?" Grace asked, all confused.

The driver had been tempted to look towards Elizabeth to confirm if that had been a joke. Alas, there was some movement in her driver-side mirror, so she buried the accelerator instead.

"They would never put in this much effort for little ole me," Grace added. "They normally hunt us down during the day."

"Why is there always something trying to kill me?" Elizabeth muttered.

When Elizabeth realised what the driver was up to, she confirmed that her seatbelt was properly fastened. Ahead, the light changed to a bright yellow, then turned red, but Grace was having none of that.

"It's *red*," Elizabeth said, but there was no reply. "R-E-D!"

Elizabeth grabbed the handle located just above her head and stiffened. When the ambulance crossed the intersection, she heard a car horn on her right transition to her left.

"That was fun," Grace giggled.

This time, Elizabeth caught sight of what was going on. Right behind them, there were two motorcycles following them through the obstacle course created by their burning a red light. Despite their head start, it would not take long for those bikers to overtake them.

"How did I miss that?" Elizabeth asked.

"Easy," Grace said with a grin. "You're only human."

If that was meant as a joke, Elizabeth did not have the time to find out. They had an enemy on their tail with no obvious way out of this mess. The last part was exacerbated by the fact that their kind was dangerous, even in human form.

"I'm going to need to feed," Grace said.

Elizabeth's mind froze for a moment when the gravity of those words hit her. This was not some mundane request to make, especially when sourced by a vampire. Still, this girl had saved her life several times in the last hour.

"Okay," Elizabeth said firmly.

"Really? I was expecting some back and forth on this," Grace confirmed. "Still, for my plan to work, I'll need a quick pick me up."

"As long as we both end up walking away from this," Elizabeth said to confirm that had been part of the plan.

"I'll need about half a pint," Grace said. "You'll feel a bit woozy at first, but you won't need to run if this all pans out."

"So, what do I do?" Elizabeth asked.

"Just hand me your wrist," Grace said. "Unfortunately, I can't explain, feed, and make this work."

In the side view mirror, the bikers were getting really big, despite the objects in the mirror being closer than they appeared. She guessed there were others lurking throughout the city, waiting for an opportunity to strike.

Still, there was a lot of conflict in her mind, because she had been warned about vampires and their lust for blood. Then again, what Clara told her about werewolves was far worse.

Out of options, Elizabeth exposed her left wrist and presented it to the driver. The child's face came in and out of focus while she concentrated on feeding and driving. Once Elizabeth felt that bite, along with the free flow of blood, she understood why vampires had willing victims.

The experience was so all-consuming that Elizabeth never realised that the ambulance had taken a hard turn to the right, nor that the contents in the back had shifted violently. She had no clue that Grace had slammed on the brakes just as a biker approached from the rear, forcing them to back off. By a stroke of luck, this corner was also packed with pedestrians. So many potential witnesses were a liability for them.

Elizabeth experienced pleasures that her mind would never truly grasp. That's why she missed that her seat belt was unbuckled, that her door was opened. It also explained why she could not remember being carried out past the sidewalk, down a flight of stairs, and left at the subway terminal.

All she knew for sure was that the pleasure was gone, along with Grace. Woozy from the blood loss, she had been abandoned, left to sway out in public. Still, there was a warm wet feeling pulsating between her legs.

"Figures," Elizabeth said. "Get shown the time of my life. Doesn't leave me her phone number."

Just outside, she heard the sound of an Ambulance's siren whirling to life. Her heart sank to the pit of her stomach, hoping that Grace would make it through the night. Although, Elizabeth was not exactly out of the woods herself yet.

"Once they find out that I'm no longer in that ambulance…" Elizabeth said and thought about her phone for the first time since this all began.

While the idea had merit, it proved to be nothing more than a huge disappointment. Her phone was waterlogged and would not power up. That meant there was no obvious way of reaching out to Clara.

"What's her number?" Elizabeth asked but drew a blank. "Fuck!"

When a young mother and her toddler turned around and glared, Elizabeth blushed and apologised, before melting into the crowd. For now, hiding amongst the masses and keeping on the move was her plan for survival.

"Where to?" Elizabeth asked, and as expected, no answer came.

# CHAPTER 7

## *THE BEST LAID PLANS OF BATS AND MEN*

Horsefeathers," Clara said under her breath.

"What's wrong, *ma chère*?" Evelyn asked from the far end of the limo.

At Clara's request, the limousine had pulled up alongside Elizabeth's place so she could check up on her friend. It was rare for Clara to show such concern, but there had been no word since the work day. Alas, there were no signs of her roommate and nothing had been disturbed since this morning.

The only detail that surprised her was the odour of wet dog from her nosey neighbour's door. Odd, seeing how Clara figured that this man was so vile, but no living creature would dare trespass on his domain.

Clara chose not to linger on that thought. Instead, she returned to the limo and focused on thumbing away a message on her phone, wondering if Elizabeth was ghosting her. Although that idea made no sense on so many levels.

"Elizabeth is not answering—" Clara said.

A series of thumps came out of the trunk which drew Clara back to reality. In response to this *faux pas*, the driver's door opened, followed by a series of precisely paced steps. *Someone is going to get it.*

Evelyn ignored the muffled sounds Horace made. This man had banked on their stopping at a light and hoped that the commotion would be enough to get help. Alas, the sound of the trunk popping open reached her ears, and just like that, everything was silent.

"Do you have any reason to be concerned?" Evelyn asked.

Clara looked up from her phone out of habit while she got a better read on this baby vamp. Alas, Evelyn was still wearing that latex suit and mask, so it was impossible to read her. Not that reading Evelyn's emotions was a snap. Like Clara, both women had spent their lifetimes honing the ability to hide behind a figurative mask.

"I… I'm not sure really," Clara replied. "She did make a reference to a dog house earlier."

"Does she make such statements often?" Evelyn asked.

Now the footsteps were heard travelling back towards the driver-side door. Once the steps stopped, the limousine shifted slightly, and the door slammed shut. It seemed that Horace would not interrupt again.

"No," Clara said. "Although, I did deserve that one."

Clara smirked when she remembered this morning's exchange and was surprised that it had not been months ago. Since she had no real need to sleep, her days could stretch on. However, the emotional toll of fighting with Elizabeth and the *incident* at the club left her with a warped perception of time.

"Some people need their space after a spat," Evelyn said.

"You think that's all it is?" Clara asked.

Evelyn giggled, her shoulders exaggerating the movement to add a bit of theatricality. This elaborate show left Clara to wonder if all of this was part of a sick joke. Either that, or Evelyn was trying to make a point.

"Have you ever come across an instruction manual for men?" Evelyn asked.

"…no?" Clara responded.

"Men are such simple creatures," Evelyn said before pausing long enough to let those words sink in. "Despite their simplicity, no one has ever written a guide that would help deal with them under most situations."

"That would be too easy," Clara said with a smirk.

She looked down at her notifications one more time just in case, but it was all for naught. Elizabeth was not responding, and she had no idea why. It was the uncertainty that made it worse, poisoned her mind, and left a bitter taste in her mouth.

"Too true!" Evelyn exclaimed. "Now imagine the magnitude of writing such a manual for women?"

"So... despite being in the dating game for four centuries, the best you can come up with is a guess?" Clara asked.

If that statement hit too close to the mark, Evelyn never let on. Instead, she giggled loudly, while nodding up and down. Those exaggerated movements were beginning to wear thin on Clara, but she knew this was all part of the act.

"Look," Evelyn said. "Why don't you come over to my studio?"

"Studio?" Clara asked, unsure of where this was headed.

Evelyn nodded vigorously before saying, "It's where I create and keep my best work."

"...and?" Clara inquired.

"You'll be giving Elizabeth some much needed space. Besides, you'll get the chance to view a project that I think you'll love," Evelyn answered.

While the idea had merit, Clara was not comfortable with leaving Elizabeth alone for the night. The last thing she needed was to come home in the morning to find her friend passed out drunk. Especially, if it was a result of Clara's desire to give her friend *some space*.

Evelyn anticipated this and said, "Let her know where you're going and that you'll come in when she heads home."

"How will that help me to figure out if she's just giving me the cold shoulder? Or has me on the hot seat?" Clara asked.

"After Marc is done securing Horace," Evelyn said. "I'll have him swing by her workplace to make sure she is safe."

That proposal had all of the hallmarks of a good plan. It was reasoned, well laid out, and included a fallback. So why was Clara still feeling rotten about accepting the offer? Still, she was tired of playing games and needed to let off some steam…

"Fuck it," Clara said in defiance of her conscience. "Lead the way."

As those words rang out, the limousine lurched forward. Evelyn pushed back into the leather seat, looked up, and unleashed a loud and contented sigh.

* * * *

Elizabeth jumped the turnstile while no one was looking and cursed the fact that her things were back at the office. That meant she was effectively without her purse, credit cards, and enough mad money to get her out of a tight spot.

"Mad money?" Elizabeth pondered, since that expression was not in her normal repertoire. "Clara must be rubbing off on me."

So, Elizabeth had nothing to her name, and given the weather, her options were also limited. If this had been summer, she could have made her way home on foot, and Clara would be there to help.

"That's assuming that Clara is even home," Elizabeth whispered.

Unfortunately, hindsight had a way of biting people in the ass, and tonight served as a particularly poignant lesson. Still, how could she have known that keeping Clara at bay would end up putting her life at risk?

After all, she could not use her friend as a crutch and expect genuine emotions to develop, let alone a healthy relationship. Would either of them benefit if her feelings of dependency deepened?

The train pulled up as she arrived at the platform. Elizabeth was not concerned about where this train was headed, not if the goal was to confuse those tailing her. She would need to make several transfers, doing so at random, which would reduce their chances of finding her.

As a precaution, she looked down both ends of the platform. No one in the area appeared to be particularly noteworthy or dangerous. Although, without a clear understanding of what was after her, that was, at best, a guess.

With a sigh, she stepped onto the train and sat down on one of the long benches. This vantage point gave her the ability to observe what was going on within the car. For now, this section was nearly deserted except for two other occupants. Both were absorbed by their phones, so they would not notice how under-dressed she was.

Elizabeth reached for her phone and tapped on the screen. After a few frustrated swipes, she remembered that her warranty was voided. This model may have been touted as water resistant, but it was never designed to survive rapids or be immersed for as long as hers had been. Having a working phone right now would have been a game changer. Given her predicament, she might even ask Evelyn, her killer ex-girlfriend, to come get her. Alas, she did not know her number either…

Elizabeth was startled awake when the train lunged forward. Her eyes darted from one end of the compartment to the other, but the situation remained unchanged.

Her heart was at gallop as a surge of adrenaline coursed through her veins. Her mind was flooded with questions, until one in particular floated to the surface. To satisfy her curiosity, she looked down at her wrist, searching for any traces of those bite marks. There were none, but her skin did tingle whenever she ran a finger over that patch.

"A half a pint," Elizabeth scoffed.

To avoid getting noticed, Elizabeth kept her phone in her hands. That way, if someone gave her a casual glance, she could feign chatting with someone over Bluetooth. For the most part, it proved to be an effective subterfuge since no one was looking for the earpiece.

Nonetheless, this was not her first-time *donating* blood. While giving at the blood bank would leave her unfit to run a marathon, this drain on her strength was far worse. *I hope she's okay.*

"So, he got drunk and punched the wall?" Elizabeth said in a normal voice.

Meanwhile, she opened and closed her eyes in rapid succession, all in an effort to rid herself of this fatigue clinging to her eyes. So far, any attempt made to stay awake was having no effect.

"No? He broke his hand?" Elizabeth said while trying to feign surprise.

With her eyes so heavy with sleep, Elizabeth opted to close just one. She hoped to rest an eye, while doing some mental math to keep her mind alert. The numbers running through her mind should have helped her focus. Instead, they were replaced by images of Clara cooking supper.

"Uh huh," Elizabeth added before furrowing her brow.

In this memory, Clara was laughing out loud, but the sounds were muffled and distant. In the background, the sizzling shrimp gave way to the somniferous clickety clack of the car's wheels striking new sections of rail. The disjointed sounds and images should have been a warning, but Elizabeth was already fast asleep.

The last thing she did was relax her grip and let her phone drop to the deck. The device impacted the floor and bounced a couple of times before landing on its screen. Farther down, another passenger looked up from their phone and chuckled. They were smug in the certainty that someone was going to wake up with a severe case of disappointment. Not only for missing their stop, but also for the panic that would set in once they realised their phone was smashed.

\* \* \* \*

Clara had no idea what to expect when she set foot in Evelyn's workshop. The only thing she knew for certain, was that it was nowhere near Evelyn's home.

Despite her theory, Clara was surprised when they drove into the compound of a large windowless warehouse. They went past that structure and entered one of the supporting buildings. From there, the limousine travelled down a ramp that led to the lowest levels.

If anything, this was a reminder that no matter how happy-go-lucky Evelyn appeared to be, her elder took a grim view of the world. It often made her wonder how their relationship worked. The differences were so vast that they may as well have been from different species.

Evelyn slipped out once the door was opened. She blew a kiss suggestively to Marc who, as usual, did not respond. Instead, he moved on deeper into the complex. From the looks of things, these tunnels were used to distribute either steam or hot water. Genius really, since it provided them with an excuse to maintain underground facilities that linked the buildings. *What a great way to avoid drawing unnecessary attention.*

Clara followed closely behind and noticed a rusty fallout shelter sign perched on a grime covered column. She had seen such signs all over the city and wondered if these two had taken over a few forgotten shelters to call home. *Wow! That explains a lot.*

She wore her costume which was covered in blood and gore. The incident weighed down on Clara, especially the fact that she could be sent into a blind rage based on a set of predefined conditions. This time she was lucky, ending the lives of creatures she deplored… for the most part. How would she react if innocents had been counted amongst the dead? Based on Eleanor's arrival, could she be so certain there were none?

"Why did you bring me there?" Clara asked when her mind coalesced around this pertinent question.

"I needed your help and believed that was the only way to convince the Council to see our point of view," Evelyn said.

Those words appeared to be so innocuous when strung together like that. Still, this was not a person who could be taken at face value. Evelyn was a schemer; one whose plans bore fruit over decades or even centuries.

"Did you expect that we'd be able to change their minds?" Clara confirmed while her mind analysed every word.

"Of course," Evelyn replied as her heels echoed throughout this maze of tunnels.

"Would that be before or after you joined their ranks?" Clara pressed.

Evelyn did not immediately respond. Instead, she stopped near a set of oversized steel panels. To the casual observer, this section of the tunnels was sealed shut. However, Evelyn's lingering presence activated a hidden mechanism which caused the two disparate pieces to move apart until they were embedded into the ceiling and floor.

"Collaboration was never an option," Evelyn said with a tinge of venom in her voice.

"Collaboration?" Clara asked, certain that a big part of the puzzle was within her grasp.

"The *council*, which is a name they chose for themselves," Evelyn said activating a series of lights, "were representatives of this nation's government."

"Wait," Clara said. "You mean—"

"That the sheep are in charge of the wolves? Correct." Evelyn answered.

The idea that certain elements of human society were not only aware that vampires existed, but also employed them, had a sobering effect on Clara. This piece of news left her feeling like a new-born babe and took her back to those early days on Earth.

She had been captured shortly after completing a mission and woke up half-naked, bound to a cold metal chair. That much had been expected for getting herself captured, but she later learned that she was being interrogated by a ghoul. At the time, she had not considered that such an alliance included other creatures.

She did not realise who this team reported to, nor considered their reach, until now. Clara had killed a government asset and disrupted operations at a black site. That meant that she had pissed off a group who had command over this nation's armies.

"So, they knew who I was," Clara said.

"Only as much as they learned from your encounters," Evelyn said. "Yes."

"So why did they let us in?" Clara asked.

"Isn't it obvious?" Evelyn asked while walking up the stairs.

Upon reaching the next level, another set of steel jaws broke apart to let them in. Even from the light bleeding out of the stairwell, Clara caught sight of easels, workbenches and tons of tools associated with art. However, it was the odour that really got her attention, especially the overwhelming smell of paint. *Does Evelyn bathe in the stuff?*

"Home," Evelyn said with a soft sigh. Since Clara had not answered yet, Evelyn took the initiative and replied, "Hubris, *ma chère*. Hubris."

\* \* \* \*

"*You shouldn't be sleeping,*" Elizabeth's internal voice said.

Her eyes were heavy with sleep. The sounds beyond her skull were muffled and reminded her of an effect reminiscent of a couple fighting on another floor.

"Did I—" Elizabeth wondered why humidity was clinging to her bottom but remembered that swim from earlier.

With a bit of coaxing she opened one eye, and the bright fluorescent lights above made the world come aglow. Everything in her vision had a halo, and given the fatigue, it made her head throb.

"I need to quit drinking," Elizabeth muttered, while longing for painkillers to dull the pain.

After a few more moments of self-torment, her vision cleared up just enough to get an idea of her surroundings. Her grand plan of keeping a watchful eye on the flow of people on this train had failed.

"Spectacularly," Elizabeth grumbled.

This once nearly vacant car was now the temporary home for dozens of passengers, providing a clue of how long she had been riding this line. How? Where? How long? What a shame, none of these questions came with ready answers. Her only option would be to chance looking foolish and ask.

For the second time in recent memory, Elizabeth heard giggling. She shot a glance at everyone nearby but could not trace the source. Given her fatigue and heightened senses, she dismissed it as an indication that her imagination was running wild.

"I should get my ass in gear and get off—" Elizabeth said.

The brakes locked down hard, leading to a loud squeal that tore through her brain and worsened her headache. She would have covered her ears, but the sudden change in motion sent her sliding down the bench. *Now there goes the idea that my wet ass was suctioned to the seat!*

She managed to grab onto the railing and watched as others struggled to do the same. The sudden deceleration enraged some passengers, leading to strings of profanity that would make a sailor blush. Others were more fearful, but given earlier events, Elizabeth assumed this was not a mechanical problem.

"Your attention—" The driver said over the train's public address system before a power blip cut off the broadcast.

Power interruptions like this were known to happen. Normally, she would lean back and relax, because there was little else to do. This time, her entire body was on edge, ready to make a run for it on short notice.

"But where would—" Elizabeth wondered.

"Debris up ahead—" The broadcast added when the system reset.

Elizabeth was about to let herself breathe a sigh of relief. That is, until an impact resonated throughout the stopped car, and everyone gasped in response. A blackout followed, one that plunged them into an inky darkness, a world entirely devoid of light. Again, Elizabeth might have been able to keep her cool, but a deep guttural howl originating from outside the train got her attention.

"*Run!*" The voice inside her head yelled.

* * * *

Clara was left with a profound sense of awe once the lights came on. Everywhere she looked there were unfinished pieces, all awaiting the skilled hands of their creator. *Evelyn's been busy!*

She noted that this studio was not dedicated to a singular craft. She was surrounded by reliefs made from various materials, wooden and stone sculptures, paintings that bordered on being photorealistic, and a few pieces of metal work tossed in for good measure. Since every project featured either landscapes or women, Clara figured there was only one prolific artist responsible for this.

"How do you find the time?" Clara asked.

Evelyn turned around and blew a kiss before giggling. The musical notes of her voice could enchant an audience, but Clara was immune to that particular parlour trick. Still, it was hard to ignore the show this baby vamp was putting on.

"I sometimes spend days in my studio," Evelyn said. "Like you, I have no real need to sleep."

"How do you—" Clara tried to ask.

"Take your clothes off," Evelyn ordered.

Evelyn led by example, removing everything except for her mask and bodysuit. The performer in her was very much alive, since every motion was fluid and sensual.

Clara was not sure what to make of this, but even with the plethora of potential weapons surrounding her, the threat remained low. She chose to be more utilitarian in this case, however, and stripped down to nothing without fanfare. This was her chance to tease and torment the hostess tonight.

"*C'est dommage*," Evelyn said, while pretending to wipe a tear from her mask's right eye.

What a shame indeed. Clara was ready to swear that she heard Evelyn biting her lip in anticipation. While there was no way to be sure, the visuals in Clara's mind were rather vivid.

"Still," Evelyn said while approaching the angel and circling her model as though committing every aspect to memory, "I often fantasise about what I would do, if I had you all to myself…"

"Have you now?" Clara asked, and could not stop herself from grinning.

"*Bien sûr*," Evelyn said before running a finger over a faded scar located near Clara's heart. "So, what's your secret?"

The act of Evelyn touching her in that way had an immediate effect on Clara. For a moment, all of the shit she had to deal with in the past six months faded into the ether.

"What do you mean?" Clara asked, while making sure that her heart rate and respiration remained steady.

Evelyn cocked her head to the side and giggled. This time, she turned around, her stride purposefully elongated to exaggerate the sway. After a brief pause, the doll raised her right arm and motioned with her index finger to follow her deeper into the studio. After a series of twists and turns, she halted her progress, once they reached a large object covered by a white sheet.

"You are nearly flawless," Evelyn said in all seriousness, "almost symmetrical, and there are few variations in your skin."

Evelyn grabbed onto the sheet and pulled it down. As the white cotton slid from the statue, Clara learned why she had been asked to strip down. Dead ahead stood her proverbial *doppelgänger*, or at least it would be once Evelyn applied the finishing touches.

This version of Clara was, for the most part, nude with the exception of a cloche hat, a long strand of pearls around her neck, and a rosary wrapped around her wrist. It was the latter that caught her eye, seeing that Father Michael's rosary had been lost since she died. The sculpture also featured her cherished derringer, an item that would have also been found at The Grand.

"How did you know about those?" Clara said while pointing at the weapons.

"You had them with you when we first met," Evelyn replied.

"*Really?* That was over ninety years ago," Clara added.

"So?" Evelyn asked with a giggle.

The statue was perched atop a small pedestal carved out of the same white marble as the rest. It did have the end effect of forcing Clara to look up to gaze upon her own splendour. This rendition had one bent knee and a hand at her back, which brought out her chest and made the derringer much more noticeable.

"So, you pieced this together using memories and the odd peak?" Clara asked.

Evelyn exaggerated a nod before replying, "You like?"

"I do," Clara said.

What was missing from this work were details that Clara had kept out of sight. The areas concealed by her bra and panties were rough. The sculptor had left enough material behind to adjust for reality, specifically, around what would make up her breasts and berry patch.

"You'll love it when I'm done," Evelyn said while sauntering down the aisle to another corner of the studio.

On her way back, Evelyn tossed a bronze object at Clara. The item was intimately familiar, although hers were not fashioned from bronze. Right in the palm of her hand, there was a beautiful rendition of a feather, but chemically aged to make it appear black.

"I just might," Clara said before attempting to give back the feather.

Evelyn shook her head while holding up her hand in protest. It appeared that this particular item was to serve as a memento. Hence, it would not be used for the finishing touches.

"So… are you going to answer my question?" Evelyn asked.

"What quest—Oh!" Clara exclaimed. "You mean, why am I not riddled with scars after living nearly twenty years as a hunter?"

Evelyn giggled before replying, "*Exactement.*"

The artist moved in closer, enough that Evelyn had to look up into Clara's eyes. The proximity did not bother either of them. In fact, Clara enjoyed the other's ability to take charge. *Has this ever happened before?*

"Years ago," Clara began. "The Tower made an agreement with the Georgians to gain access to certain technologies. So, we ended up in possession of a series of medical devices that were not only capable of healing those on the verge of death, but could also fix flaws."

Evelyn cocked her head and imitated the thinking man's pose for the second time tonight. Her latex hand slid over the whole of Clara's bare chest before focusing on that scar.

"Before going after Drusilla, I had been recalled to the Tower. A secondary objective was to undergo a treatment," Clara said.

"So, *this* happened after your death?" Evelyn inquired.

"It did… yes," Clara answered bluntly before grabbing Evelyn's hand. "Although, this scar is fading with every passing day."

"So, you are flawless by design?" Evelyn asked and used the opportunity to interlock their fingers.

"They believed it would give us an advantage when hunting your kind," Clara said.

"Well, it certainly worked on me," Evelyn said with a giggle.

"I've always preferred the look of a natural beauty," Clara said, assuming that Evelyn possessed a treasure trove of flaws that could be discovered over a lifetime.

Nevertheless, the bodysuit and porcelain mask only served to hide that natural beauty. She was faced with a life-sized doll, one who could not emote due to the limitations inherent to the costume.

Still, Evelyn had something else in mind. With a hand to spare, she shifted just enough to glide it freely over Clara's tummy and down between her legs. While sensual, it also gave the artist the added benefit of getting to know her model intimately.

"Let me have you tonight. I want—I need to find your every flaw," Evelyn said softly.

"What do I get in return?" Clara asked.

Evelyn answered by creating the shape of a smile with her spare hand and relied on the skilful exploration of Clara's berry patch to signal her intent. Upon finding that stiffened cap, Evelyn straddled it with her fingers and sent a wave of pleasure coursing through her partner's body.

"Never mind…" Clara moaned.

# CHAPTER 8

## *FROM CLOUD NINE TO THE UNDERGROUND*

While the voice in Elizabeth's head was right, the slight rub of the plan was actually getting off this train. The compartment did have a bit of light, mostly from those who turned on their flashlight apps. That was all well and good except that her own phone was nowhere to be found. *What good would it do anyway?*

How the hell was she going to make it through these darkened tunnels? Besides, whatever came looking for her at work was clearly not bothered by poor lighting. Elizabeth did not know much about werewolves but assumed this group was not looking to take her out on a coffee date.

A second impact to the train sent people into a full-blown panic. Elizabeth kept her hand wrapped around the railing, her eyes searching the area until they were drawn to something. Near the back of the compartment, a phone was blinking blue. Her eyes widened, her heart raced, and she closed her eyes.

"*Now!*" The voice exclaimed.

"Now," Elizabeth whispered.

Elizabeth snapped up and slipped past the other passengers. When she got near the phone, she faked tripping over her feet, grabbed the device, and tore on through to the next compartment.

People in this compartment were just as concerned. To reduce her chances of having a panic attack, she slowed down and nudged her way through to the back. As a precaution, she pocketed the phone since this would be the linchpin to her plan once she made it outside.

On her way, she passed a young woman who seemed suspiciously calm, a brunette of average height, one with worn out clothes that were several sizes too big for her. For a moment, their eyes locked on one another, but there was nothing familiar about this girl. Elizabeth continued with her attempt to reach the back door before those looking for her figured out what she was up to.

While nearing the last compartment, something scraped against the train's side behind her. Her mind conjured up imagery of a handful of claws tearing into the soft metal. It would not be long before they breached the doors to gain entry. *They are so fucking with us.*

"*Keep going*," the voice urged.

Despite the risks, Elizabeth entered the last compartment and saw fear lingering in the eyes of the passengers. She kept a smile painted on, partially to allay their fears, but also hoped that faking courage would have a positive effect on her.

The vibe in this compartment took a turn for the worse when blood curdling screams came from out front. It would not be long before panic spread throughout, so Elizabeth pushed her way through the remaining passengers and stopped at the last exit door. When the door would not budge, she located the emergency door release.

Tired of waiting, she pulled open the panel and reached for the red lever. Elizabeth paused, closed her eyes, and waited patiently for a sign. Her hands shook in anticipation and she desperately wanted to run. Opening these doors without a distraction would be sure to get the wrong kind of attention.

The screaming did not last long up ahead. Elizabeth figured they were either too afraid to scream or had been silenced. Since there were no signs of people running outside, she worried it was the latter.

"What are you waiting for?" Some man said. "Pull the fucking lever."

"Wait for it," Elizabeth said calmly.

"Wait for what?" The man pressed.

Elizabeth raised her hand with an index finger pointing towards the ceiling. She needed him to be quiet long enough to hear an opening, and it soon came in the form of claws digging into the side.

"Just about…" Elizabeth said.

Once the sound of a metal door being stressed reached her ears, Elizabeth pulled on the lever which released the locking mechanism. The man pushed her out of the way and jumped out into the thick blanket of darkness.

Elizabeth followed suit but slipped around the back, giving the opportunity for her eyes to adjust. While it would not give her night vision, it was better than stumbling through the dark.

"*Stand still,*" the voice said.

As directed, Elizabeth dared not move. While that man ran off into the void, a series of thumps followed. In a flash, a large mass of darkness moved past her and overtook the man.

While glad of being spared the visual details of his death, she wished that life came equipped with a mute button. No living being should be forced to hear those god-awful sounds: the pleading, the breaking bones, and tearing flesh. *No wonder those up front went quiet so fast.*

"*To your left,*" the voice said.

She turned her head and saw the outline of a rectangular frame in the shadows. Chances were that this was an exit, alas, one located between the train and the feeding frenzy going on up ahead. Elizabeth had a choice, but running or sneaking towards the doorway were both highly undesirable options. *Still, it's better than waiting around for that thing to start looking for seconds.*

After taking a deep breath, she focused on the exit and walked calmly towards the door. Just behind her, there was the sound of a door being ripped from its hinges, followed by a fresh round of screaming. Despite her instincts urging her to run, Elizabeth maintained a measured pace, letting all of that chaos drown out any sounds she made.

"*Hold,*" the voice said.

Ever the dutiful soldier, Elizabeth stopped midway between the door and the train. She was out in the open which was the last thing she wanted. Elizabeth wanted to bolt, but the chewing sounds up ahead had stopped.

On a hunch, Elizabeth slipped her hand slowly into a pocket and pulled out that phone. To prevent giving out her position, she kept the screen against her leg to conceal the periodic blue glow. She waited like this until the door leading into the final compartment was about to give way.

That was when she pitched the phone further on down the tunnel, beyond where the werewolf and his meal were located. On impact with the ground, the screen came alive and bathed the tunnel in white light. Alas, that light caught two women trying to escape down that tunnel. *Oh no! I just got those two killed.*

Elizabeth waited for the creature to take the bait, then bolted towards the door. When she reached the doorway, she grabbed the silver handle and pulled. To her surprise, the door gave way, and without hesitation she slipped inside before closing it behind her as gently as she could.

Unfortunately, it would not be long before her ruse was noticed, so Elizabeth looked around for something, anything to help her. A shame she had to expend her sole source of light to get inside. The screen from that phone would have at least given her an idea of what was inside, namely if this happened to be a communications closet with no other exit or a utility tunnel that led to freedom.

"Thank the lord! Someone else made it," a woman concealed in the shadows said.

Elizabeth yelped before backing away from the source and almost slammed into the door she came from. She grasped her chest and struggled to breathe. Given the shock, it took a moment for her mind to process those words.

"Oh! So sorry," the woman added.

The woman's face then came into focus once the screen from their phone came to life. After a few taps, a bright white light bathed the room and filled in the details on the individual behind the voice.

"I'm Adrienne," the woman said but kept a healthy distance.

Elizabeth looked over this woman who appeared to be in her forties based on the blonde hair with streaks of white running through it. She would have been a betty back in the day, but time had not been kind. Given how scrawny she was, Elizabeth wondered if there was a history of drug use. The fact that she was dressed up like a biker chick only reinforced that prejudice.

"Elizabeth," she said in reply while her eyes took in more of her surroundings.

"I know," Adrienne said.

"What? How would you—" Elizabeth asked.

The door behind Elizabeth opened up which caused her to pivot, lose her balance, and fall straight on her rump. When the stars cleared from her vision, a foreboding creature was towering over her, covered in hair and gore.

"Who do you think's been chasing you all night?" Adrienne asked.

"*We are sooo fucked,*" the voice said.

* * * *

Evelyn smiled taking in the beauty of her latest conquest. Just above, Clara's freshly shaved berry patch was glistening in the pale light. She watched as her legs quivered from the latest orgasm that rocked through her partner's body.

With her back against the base of the statue, and Clara's chest leaning over her to rest her arms against the pedestal's base, Evelyn had an ample view of those tight breasts, defined abs, toned arms, and most importantly, that overwhelmed look etched on her face. It was the latter that really got Evelyn excited. She also enjoyed the sight of those pulsing veins in the neck and forehead, all of which were flush with blood.

Once Clara's body began to relax, Evelyn giggled before sliding a hand between Clara's thighs and ran it straight down that slit. Even that small amount of stimulation was more than enough to make Clara convulse. This was precisely where Evelyn wanted her lover to be.

"You've been a good girl," Evelyn said softly into her lover's ear.

Clara swallowed hard and bit her lower lip. Given her current state of mind, the best she could manage was a slight nod. Her mind struggled just to keep her knees from buckling.

"You know that I'm not done with you yet?" Evelyn asked, every word sounding like a musical instrument played with a cunning hand.

The only reply Clara could muster was shaking her head, pleading for a break to catch her breath. Still, her breathing quickened, anticipating what was about to come despite her weak protests. Evelyn's lover knew full well who was in charge.

"You need this, don't you?" Evelyn asked.

She moved slightly forward, close enough that her nose was just inches away from Clara's clit. Evelyn then reached for a long strand of pearls, the ones used as a model for the statue, and wrapped them around Clara's leg. She pulled one end of the strand and rolled the beads ever closer to that slit.

Her partner shivered in response and stiffened in anticipation. Still, this was not her ultimate goal, just a way to introduce a new toy. Once the pearls were nearly between Clara's legs, she closed them on instinct, which shifted the beads directly over the clit and between her labia.

Evelyn giggled and let one side go, allowing the entire strand to become soaked in those warm juices. She brought her other hand to Clara's *derriere*, her fingers travelling between those cheeks until they found that distinctive star which Evelyn had neglected.

When Clara tightened up, Evelyn said, "Now. Now. *Ma chère*, have a little… faith."

Clara did relax, but only slightly, so she rubbed the first bead in the strand around the star. The motion was light and expertly done, knowing full-well that more coaxing was needed.

Evelyn looked up so her voice would carry and whispered, "Relax. Soon I'll have you dripping in come. Let your body serve as my instrument."

When feathers rubbed up against her legs, Evelyn pushed in the first bead. Despite her precautions, its insertion caused Clara to stiffen. She repeated the process for the second and third time until Clara moaned with every insertion.

"Good girl," Evelyn said with a giggle, before wrapping what remained of the necklace around her wrist.

Her bound hand slid down a few inches, enough for her two longest fingers to venture into Clara's warm and welcoming crevice. This time, she took it nice and slow, letting Clara gasp as the whole of her body gave in to the stimulation.

"Did you miss me?" Evelyn asked, her fingers pressed against that distinct patch of skin facing towards her.

"Mmmmhmmm," Clara managed to say.

Once again, Evelyn smiled despite her overstimulated partner beginning to settle. Clara needed to come down a bit, if only to send her straight into the stratosphere.

"I could stop?" Evelyn teased.

"No!" Clara exclaimed for the first time in an hour.

Evelyn giggled and chose that moment to rub that spot, feeling the walls around her fingers tighten. Meanwhile, her other hand reached behind Clara and brought forward a purple wand with bunny ears.

"Now be a good girl," Evelyn said. "You need to come so hard that you push me out. Understood?"

Evelyn turned on the wand, using the vibrating fork to stimulate the inside of Clara's thighs. Again, the intent was to introduce her partner to a new source of stimulation. It would give her a chance to acclimatise before applying it to just the right spot.

Clara moaned even as the pressure relaxed around Evelyn's fingers. That's when the wand sailed over the curves of Clara's body until it straddled her partner's clit.

Just above Evelyn's head, Clara responded by throwing hers back. While fer face was out of sight, her breasts became neatly outlined by the overhead lights. Those hard nipples beckoned. Alas, she would never be able to taste their salty goodness, not without risking her life.

So, Evelyn focused all of her attention on Clara, paying particular attention to her heart rate and breathing. That permitted her to adjust what she did so the two would rise in lockstep.

From a distance, Evelyn would have witnessed those wings expand. They rose from off of Evelyn's legs until they unfurled horizontally. Only then could Evelyn see them, their shadow growing perpendicular to her.

That's when Evelyn stopped cold, dropped the wand, and let her remaining hand slip down from between her lover's legs. That motion caused the beads to pop out one after the other and added to all of that bottled up passion, the culmination of which finally pushed Clara past the finish line.

She came hard and her wings expanded to their full size, just before her knees gave out entirely. The exhausted angel fell forward onto Evelyn and remained like that for a while. Clara used this reprieve to suck in as much air as her lungs could handle.

As her heart rate returned to normal, Clara wrapped her arms around her mistress. Only then did she realise that Evelyn was not entirely there.

"Is everything alright?" Clara asked.

Evelyn did not say anything nor move at first. Given the bodysuit and mask, Clara lacked all of the normal tells that would indicate if something was wrong.

"Evelyn?" Clara asked.

It took a moment longer, but Evelyn eventually breathed in through her teeth and giggled. She wrapped her arms around this warm and welcoming angel. Her eyes, distant and glassy, they were thankfully hidden behind the mask's screen.

"Sorry," Evelyn said. "That was something else."

"Ab-so-lute-ly," Clara replied before a pause. "I'm pretty sure that my first taste of ambrosia paled in comparison."

"Glad I could be of service," Evelyn said grinning, despite the mask concealing the effect.

Clara let out a long-contented sigh, cuddling the latex doll at her side. The memory of that orgasm created aftershocks which rippled through her body.

"Wait," Clara said. "Were you talking about one of your own?"

Evelyn pushed her mask against Clara's lips and made a kissing sound. While not ideal, that was the best they could manage.

"Yes, I did," Evelyn said.

"How?" Clara pressed.

"All in my mind," Evelyn said. "The sight of your entire body convulsing, including those magnificent wings… was more than enough."

"Glad I could be of service," Clara mimicked.

Evelyn leaned in for another kiss and rested her head on the floor. For many, the cold seeping out of the concrete would have ruined the mood, but the cold never bothered the dead anyway.

Still, there was something gnawing at her. It was fortunate for Evelyn that Clara was too busy basking in the afterglow to notice.

* * * *

"You've been chasing me?" the confused Elizabeth asked since none of her sins warranted this level of response.

While that thing behind her fit the profile of a monster, the woman before her did not. Clearly, this world hidden from humanity was far more nuanced than Clara had led her to believe.

Adrienne cocked a brow. The idea of being questioned had a distinctly negative impact on her demeanour. Elizabeth caught the change and cringed, knowing full-well there would be a penalty for this perceived slight.

"I'm sorry—" Elizabeth said.

The hard slap across Elizabeth's face was more than she deserved. It stung, sure, but it could have been worse. That thing standing behind her could easily bite her head clean off.

Instead of trying to talk her way out of this situation, Elizabeth opted to watch and wait. Only through observation would she be able to find vulnerabilities and exploit them to her advantage.

She lowered her gaze, and kept quiet, all the while remaining alert to any and all commands. Given how these animals had torn up the subway and killed potential witnesses just to get at her, it was safe to assume they were not in the mood to play games. *Why the fuck would they put so much effort into finding me?*

She had to assume that werewolves were not normally interested in social workers, unless they had unknowingly interacted with the group. *Or is it a pack?* However, these were the first creatures Clara encountered when she fell to Earth. So, either that was a wild coincidence or that was a factor. One way or the other, there was no point in assigning blame. *What good would that do?*

"*Humans*," Adrienne said. "So pathetic. So weak."

When one of the werewolves chuckled like a hyena, Adrienne shot it a dirty look and everyone nearby went silent. Now, that exchange was telling, but Elizabeth needed more to work with…

"William," Adrienne said while looking towards the towering monstrosity standing behind Elizabeth. "Make sure she gets delivered to the den unharmed."

Without warning, a large clawed hand grabbed Elizabeth by the shoulder and despite being six feet tall, she was lifted right off her feet. The last time she experienced such a display of strength, she had been six or seven years old. *Shit! That's just fucked up.*

"Now. Make sure you get someone else to do it," Adrienne added. "An alpha should never take on menial tasks."

That heavy hand left Elizabeth's shoulder, and for the briefest of moments, she thought of making a run for it. Who would not? Still, she knew it was foolhardy to fuck with anything capable of outrunning and ripping her to shreds. This exchange merely reinforced the need to continue observing.

This time, it was another who grabbed Elizabeth by the shoulder, but smaller in stature. She remained in place, waiting for direction and that came soon enough.

"Move it," the gruff man barked.

In that voice, Elizabeth detected a hint of annoyance and disdain. Clearly, not everyone was happy with the current situation. Or did that tone stem from a deep sense of disenfranchisement? Elizabeth moved forward in a straight line until she was nudged into a new direction.

She opted to take a peek at the man. His long unkempt beard and hair were a given, but the dark patches under his eyes indicated severe fatigue. She supposed that the act of turning into a werewolf was stressful on the body and mind.

Still, it was what he wore that bothered her. He had on a pair of wool suit pants, a god-awful plaid shirt, and a stained winter jacket, all a few sizes too big. This mishmash of clothing assaulted the eye, not for the poor taste in fashion, but the fact it had been pilfered from his victims.

This time, the man slipped ahead of her to lead the way. She followed him down the tunnel devoid of all-natural light, and wondered how bad this would get before it got better.

"I have to meet our informant," Adrienne said. "You know what needs to get done before we leave here."

Elizabeth may have been unsure about a great deal of things, but she had no doubt that this would not end well for those left on that train.

"May God have mercy on their souls," Elizabeth mumbled, which was the most respectful thing she could think of to say.

"There is no God," the man replied.

With those words came Elizabeth's first real lesson. Werewolves had superb hearing, no matter what state they were in. *So why was Adrienne talking so loudly?*

\* \* \* \*

Once Clara descended from cloud nine, she adjusted her position to get a better view of Evelyn. Meanwhile, her arms remained wrapped around her doll, and she stared into what would have been those piercing green eyes before smiling.

"A thought occurred," Clara said as though waking up from a dream.

She sensed Evelyn shift to get more comfortable. In reaction to that statement, the doll moved a finger to her chin to highlight her curiosity.

Clara chuckled and added, "You essentially did all of *that* with both hands tied behind your back. Didn't you?"

Evelyn giggled, the whole of her body reacting for heightened effect. Clara kept on smiling while the other nodded in agreement.

"I'd hate to imagine what you'd have done to me without restrictions," Clara said.

"Hate is such a strong word, *ma chère*," Evelyn finally said.

"True," Clara replied. "I was trained to never lose myself in any situation."

"*Vraiment?*" Evelyn asked in a mocking tone. "It's a wonder your order was able to retain a membership."

"Compared to a regular convent, we had it pretty good," Clara quipped.

That line dredged up memories from her time at the Tower, specifically of how often hunters and acolytes went missing. It was true that some of them had paid the ultimate price to fulfil missions. Still, more often than not, hunters simply walked away.

That was a dilemma that Clara was intimately familiar with. She had the choice of dropping her weapons for a chance at a normal life. Alternatively, there was the option of moving forward with her training, knowing that an unpleasant death would likely follow. For her, the choice had been simple; how could anyone live a normal life knowing what lurked in the shadows?

"It's been a while for me," Clara said to change the subject.

"Weeks? Months?" Evelyn asked.

"A *lot* longer," Clara said.

"Oh?" Evelyn said before the answer popped into her mind. "Ohhhhhh."

"Yeah…" Clara said. "So, I needed this."

"It was an honour," Evelyn said, before caressing Clara's face with a free hand.

There was a lot about this period of intimacy that Clara needed. That primal connection with her body and the ability to let someone else take charge, these were all crucial to reconnecting with her humanity. Evelyn had been there at just the right time to collect the spoils.

Still, this impish woman, capable of creating such intense beauty, was just as skilled at unleashing unspeakable horrors. For now, they were aligned, but Clara knew a lot of the puzzle was missing. That much was obvious given their outing.

As beautiful and fulfilling as this moment was, Clara was left with the impression that all of this had been planned, a series of events neatly aligned to reach a goal, a bit like dominos falling in sequence to form an image after being toppled over. In hindsight, it was obvious that she should have dedicated more time to resolving issues with Elizabeth. Was it even possible with all of this pent-up sexual tension? Was that not just begging for failure?

Clara's relationship with Elizabeth was out of balance, all stemming from being honour bound to look after her friend's safety. Elizabeth's growing dependency further stressed the relationship, which introduced a dynamic that was toxic for both.

The fact that Clara had given in to her baser urges would only serve to complicate matters. Still, this would also force her to face this situation with Elizabeth head on. Or, would the guilt that was sure to follow come into play and poison the well? These were questions that she desperately wanted to avoid, at least for a couple of hours more.

"I'm pretty sure you have that backwards," Clara said, as the mere memory of what Evelyn did was enough to send a shiver down her spine.

Evelyn may have limited her senses due to the presence of that body suit, but she was able to take in the scent of her partner's renewed arousal. That truth was enough to set a smile on those concealed lips.

"No," Evelyn said. "I thoroughly enjoyed watching you come over and over again."

Clara adjusted her position to get comfortable, nuzzling into Evelyn's neck. Normally, the air would grow warm and make breathing difficult, but that was not a concern here. Lastly, she shifted one of her wings to cover them.

"So, I was a good girl?" Clara teased.

Evelyn giggled while caressing Clara's shoulder length hair. Every so often, she would come across a knot in her hair, which made Clara wince. Still, the reactions grew more subdued with every occurrence.

"Such a good girl," Evelyn whispered.

"Mmmmhmmm," Clara said before nuzzling in deeper.

Soon Clara's breathing turned soft and deep as she surrendered to Morpheus' soothing verses. That left Evelyn alone with her thoughts, free to ponder the ramifications of this evening's complications.

\* \* \* \*

Adrienne watched another one from their pack revert to his human form. She checked her mobile and realised that the sun was about to rise. Alas, that was the best they could get of these louts, at least until tomorrow when the moon reached its apex.

"Get some clothes on," Adrienne sneered.

When the peach-fuzz wielding teenager gave her the evil eye, she smirked. The cold look in her eyes was a firm reminder that repercussions were severe for those who did not fall in line. The pack had learned that the hard way when William gained control.

William had the bravery, brutality, and brawn to make him a feared member of the group. What he lacked was guile and a keen intellect, both of which his mother had in excess. Under her guidance, any hint of dissidence was put down without mercy.

"Yes ma'am," the adolescent replied and ran off towards the train.

She eyed that milky white moon giving way to the sun on her app and huffed. She had other matters to deal with, and it would not be long before emergency response teams converged on them. As planned, their diversions had effectively slowed down response times throughout the city. A great deal of resources would be expended to deal with their chaos.

"Send her my way!" Adrienne barked.

The adolescent jumped before running off. She chuckled at his lily-white ass before focusing on the phone.

After a minute or two, a pale and sickly looking individual stepped off the train and headed her way. The individual was thin, and obviously suffering from malnourishment as judged by those sunken cheeks and ashen skin. The clothes were several sizes too big, an *outfit* with enough spare material to serve as a sail. *How on earth do those pants stay up?*

"Aunt," Julia said meekly.

The feminine undertones in that voice were the only clue that the speaker was a woman. Without it, she could disappear amongst the cities downtrodden without raising a brow. For the most part, men did leave her alone, well, except for that creep who had a thing for kids…

Adrienne ignored the new arrival, engrossed by the contents of her screen. She even giggled once or twice for effect, showcasing the importance of her time compared to that filth waiting at the door.

Julia coughed and watched for a reaction. When none came, she realised that this entire exchange would have to be done formally. Defeated, she sighed softly, kneeled, and forced her eyes to focus on a point midway between them.

"Den Mother," Julia said.

As though on cue, Adrienne looked up from her phone but flashed the five-minute hand signal. This response forced Julia to remain in this uncomfortable position, requiring her to bow before what was once a choice piece of ass, yet well past her best before date.

"I'll never understand what Dad saw in her," Julia muttered.

That statement fortunately did not elicit a response. The last one who dared make such remarks ended up eating their own tongue. Adrienne would not tolerate anyone questioning her place nor authority within the pack.

Adrienne eventually looked up from her phone, but to torment the other she first scanned the room. It appeared as though she had forgotten the reason for Julia being there, and this sham went on for a moment until she chose to acknowledge her.

"Julia," Adrienne said. "So, you're the one who sent us that tip?"

"Yes," Julia replied. She then thought it best to add, "Den Mother."

Adrienne grinned because she could almost hear Julia grinding her teeth every time that title was used. A lot had changed since the altercation which led to the death of her lover. Despite being left behind, Julia had been found safe and sound at the bar. In a stroke of luck, the head trauma also left Julia with a fractured memory. That gave Adrienne the opportunity to lay seeds of doubt about Julia's role in the alpha's death. Who could trust one of their own who left that club without a scratch? Doubt turned into mistrust, which made it easy for Adrienne to sway opinion and get her lover's daughter shunned. Yet, here she was, trying to bribe her way back into the pack.

"So… you want a medal?" Adrienne asked.

The young woman's eyes bulged when that statement registered. She then understood that Adrienne had no interest in allowing a link to the old alpha to return. It could easily upset all of their hard work.

"I was—" Julia said.

"You were?" Adrienne interrupted.

"I w—" Julia replied.

"Speak up," Adrienne said to interrupt. "I can't hear a word you've said."

Adrienne observed how Julia's fists clenched and relaxed. The girl's eyes were closed, all in an attempt to cool the blood coursing through her veins. Such coping mechanisms might have worked if the Den Mother were inclined to cooperate.

"I—" Julia tried to say.

"Can someone get her a pen and some paper?" Adrienne asked with a sickly smile. "Looks like you—"

Julia opened her eyes and gave those facing her a great view of that hate burning within. The taunting had worked, Adrienne was faced with a proverbial bull ready to charge. Still, the *Den Mother* was not happy, or at least not yet. To push things over the edge, she stuck out her tongue.

"You cunt!" Julia yelled, pushed herself up, and charged.

As expected, the ruckus was more than enough to get noticed by those nearby. Adrienne appeared unimpressed by this show of strength, so much so that she brought her phone in line with her chest and tapped on the screen.

The flash from her phone lit up the room, creating a strobe light effect. For a brief moment, Julia felt like she was moving from one frame to another like a celluloid film strip. While such a tool could blind and distract, the effect was severe for those recovering from a concussion.

Julia hesitated, leaving ample opportunity for Adrienne to land a blow on her shins. The impact was immediate and brutal, especially for someone not expecting it. Then, without mercy, Adrienne dropped her phone and followed through with an uppercut.

The impact connected just below the chin and sent Julia flying backwards onto the tile floor. Her head made contact first, which would not help matters.

As expected, none who witnessed the altercation interfered. Such was the custom when one was challenged for dominance. By goading Julia into making the initial move, Adrienne had been able to attack openly, and no one would bat an eye if she chose to slit her throat.

Adrienne licked her lips in anticipation, just as an idea popped into her head. There were uses for someone like Julia, some that might be leveraged into an even greater win.

While Julia was a threat as long as she lived, potential windfall from this gambit led her to consider an alternate path. She grabbed her phone, and made sure to kneel right by Julia.

While pretending to play a game on her phone, Adrienne said, "You lost this round. Still, if you were to bring me the head of the one who killed my *lover…*"

Adrienne left it at that and got back on her feet. For effect, she spat on Julia's face and laughed. The sound of her cackling echoed throughout, creating the illusion of a crowd mocking Julia.

"Even *I* can show mercy," Adrienne said aloud for the benefit of those nearby. "Now. Get that filth out of my sight."

With those words, Adrienne turned away from the fallen girl and faded into the shadows. That whisper had planted a seed deep within Julia's subconscious, one that would soon take hold and bring forth the foundations of a plan. Despite the drool rolling down Julia's cheek, she smiled weakly before losing consciousness.

# CHAPTER 9

## *A FRESH PERSPECTIVE*

C lara's eyes opened up in a flutter, and once again she was confused as to her whereabouts. The room was dark with nothing more than the red glow of a distant exit sign to light the way. Clara rubbed the sleep from her eyes, which gave her a better view of her surroundings.

Despite starting out in life as a human, her eyes could cope in low light situations. The first thing she made out was the doll-like creation at her side. That was enough of a reminder to put everything into focus.

"Horsefeathers," Clara swore under her breath.

Evelyn giggled before running a hand across Clara's cheek. Despite the gesture being soft and gentle in nature, Clara found herself evading the attempt.

"Something wrong?" Evelyn asked.

"Nothing… really," Clara answered and put on a warm smile.

In truth, Clara was annoyed for failing to heed to her own warnings. Last night turned out to be prophetic, and despite desperately needing the passion and intimacy, guilt crept in the moment those needs were quenched.

"*Ma chère*, do not take me for a fool," Evelyn said dryly.

Evelyn then slipped out from under Clara's wing before pushing herself from off the floor. The motion curved her back, which defined the shape of her breasts and ass. For a moment, Clara wondered if this woman was capable of turning off her flirtatious nature.

"Ah," Evelyn added. "It feels divine to stretch my back and muscles after a night on the floor."

"Night?" Clara asked, confused.

The reply was not immediate. Initially, Evelyn moved her legs forward enough so that her thighs were perpendicularly aligned to the rest of her body. Without a doubt, that position would have given some lucky soul a spectacular view of her slit. Alas, the body suit just left behind an impression of the glory that was.

"*Mais oui*," Evelyn said before getting on her feet. "You woke, up when the sun passed over the horizon."

"How do you know?" Clara asked while getting up.

"Because I'm a creature of the night," Evelyn replied. "You woke up, just as I was feeling the need to doze off."

Clara never thought about the reasons for her waking up when she did, let alone that it was tied to the solar cycle. However, she was capable of resisting the urges to sleep like Evelyn was doing right now.

"Sorry," Clara said.

"To which?" Evelyn asked with a giggle.

Clara cocked a brow before saying, "Both... actually."

"No need to be sorry on either account," Evelyn replied in those musical tones. "You may have spent a lifetime hunting my kind. It does not mean you know every nuance associated with those who haunt the night."

Their first meeting had been proof enough of that. Clara had been an independent hunter back then, still living within the limitations of her humanity. While her mission had been successful, she caught the eye of this devastatingly beautiful vampire standing before her.

Clara could have easily ended up dead or turned, however, she had been spared for reasons that were beyond her. Still, that meeting served as a wakeup call, a clue that vampires were far better organised than previously thought. That, and how a select few were able to indulge in food without becoming violently ill.

"True," Clara said with a smirk.

"As for the first matter," Evelyn said to get back on track. "Let me guess... you are ridden with guilt?"

She opted to keep a stoic appearance at the mention of the emotional turmoil she was only now coming to terms with. The Tower had trained them to keep their true selves hidden at all times. Funny how that had never been a problem before. Although, they never trained her to deal with the complexities associated with *going native*, or how to cope with the feelings developed while watching over her friend.

"Nailed it," Clara said, opting for the straightforward approach.

"I knew that going in," Evelyn said.

"Really?" Clara questioned while those words sunk in.

Evelyn exaggerated a nod and approached. Better prepared, Clara did not back away and let this doll sit beside her.

"Your eyes are set firmly on Elizabeth," Evelyn said before falling into a hug. "I knew that I'd be playing second fiddle once you got what you needed from our tryst."

Clara looked down and caressed the doll's hair. While the hair felt real enough, it was nothing more than an elaborate wig. The act should have been soothing, but the artificial nature of this situation began to wear thin.

"Besides, how could we manage... really?" Evelyn asked before giggling.

She was about to say something, but a stray thought entered her mind. Again, it felt as though this situation had been purposefully constructed, just like her lover's overall appearance. For all intents and purposes, she had spent last night getting off on a very sophisticated sex toy. Her lover may have been flesh and *blood* underneath, however, she was plastic on the outside and something else entirely at the core.

*"One day you'll wake up and see me for the monster I am,"* Evelyn had said on the day they met.

While Clara had not forgotten this lesson entirely, she did choose to ignore it. The entire contrived situation was designed to get her vulnerable, just enough to lower her guard. *I wonder if this is Evelyn's modus operandi?*

"To what end?" Clara wondered. "For the exploit? For the emotional blackmail and leverage that could conceivably be gained? Just to fuck an angel and live to tell the tale?"

Clara's eyes widened for a split second before pulling away. Evelyn did the same, returning to the base of the statue that would soon bear Clara's likeness in frightening detail.

"So, you aren't bothered by this?" Clara said, opting to stay the course.

In that moment, there was a burning desire to extricate herself from this studio and get home. Given the time of day, Elizabeth would likely be at home and hopefully sleeping. That would give her the opportunity to not only confess her sins, but to talk about their feelings? *What if she turns her back on me?*

Any relationship founded on lies was bound to fail. Lies begat more lies, and eventually, neither side had a grasp of the truth. It was better for Elizabeth to see Clara as the flawed creature she really was.

"*Non,*" Evelyn said. "It was a beautiful experience, one that I'll cherish."

"But…" Clara said in anticipation.

Evelyn giggled before moving deeper into her studio. Once she reached a work desk, Clara heard the click of a toggle-button.

"Yes, Madame Chartres?" a voice said on the intercom.

"Can you come to the studio please?" Evelyn said.

"Right away, Madame," the voice replied.

Clara looked around for her soiled costume, but it was lost in a maze of art. This made getting dressed rather difficult, doubly so once she realised that her actual clothes were somewhere else. *That includes my damaged boots.*

"Aww nertz," Clara said.

"Are you worried that you hurt my feelings?" Evelyn asked.

"Not precisely," Clara replied while searching the area for something to wear.

"*Reviens une minute, veux-tu?*" Evelyn said in a stern voice.

When Clara popped out from behind a row of paintings, Evelyn giggled. She then shifted out of existence and reappeared just in front of the angel.

"Or I can come to you," Evelyn added. "Don't worry about getting dressed in… that costume. I've taken care of it."

"Familiar territory for you?" Clara asked.

Evelyn ignored that comment and said, "My assistant will be bringing in your own clothes momentarily."

"Thank—" Clara said.

Evelyn gave Clara a peck on both cheeks. Each kiss was accompanied by the expected sound but not the feel of it. Again, this beautifully executed situation only served to confirm that this had all been staged.

"No need," Evelyn said. "I do want you to keep one thought in your mind."

"What is it?" Clara asked.

In the background, the soft steps of a woman approaching gained clarity. Clara looked down at her nudity which served to showcase how exposed she was.

"We are still here for you," Evelyn said. She then got onto the tips of her toes and whispered, "Now, if you ever want to do this again, day or night, I'm game."

And with that a door opened, flooding the room in white light. In the distance, Clara made out the silhouette of a stern looking woman who was holding her things. Even those tell-tale boots adorned the pile.

"You'll be the first to know," Clara said.

Evelyn ventured deeper into her studio and disappeared from sight. Always one for theatrics, Evelyn's giggling reverberated off of walls, creating a haunting effect.

"That girl knows how to make an exit," Clara said, but the assistant did not say a word.

* * * *

Julia was lost in a dream, one where they were holding a banquet in her honour. It even featured a spit roasted remains of a police officer, although some in the pack preferred to use the term long *pig*. Really the difference hardly mattered once the bitterness of beer reached her tongue.

"All for me?" Julia asked, wearing a big toothy smile.

Adrienne knelt in the corner, and it was clear from her face that this woman looked positively miserable cleaning the floor by hand. She also guessed that the guest of honour had worsened her mood.

"Miss?" A muffled voice asked.

Julia turned around to look but found no one there. Given the situation, she shook off her confusion and paid attention to the festivities.

"Here! Here!" Her father bellowed.

When the crowd simmered down to a dull roar, the alpha said. "You know that I've never been one for speeches."

Several laughed at those words because her father took pride in being a man of action. He would sooner rip out the spine of an irritant than try to reason with them. Although, that was not entirely true. He always had ample time and patience for his children, namely William and Julia. He would often regale them with tales of his youth-fuelled exploits. To his children, those stories were the fairy tales they grew up with.

"Lady?" That same muffled voice asked a second time.

This time she ignored it, choosing instead to focus her attention on the silver haired biker before her. The long shaggy beard and hair complimented his muscled exterior. This was a silver aged version of the 'mountain man' from that song their father used to play. Or at least, that's how he told it. In truth, it was the 'monkey man,' he just liked his version of the song better.

"So, I'll just say that I'm proud of my daughter," her father said.

He then looked at Julia with a twinkle in his eyes, one that would only be explained away by some lame excuse. The emotion welled up within her, and she fought to keep from becoming an emotional wreck.

"For bringing me the head of that whore who tried to kill me four months ago," her father added.

Her brother approached the head table with an oversized tray. He smiled, placed the tray gingerly on the table, and bowed. William was happy, she could tell from the genuine smile on his lips.

"Time to wake up," the muffled voice said.

Once more, she opted to ignore the voice. Instead, she eyed the tray as he lifted it from the serving plate to reveal the severed head of a woman. While the skull had been cut open to give access to the brain, the top part had been replaced for aesthetic reasons.

The skin was nice and golden brown, including the plucked scalp. What had once been a pair of soft lips were dry and blackened. Julia was certain that they would taste like smoked jerky. So much so, that the idea of feasting on them made her salivate.

"As our guest of honour," her father said. "I'd like her to have the first taste!"

Meanwhile, her father peeled back a dry eyelid to reveal the eye and buried a steak knife into its side. This gave him enough leverage to pop out the eye intact, including part of the optic nerve.

"For the love of my life," her father said gently while handing over the knife.

No one else heard those words, but they meant everything to her. She turned the eye to find the iris intact. Surprising, since it had been in an oven for several hours. Julia then looked at that steel-grey eye and sucked on the optic nerve endings.

Thunderous applause followed, growing in intensity as she pulled in the rest until her lips rested against the blade. Without fear, she withdrew the knife and smiled, revealing the eye caught in between her teeth.

"Last chance," the muffled voice said.

This time, those words were accompanied by a sharp jab to her ribs. The pain was so intense that she pushed her chair back and slammed against the cold floor.

No one in the room, including her father, appeared to notice.

* * * *

As the cab pulled up to the curb, Clara scanned the windows down the alley for any signs of activity. Other than a dim light originating from their kitchen, the place was dark and uninviting. So, either that meant that Elizabeth was asleep, or she never made it home last night.

"How much?" Clara asked.

"No charge," the cabby replied. "They paid up front."

Clara smiled, and slipped a twenty to the driver. While certain that Evelyn had paid the gratuity, she was interested in showing her appreciation for the effort.

"Hey. Thanks," the cabby said in response.

"No. Thanks for the ride," Clara said while leaving the cab.

While standing at the curb, she closed her eyes and focused. The sounds of the city disappeared one by one, until all that remained were heartbeats. The building was always full of people this early in the morning, and two located in the same unit were beating wildly. It did not take a cardiologist to figure out what those two were up to.

Clara smiled at the thought of waking up in bed with Elizabeth. Her eyes conjured up the imagery of those breasts rising as she breathed in. All the while, feeding off their desire for one another, it would take no time at all for their heart rates to be racing too.

"*Not the kind of ride I was hoping for,*" the cabby said as the man caught sight of that smile. "Hey. Wait a minute, you forgot your feather."

She was momentarily confused by that statement since her wings were hidden within that greatcoat. Eventually, her eyes widened as she caught sight of the brass feather and she reached in for it.

"Thanks," Clara said.

Clara then checked around and found a gaggle of people standing outside their building. There was also a maintenance crew working down the alley. Disappointed that she could not stretch out her wings, she sighed and walked in through the front door.

The rest was all part of her routine: checking the mailbox for correspondence, looking over the notice board, walking upstairs while skipping every second one. She even smiled at the nosey neighbours who opened their doors to gaze upon the late arrival.

Only once Clara passed the mustard plaster's unit did she pause. The odour of wet dogs that wafted in from the unit was noticeably stronger now. Again, the scent was familiar, but she could not remember why.

This man must have taken in a stray because this generally unpleasant man rarely missed an opportunity to leer at her. If anything, she was tempted to leave a dog cleaning service gift card, and call this a victory.

So, she pushed on, paused at their door, steeled her resolve, and slid back the deadbolt.

"Now or never, girl," Clara said softly.

Despite there being no heartbeats near their place, she opened the door carefully to avoid waking Elizabeth. As light from the hallway bled into the living room, she glanced inside, but found no traces of her friend.

"Okay," Clara said before stepping inside, immediately lobbing off those damaged boots.

With nothing more than her two layers of socks to cover her feet, she crept up nearer to the bedroom, took a peek, and found the bed undisturbed. Now that her suspicions were confirmed, Clara was both relieved and worried.

Relieved that this much needed conversation could wait, it gave her the opportunity to run through variations of what she needed to say. Then again, this reprieve also forced her to dwell on the guilt, and that would worsen her mood until the opportunity came to get it off her chest.

"Where is she?" Clara asked while checking her phone for the tenth time since getting in that cab.

There were no new notifications from Elizabeth. That in itself was unusual, since she normally kept Clara informed when the plan changed. Still, the fight could easily explain the deviation from the norm. *So, where is she?*

She considered restarting her phone, but there were several notifications from other contacts, including Evelyn. When she checked the latter's message, she found an image waiting for her.

It was a picture of Evelyn and the statue. Both were nude, but the artist was taking a selfie while holding a chisel. Since this picture was centred on the statue's berry patch, Clara guessed what section of this work would be getting details added today.

"She certainly got a great view of it last night," Clara said and chuckled.

Despite the smile, Clara was hurt, and even felt dirty. Evelyn's picture was exactly the type of reminder she did not need. Although this proved that Evelyn was not bothered by Clara giving her the cold shoulder.

"At least I'm not fighting a war on two fronts," Clara said.

Although, a no-win scenario did have a tendency of clearing her head. Why worry about everything that was going wrong with life when her very existence was in jeopardy?

"Alright." Clara said after settling on a plan. "Get these boots replaced with a pair in the closet, grab a quick bite, then have a nice long shower."

While Clara made her way into the kitchen, she deleted Evelyn's thread, including that selfie. For one, she was doing it out of respect for her friend, and she also wanted to avoid taking a cold shower…

* * * *

Julia woke up in pain with her arms protecting her tender midsection. Before taking a dip, a police officer grabbed her by the arm.

"Whoa there," the officer said.

As the crepuscular light shone into her eyes, she froze. For a moment, she stopped breathing until it dawned on her she was out of that subway tunnel. That meant this particular officer might not be out to arrest her.

"Where am I?" Julia asked, without the faintest clue as to why water was trickling in the background.

"Are you okay?" the officer asked. "Do we need to take you to the hospital?"

Julia's eyes widened when the word *hospital* registered. Her kind had no need for a series of invasive tests that might lead doctors to realise that she was not entirely human. Still, the world came into focus, and she noticed that she was dealing with a female officer. All the while, her all too serious partner remained in the background holding a baton.

"Figures," Julia muttered. "No, ma'am."

"Are you sure?" the officer asked. "Did you blackout at a bar or club?"

Julia chuckled nervously since it was plain as day that anyone dressed like her would not be going clubbing. Still, she had to appreciate the compassion that this one was showing.

"No, ma'am. I got lucky last night when someone dropped a whole wad of cash into my cup…" Julia lied.

A total fabrication, but one she hoped would shake this officer loose. She had no desire to spend time in lockup or be carted off to a hospital. Besides, they might have her committed if her erratic behaviour kicked in on account of her migraines.

"Alright then," the officer said in a tone that hinted that she had just lost a bet. "I want you cleared out of this park by the time we circle back. Understood?"

"Yes, ma'am," Julia said while nodding.

She was half-tempted to ask which park this was. However, a quick glance at the partially frozen fountain behind her and the skyline was all she needed. *That means I'm close.*

The image of Clara's head cooked to perfection clawed its way back to the forefront of her mind. While a dream, the sight of her father had been desperately needed. But it also reminded Julia of the loss, and it felt like that *woman* had taken him away for the second time.

"I'm going to enjoy tearing into you as you scream for mercy," Julia said before licking those lips.

A man passing by looked up from his phone. For a moment, they eyed one another, but he quickly lost his nerve and made a hasty retreat towards heavily frequented areas of the park.

"They'll love me... worship me... when I bring them her head," Julia said.

She then lifted up the collar of her frayed jacket to keep her neck warm. She had a hunch that the wind would pick up and make it difficult to hunt with chattering teeth. Fortunately, the course she plotted would take her far away from those officers or the man with frayed nerves.

"I still got it," Julia said.

* * * *

A young man named Vincent sat on a lounger in a room that reeked of mothballs, analgesic cream, and death. He was surrounded by clutter, mostly memorabilia from the former occupant's glory days. Such collections were a sure-fire way to remind anyone how getting old sucked.

The only redeeming quality of this place was the recliner. While threadbare, this chair was comfortable, not surprising seeing how this was the throne to this tenant's masturbatorium. This hoarder had amassed stacks of porn, all neatly piled up right beside the television, and given the opportunity, Vincent would indulge.

Instead of keeping an eye out, he fell asleep and remained as such until a loud clang resonated throughout the outside hallway. The noise roused him from his fatigue induced stupor which left him momentarily confused about his whereabouts.

"Oh yeah," Vincent said while pulling out his phone.

He found the right contact, and his eyes twinkled in celebration at his own rapier-like wit. 'Queen bitch', the moniker he chose, fit that woman to a tee. Besides, the recipient would never know, which meant there were no risks. With a smug look on his face, he typed.

> Vincent: Subject has arrived. 🐱

To celebrate a job well-done, he decided to peruse the old man's collection after completing this task. Really? Did anyone ever need an excuse for porn?

# CHAPTER 10
## *A DAY WITH THE INDOOR AVIATOR*

Julia had not stepped inside Clara's building before today. It was best to keep away from prying eyes, and distance permitted her to keep an eye out for that murderess and her so-called *roommate*. That way, they could carry on with their lives, while Julia gained intelligence without detection.

Surveillance. That task was made far easier due to the opposing building being condemned, an address that gained notoriety for being the site of several ritualistic murders.

This time, there was a real need for her to take the initiative. She knew that Clara would be taking a shower, which meant that she was alone and isolated from her wide array of weapons. This would be her best shot, and she doubted a better opportunity would present itself before Adrienne lost patience.

"Get in," Julia said while visualising her plan. "Grab a knife."

While Julia's objectives were straight forward, maintaining an element of surprise was the problem. That woman killed her father on a cold autumn night… naked! The thought of facing an armed opponent *that* skilled made her cringe.

"Yeah… easy," Julia said and then gulped.

She considered adding a witty one-liner to get pumped up, but such words would only ring hollow. This was her chance of exacting her revenge and to be welcomed back into the pack. Surely the rewards were well worth the risk? *As long as Adrienne follows through on her promises.*

After mulling over the scenario, she slipped off her boots and placed them beside the open window. The damned things were big and clunky, to the point of nicknaming them her *moon boots*. They would make an awful racket while trying to sneak across that wooden floor.

"Besides," Julia said. "I'll be able to get my boots and jacket later, once I'm done."

That thought brought a smile to her lips. This winter had been hard on her, the result of spending most nights out under the *loving care* of mother nature. That's why a twinge of pain shot through those cracked lips when she smiled. She licked them to taste the fresh blood which helped her to get into the zone.

Her next step was a bit more challenging. She pulled herself up onto the metal railing and balanced herself on the thin ledge. While werewolves were not known to be particularly graceful, that trait was reversed while in their human form. Sure, she was not super strong, fast, or dextrous in this form, but these aspects were tweaked in her favour. That also included her ability to—

"Jump," Julia whispered prior to vaulting over the void between the buildings.

As expected, she dropped a level beneath Clara but grabbed on to the railing from below. The momentum forced her to swing towards a window. Julia spread her legs and straddled the window frame. Despite bending her knees, her body continued to drive forward, pushing her ass dangerously close to the delicate glass. Shit! *Breaking that window would be like breaking down the door.*

"Fuck," Julia let slip as her mind processed what might end up going wrong.

With luck on her side, she managed to arrest her trajectory less than an inch away from the glass. Julia pushed away from the window and let herself hang loose. Even in this position, she barely felt the railing with her toes. Before letting go, she ensured that no one was looking, glanced at her feet, and fell. Still, she almost lost balance which forced her to grab on to the stairwell leading up.

This time she bit her tongue and tasted the iron of her blood. She slid along the railing and transferred her weight onto the steps. As a precaution, one step was taken every time a car rolled by until she reached the window. Based on observations, Clara made use of the middle window to fly in and out of because it led directly into the living room.

She peeked out from the edge and found the area was deserted. Julia pushed up to open the window and it mercifully did not squeak. However, noises from within did spill out onto the streets.

"No one to talk with," Clara sang from inside the shower.

Julia opened the window just enough to slip on through. She had no desire to risk making a racket, but there was an impetus to get this over with. After all, Clara would not be in the shower forever.

"All by myself," Clara continued, singing a song that preceded Julia by sixty years.

As water splashed in the shower, Julia froze. When it was followed by the sound of a shampoo bottle being popped open, Julia pushed on. By then, Clara had shifted to humming the tune.

In the kitchen, Julia noticed that there was a plate full of food. French toast, bacon, along with fruit and a homemade potato hash. Just to the side, there was a small bowl for syrup and butter. The sight of this *feast* made her wonder when she last had a decent breakfast.

"No one to walk with," Clara sang.

Julia noticed the simple note left by the plate, a message for someone that would not make it home. Not today, or ever. Although, that was an assumption based on the pack moving forward with their plans.

On the corner of the island, she found a knife block. Without hesitation, she cycled through the knives until she found one with a heavy blade and handle. A weapon that would permit her to slash and stab away to her heart's content.

"But I'm happy—," Clara added before slipping back into a hum.

This time, when the water splashed, Julia realised that Clara was rinsing out the product in her hair. That allowed her to sneak towards the bathroom door, the glow from the lights on the other side stretching out into the living room.

Once again, she heard a bottle being cracked open. That must have been the conditioner because that was followed by an indeterminate pause to let it work its magic. For a split second, Julia was envious of someone who could shower whenever they wanted. In turn, that emotion helped to motivate her.

"—in the shower," Clara added.

Julia reached for the door knob with her left hand, while holding the knife in her right. The metal was cool to the touch, as she turned it over ever so slightly.

"Still I'm always misbehaving," Clara sang on. That voice came off as cocky, even in the shower.

Julia contorted her body to continue with the motion without using both hands. She could not chance being disarmed while opening that door, especially in an effort to keep the knob from springing back.

Once the latch was home, her heart rate climbed. Sweat rolled off her brow as she worried her that her hand might slip if she were not careful. She carefully shifted her body back to normal.

"Now. Now. N—" Julia uttered under her breath while trying to push open the door.

Instead, the door opened from the inside, with enough strength that her hand jotted free from the doorknob. Right before her was the soaking wet angel, one who also had a double-barrelled shotgun pointed straight at Julia's face.

"I'm savin' these slugs for you," Clara sang.

While those beautifully sung words hung in the air, it served to contrast Clara's appearance perfectly. This woman normally appeared to be jovial and full of life. However, her furrowed brow and piercing steel-grey eyes told Julia all she needed to know: this woman was *not* in the mood to be fucked with.

"Fuck," Julia whined before dropping the knife.

\* \* \* \*

"Figures," Vincent said.

All of those videos were nothing more than a visual tease. Not one disc contained anything more *risqué* than a soapy topless car wash. He would have killed for a single video that featured a blonde gagging on a monster cock.

While reaching for his phone to see if he could leech off someone's Wi-Fi, he heard a commotion outside. Seeing that all the networks were protected, and this porn would get him nowhere, he peeked out the window. This time, when he cocked his head just right, Vincent saw a scrawny brunette hanging from the edge of the fire escape.

"What's she doing here?" Vincent wondered, remembering to report the incident.

> Vincent: Julia is here. 😨

There tended to be delays when reporting via text messages, which turned out to be a bit of a feature when dealing with that bitch. Normally, he passed the time on Bealzabook, or at least he could when there was data left on his phone.

> Queen Bitch: Just arrived?

> Vincent: Just outside the target's apartment.

> Queen Bitch: Excellent. Report back if the situation changes.

He looked up from his screen all confused. Everything about this situation smelled, but he could not lay a finger on it.

"Do you have any idea what's going on?" Vincent asked the old man.

Despite the old man's head being turned at an unnatural angle, it was those glassy eyes and protruding vertebrae that were a clue on to his health.

Getting in was normally a breeze. Vincent had gained access to this building by bringing in takeout that he pinched from a local restaurant. People rarely questioned food deliveries, less so when they coincided with meal times.

"What? You don't know?" Vincent confirmed.

This man's bark turned out to be louder than his bite. Who threatened to call the cops over a delivery made to the *wrong* address? Well, they both knew the answer. A miser who steadfastly refused to pay. Or had he sensed the cool chill of the reaper?

"Great chat," Vincent said just as Julia entered the unit. "You know? You're a lot more fun this way."

* * * *

Clara had a finger on each trigger, and even with her light touch, the mechanism shifted. These hair triggers were unpredictable and, most importantly, dangerous for those on the receiving end.

She ignored that water dripping off her body, since such discomforts were, after all, temporary. Besides, depending how all of this panned out, the fact that she was already wet would only make it easier to clean off. Fortunately, her assailant had voluntarily disarmed herself, and that did a lot to diffuse the situation.

Clara slowed down time until individual droplets of water striking the tub's porcelain were heard. She used this opportunity to check out various ingress points. First, she confirmed they were alone, followed by the position of the deadbolt.

The door to the bedroom had not been moved, meaning this girl had not slithered her way through there. That left the living room, and the cool breeze originating from that direction confirmed her hunch. Still, the ladder had not been deployed. She would have known, because it made enough noise to wake up the dead.

That missing piece of the puzzle is what made this incursion interesting. Did she come in through another unit? Or leap across the alley? The latter would be quite a feat for a human in peak physical shape. Since the girl standing in her living room was clearly not, it hinted that this specimen was something else entirely. *What then?*

Clara used this opportunity to size up her opponent. The girl was a bit shorter, while her dark brown hair was oily and matted. Her gaunt cheeks and unhealthy waxen skin did little to compliment the overall look. This was not the first homeless woman she had come across since falling to Earth but, as far as she knew, none had any reason to tempt fate.

Then it hit her, or at least the smell did. This girl had been the source dogging her since yesterday. *How is that pertinent?*

With no other way to passively get any answers, Clara returned to normal time. She needed to open a dialogue and see how cooperative she would be.

"So, you jumped across that alley?" Clara asked with a wry smile.

Julia's deep brown eyes opened up a smidge to reveal a twinkle. Once it registered that Clara was not going to shoot, she cautiously opened them entirely, before nodding.

The non-verbal response irked Clara, a holdover from her evening out. While Evelyn had to overact to get her point across, this one's reactions were so muted she may as well have been looking at a painting. With no other option, Clara opted to pursue her current line of questioning.

"Impressive," Clara said.

"Really?" Julia questioned.

"You could have gone to the Olympics with a jump like that," Clara pushed, with no expectation of hearing the truth.

"Something like that," Julia said while focusing on those two inky black openings in the barrels.

Clara did not know what to make of this situation. Clearly this woman was not human, or at least not entirely. Even an experienced long jumper would have had trouble crossing that divide, and even they required some distance to gain speed. She decided to follow a hunch.

"Or is all of this a show of how obedient you are?" Clara said with a grin that bordered on a smirk.

Julia's eyes and narrowed, her jaw muscles bulged out, while those lips thinned. That comment managed to hit a nerve which deepened Clara's suspicions.

"Bitch!" Julia hissed.

That word, and most importantly how it was delivered, was the final piece of the puzzle. That word carried with it a hate—so much hate—that even a body count rivalling the Great War would not quench that thirst for revenge.

"So, you managed to find me?" Clara asked to confirm her suspicions.

Julia rubbed her temple. The headache she managed to keep at bay was about to assert itself. Great, a migraine would be sure to complicate matters.

"Surprised?" Julia asked.

"No," Clara said honestly, lowering her point of aim before taking a few steps back into the depths of the bathroom.

When Clara reached the counter, she felt inside the top drawer and pulled out a bottle of pills. She then tossed it to Julia and found a spot on the counter to lean against.

Julia looked at the bottle with wide eyes, lined up the arrows, and popped the cover. Without bothering to count, she swallowed half the contents of the bottle and munched down on the pills. Clara looked on, mildly horrified by what she witnessed.

"Get those often?" Clara asked.

"Ever since you fucked me up," Julia said bluntly.

"How did I—" Clara said just as something crashed into the living room.

Based on Julia's reaction, she had not been expecting it either. The girl was half-turned towards the source before dropping to her knees to cower. That was an expected response in Clara's mind, since the loud crash would have likely worsened the headache. Clara grabbed her weapon and accelerated her reaction time enough to hone her reflexes before pushing off from the counter.

Just as she approached the door frame, the beast came into sight. Bearing down on her was a werewolf, or at least something that resembled one. It had the hair, snout, and claws, but lacked a significant amount of bulk. The presence of a few patches of bare skin implied that the transformation was incomplete.

Clara did not hesitate, bringing the weapon in line with this new threat and pulling both triggers. The weapon roared to life, but despite a direct hit, the oversized pellets bounced off harmlessly.

"Horsefeathers," Clara swore.

Back at the Tower, Professor Stephens had taken a great deal of time delving into their anatomy. These were powerful and massive creatures, blessed with overlapping ribs and accelerated healing. Werewolves ignored pain better than their best hunters. When weighing these factors, why assume that it would slow down when dealt a lethal blow for humans? *I'll need to stock up on armour piercing rounds for next time.*

Clara moved until the door frame blocked his path. With any luck, that would slow him down while momentarily keeping Julia away from the eye of the storm. The wrinkle in her plan turned up when the werewolf did not alter course, continuing on a straight path for the girl.

"Get back behind this wall!" Clara yelled while withdrawing behind the counter.

This time, she pulled out a fresh pair of shells from the back of the top drawer and ejected the spent casings. She slowed down time long enough to load both barrels before the old ones bounced off the floor. Meanwhile, she kept an eye on Julia who was nearly in a foetal position by now. This poor girl was covering her ears as though ignoring this chaos would make it go away.

"Just ducky," Clara said, once it became clear that Julia was also a target.

Without another option, Clara jumped forward, grabbed Julia by those filthy clothes, and pulled her up from the floor. Her foot nearly slipped, but she managed to pivot the girl through the door and straight into the tub. To prove her suspicions, the werewolf immediately veered directly towards her.

"Awww nertz," Clara whined. "Why can't these things attack when I'm presentable?"

At that point, the thumps from its steps were shaking the floor, sure to rouse the neighbours. Clara kept an eye on the beast, and before he could reach her with his clawed hands, she slipped behind the wall.

While powerful, it lacked a certain amount of grace. The damage it caused would make one hell of a mess, but that was unavoidable now. Either way, werewolves were not known for being house trained.

Behind the wall, she counted the thumps and the interval between them. A normal person when approaching a wall at a run would slow down. People had a natural aversion to serious injury. This one actually sped up, causing the door frame to splinter as it ploughed right through the wall and frame.

Clara smiled, focused and watched as the splinters slowed down to the point of being frozen in mid-air. Her ability to linger at this relative speed was somewhat limited, so she slipped around the werewolf, went through the doorway and stopped at the front door.

This time, it was *her* turn to charge. She pushed herself away from the wall and used her wings to give her a boost. When she made contact with the werewolf, both were pushed beyond the bathroom and driven clean through an exterior brick and mortar wall. This private little fight was now on display for all the world to see.

"What a rush," Clara said while exiting the cloud of debris.

With a controlled flap of her wings, she slowed down her descent long enough to witness this beast falling face-first into the pavement. Despite a three-story drop, that would not slow him down, not without some coaxing.

Clara tucked in her wings and dove towards the falling werewolf. First came the sound of the beast belly flopping against the pavement. Second, came the high-speed impact to its side. The fractured ribs sounded just like a beam snapping in half.

The creature roared, and the adrenaline burst that coursed through its veins allowed it to push Clara off with a single shove. In response, she used her wings to alter her trajectory and set foot near a parked car.

While Clara still had the shotgun in her hands, those last two rounds had been ineffectual. That meant she would need to wait for an opportune time, one that might never come. Still, despite all of her strength and speed, she was at a disadvantage even against this runt.

So, she smashed the driver-side window, reached inside for the handle, and opened the door. She then sheared the door clean off and wielded it like a shield.

Fifteen yards away from her, the werewolf panted heavily. In this weather, its breath turned into a thick fog that reminded her of horses keeping warm during the dead of winter. Clara did her best to ignore the elements, but being naked out in the streets was not ideal for long term survival.

"Oh baby!" Some random bystander said in jest.

When Clara and the werewolf turned their heads towards this witness, their glares were enough to convince the man to exercise the better part of valour and run. Unfortunately, there were more than enough witnesses to go around, most of which were peeking through their windows.

"Are you afraid that you'll break a nail?" Clara asked to taunt the beast.

Clara needed this creature to get mad, specifically, to the point of clouding its judgement. Only then would she get the upper hand. One problem: this one was not taking the bait.

"Just enough humanity left to have some common sense, eh?" Clara whispered and grinned. "Well, it's time to take the war to you."

Her wings unfurled to their full size and blotted out the sun. Her shadow stretched out beyond the creature, and the drop in light intensity forced it to squint. *Say, that might just come in handy.*

When the annoyed werewolf roared, Clara mocked it. She then opted to push into a sprint, wielding the car door in one arm and her weapon in the other. Every step she took caused the sun to appear momentarily over her wings, enough to create a strobe effect. As she leapt into the air and flapped her wings, the werewolf was visibly befuddled, enough for her to avoid detection as she soared over its head and landed feet first just behind him.

Clara whistled and taunted, "Here boy!"

This time, the werewolf took the bait, turning its head first while the rest of his body followed. However, Clara did not hesitate. She lunged forward and ploughed into the werewolf to exploit the shift in balance.

The impact caused it to lurch to the side, but that was not enough to send him crashing down. Clara shot off one round at the creature's foot and watched as the slug pulverised tissue and bone.

Despite the howls of pain, it simply made use of its bloody stump to remain balanced. Irked at the creature's stubborn nature, she tossed her weapon into the air, grabbed the door with both hands, and swung it across that thing's head.

The impact was deafening and left a dent in the door's metal exterior that looked right at home in a high-speed pileup. This time, the werewolf went crashing down like a log.

"Tiiiiiiimmmmmberrrrrrr!" Clara yelled.

She looked up, waited, and grabbed her weapon a couple of yards back from where she stood. With one more cartridge, she casually walked over the werewolf, the sway in her hips subtle but alluring. She kicked its wounded side for good measure, but the hit barely registered to the beast.

"First lesson," Clara said. "Vampires can be killed primarily with sunlight or decapitation."

Clara then looked up at the sun and felt alive. It was as though this heavenly body was nourishing every cell in her body.

"Clearly, the sun won't do much to you," Clara said.

Without another word, she pointed the barrel at the base of its skull and fired off the last round. This time, the effect was both graphic and final. As a reward, Clara ended up covered in a thick layer of blood splatter.

"So, what's the second lesson you say?" Clara asked. "It turns out that decapitation is pretty much universal," she answered herself with a chuckle.

* * * *

While the exhausted Elizabeth slept, her ride hit a bump and sent her airborne. Her mind never registered the airtime because she was caught in a world of dreams brought on by a combination of physical and mental exhaustion. She might have slept the entire way, if not for the fall that invariably followed.

The fall roused her. Elizabeth's eyes opened in a start, wide and wild. They darted from point to point before her ass hit the hard metal surface of the van's floor.

That pain worked like a slap across the face. Unfortunately, waking up in this matter, from an empty stomach and from a deep sleep, left her head pounding. To ease her pain, she reached up to massage her temples but could not separate her hands. Being bound, like headaches, was becoming a bad habit, one she could do without.

"I told you to avoid that pothole!" the passenger named Eric yelled.

Elizabeth glanced in that direction, but there was little to see. Other than a small sliding window, there was no access to the back. Still, that left her free to look over the rusting interior and eavesdrop on the conversation.

"Did you see the one right beside it?" The driver asked, the one they called Sam. "It could have swallowed us whole!"

She figured they were driving over a dirt or gravel road. The rock chips pinged within the wheel well, and the road itself was loud, doubly so when they travelled up hills with a surface built like washboards. The fact that these two were treating their trip like a rally race was not helping matters.

"Gets rougher every year," Eric said.

"No kidding," Sam said sarcastically. "Pretty soon only off-road vehicles will be able to make it up this far."

"That will suck," Eric stated.

"Yeah," Sam added. "Will be a *lot* harder to get supplies in. Not to mention, fewer tourists…"

Elizabeth wondered why the driver complained about that last point. People who lived this far off the beaten path were seldom interested in random visits. Of course, that was assuming these two were human. *What the fuck do I know about werewolves?*

"Remember that teen with the big booty who backpacked up the mountain with her boyfriend to make a sex tape?" Sam asked.

"Fuck yeah!" Eric replied. "The meat was falling right off the bone when the dinner bell rang."

She imagined those two drooling over the idea of eating another sentient being and felt nauseous. Had Elizabeth known what those two had done before ending that girl's life, she would have vomited… everywhere.

In that moment, Elizabeth understood a vegan's point of view. After all, the difference between hunter and hunted when both involved sentient beings was a thin line at best. Then again, with the way her stomach was growling, she would eat anything offered, no questions asked.

"Yeah," Sam said. "She was fun."

"The one out back is pretty sweet too," Eric added while sounding giddy as a schoolboy.

"The difference is," Sam said, "he'd skin us alive."

"Bill doesn't care," Eric stated. "Does he?"

"*She* does," Sam replied. "So, *he* does."

Since they were speaking without context, it made the conversation hard to follow. Elizabeth did know one thing for sure: someone went through a lot of trouble to ensure that she got there unharmed.

Still, a few answers would be nice. Were they talking about Adrienne, that rail-thin woman from the subway tunnels? There was something about this one that made Elizabeth's skin crawl, and she had met some pretty disturbed individuals in her line of work. That one? *Wow!*

Then again, she had yet to meet someone from this group who would not need a whole lot of therapy. She supposed that should be expected for those who had humans on the menu. After all, would it be difficult for a wolf to integrate with a flock of sheep? Who would willingly take orders from those better served with a bottle of Pinot Noir?

"That sucks," Eric said. "Having a bit of fun on the side is a big reason that I'm—"

"Don't," Sam interrupted.

"But—" Eric tried to argue.

"Just… don't," Sam said. "You never know who might be listening."

"You think—" Eric asked.

"I don't know what to think," Sam said sternly.

For Elizabeth, that exchange revealed a great deal: a clear sign that the dynamics of their group had changed and that they were adjusting to the new normal. The fact that not everyone knew how to toe the line or understood the rules meant that order and punishment were arbitrarily applied.

"Then what?" Eric asked.

"Haven't you noticed that the old gang aren't around anymore?" Sam asked.

"Well… yeah…" Eric replied.

"Sooo…" Sam said.

"Sooo?" Eric mimicked with no intention of putting any thought into this conversation.

The driver sighed, which left her with the distinct impression that he was staring down his counterpart. A strong grasp of both logic and reason were not universal traits, and this man was learning this lesson the hard way.

Sore from being in the same position for so long, Elizabeth shifted slightly. Her foot slipped on the piece of rebar, causing her to kick the opposing wall. The sound deafened her and winced even though the change of position was doing wonders to ease the pain.

"Just watch it okay?" Sam asked.

"You know me," Eric replied with a grin.

"That's why I'm warning you," Sam said. "This place wouldn't be half as bearable without you."

"Thanks, bruh," Eric said.

"Anytime," Sam said. "So… you think they'd notice if we tag-teamed her?"

"But you said—" Eric said.

"Never mind what I said," Sam replied. "We are literally in the middle of nowhere. "

"What if she talks?" Eric asked.

A good question to ask, but one easily answered. They could blindfold her, knock her unconscious, or simply make a convincing threat. How would she be able to tell friend from foe? *Especially amongst this bunch.*

How could anyone in her position forget that humans were just another source of protein for them? She doubted any university professor had ever detailed this type of power imbalance in their lectures. *They probably should!*

The truck was beginning to slow down, which left her with some options. First, she could stay here and take her chances with Tweedledee and Tweedledum. That option left a lot to be desired.

"She won't," Sam said. "Not if we do this right."

The other option was more in Clara's domain. Feign being asleep and gouge their eyes out when they were close. While the idea had a satisfying end, her human strength and non-existent fighting skills weighed heavily against her.

"Oh!" Eric exclaimed excitedly. "You mean what's in there?"

Elizabeth did not like the sound of that. This left her with the third option, and her window of opportunity was limited. Attempt an escape when the truck slowed down to a near-stop. That might let her get off this truck unharmed, and with a lot of luck, she might find her way out of these woods.

"Yep," Sam said. "She'll be begging us to stuff her at both ends."

The truck continued to slow down, so Elizabeth looked at the two hinged doors at the back of the van. Freedom, or at least *her* chance for it was just on the other side. Without much thought, she got onto her feet, steadied herself to the best of her abilities, and waited a moment longer.

When the brakes squealed, Elizabeth got some speed and rammed those doors. In all honesty, she had been expecting a great deal of resistance, but they flew open on the first go. At first, she was blinded by the sunlight while the doors struck their respective sides, sending out a loud clang. *Great. I may as well light the fires of Gondor.*

Elizabeth stood there stupefied, or at least did until the van lurched forward. That motion was just enough to send her flying out the back and into the mixture of mud and slush. Instantly, her skin turned to goose bumps and would soon be suffering from hypothermia if she did not warm up soon. *Again?*

"Bravo!" Sam exclaimed while giving her a limp wristed applause.

Elizabeth stood up from the filth just as a light mountain breeze picked up, sending a shiver down her back. If her teeth had not been chattering, she might have managed to genuinely look mad. As it was, neither of the men were particularly impressed by her escape attempt.

The other man named Eric, the one she assumed to be the passenger, approached. He removed his jacket and placed it over Elizabeth's hesitant shoulders. For now, it was warm, although the jacket would only do so much to stem the tide.

"Here," Eric said, while handing off a wad of cash to Sam.

"I told you she was awake," Sam said.

"How do you always know?" Eric questioned.

"It's a skill, man," Sam said. "Now we have a bit of a hike ahead of us…"

Elizabeth could not see much from where she was. They appeared to be outside an industrial complex, one surrounded by several structures. Nothing here was particularly noteworthy: dull, grey, rusty, and abandoned.

Initially, she wondered why they were leaving the vehicle here but realised the buildings were the perfect hideout. This far out, they would only need to worry about aerial reconnaissance, and concrete structures worked wonders to hide activity within.

"Lead the way," Sam ordered as Eric pushed her on the shoulder.

Elizabeth lurched forward. At least that would help her warm up, and hopefully the sun would lend a hand as well. A shame they appeared to be heading towards a huge mound of mining debris. Wherever they were headed, Elizabeth was pretty sure it was not a five-star resort.

# CHAPTER 11

## *GLOBE AND MAIL MOMENT*

"V incent," Julia muttered in her sleep.

Despite being covered with nothing more than a loose sheet, Julia was bathed in sweat. It was enough for the white fabric to appear translucent.

"Noooo," Julia said as though she were far away.

Her jaw tightened, grinding her teeth while her head jerked from side to side. Unconsciously, her hands probed the bed until they came across a pillow. She latched onto it and hugged it for comfort, but this dream was not over.

"Vincent!" Julia screeched before her body shot straight up.

The sheet clung to her skin, which arguably maintained a modicum of modesty. However, Julia was caught between the dream realm and reality. Unaware that she was awake, anxiety poisoned her thoughts. Her breathing grew rapid while skirting the edge of hyperventilating.

A stray sound forced her eyes open, and darted across the non-descript hotel room. This place was not by any means luxurious, but compared to what she called home, it was palatial.

Her eyes spotted a glass of water at the bedside. Julia reached for it, but in her haste, spilled some of the contents. Normally, that would bother her since clean water was in short supply on the streets, but she was so thirsty. Once the glass came to her cracked lips, she greedily gulped down all that remained.

"Ah," Julia said, letting the glass drop between her thighs.

Now that her base needs were met, Julia's ears perked up. Farther down the room came the sound of running water, a big hint that she was not alone. The presence of a second bed only reinforced that notion.

"Why would someone bring me here?" Julia asked, while racking her brain as to why anyone would be so altruistic.

Of course, when she looked down and noticed that she was effectively naked, another theory gelled in her mind. The thought of it made her skin crawl, that someone was out to take advantage of her and had undressed her while she was unconscious. It was hard enough living on the streets. What did she do to deserve this?

In anticipation of that slimy guest's return from the bathroom, Julia slid off the bed. Alas one of her legs was bound, so she lost her balance in the attempt. Julia fell forward and crashed head first into the laminate floor.

"Fuck!" Julia yelled as stars filled her vision.

That word caught the attention of whoever was in the shower. The flow of water was immediately cut off, followed closely by the curtain being drawn. Julia sensed that her window of opportunity was gone. Still she looked over her binding just in case. The knot had been made by an expert, which meant that she would not be going anywhere… not with that around her leg.

A bright white light flooded the room when the bathroom door opened. While ignoring her worsening headache, Julia made out a long and slender silhouette. She thought it would be a burly man, but those curves were clearly feminine, and that's before those wings came into sight.

"Oh shit," Julia whined.

The silhouette unleashed a coquettish laugh that filled the room. That only served to enrage Julia, but in her current state, what could she do?

"I'm sorry," Clara said. "I thought you'd be asleep a bit longer, and I wanted to wash up before you woke up."

"Why?" Julia asked. "You were planning to dazzle me with your fashion sense before slitting my throat?"

"No," Clara said firmly.

Clara reached inside a nearby drawer and pulled out what looked to be a throwing knife. Julia eyed the angel moving towards her and backed away instinctively. Without even batting an eye, Clara lifted the mattress and cut Julia's binding from that end.

"There," Clara said. "You can leave."

This situation felt all wrong. Too easy, a convenient trap for Julia to fall into, one designed to worsen the eventual sense of betrayal.

Sensing what the other was thinking, Clara flipped the knife around so Julia could claim it and said, "Your clothes are drying in the bathroom."

"Sorry, did you say *drying*?" Julia asked.

When Julia did not reach for the blade, Clara dropped it on the mattress. The angel then sat on the office chair in the corner near the old-style tube television. Since the back was high, she was forced to sit upright, a slight distance from the back, to accommodate those wings. Only then did Julia notice that her captor was naked.

"Your clothes were filthy," Clara said. "So, I gave them a quick scrub with a bar of soap before grabbing a shower."

"Why would you even?" Julia asked.

This time, she became aware of her own nudity. Suddenly self-conscious of it, she sat on the edge of the bed near the knife and reached for her sheet. Since the sweat soaked fabric made her cringe, she opted instead for the comforter scrunched up at the foot of the bed.

"Why not?" Clara asked in return. "There is plenty of hot water if you want to shower or bathe."

Julia raised her left brow in surprise. This woman was not behaving in the way she expected, just like earlier when Clara wasted the opportunity to unload both barrels. Why was her father's killer being so civil?

"I want to gouge your eyes out," Julia let slip.

Clara did not move, remaining as naked and vulnerable as anyone in her position could be. Julia even noticed water droplets gliding off her skin.

"I said—" Julia said.

"I know," Clara said.

"You're not bothered by that?" Julia questioned.

"Why would I be?" Clara said to lob the question back in Julia's court.

"Just fucking give me a straight answer!" Julia snapped.

The foundations of a smile appeared on the left edge of Clara's lips. It was a cocky sort of smile that was sure to escalate matters.

Julia grabbed the knife and held her free arm against her chest to keep covered before leaping off the bed. As the comforter pulled away, the empty glass rolled off the mattress and shattered against the floor.

She ignored the chaos she unleashed and crossed the void between them in an instant. Again, Clara showed no signs of worry, which fanned the flames within Julia's soul. She gripped the handle of the knife and held the blade perpendicular to Clara's throat. The blade was high quality and sharp, so it would not take much to finish this bitch off.

"You'd kill an unarmed opponent?" Clara asked in a steady voice.

"You killed my father!" Julia yelled.

"Yes, I did," Clara replied.

"Why?" Julia asked.

"Because he was dangerous and was trying to kill me," Clara said.

Her grip on the blade was so tight that her knuckles were white. The tighter the grip, the harder it became for her to control. Still, Clara did not appear to be worried in the slightest.

"I hate you!" Julia exclaimed.

"I know," Clara said. "I'd feel the same."

"Then why aren't you fighting back?" Julia pressed.

"Because you're not my enemy," Clara said softly.

That statement hit her hard. This woman had killed two werewolves. How did that not make them enemies? The thought of this certainty turning up false was mind blowing, a foreign concept in her mind.

"So, who is?" Julia asked, half-expecting Clara to mention that vampire whore.

"The same as yours," Clara replied in a strangely soothing tone.

Did Julia have an enemy? While the pack shunned her, that merely meant she was not worth the price of a bullet. Only the death of a fellow pack member, the most grievous of crimes, warranted death.

"So why was Vincent…" Julia said after realising that aspects of her dream were actually latent memories.

Clara looked up so that her steel-grey eyes were locked onto Julia's. They remained like that while the young woman's mind connected the dots.

"Adrienne…" Julia said before letting go of the knife.

Such a realisation felt like a punch to the stomach. Not only did Adrienne goad her into making a move against Clara, but she also had the gall to order Vincent to clean up any loose ends. That meant her half-brother sanctioned the attack. *What a bitch!*

When Julia's knees gave out, Clara moved in like a blur and grabbed her. Instead of a slap, or even a fist, she wrapped arms around Julia just in time for the waterworks.

"There… there…" Clara said softly.

Julia collapsed further into Clara's embrace. The latter wrapped her wings around the crestfallen gal, which effectively cocooned them. Despite being in the arms of a stranger, for the first time in ages, Julia felt cared for.

\* \* \* \*

Adrienne looked ahead at the dirty, snow-covered road winding a path through the wilderness. This may have been the path less travelled, but she was intimately familiar with every twist, turn, and bump.

"I told you to slow—" Adrienne snapped.

Sure enough, they hit a bump, and those in the jeep were jostled around like rag dolls. At this speed, this stretch of rotted out road was known to cause breakdowns. To avoid a similar fate, Adrienne had almost bitten her tongue off.

"Sorry," the driver, Jeremiah said.

Adrienne glared at the driver. Her eyes were so focused on the source of her fury that everyone felt the chill in the air. Her thin lips pressed together to the point disappearing, looking more like a healed scar. The effect was more than enough to make Jeremiah slink into his seat and slow down.

Certain that her message was received and understood, Adrienne returned her gaze out towards the road. At this time of the year, they generally restricted their travel to the night, seeing as there was no foliage to camouflage their passage, except for a few stray leaves that clung stubbornly to some random tree branch, their red or orange tinge serving as a testament to the passage of time.

Adrienne loathed winter, or the dead season as she called it. This season extended from the time the trees went bare to when they bloomed again. That's when the cold seeped into her bones, aggravated by hanging out in an abandoned mine.

The mine served as their base of operations for the pack. They had plenty of space, which gave them room to expand. It was also isolated from any large settlements, and with a little bit of *ingenuity* they made the place fairly comfortable.

"Except for this damned cold," Adrienne muttered and shivered just thinking about it.

"Erm," Jeremiah said. "We are almost there."

"Thank you," Adrienne replied in a neutral tone, which further served to worry the driver.

She was well aware that they were near the base camp, notably the complex surrounding the mine. The buildings once served as offices, ore processing, and maintenance facilities when this mine was in full swing. These were now used to support their pack, and the vehicle bays were perfect for hiding anything they could bring up here.

As they approached the garage, the doors were opened by sentries waiting inside. The building was well-lit, so she noticed the van, which meant their prisoner was already here. That was fortunate since she was in no mood for complications.

With the sun directly overhead, there were no concerns with bleeding white light into the sky. The windows were either boarded up or painted over to avoid giving away their presence.

Once their ride came to a stop, Adrienne popped open the door and stepped out. The crisp mountain air caressed her cheeks, which emphasised how hot and stuffy that jeep had been. She closed her eyes, sighed softly, and let the moment sink in.

When her eyes opened, William was standing directly in front of her. Her boy was a man: tall, muscular, with thick black hair and a beard. The latter was kept neatly trimmed, in accordance with her wishes. When she looked into those deep blue eyes, she saw a twinge of fear reflected back at her. She knew at once that he had bad news. *Great… what now?*

"Anything wrong?" Adrienne said in a soft and soothing voice.

The tone had the desired effect, which helped William to relax. Still, the impending bad news lingered in the air, so Adrienne's mood was liable to change. No creature on earth could hope to contain her fury when enraged.

"Vincent was featured on the news," William said flatly.

"His kill made the news?" Adrienne asked.

"N-N-No," William stuttered as the corner of his eyes welled up.

Adrienne scanned the room and noticed there was a small group congregating in the corner. She gave them a dirty look and marched off to the nearest office.

"Come," Adrienne barked.

William followed her lead, something unheard of until now. The alpha was expected to lead, to fight, and in some circumstances, lay down their lives for the good of the pack. William shedding a tear for one of their fallen might endear a few of the remaining bleeding hearts. However, those who held the balance of power were sure to think otherwise.

Adrienne gave her boy a stern look before slapping him hard across the cheek. The sound resonated throughout the office and beyond. It was time for him to *man up*.

"So, what happened?" Adrienne said.

"It happened a couple of hours ago," William said.

"That's not an answer, William," Adrienne said, testing an old-fashioned wooden office chair, one fitted with four legs instead of the standard five.

While the wood creaked from her weight, she was nonetheless able to sit down. There were no other chairs in this room and the power imbalance suited her just fine. After all, William was not actually expected to show independent thought.

"He must have made a move against the harpy," William said. "The two of them ended up in the street."

"Out in the open? For everyone to see?" Adrienne asked to confirm.

That in itself was not necessarily a bad thing. Vincent was a shit disturber, one who challenged the status quo. His loss meant one less loose end for her. *So why is William bringing this up?*

"He turned before the attack," William said with a gulp.

Adrienne's eyes opened wide, dumbfounded that a werewolf had managed to change in broad daylight. As far as she knew, such a feat had never been done.

"The transformation was not complete, but it was more than enough to get noticed and trend on social media," William added.

"What!" Adrienne yelled. "I hope that he was successful, at least?"

"No. *She* got away after the fight," William said. He could not stand to look her in the eyes.

Adrienne was not sure what to say. The one responsible for her husband's murder was still out there with fresh blood on her hands. Vincent had been a fool to pull that stunt during the day.

Her orders had been clear: leave no one alive. Considering that he was well-armed, that idiot should have broken down the door and taken the occupants down in a hail of bullets. Even if they caught him, the media would have easily bought that these deaths were gang related.

The fact that he opted to transform prior to the attack complicated matters. He wanted to feed his primal urges, to face his opponent in hand to hand combat, and tear that woman apart. All for what? To reclaim his pack's honour? In other words, Vincent had done exactly what she ordered him not to do.

"Thank you, William," Adrienne said after taking a few moments to collect her thoughts. "I need a bit of time to think. Would you mind closing the door on your way out?"

"What about the harpy?" William asked, immediately regretting showing a lack of faith in her plan.

"Why don't you let me worry about that?" Adrienne replied with a strained smile.

This time William did not say a word. Instead, he nodded and closed the door behind him.

"That's the first thing that's gone right so far," Adrienne muttered.

They risked exposure to capture that winged demon, and that included leaving a wave of destruction all over the city just to find her friend. Then, that idiot revealed his true nature for the world to see. Adrienne wondered if that winged menace would take the bait now?

"Still, it might just as easily embolden her, enough to drop her guard," Adrienne thought.

There was a full moon tonight, so everyone in the pack capable of changing, would. That *bitch* was about to experience the terror of being hunted down by a pack of werewolves.

# CHAPTER 12

## *LONGER AND DEEPER*

J
ulia leaned forward so the hot water was aimed between her shoulder blades. The soothing heat radiated throughout her body, massaged her muscles, and relieved tension.

"My god," Julia moaned as droplets of water slid down her bangs, nose, and jawline before dripping off.

When was the last time she had an opportunity like this? Julia never lasted long in a shelter since she could not deal with the strings attached in getting a bed. She had the heart of a werewolf, and that meant the call of the wild was forever whispering in her ear.

Ever since being shunned by the pack, she had to ignore that call. While the wilds remained expansive, she was hesitant to lose herself in them, fearful of crossing paths with another member of her pack. Given her emaciated state, one which prevented her from transforming, she was ill equipped to defend herself.

Julia looked up at the clear shower curtain and noticed that it was fogged up with vapour. Her hand ran across the material and caused droplets to form and ripple down.

"So wasteful," Julia mused. "So glorious!"

Like all good things, her foray into the realm of bliss had to come to an end. In the background, she heard a knock at the door, a sound that reminded her of all the things that needed doing.

"Is everything okay?" Clara asked, her voice muffled by the door.

"Everything!" Julia exclaimed. "Everything is great. Just give me a few more minutes… to indulge," she added after adjusting the volume of her voice.

"Take your time," Clara said and she imagined the speaker walking away.

"When was the last time anyone bothered to check up on me?" Julia asked herself.

A good question, although the answer was a bit depressing. The city's homeless were invisible, and she was by no means an exception to that rule.

On the counter beside the tub, there was a fresh razor and lotion. At first, she grimaced at the thought of shaving. The idea of conforming to social norms did not interest her, doubly so if it pleased *that* woman. But it *would* give her reason to linger in this water a while longer…

"Might do me some good to feel a bit more… human, anyways," Julia whispered.

Since she could not change, it made sense to embrace who she appeared to be. She lathered up her legs, grabbed the razor, and ran the head against the hairs' grain. A clear patch of white skin appeared, along with a deep gouge.

Julia winced when the water interacted with the cut. Still, the pain was temporary since the wound closed up before the blood washed away.

"Well, a bit more than human," Julia said with a smile until she realised how much was left to shave.

"Oh boy," Julia said.

\* \* \* \*

Clara was once again sitting on the office chair. One of her pistols was broken down into its individual parts, neatly laid out on the desk. Every part gleamed in the light, courtesy of the thin coat of oil. The assembly and disassembly of weapons was something she was intimately familiar with. Hunters for the Tower did not progress with their training, or survive for long, without mastering this particular skill.

The shower went silent which meant that Julia was either done with her shower or the hotel's cistern was bone dry. Either way, other familiar sounds followed suit, so her recommendation for a shower turned out to be a rousing success.

Since the weapon was ready, Clara reassembled the pistol and completed a function test. When satisfied, she inserted a fresh magazine, chambered a round and applied the safety. In situations like these, it paid for a gal to maintain a healthy dose of paranoia.

When the door to the bathroom opened, Clara slipped the pistol into the desk drawer and spun around in her chair. The world blurred as she moved into position, but her eyes quickly settled on the young vixen walking across the floor towards the bed. The overpowering smell of wet dog was gone, although the bed still reeked of it.

"Feel better?" Clara asked.

"Much," Julia said while ensuring the hotel towel stayed on.

Since this gal was still soaking wet, Clara had no trouble imagining that the towel would not be going anywhere. Still, modesty was a welcome change of pace from their last couple of exchanges.

"I took the—" Clara said.

Julia squealed when she caught sight of fresh clothes on the bed. Every item was neatly laid out, from a new sports bra to a pair of leather boots. The latter Julia recognised immediately because they had been hers the night they met.

The excitement had electrified the air, but they soon became aware of the impasse. With the bathroom being a proverbial flood plain, changing in there would be quite a feat. To make things easier, Clara smirked and turned her back on Julia, using the opportunity to clean her shotgun.

"Thank you," Julia said quickly.

Those words were followed by the sound of the towel puddling around her legs. Julia opted to slip on panties, bra and stockings before giving the rest of her attire a look.

"Anytime," Clara said, remembering how hunters would change in front of their partners.

Hunters were initially paired off, and for their survival, checked on each other to ensure that no detail was missed or glossed over. Of course, Julia was not a partner. Heck, she barely qualified as an ally.

"*Inimicus inimico amicus*," Clara muttered in Latin as a way to avoid being understood.

While having a common enemy could forge an alliance, it often brought forth the winds of uncertainty. How long would it be before old grudges returned to the forefront of Julia's mind? Her partner had plenty of reasons for wanting revenge, so Clara would need to hedge her bets.

"What was that?" Julia asked.

"Oh nothing," Clara said. "I was just reciting a prayer."

"You pray?" Julia asked.

"Most nuns do," Clara countered.

"You—a *nun*?" Julia flubbed.

"Surprised?" Clara deflected.

Julia paused while deep in thought about this truth. When those eyes began to twinkle, she picked up the plain black blouse. Her long slender fingers slid over the fabric, and it gave her a shiver.

"Wow," Julia said under her breath. "I've never seen nuns waltz around naked, hunt mythical creatures… or fuck vampires."

"Our order, by design, was a *bit* more relaxed than most," Clara said and did not ask how she knew about the interlude they had back at the studio.

"No kidding?" Julia added absentmindedly. "So, what did your order excel at?"

Clara did not immediately answer. Instead, she laid out the components of her weapon on what was once a towel. Now was the time to oil, brush, and wipe away excess carbon.

"We excelled at infiltration, information extraction, killing mythical creatures, and using sex to forward our goals," Clara answered.

"So, fucking a vampire fits into this how?" Julia asked while she sized up a pair of black denim jeans.

"Like I said," Clara replied. "I'm flexible."

"I bet you are," Julia said and smirked before sliding her left leg into those pants.

Clara wondered if there was a point to all this banter. At face value, Julia was taunting Clara in an effort to elicit some sort of response, not wholly unexpected, really, since that was exactly what she would have done. Still there was something else, but what?

"Besides, aren't nuns supposed to wear..." Julia said while snapping her fingers in an attempt to jog her memory.

"A habit?" Clara confirmed, which conjured up memories of that uniform she wore as an acolyte.

"Yeah!" Julia replied, and slipped her foot into the proper pant leg. "One of those."

Clara chuckled, and used a hand towel to wipe the parts of the weapon dry. Habits were not a regular affair for her order, and for a good reason. Although, plenty of their instructors wore those, conforming to their orders.

"That's a tough one," Clara said. "You could say that the habit actively prevents us from hiding in a crowd or diminishes our *powers of persuasion* to gather intelligence."

"So, fucking that vampire was nothing more than an attempt to get something out of her?" Julia asked, smirked, and zipped up her pants.

Since it was time for the truth to come out, Clara spun her chair around to face Julia. Without much thought, she stood up and walked towards the vixen. Julia's eyes widened; her desire to bolt grew with every step. Despite the calm demeanour and the sensual sway of those hips, Clara did not betray her intentions.

Once within a foot of one another, Clara stared into those wild eyes, while her right wing reached out to enclose the other. From this point, for better or for worse, Julia was at the angel's mercy.

"You keep mentioning *fuck*," Clara said in a husky voice. "Is this something you'd like… to explore?"

"I-I-I…" Julia replied as her mind appeared to be disconnected from the speech centre of her brain.

Clara smiled and leaned in close. While Julia could feel those soft lips move, the speaker sounded far away.

"Besides, she *fucked* me," Clara said. "Would you like me to show you what she did?"

"N-N-No," Julia replied.

"Are you sure?" Clara taunted. "Those orgasms were really… *really*… intense."

Julia's features reverted to a neutral state before cracking a smile. She then turned her attention to those wings and noticed the feathers were black like coal.

"Nice wings," Julia said with a giggle.

Clara returned the smile and tucked in her wing, certain that this exchange was an excuse to probe for weaknesses. How a werewolf came to possess that type of training was a mystery. Could life in a pack really be that dangerous?

"Thank you," Clara said. "They are the bees knees, aren't they?"

"Yeah," Julia said to play along.

"Nicely done by the way," Clara said.

The young woman leaned back enough to fall onto the bed. To her left, she saw those leather boots, the ones Clara had absconded the night her father died.

"Thank you?" Julia confirmed while eyeing the boots.

"So, why were you trying to push my buttons?" Clara asked on the off chance that the other would cooperate.

Clara looked over the spectacle unfolding before her. Her choice of boots had been a gamble, a symbolic gesture, but one that the other was not yet ready to deal with. It might have been easier to leave them back at the apartment, the one crawling with bulls by now.

"I don't like vampires," Julia answered softly, her hands trembling.

"Clearly," Clara said. "Surely, there is more to it than that?"

"What gave me away?" Julia asked to deflect.

"I have about a century on you," Clara said nonchalantly.

"Pffft. Like age alone ever explained anything," Julia said.

Clara sensed that statement was loaded and guessed that all of this was centred on someone older, one who pushed her buttons recently. Perhaps the power dynamics of the werewolf pack was more complex than she believed possible.

"No," Clara said. "However, experience teaches us a lot."

"Not for everyone," Julia said dismissively which strengthened her hunch.

"How did you know my *friend* was a vampire?" Clara asked, implying that Evelyn was not necessarily an ally.

"They smell like death," Julia said flatly.

"Really?" Clara confirmed. "I've never noticed it, myself."

"Our sense of smell, even in this form, is far more acute," Julia replied. "I can pick up a drunk from a mile away. Twice that, if a guy wears that body spray featuring fallen angels in their commercials."

Clara dismissed the fallen angel comment as nothing more than an unintentional pun. Both had gaps in their knowledge; that much was clear based on their heart-to-heart chat about nuns.

"So..." Clara said. "What do I smell like?"

"I'm not really sure," Julia answered.

Julia's eyes rolled to the ceiling while that question simmered in her mind. That facial response was a sign that the truth was far more nuanced than anticipated.

"Right now, you smell like crisp mountain air with a hint of autumn," Julia answered.

Clara cocked an eyebrow before saying, "Right now?"

Julia nodded and eyed the long winter jacket. While not stylish, it would keep her warm, even in a nor'easter.

"Yeah," Julia said. "That's why you were hard to track. Your scent tends to change. But it has never been offensive or pungent."

That particular detail was something Gabriel neglected to mention. Chances were that these odours were designed to disarm the people they interacted with, all to gain trust. That scent probably originated from Julia's childhood memories, a way of manipulating strangers with minimal effort.

"Ingenious," Clara muttered. "How does my roommate smell?"

Julia's focus lingered on that coat, so this particular question clearly hit a nerve. Up until now, Julia had not seen Clara enraged, and as judged by her father's untimely death, it was best to avoid doing so.

Clara slowed down her reaction time, forcing herself to go through the excruciating torment of watching someone's emotional cues in slow motion. Still, it permitted her to see every reaction without giving away what she was up to.

"Hair products and alcohol," Julia said absentmindedly, but her heart rate and respiration were sky high now.

Normally, Clara would have wondered how such an innocent question could bring about that kind of response. This time, it was clear that fear of follow-up questions had been the trigger.

"She has been hitting the drink hard these days," Clara said in a slow and deliberate tone that would appear natural.

"She has," Julia said in confirmation. "You've been giving her a hard time?"

When Julia's heart rate dropped in response, Clara smiled and decided to further test her hypothesis.

"You know why she hasn't been answering her phone," Clara said in a neutral tone.

Those deep brown eyes glided over the bed and settled on Clara's face. There they lingered for a fraction of a second before shifting her gaze towards those boots. That motion was met with a drop in respiration, as though the air between them had cooled by a good twenty degrees.

"The pack..." Julia faltered.

Clara's heart sunk to the pit of her stomach. It was one thing to guess, but another to have it confirmed. Since this group had a hostage, that changed the situation. Although, the end result remained the same.

Satisfied that she was on the right track, Clara returned to normal time. All that she needed was to keep pushing for more information.

"Do you know where they took her?" Clara asked calmly.

Julia visibly winced, responding as though expecting retribution, nothing out of the norm for someone being asked to betray their family and potentially burn a few bridges.

"Up north," Julia whispered.

Clara cocked her head to the side before saying, "Outside the city?"

"Yes," Julia replied, almost managing to sound normal while doing so.

"Where?" Clara asked.

"Abandoned iron—mines," Julia replied faintly.

"Do you know the way?" Clara asked.

Julia gulped, nodded faintly and said, "Uh huh."

Either this girl was an expert at lying, or she was speaking truthfully despite the potential ramifications. The thought of a pack of werewolves choosing such a remote site fit in well with her view of them being social outcasts. It also worked beautifully from a strategic standpoint, and given her current list of allies, limited her options.

"Do you guys still use that clubhouse near the outskirts of the city?" Clara asked as an aside.

The tone of voice was so casual, so relaxed, that most would think it was an afterthought. Sometimes it helped to conceal the full breadth of their plan, especially when faced with an unreliable ally.

"N-No," Julia asked. "It... it was abandoned shortly after the attack... why?"

Clara shrugged to show disinterest, but Julia's heart rate gave her all she needed. They still had some sort of presence at that dive bar, a foothold in the city from which to carry out their business. Why not? In their position, Clara would have done the same.

"I was just curious. I want to avoid falling into a trap." Clara said. "As an aside... do you still get headaches?"

"Yeah?" Julia said. "Ever since you kill—"

Clara kept quiet, seeing that it would be foolhardy for her to reopen that wound or to attempt to explain it away. Still, Julia needed to remain committed to the operation, and adverse reactions to light and sound made her a liability.

Clara reached for something in her pack. The moment that bag was opened, an unearthly golden hue lit up the room. Clara hummed a ditty from the Twenties as she dipped a small cup into the liquid.

"So... you aren't human?" Clara confirmed while holding onto a clear cup with a golden elixir swirling within. "Right?"

"You know I'm not," Julia said. "What is that?"

The sight of the contents of that glass made Julia uneasy. Clara kept on smiling to ease the words that would soon resonate between these walls.

"I was stabbed recently," Clara said. "It would have killed me if it weren't for this stuff."

"What is it?" Julia asked. "Some sort of experimental drug?"

Clara chuckled before answering, "Ambrosia."

"That stuff doesn't exist," Julia stated unequivocally.

"But vampires, and werewolves do?" Clara replied before dipping a lone finger in the cup. "Stick out your tongue please."

"Why…" Julia said but did not finish her question.

Once Julia realised what had been said, denying the existence of such a substance was ludicrous. The world was full of secrets, and neither of them had all the answers.

Julia ignored her fears, closed her eyes, and complied with Clara's direction. A moment later, something brushed lightly against the tip of her tongue and sent an electric current flowing through her entire body. When she opened her eyes to see what was going on, there were streaks running through her field of vision.

"Whoa!" Julia said.

"Good?" Clara asked.

"Umm," Julia said as her mind struggled to come to terms with what happened. "Yeah."

"Feels like an intense orgasm?" Clara asked.

"Ummm," Julia replied.

"More subdued?" Clara guessed.

"Yeah?" Julia said.

When Clara heard that reply, she left the plastic cup on the bedside table. She then walked away and returned to her weapons maintenance. This left Julia free to decide how to proceed with the remaining contents.

She slid deeper into the bed, enough that her back would be propped up with pillows, and eyed those boots. Since she was still not ready to deal with that, Julia grabbed the cup. For a moment, she stared into the golden liquid and with nothing more than hope and speculation, swallowed it all in one gulp.

This time, she experienced the best orgasm of her life, followed by another, and another until she slipped into unconsciousness. When Julia began to breathe deeply, Clara smiled. She then prayed that this experiment would not end up with unintended consequences.

\* \* \* \*

Adrienne rode the funicular, known as a man-skip, towards the lower levels. The steep angle of their descent was barely noticeable, since passengers travelled standing up. The riveted metal contraption looked like a toy car with steel wheels that maintained contact with the rails. The driver controlled everything from the centre, while passengers rode under a canopy at the top.

She stepped off the skip when they reached the level and needed time to orient herself. Every level was similar, and the nuances were very subtle, which could get people into trouble. Overhead, less than half the lights were working, stretching out the shadows and making it hard to see anything.

"Ugh," Adrienne said in disgust.

She considered reaching for the compact flashlight concealed within the depths of her coat. While most of the pack could easily make their way through this level, she could not. Like any other human, her eyesight was quite poor in low-light conditions.

Word of her using a flashlight might get around. It was hard enough to be a den mother, doubly so when her human weaknesses were on display. William needed her to be strong and to guide him through these troubled times. For that, she would not let her humanity stop her.

In time, her night vision would assert itself. Unfortunately, these ceilings were so high that the naked lightbulbs of white light appeared as a tapestry of stars. She knew that in one-hundred yards on her left there would be an expansive room, one that once served as a heavy equipment maintenance room.

When this mine was operating at full-swing, that space had been manned and secured. Today, those traits made it the ideal location for their prisoner. The thick iron doors would not only hinder an escape attempt, but also prevent a breakout.

Adrienne turned, and kicked off her journey through what had once been a thriving mining operation. She loathed the lower levels because of the high humidity that clung to her skin and invariably left her with an intense desire to shower.

"That's why the lights are always shorting out," Adrienne muttered and made a note to bring that up with William.

As the crushed rock gave way beneath her footsteps, Adrienne unzipped her leather coat to cool down a bit. To think, not five minutes ago, she needed that jacket to keep from freezing.

A few minutes later, Adrienne stood in front of a heavy iron door. She peeked inside through the barred peep hole, and in the far corner of the room, atop an old workbench, that troublesome woman was curled up and asleep.

Adrienne smiled at the sight of her plans coming into focus. It may have risked the exposure of their kind to pull off that raid, but now they had all the leverage they needed to lure in their prey. All they needed was to wait and spring the trap. Soon they would be sucking the marrow from her bones.

"After that, the pack will follow William to hell and back without question," Adrienne said, while observing the sleeping woman.

The idea of this woman resting peacefully gnawed at her. This one had managed to evade their forces for the better part of the night. That alone pissed her off, so Elizabeth sleeping so peacefully simply would not do.

She slid the thick steel rod, and heard the friction grind away the rust. The motion was slow and deliberate to avoid ruining her surprise. After all, what was the point if she could not have a bit of fun?

She then pushed against the door, at first lightly, and when the door resisted, gave it her all. The hinges eventually gave way with a loud snap resonating throughout the room. Still, the captive did not stir.

"Better not be dead," Adrienne muttered. "Or in a coma."

In either situation, whoever was responsible would end up with hellfire being rained upon them. There was nothing worse than fighting a cornered predator with nothing left to lose. Especially an opponent who could defeat one of their own, unarmed.

She stepped into the workshop. By then her eyes were adjusted to the reduced lighting. She made out Elizabeth's chest expanding and contracting with every breath. *Good, that answers one question.*

Adrienne smiled, gave the workbench a once over, and concluded that it would never budge. The thing was made of solid steel and anchored to the rock. So, kicking it out from under Elizabeth was not an option.

Instead, she climbed onto the bench, steadied herself, and kicked Elizabeth square in the ass. The impact sent their prisoner flying right off the table. Since the latter could not move her arms, she had no ability to cushion the fall. Thus, Elizabeth landed chest first, followed closely by her chin which slammed against the rock floor.

After hearing a loud thump, Adrienne peered over the table to find Elizabeth bleeding from a cracked lip. She noted that flow of blood subsided as her breathing turned deep and slow.

"So that bitch was faking," Adrienne said.

All of that meant this woman had been paying attention the whole time, although it was too late to find out what she knew. Her need to inflict pain on another would prevent interrogation. *Still, it was so worth it.*

"I guess you won't be snooping around while I'm away," Adrienne said. "Will you?"

Adrienne cackled before jumping off the bench. Out of spite, she kicked Elizabeth in the ribs and walked away. In her mind, that was letting her prisoner off easy.

# CHAPTER 13

## *THE ENEMY OF MY ENEMY*

C lara sat in her truck, looking out towards the dive bar down the street. From within, she heard the familiar dull thumping of the jukebox, along with five steady heartbeats.

That did not necessarily prove that Julia had lied. However, the motorcycles parked in the alleyway, the scent of wet dog, and the worn-out memorial to a man she killed were far more damning.

"Guess it's time to get a second opinion," Clara said before stepping out of the truck.

Once her feet touched the pavement, she reached back for her shotgun and slipped it in between her wings. That way, the bulge was concealed at the cost of making her look heavy set.

Next came her long leather coat, long enough to hide those wings. She slipped it on and adjusted the wings until they fit in comfortably. Lastly, she picked up a pair of panties, eyed them warily, and pocketed them while ignoring their stench.

Ready, Clara crossed the street casually and reached for the door. It all seemed too easy, as though this were a trap. The thought had crossed her mind, but she needed to confirm the intelligence. Besides, she was in the mood for a fight, and this might just be her ticket to getting what she wanted.

"Let's have some fun," Clara said with a smile.

When she opened the door, the dull thump was joined by the rest of the tune. While the song was considered an oldie by today's standards, it had been released thirty-years after her death. Its dark mood left her thinking that it suited this place's sombre tone perfectly.

The establishment had not changed, which included the pool tables and wooden bar with an array of cheap booze behind the counter. The place was aglow in neon, advertisements for various common brands making the lowliest of speakeasies in her time appear highbrow.

The bartender barely looked up, polishing a glass with a cloth of questionable cleanliness. Meanwhile, two cigarette smoking bikers were playing a game of pool, while a haze of blue smoke obscured the view.

The remaining two sat on worn wooden stools near the bar. Figuring that proximity would make things interesting, Clara navigated past the empty tables, heading towards the bar. She noticed the place was littered with discarded peanut shells. Those were either a new addition, or the waitress had been on an extended vacation.

Clara sat on a stool, which creaked and hawed. She smiled, while pretending to look over the assortment of bottles arrayed behind the bar.

"So, what will it be?" The bartender asked.

"I don't suppose that you could make a Bee's Knees?" Clara asked, before biting her lower lip, hopeful the answer would be in the affirmative.

"Whatcha see is whatcha get," the bartender replied.

"Oh," Clara said with a faux pout and shifted back on her stool before reaching for something in her front pocket. "Whiskey, and leave the bottle," Clara added before dropping a crisp hundred-dollar bill on the bar.

The bartender's eyes widened at the sight of cash, but there was no reply. Instead, he reached to the back row and grabbed a bottle of whiskey along with three shot glasses. He then proceeded to fill them, pocketed the bill, and went to refill some drinks.

"Thank you," Clara said lightly.

At that point, the other patrons were beginning to take notice of her presence. The change was subtle. Those playing pool had slowed their game, using the opportunity to figure out what the new arrival was up to. There were several valid reasons for this change in behaviour, but sniffing the air? Now *that* was noteworthy.

Clara kept her heartbeat steady, while eyeing her first glass. She reached for it, swirled the dark amber liquid and sent the contents straight to the back of her throat. The liquid burned as it worked its way down to her stomach.

The bartender was caught by surprise, expecting her to cough or wheeze from an adverse reaction. Truth be told, this was not her first time indulging in alcohol of questionable origin.

"That's pretty good for coffin varnish," Clara said before adopting a large grin.

The two at her side had given up any pretext of subtlety. Clara felt their eyes burn a hole through her skull, which tended to happen when they figured out that she was a threat. However, there was something off about their reaction and she suspected that it had something to do with the contents of her pockets.

After an overt sniff, the man closest to her stood from his stool and approached. With the exception of the bartender, everyone else's heart rates rose. She knew they were itching for a fight, and chances were that everyone was armed.

Clara downed another shot of whiskey and caught a glimpse at the man closest to her, tall, burly, sporting a beer belly, and the characteristic bulge of a pistol fitted around his leather chaps. *So far, no one has their weapons drawn.*

"You're not welcome here," the chap-man said.

Out of curiosity, Clara turned to face him and smiled. As expected, that managed to annoy him, so she flashed him a cocky grin to bring things to a boil.

"Funny. I didn't see a sign when I walked in," Clara replied.

"I said—" the chap-man said.

"Hey—dude," the bartender interjected.

Clara watched how the bikers focused their ire on the bartender. Their collective glares were enough for him to stand down, and he backed away with his hands held up high. Fortunately, that identified him as a non-combatant. Still a lot could change as the situation developed.

"Whiskey?" Clara asked.

The man twitched at the offer. Clearly, Clara was violating some sort of unwritten rule. So, was it because of her gender? Or was it the bloodline they mistakenly attributed to her?

"I'm soooo going to enjoy this," the chap-man said.

Clara had been expecting trouble the minute she walked in and was entirely disappointed that none of these *fine gentlemen* had thought to stretch out this bit of foreplay. *So typical of men.*

When the chap-man threw the first punch, Clara barely moved. Instead, she reached out with her left hand, grabbed his fist, and stopped it mid-motion.

With his punch stopped, the chap-man took more time than reasonably expected to figure out what happened. A deer in the headlights look fell on his face after realising that his arm would not budge. To antagonise him, Clara's smile melted into a cocky grin.

"Enjoy what?" Clara asked. "Being punched by a little girl?"

Those words had no time to sink in because the remaining bikers advanced on her. Clara jumped off the stool and sent it flying back against the wall. Now, it was her turn, and her fist connected against chap-man's jaw, sending him into a tailspin. The man was out cold before he reached the floor.

In response, the chap-man's partner drew his pistol. Clara pushed her wings against the fabric of her coat, which forced the Velcro to give way and let her wings expand. To up the ante, Clara reached for her shotgun and turned his back on the pool players.

The look on the partner's face was priceless. He had a clue who he was dealing with. His senses may have told him this was an outcast who deserved retribution, but those wings blew that theory out of the water.

"You!" The partner said.

"You were expecting Julia?" Clara asked, impressed that rumours still travelled faster than light.

When confusion clouded his eyes, Clara realised that this was not the same pack. He could classify scent based on pack but could not identify an individual. While this reduced her chances of gaining some insight on *her situation*, there was still a lot of fun to be had.

The partner responded by taking a few ill aimed shots. Unconcerned, her wings reacted as though they had a mind of their own and blocked the shots. The projectiles slammed against the tight mesh created by her feathers and dropped harmlessly to the floor.

That took the wind from his sails. The partner's shoulder, slumped, his arms fell limply to the side, and the pistol slipped from his fingers. Even his jaw would have done the same, if it were not physically attached to his skull.

Sensing that their weapons were ineffective, the two near the pool table broke their cues over their knees, chose the sharpest ends, and charged. Such a tactic had merit. Attacking from two directions certainly made defence more challenging. However, screaming like berserkers running into battle did not help their cause.

From the partner's point of view, Clara had been facing him and blinked out. She was there one moment, gone for less than a second, and reappeared in her original position.

While his mind struggled to come to terms with what he saw, this visual anomaly was then followed by two shots from her shotgun, which caused his ears to ring. The constant hum was enough to effectively drown out the screams that followed.

"Wait here please," Clara said as she broke the breech to reload.

The man heard nothing more than the muffled *waw waw* of her speech. His mind deciphered the words, and he nodded mechanically. This time, Clara could be seen turning her back to him slowly, but not before kicking the chap-man in the side, just to make sure he was not faking.

"Now. Now. There is no need to cry," Clara said to the two who had been playing pool, as they writhed in pain. "Those are only flesh wounds," Clara said while loading two slugs, which were sure to make one hell of a mess.

The fact that the wounds were healing right before her eyes confirmed that they were not human. Clara lined up her barrel with the first man and pulled both triggers. Once the headless corpse stopped moving, she repeated the same with the other.

"Peace and quiet," Clara said, before wiping off splatter from her cheek. She then turned to face the partner, reloaded her weapon, and said, "So, werewolves?"

When the man did not immediately respond, she leaned in closer and yelled out every syllable. This time he nodded.

"Know that man from the mural?" Clara asked in a deliberate manner.

The man nodded slowly to reduce any chance of him appearing as a threat. To be honest, there was little left for him to do, other than shit himself.

"Your pack?" Clara asked.

The man shook his head, and that confirmed her suspicions. Still, there might be a few more nuggets of information to be gleaned from their encounter.

"Do you know me?" Clara asked.

"Kinda!" The partner yelled in an attempt to drown out the buzzing in his ears.

"How?" Clara pressed.

"Word on the streets!" The partner yelled.

That meant they knew of her, but nothing more than rumours and innuendo. She might be able to use that to her advantage, depending how all this played out.

"Who did you think I was?" Clara asked.

"One of his!" The partner yelled, the strain causing his voice to crack.

"So, the one on the mural?" Clara confirmed.

The man nodded, which dropped all of the pieces in place. Julia's panties reeked of someone who belonged to a rival pack. The attack would have happened regardless. It was the reasons for which that differed.

"Know where they are?" Clara asked.

When confusion set into his eyes, Clara looked around and spotted a laminated map of the state next to the faded outline of a payphone. These days, only the bare wires served as a monument to a monolithic device. *To think that I used to be in awe of these when they first showed up.*

Clara pointed at the map and repeated her question. This time, the partner caught on, nodded and walked over backwards to keep an eye on Clara. When he got close enough, he searched the map for specific details and pointed to a spot with his finger.

"There?" Clara asked.

When the man nodded, she pulled out her phone and took a picture of the area. While she had a knack for details, describing the map's particulars over the blower was her special place in hell.

"Go." Clara said, while waving her shotgun in the direction of the door. When he hesitated, she repeated the gesture and yelled, "Get out of here!"

The man nodded vigorously and yelled, "Thank you!"

When he turned to face the door, Clara gave him both barrels. A small part of her felt bad for the deception, but she needed it to look like his death was connected to the earlier two. *Besides he saw my wings, and that changes the narrative.*

Clara returned to the bar and looked over the side. She found the bartender cowering in the corner, which was problematic. To alleviate his fears, she broke the breach of her shotgun, and left it open on the bar for him to see.

"If I were you," Clara said, "I'd get the hell out of town and never come back."

As expected, the man did not budge. Clara slowed down time just long enough to appear at his side.

The sight of her materialising out of thin air had the desired effect. He screeched as though he had seen a ghost and bolted out of the front door.

"That should motivate him," Clara said.

Sure, it may have been an empty threat, given that he was human. How fortunate for her that she neglected to mention that part.

Clara searched through the carnage to pick up the empty shells and discarded wads. That would prevent anyone from connecting this scene to her weapon. Even with these precautions, Clara would have to ditch this weapon, and soon.

Afterwards, she pulled those panties from her pocket and wiped down surfaces she touched, her seat, and the bodies. While Clara could not tell the difference, she suspected a pack of werewolves would form a picture of what happened.

Lastly, she grabbed her weapon and loaded it with bird shot. Without much thought, she fired both rounds into chap-man's rump and smiled at the sight of the new moon rising.

"Now we have a witness," Clara said before leaving the bar.

Despite the wounds, chap-man was still down for the count. Clara was certain that she would be long gone before he was in any shape to tell the tale.

On her way out, she noticed that the memorial was more washed out than worn. Either someone had made a deliberate attempt to erase the rival pack's alpha from the wall, or as judged by the stench, preferred to use it as a public urinal.

"The enemy of my enemy," Clara said.

* * * *

Julia was running through an open field as the long grass cooled her paws. At this time of night, the dew had settled on the blades of grass, and soon her fur would be soaked.

The rest of the pack was up ahead with the bigger males leading. When the alpha caught the scent of their prey, the males split off in two directions.

The pack surged when they crested the hill and sighted the valley floor. With the full moon high in the sky, her eyes caught every detail as though it were high noon. In fact, she quickly spotted a woman running away from the main group.

Now that their cover was blown, the main body yelped and howled. This cacophony of horrors served to distract their victim while the males approached from the side.

With their prey in sight, Julia saw nothing else. Even this far out, she made out the dirt covered brown hair, loose fitting clothes, and oversized boots. They hunted down vagrants on a regular basis, but something about this one seemed familiar.

This one was smart, knowing that her only chance was to give it her all, and would not look over her shoulder. Still, such tactics rarely worked against a numerically superior foe, and the pack always got their kill.

As expected, she spotted the males driving in. Their prey caught it too, and by then it was too late, even for an Olympic-class sprinter. Defeated, she stopped running and dropped to her knees. The breeze carried the sweet smell of defeat... so why was Julia not feeling the thrill?

The alpha got onto his hind legs, towering over the woman as he approached. The confident sway in William's gait implied a great deal of pride. Despite executing a flawless chase, this one was not about to cooperate, instead she leapt up and charged the main body.

"Julia!" The woman shouted.

That's when Julia saw the details of that face, the spitting image of herself in human form. How was this possible? Why would they betray her like this? Was this a look—

A shot rang out in the night closely followed by a pink mist that replaced her copy's head. What was left of the body collapsed to the ground, falling like a rag doll casually tossed away by a toddler. William then knelt down, and with his powerful fist, punched a hole through to the chest cavity. The alpha rummaged until he found what he sought, grabbed ahold, and tore out the heart.

Unexpectedly, the muscle continued to beat. The shock of the imagery caused her to dig her claws into the ground. Meanwhile, a silhouette crested over the opposing valley wall, carrying a high-powered rifle. Julia knew the shooter, and Adrienne was by no means an ally.

William lifted the heart into the air, basking in the glow of adoration that came from being the alpha. The group howled at the moon, a sound she normally cherished… now, she cringed.

Julia considered slipping out of sight while the pack was busy with their feeding frenzy. Alas, every member of the pack was facing her, their predatory eyes focused on her.

"Get her!" Adrienne barked.

* * * *

Julia shot up into a sitting position; the blanket that Clara covered her with was piled up around her waist. She reached for her chest, feeling her heart trying to break free from its cage. She gulped in the air as fast as her lungs could take it, and once she caught sight of the room, realised it had been a dream.

"Fuck me," Julia said. "She screws me over any chance she gets, even in my dreams."

When her breathing slowed, Julia ran a hand through her hair and realised that another shower was on the horizon. She was soaked in sweat, which fit in with what she experienced during the dream.

"It felt so real," Julia said with a hint of disappointment.

She would have given up anything to be back with her pack. Still, the image of Adrienne holding that rifle served as a stern reminder that the life she had known was gone. Adrienne and William would see to it that she never rejoined the fold.

"Clara?" Julia asked once she realised that the angel was being quiet.

When no answer came, Julia scanned the room for signs of life. It was dark in here, and only a thin filament of white light from the curtains cut through the room. Julia was alone, that much was clear.

Despite wondering about Clara's whereabouts, Julia was overwhelmed by a wave of fatigue. Unable to fight the urge, she leaned back into the bed, pulled up the comforter, and closed her eyes.

"I wonder where…" Julia tried to say before slipping back into dreamland.

# CHAPTER 14

## *LOUD AND CLEAR*

T he high-pitched scream carried throughout the mines, a sound feared by vermin and predators alike. The scream persisted to the point of appearing supernatural in nature and conjured up imagery of a banshee. This lonely sound was soon joined by others, like the breaking of glass and furniture.

"Mother," William said in a calm voice.

Adrienne stopped cold, before gently placing the plate back on the table. She brushed some dust from her clothes, closed her eyes, and took a deep breath. After a pause, she exhaled, opened her eyes, and managed to look like a new woman.

Despite all of that effort to calm down, her smile remained tight and forced. Her eyes were thin slits and burned like raging inferno. Even William had no memory of his mother losing her cool like that.

"Thanks, dear," Adrienne said in a sickly-sweet tone. "Can you repeat that? Please."

William's head jerked back unexpectedly, certain that this had been passed on properly the first time. Still, with her temper so close to the surface, it paid to humour her.

"Someone hit the old club house," William said calmly. "They blame us for the incident."

"One... of... our... own?" Adrienne confirmed, because she knew that was impossible.

"They could smell the—" William said.

"Smell?" Adrienne asked. "Accusations are being levelled against us based on nothing more than odour?"

While Adrienne knew that werewolves had a superior sense of smell, the idea that three deaths and a near-castration were being pinned on them for something as innocuous as scent, struck her as ludicrous.

William nodded and said, "Female."

"Are all of the women accounted for, William?" Adrienne asked, despite knowing the answer.

"In accordance with our plan, everyone joined us back here," William said.

"William, while that's an excellent answer…" Adrienne said. As he began to smile, she added, "…that's not what I asked."

Without realising, William took a step back and hit his head against the stone wall. The likelihood of his mother going off was exponentially greater.

"We did a headcount—" William answered.

"Excellent. So, *all* of the women were accounted for?" Adrienne asked.

William gulped before answering, "Except for Julia."

"Julia," Adrienne said as her jaw muscles tensed to the point of her teeth straining.

"Yes, Mother," William said.

"Do you think it likely that your scrawny skank of a *half*-sister could dispatch three *males*?" Adrienne said with her hands balled up into fists. *Although, she would sure as hell fuck them.*

"Well… no?" William guessed.

"So?" Adrienne asked.

"Soooooo?" William asked, because he was not following.

Adrienne pounced and pummelled William with both fists. He may have been as imposing as a brick shit house, but there was power and rage behind those fists. Instead of fighting back, he stood there and took it, which made matters worse.

"That means she had help!" Adrienne yelled and did not care if the world heard every word. "You witless oaf! That winged harpy is behind all of this!"

"Oh?" William said at a near whisper.

"Fuck!" Adrienne yelled. "The last thing we need is a turf…"

She paused in the middle of a thought. Her eyes jumped from point to point, as though each spot contained an encapsulated thought. Her eyes eventually settled on a spot while adopting a sickly smile, one that chilled the air.

"William," Adrienne said calmly.

"Yes, Mother?" William asked.

"I want three *volunteers* to go into the city. They are to find a woman that roughly fits the description of our hostage," Adrienne said.

"And bring her here?" William asked.

"No… fuck her up," Adrienne replied before adopting a smile so disturbing that it would make a death row inmate uneasy. "I want it bloody, violent, and public."

"Why—" William asked.

"I want the lemmings to record the assault and stream it online. That means one of the local channels will be sure to report on it," Adrienne said.

"Send a message?" William asked.

"Very good, William," Adrienne said. "After they complete their mission, I want you to make an anonymous call. Tell them that more will die at sunrise unless our demands are met."

William was tempted to ask what their demands were. Doing so might lessen her rage if her instructions were followed to the letter. However, he had no interest in knowing more.

\* \* \* \*

Julia stood at the foot of a little pond, looking towards an island. There was a tree growing at its centre, big enough to tower over those nearby. A stream fed the pond on one end and transitioned into a series of waterfalls on the other. The trickling was both gentle and constant, a reminder of simpler days, and a testament to those precious moments of her youth.

She had several fond memories of leaping from rock to rock to get to the island, all the while wearing an adorable flowery dress and a pair of rubber boots. This was her kingdom, a refuge from the constant reminders of the need to grow up. *Whoa. I can get onto the island with one step now?*

"...*old mining operation north*..." A voice carried by the wind said.

Julia furrowed her brow when something brushed against her cheek. Curious, she rubbed her face and felt a tear.

"I'm crying?" Julia asked. "Why am I crying?"

Julia retreated from the water and stopped near a tree stump. There she sat. The moss and grass beneath her rump turned out to be soft, while the stump provided her with ample back support. From this vantage point, she had a great view of her childhood hideout.

"...*back home I'd let the sea*..." a voice in the wind added.

A quick scan of the area confirmed that she was alone. She was surrounded by birch trees deep in the woods, left to her own devices. This moment helped Julia to realise how much she missed being out in nature.

For one of her kind, the city was nothing short of a death sentence. Even the patches of forest found at the edges of the city were diseased compared to the deep woods. Julia had been banished, which barring her from visiting her refuge, and that punishment was starting to take its toll.

"...*really?*" The wind asked.

Conceptually, Julia had no idea how the wind could ask questions. Instead of racking her brain, she concentrated on the little waterfalls and relaxed.

At one point, Julia imagined herself as a child, sitting on that island, playfully splashing her feet in the pond. Emotion swelled up from within, and she wept at the innocence stolen from her.

"*...as much...I trust you...*" the wind carried on, but Julia was not paying attention.

At first, she wanted to lay the blame on Clara for the loss, but that was not entirely true. This beautiful corner of her life had been taken from her well before they crossed paths. Someone else had been chipping away at the pack's harmony for a long time now.

Julia clutched a tuft of grass and yanked it free from the ground, roots and all. Julia narrowed her eyes and wondered why everything she touched had the consistency of cotton.

"*...remember that...thumper...*" the wind echoed.

"Hello?" Julia asked to no avail.

On a hunch, she reached out to a nearby moss covered rock and it too felt like rough textiles. In fact, everything else around her was the same, except for a small patch near her feet that had the texture of wool.

"What the fuck?" Julia swore.

As confusion set in, the wind picked up and began to howl as though responding to her distress. Why were the trees unaffected by such a stiff wind? Despite the disconnect, the wind changed in both pitch and tone, and varied over time. *Is that a melody?*

"*...misbehavin'...*" the wind sang.

"So, the wind sings now?" Julia asked before having a moment of clarity.

That spark of insight set off a firestorm in her mind. The world before her was set aflame and consumed everything until it turned to ash. All of that soot was then whisked away by the wind, leaving her alone in a void.

\* \* \* \*

While Elizabeth's head throbbed, the bulk of her pain was centred on her nose. She grimaced and took in a deep breath through her mouth to avoid another jolt of pain, but instead, inhaled whatever shit covered the floor.

The reaction was both immediate and brutal. Her eyes opened wide as though she were about to suffocate. The violent reversal came next, one that forced her to cough and spasm, which only worsened the agony.

The coughing persisted and made her eyes tear up. All the while, the pain and urgency for air led her to pray that this torment would end. It was bad enough being tossed from a workbench, but to endure this? *What the fuck did I do to deserve this?*

"Shit," Elizabeth managed to say after she got her first lungful of air.

She tried to wipe the grime from her face but remembered that her hands were bound behind her back. *God, talk about an itch that can't be scratched.* That realisation only made things worse, and if it went on unchecked, it could evolve into a full-blown panic attack.

"*Calm down,*" her internal voice whispered.

Those words had been delivered at precisely the wrong time. While true, Elizabeth was rather resistant to the idea of relaxing. She was tired, sore, and had the motherlode of all headaches. If this was not the ideal time to break down and cry… *when would it?*

"*Clara knows,*" the voice added.

"What?" Elizabeth asked herself.

How could Clara know about her kidnapping? Even if she did, how would she know where to find her? Based on the journey to get here, this place was pretty remote and desolate.

"*Grace told her,*" the voice said.

That might explain the how, however, that did nothing to help Clara narrow down where this mine was located. She was native to these parts and had no clue that this place even existed.

"*Are you willing to stake your life on that?*" *The voice asked.*

Elizabeth had to think about that, since giving up hope now would do nothing for her. That much was grudgingly obvious, even if she loathed to admit that her dissenting voice was right.

"So, what now?" Elizabeth muttered.

Just outside the door, something big moved. Elizabeth scooted against the workbench before figuring out the source and realising the futility of her actions. She guessed that hiding against anything smaller than a tank would do little to slow a werewolf down.

"What's that?" Elizabeth asked herself.

Something was poking her in the back. At first, she ignored it, but the longer she remained in place the more intense the pain became. So, Elizabeth rolled away from the workbench, enduring the discomfort of putting all her weight on her bound hands to get a clear view.

Even in the dim light, Elizabeth made out the skeleton of metal plates and tubing. This assembly must have housed machinery and while that was not particularly noteworthy, the broken tubing protruding outwards, was.

As a precaution, she reached her hands higher up her back until she reached the source of her pain. A part of her expected to feel blood, but the area was dry. Although, her blouse was a write off.

"Dammit," Elizabeth muttered while straining to get up into a sitting position.

"*You'll feel better once your hands are free,*" the voice said.

Elizabeth had to admit that she would. The ability to breathe normally through her nose would also do a lot to improve morale. Right now, doing so was painful and laboured because swelling prevented proper airflow.

"How odd?" Elizabeth asked herself, before adding up how stress and a potential concussion made up major elements in this equation.

Once back in position, Elizabeth moved her hands into place and rubbed against the sharp edge of the tubing. The first few passes were imprecise and proved challenging to avoid injury. The odd angle needed to make a cut made it a painful manoeuvre. On the plus side, it would keep her mind busy, and most importantly keep her alert.

*"Don't worry," her internal voice said. "I can keep you company."*

"Just what I needed," Elizabeth thought as giggling echoed throughout her mind.

\* \* \* \*

Julia heard a knock at the door, and faced the source of the sound to investigate. The first thing she did was confirm that the sliding bar was in place, along with the privacy lock. With both in place, no human would be able to get through without giving it some effort.

"Can you get that?" Clara asked from the shower.

"Huh?" Julia said, surprised that the other could hear the knock at all.

Her sense of hearing was sharper than the average human. As a werewolf, she could hear just as well as any wolf, including those annoying dog whistles. Since Clara caught that knock, that meant that she also possessed enhanced senses. Obviously, her upgrades went beyond being fitted with a pair of wings.

Someone knocked on the door for the second time. Julia sighed, slipped out of those humid sheets, and found her footing. She sniffed her underarms, curled in the corner of her lips, and tightened her nose. While she hated to admit it, another shower was most definitely called for.

She reached the door, peered through the peep hole and found a middle-aged woman of Asian descent on the other side. She held a bunch of bags in her hands, and the black skirt, jacket and white shirt marked her as a member of the hotel staff. On her jacket there was a cheap plastic name tag that said, 'Hello. My name is Ming.'

The smile on Ming's face left her unsettled because many who wielded such facial adornments were known to take advantage of her. Julia had to remind herself not to take it personally, since smiling came with the job.

"Yes?" Julia said.

The woman did not seem surprised by the voice. She simply raised a bunch of bags to eye level. These bags were not from stores known for their fashions, but from outdoor outfitters.

"Clara asked me to pick up some items," Ming said with a faint accent.

Julia hesitated for a moment, wondering why Clara would not have done the supply run herself. Then it dawned on her that the fight was streamed all over the Internet. That kind of exposure would make sneaking about the city… difficult.

So, she turned the lock and opened the door while leaving the crossbar in place. A beam of bright white light shot into the room and straight into her eyes. She instinctively closed them, fearful that a migraine would wash over her, but nothing happened.

Opting for caution, Julia opened her eyes bit by bit until the hallway came into focus. Despite the sight of a new face, Ming did not appear to be worried.

"You must be Julia," Ming said, although that was not a question.

"Y-Yes," Julia answered while dismissing all thoughts that this was due to some form of supernatural ability.

"Here are new outfits for you and Clara," Ming said. She then took one quick look at Julia and added, "Are you hungry?"

As though responding to a command, Julia's stomach growled, so she replied, "Starving."

Ming nodded, left the bags where she stood, and walked away. Julia waited for the steps to fade off into the distance before opening the door. This gave her the opportunity to get a good view of the floor, conveniently under construction. Half of the room doors had been removed and stacked neatly in a pile near the elevators. Given a couple of weeks, she figured that every door on this floor would be gone.

"Smart girl," Julia muttered before grabbing the bags.

"That was Ming?" Clara asked.

The voice originated from directly behind her and sent Julia's heart rate soaring. Meanwhile, she wondered how anyone could get the jump on her. When she reached for her chest, a couple of the bags shook loose from her other hand and fell towards the floor.

"Looks like it," Clara said and grabbed those bags in mid-flight. Once she realised that Julia had been startled, she added, "Sorry!"

Julia took a series of deep breaths to calm down before turning around. Just ahead, Clara was standing before her sopping wet. Julia looked down at her feet to avoid seeing all that nudity. While it did nothing for her, doing so seemed respectful.

Clara dropped the bags on the spare bed. She then sorted the items into a series of neat piles.

"How do you move that fast?" Julia asked.

"Comes with the job," Clara said as the piles took shape. "I hope you like black."

"Suits me fine," Julia said while avoiding looking at anything soft, white and glistening. "Why?"

"Just drop those bags on my bed," Clara said. "I assume you'll be taking another shower?"

"Wait… you can smell me?" Julia asked.

"Of course," Clara said. "You've had a pretty rough go of it since I left."

"Speaking of which. Where did you go?" Julia asked.

"I figured you'd be out a while. So, I visited the club house," Clara said honestly.

"I told you we didn't use that place anymore," Julia said.

"You did," Clara said. "Still, I had the time to spare—"

"Anyone left breathing?" Julia asked, grinding her teeth in between words.

"Yes," Clara said bluntly.

"Did you attack—" Julia blurted out.

"They made the first move," Clara said while grabbing the additional bags to sift through. "A gal has to look out for herself after all."

"Why?" Julia said.

"It seems they don't like you very much," Clara said.

"Me?" Julia said.

Clara paused her triage operation long enough to pull out the panties from her coat which was draped across the office chair. Julia cocked a brow at the sight of them. That was enough for her to figure out the rest.

"It appears that you're not universally loved," Clara said bluntly. "They also know where your pack is located."

"Really?" Julia asked while looking into those steel-grey eyes long enough to get a sense that she was telling the truth.

Clara walked back towards the bed, forcing Julia to avert her eyes. The anxiety would make her grind her teeth, and that could bring on a headache.

"So, what do you need me for?" Julia asked once she figured out what Clara's scouting mission really meant.

Clara smiled, a sign that this was the question she had been waiting for.

"Other than being a guide?" Clara asked.

While Clara went through the clothes, Julia observed what was sorted. Half of the four stacks appeared to be identical and contained everything one needed to conduct clandestine operations. These outfits were built around layers, some designed to keep the wearer dry, while others provided warmth. Every item was matte black, including the boots.

"Hmmm. Yeah?" Julia confirmed.

Clara picked up a stack and brought it to Julia. She noted that this outfit differed mildly from the one Clara would wear. There was an additional layer that would keep her warm, even when submerged in water.

"You need me for something?" Julia confirmed.

"Now you're catching on," Clara said before returning to the bed.

Julia got a look at the remaining mounds. One was similar to hers, but bigger. Another pile contained assorted gear and was topped with a backpack. The presence of the pack near the set identical to hers strongly implied that she was going into that mine.

The pile that Clara would wear featured knee pads, shin guards, and webbing that permitted her to transport a wide array of *toys*. That choice of clothing made it obvious that their objectives differed greatly. Primarily, that stealth was out for Clara.

"I'm going after your friend?" Julia asked.

Clara nodded and grabbed a black sports bra. When she put it on, Julia was finally able to look up from her bare feet.

"Right," Clara said.

"You're going to be the bait?" Julia asked.

"Of course," Clara said with a grin.

"Why would you do that?" Julia asked, since it was suicide for anyone to deliberately taunt a pack of werewolves.

Clara slipped on a pair of thermal underwear and the room's phone rang once. Without additional direction, Clara reached towards the nightstand, grabbed the remote, and turned on the television. After a brief chime, the image came to life.

Julia's eyes adjusted to the new light source, and she noticed that the television was tuned to a local channel. Despite this being prime time for soap operas, the news was on.

*"Again. An anonymous source claiming to be the leader of this group called and stated that there would be more dead… if not delivered by sunrise," the news anchor said before Clara muted the television.*

Julia watched the scene unfold before her. A group from her pack had ploughed through a crowded market with an old van. They then zeroed in on some tall Asian chick and beat her senseless. By itself, that would have been enough to send a message, but they allegedly disembowelled her in public. This confirmed for Julia that it was no longer *her* family.

"Does it look like I have a choice?" Clara asked.

"No," Julia whispered.

"Alright then," Clara said. "Now get washed and dressed. It does not pay to be late to this kind of party."

"Alright," Julia said before thinking of something. "Why the dry suit?"

"A Scroogle search informed me that tunnels in abandoned mines are prone to flooding," Clara said while the glow in her eyes dimmed for a moment. "I figured they would keep her in the lowest levels."

Julia had to admit that the angel had a point. Although, the tunnels were mostly dry these days, courtesy of the *engineer*, a man their father kidnapped and castrated to emulate what humans did to their pets. The pack kept him locked up in the power house attached to the dam. After some *coaxing* from the group, he managed to get one of the turbines working again.

"Good idea," Julia said and left it at that.

The young woman tried to remember the last time she showered twice in one day. It was a luxury to be sure, one that she would rather not grow accustomed to. Still, why not enjoy it while she could?

* * * *

"Do you think she got the message?" William asked.

Adrienne did not reply, since she was engrossed in the news report. It was clear that this woman revelled in the violence and the carnage they unleashed for no reason other than wishing it to happen. There were other ways of getting such a message across, like going after that corpse whore. Still, in her mind, this was a powerful message, one that would serve as the foundations for a legend.

"She got the message," Adrienne answered before adopting a sickly smile.

"How—" William asked, as he looked away.

Adrienne slapped her son across the cheek, the sound of which reverberated off the walls. William bit his tongue to focus on his pain and did it until blood filled his mouth. Once the feelings of running away subsided, he swallowed hard and faced her.

"You *always* look people in the eyes when you talk to them," Adrienne said.

"Yes, Mother," William mumbled.

"Sorry, I didn't hear that," Adrienne said sharply.

"Yes, Mother," William said while making sure to enunciate every syllable.

"That's my boy," Adrienne said before kissing him on the cheek. "Now. I want you to rally your troops."

William looked outside at how sunlight filtered through the clouds. Until now, the pack had been ordered to stay underground to avoid giving away their position. Now, he would rile them up to whip them into a frenzy, looking for any excuse to kill.

"Mother," William said. "We should wait for twilight."

While those words were soft and showed a genuine concern for her ultimate plan, they poisoned Adrienne's mind. Her lips thinned out until they disappeared while the fire smouldering in those eyes erupted once more. Despite the fury raging so near to the surface, William stood his ground and bit his tongue to conceal any hint of fear.

"That's fine, dear," Adrienne said with a big smile and walked away.

William blinked several times in rapid succession but did not follow. Instead, he remained behind until her steps were faint. Only then did he spit out the mouthful of blood. While exposure to the air caused the open wound to tingle, William knew that it would heal over in minutes.

Meanwhile, he counted his lucky stars that she backed down. He knew that speaking with a nearly severed tongue would have destroyed all credibility.

# CHAPTER 15

## *MOVING PIECES*

So how did you meet Ming?" Julia asked as they flew past the highway traffic.

Clara considered asking where that particular question came from but thought better of it. After all, Ming did provide shelter, room service, and supplies as well as arranging for a hotel rental car. That exposed her to considerable risk. However, Clara did not see the need to share that Ming was not her real name.

"She's my friend's distant cousin," Clara said. "That, and I did her a big favour earlier this year."

"A favour?" Julia asked.

Clara nodded before doing a shoulder check to change lanes. At this time of day, the traffic was getting heavy, so they needed to clear the city before its arteries turned into parking lots.

"Yeah," Clara nodded. "I got rid of a poltergeist for her."

"Those don't exist," Julia retorted and immediately regretted making such a statement.

"You know," Clara said, "for a werewolf, you don't have much of an open mind."

"Sorry," Julia said. "No one's ever mentioned ghosts or poltergeists outside of campfire stories."

"Did they mention black winged angels?" Clara asked. "Old gods? Or how an angel of death ferries souls to their final destination?"

"N-No…" Julia said softly.

"I wasn't aware of those either, or at least until I died, that is," Clara said with a chuckle. "Ming's family believes in evil spirits, so she was receptive to the idea when she saw the signs."

"You killed it?" Julia asked.

"I'm not sure that they can be killed, honestly," Clara said. "That particular topic was curiously missing from our lectures."

"So how did you deal with it?" Julia asked, focusing on the features of Clara's face to avoid thinking about all that high-speed manoeuvring.

"Any guesses?" Clara prodded.

"No clue," Julia replied.

"None at all?" Clara countered.

"Yeah… nope," Julia tossed back.

"Really, you can't even come up with a teensy-weensy little guess?" Clara said in a mocking tone.

Julia began to grind her teeth but caught on. The attempt to annoy her was purposeful, not to get under her skin, but to lighten the mood by turning this exchange into a game.

"You pissed it off?" Julia asked.

"Yes!" Clara exclaimed. "Forced it to expend all of that pent-up negative energy on me."

"Dangerous?" Julia asked while thinking of all those horror movies she had seen that covered the subject.

"There—" Clara said as the collision alert chime went off, forcing her to steer the car violently into the neighbouring lane. "There are reasons why this floor is under construction."

While there was a lot to be said on this subject, and the journey as a whole, silence nonetheless filled the air, serving as a sombre reminder that they needed to get there in one piece.

After crossing the river, the traffic tapered off. Still, Julia was not precisely sure of where they were going. While this car came equipped with every luxury available, it lacked the suspension, wheels, and clearance needed for off-road travel.

"Are there—major—routes to—mine?" Clara asked before flooring the accelerator.

Julia caught sight of something unusual, one moment, the angel looked out to her left for a shoulder check, and in a blur, faced the road once again. Clara must have been driving in an accelerated state, blessed with reaction times that humans only dreamed about.

"There is the road that leads in from the South," Julia replied while focusing up ahead, but a wave of nausea hit her.

At this speed, the cars on this part of the freeway were falling behind them as though they were parked. It seemed that Clara really had no time to waste.

"Used—often?" Clara asked in a manner that implied she could no longer dedicate effort towards speaking normally. That ability must have required a great deal of concentration and risked their safety.

"That's our main way in or out," Julia said.

The car jerked into the next lane hard enough that Julia was sent crashing into the passenger door. Sure enough, this was repeated several times to clear a cluster of slow-moving vehicles spanning three lanes. A few honked in protest, but they sounded far away by the time the sound reached them.

"What about—road—less travelled?" Clara asked.

Julia chanced looking over to the dash and found it hard to believe that the needle had nowhere else to go. Currently, they were tearing through miles in less than thirty seconds. Whoever said that getting there was half the fun, clearly had not ridden shotgun with Clara.

"There's an old road that runs along the river from the North," Julia said.

"But… this thing won't stand a chance."

As though on cue, Clara eased off on the throttle to let the car coast. On her right, there was an off-ramp leading to an industrial park.

"Goes by—old dam?" Clara asked.

"How did…" Julia wondered. "Wait. You had the time to find some aerial shots of the site?"

Clara laughed and, this time, used the indicator before taking the exit. Had they gone any faster, their car would have been launched into the air when it hit the slope.

"You did sleep for some time." Clara said. "You know?"

"Fair," Julia said.

The car turned off the main artery and came along a series of small warehouses that overlooked the river. Once the car came to a complete stop, Clara killed the engine and exited the vehicle.

From the back, Clara pulled out the contents of the trunk and walked inside. Julia unbuckled her seat belt, and opened her door just as one of the bay doors rolled open.

Clara did not wait for the door to retract all the way, instead, she tossed Julia a rag saying, "Wipe down the doors, dash, steering wheel, shifter, and anything else you can think of."

When Julia did as asked, she noticed the distinctive odour of gasoline. Just outside the car, there were two jerry cans with their caps removed. Julia easily followed how this would unfold.

The angel removed the plate before entering the warehouse. This left Julia to do the same on the front. Clara then walked inside and left Julia to finish.

"Thank you, Marc!" Clara yelled.

The sound of a big engine's grunt came from within, and a lot of love with the throttle was needed before it purred. Moments later, a large truck with a lift kit exited the bay.

"That's more like it!" Julia exclaimed.

Clara pulled up nearby, killed the engine, and jumped out of their new ride tagged with the rental's plates. Clara tossed the keys to Julia, slipped on a pair of gloves, and proceeded to soak the inside of the car with gas.

"What are these for?" Julia asked.

"You're driving," Clara said before tossing the empty jerry cans into the car and shutting every door save for one.

"Me?" Julia said.

"You know the way?" Clara confirmed.

"Yeah," Julia said but did not move due to the emotional impact associated with being given that much trust.

"Besides, you'll need the truck more than I will," Clara said while wiggling her wings.

That's when a big part of the plan fell into place. Clara would be able to fly towards the mine. Julia would need to get closer using the truck and then huff it out on foot when near.

"How did you manage to plan all of this?" Julia asked with a grin.

She backed away once Clara lit up a road flare. A moment after dropping the pyrotechnic item into the car, they heard a loud whoosh. This sound was followed by bright yellow flames that melted the surrounding snow.

"Plan?" Clara asked with no indication if this was a joke or not. "Well, get comfortable," Clara urged.

Julia looked at the keys and felt a rush of excitement. It took all the self-control she had to hold back from running towards the truck. Meanwhile, Clara went into the warehouse and pressed a button to shut the door. This time she walked out with a heavy bag in hand.

Unlike the other bags they had stowed behind the bucket seats, this one would not fit. Clara dropped it into the truck bed and used some ratchet straps to secure it before sliding the tonneau cover into place.

Once Clara was seated, she caught sight of Julia's mischievous smile. It was infectious enough to bring a smile to her own face.

"Try not to have too much fun," Clara said.

"I won't make any promises that I have no intention of keeping," Julia said. "Now, hold on!"

\* \* \* \*

Elizabeth's eyelids felt as though they weighed a ton, so much so that her mind began to wander into the dream realm. Despite the exhaustion, she changed her position slightly to get some blood flowing through her numbed arms. The act of cutting a rope with a sharp object turned out to be a long and painful affair. Who would have guessed that movies and reality differed?

While she had more freedom around her wrists, Elizabeth still had to get some slices in. Initially, she had been able to maintain the position for minutes at a time, but pain shot up with every iteration, and right now she dreaded even thinking about it.

That explained why fatigue was beginning to take hold. She was caught in a paradox: to cut her way free she needed to rest, but to stay awake, she had to keep busy. There were no other options in her situation. Besides, any plan that she could think up, required free hands.

In an attempt to compensate for her fatigue, she closed one eye and kept the other wide open. The intent was to rest one eye at a time and watch out for trouble.

"Just a few more minutes…" Elizabeth muttered while her second eye slammed shut.

"*Wake up!*" Her internal voice screeched.

That disembodied yell managed to trigger her flight response, and just like that, her eyes shot open. Now that adrenaline was pumping through her veins, Elizabeth knew that she had been granted a brief reprieve before the urge to sleep hit her again.

*"You need to work on those bindings," the voice reminded her.*

"Who asked you?" Elizabeth questioned, annoyed at being nagged.

She loathed situations like this, ones where the last thing she wanted to do turned out to be the smartest move. Elizabeth did not know what was going on, or if Clara even planned to make an entrance. Uncertainty came with the territory, but she could not rely on being saved this time.

All she needed was a bit of time and a lot of luck. The first was plentiful for the moment, and the latter required a leap of faith. Elizabeth tightened her jaw, closed her eyes, and despite the impending pain, forced her arms back into position.

This time, she focused on rubbing her bindings against that sharp metal edge. Her eyes streamed tears, but she persisted and even pushed in hard enough to chance a gouge on her wrists.

*"With great risk comes great reward," the voice said.*

"Fuck..." Elizabeth said before the bindings around her wrists went slack. "Yeah?"

Elizabeth opened her eyes, leaned forward, and struggled with her wrists. The bindings initially resisted, but the rope quickly slipped off. The first thing she did was move her arms to the front, a motion which was greatly appreciated by her sore joints and muscles.

"Now what?" Elizabeth wondered.

*"You'll need a weapon," the voice said.*

"No kidding?" Elizabeth asked.

One would think that her alter ego could come up with some helpful advice. Rummaging around through the workshop might turn up something useful, but that guard lurked just outside the door. If he caught on that she was loose...

*"What if Clara is not the one to come for you?" The voice asked.*

"What?" Elizabeth said aloud causing the guard outside to stop pacing.

As a subterfuge, Elizabeth began to snore softly. Feigning sleep was one way to sell her outburst. What she needed was the proverbial cherry on top.

"Who wears… army boots… cocktail dress," Elizabeth said in between some snore-filled breaths.

While the guard tsked before moving on, Elizabeth continued on with her charade. All the while she kept her eyes open for any signs of trouble.

*Right on cue, the voice said, "You know? Clara may need to send someone else down here to get you."*

This time, Elizabeth had no choice but keep quiet. So, she thought it over and realised that this was a likely outcome. The question that came with this flash of insight was obvious. How would she be able to tell the difference between her saviour and her executioner?

*"Just wait for it,"* the voice said.

Elizabeth cocked an eyebrow and stopped snoring. Again, her mind was left to digest the significance of that particular nugget of information. Once she realised that her charade might come to light due to this brain fart, Elizabeth started up again after a sputter. *What—*

The words from her inner-voice turned out to be prophetic. The first thing she heard was the sound of the guard bracing himself against the wall. His breathing became uneven and pained, although that was before the horror show really began. Next came a whole slew of noises that her mind was ill-prepared to process.

First was the sound of bones being dislocated, which coincided with tearing fabric. Knowing that these were werewolves did help her to guess what was going on. But what were those wet plops interspersed between screams of agony?

*"I don't think you want to know,"* the voice said.

"No shit," Elizabeth whispered, guessing that she would eventually find out.

In the distance, there came a howl. While faint, the effect it had on her psyche was immediate. The monster went silent, as though waiting for confirmation.

Once more, a howl rang out through the cavern, one that echoed throughout the tunnels and walls leading to her *cell*. That howl was followed by another, and another, until the pack *sang* as a chorus.

This time the guard grunted and ventured deeper into the tunnel complex. Elizabeth figured the pack was being called to assembly and hoped that Clara had yet to make her grand entrance. After all, there was still work to be done.

"*That's the spirit!*" Her inside voice exclaimed.

\* \* \* \*

Julia enjoyed the freedom of being out on the road. While she preferred to be out on a motorcycle or even running on all fours, this truck was pretty sweet. Heck, compared to her preferred modes of travel, this thing was a tank.

Up ahead, were the vestiges of the sun that set about a half-an-hour ago, the sky changing from blood filled clouds to a sea of dark blues and purples. This was her favourite time of the day, the proverbial dawn for all nocturnal beings. Without even realising it, Julia closed her eyes, feeling the pull of a celestial body that was about to make an entrance.

"Do I have a reason to be concerned?" Clara asked.

Julia smiled and opened her eyes just as silvery light peeked over the horizon. There was something spiritual about the moon appearing from over the horizon. A shame that she was unable to transform tonight.

"Yeah," Julia said with a sigh. "I miss my old friend."

"Are you too thin to change?" Clara asked.

She took her eyes off the road long enough to note that Clara was smiling. Despite this being an honest question, one based on curiosity, it took a bit for her to calm down. The pack often ridiculed those who lost the ability to change, and that was the way they broached that subject.

"How did you know?" Julia said through a strained smile.

If Clara was aware of the maelstrom of emotions within Julia's heart, she never let on. Instead, she faced the windshield, enjoying the last few moments of pavement before going off road. As a precaution, they had driven through this stretch of road without lights, and that certainly caught a few by surprise when they drove by.

"Our order managed to capture a couple of werewolves over the course of their history," Clara said.

"Really?" Julia confirmed, since she could not imagine a situation where a werewolf could be captured alive. "I find it hard to believe that they lived long."

Clara nodded before saying anything else, "They never went into detail on the how, or why, but our professor stated that females who were too thin to have a menstrual cycle, also lost their ability to change. Even under the full moon."

Julia thought back and tried to remember the last time she experienced her cycle. Had it really been that long? It annoyed her that this one knew something about werewolves that she did not.

"Wait," Julia said. "How did you know?"

Clara chuckled and opted for the simplest version of the truth before answering, "I *did* see you naked earlier today."

"Oh yeah…" Julia replied as her eyes widened with the realisation that all of this mess started less than a day ago.

The moon, by now, was well over the horizon. Its silvery light reflected off the snow and illuminated the landscape. Even in human form, her eyes were capable of picking up a lot of detail, and she figured her passenger could as well.

"So, what's your plan?" Julia asked to change the subject.

"The road takes us by the dam?" Clara asked.

"Yeah," Julia confirmed.

"Good," Clara answered. "You can drop me off, and I'll make my way from there."

From the dam, Clara would have a clear line of sight all the way to the mine's outbuildings.

"Wait," Julia said. "You might end up meeting the engineer."

"You mean… someone lives at the dam?" Clara asked, but managed to look completely unfazed by the news.

"Well, more of a pet really," Julia said without thought as to how that statement would come across to an outsider. "He's locked up in the powerhouse and keeps the turbine running in exchange for scraps."

"I see," Clara said flatly.

Julia's mouth gaped open before glancing at Clara who did not seem bothered at all. The lack of visible response on the passenger's part actually left her feeling uneasy.

"Guards?" Clara asked before popping open the glove compartment to get at a rosary within.

It took a moment for that question to sink in. Julia had been too preoccupied by her perceived slight to realise that Clara was focused exclusively on her mission. *Wait… why is she praying?*

The passenger ran her fingers mechanically over the beads. With every pause, she would utter a short prayer in an unfamiliar language. Whatever she was doing, it appeared to be purely based on habit.

"The dam is too remote for that…" Julia said.

Clara paused for the briefest of moments and said, "So?"

Once more, there came a question that managed to confuse Julia. How could Clara pick up on things that she had yet to consider? Especially while deep in prayer? *Again. Why was she praying?*

"…so, I have a feeling that the pack will be nearer to the mine entrance," Julia said.

"Really?" Clara said before moving on to the next bead.

"Werewolves don't fight defensive wars," Julia said honestly. "We travel and hunt as a pack."

"So, I won't be able to talk my way out of this?" Clara said with a smile before pocketing the rosary.

"Have you ever?" Julia countered.

"Well… once?" Clara said without certainty.

Julia giggled and said, "See! You're not even sure."

They approached an intersection with a well-maintained logging road on the right. Since that was a gravel road, travelling down that path would be relatively easy. However, the one to her left was nearly invisible. Little remained of this road, other than two distinctive parallel dips that led into the woods with shrubs on either side.

"The road less travelled," Julia said before shifting the truck into four-by-four.

"Is that what you call a *road*?" Clara asked.

Without saying a word, Clara rolled down her window and tossed something out. The sleight of hand had been so fast that Julia had no time to guess what it was.

"It will be once we tear through all of this overgrowth," Julia said.

She floored the accelerator and sent the truck into the ditch. The truck's shocks sent them rocking back and forth, while shrubs, branches, and rocks collided with the skid plate. Since Clara was not driving, the best she could do was make sure her seatbelt was taut before their vehicle was swallowed up by the forest.

"Here we go!" Clara exclaimed.

On the road, the blue LED light of a phone illuminated the sky, a sight remnant of a firefly out at night, which was completely out of place in the dead of winter.

\* \* \* \*

Elizabeth's legs wobbled as she pulled herself off the ground. She had been sitting for so long that her legs were numb and tingly, which created a disconnect in her mind.

"Come on," Elizabeth said.

Frustrated with her current state of affairs, she slammed a fist against a leg and never felt a thing. That was temporary, however the pain would soon come a knocking once the tingling subsided.

"Think," Elizabeth said, loud enough to figure out if something was out there.

No response meant that Elizabeth was left with three options. The first was obvious, give in and fall asleep. Chances were that she would never wake up, especially if she made sure to hit her head *just* right.

"*A bit boring,*" her internal voice said.

While she disagreed about the *boring* bit, she *would* die a victim. A woman ever in need of saving, even until the bitter end.

*"Someone who doesn't deserve a woman like Clara," the voice added.*

If anything, Elizabeth was pretty sure of one thing: she needed to stand on her own two feet. Funny how that thought was both figurative and literal at the moment. That meant she needed to crack on with one of the remaining options.

*"Fashion a weapon or try to get that door open?" Her inside voice confirmed.*

"Door," Elizabeth said.

"*Are you sure?*" The voice asked.

"Yeah," Elizabeth said annoyed. "If I know what I need to get out of here, then I can search for both."

When no smart-assed remark came, Elizabeth pushed off the workbench. For a moment it looked like her knees would give out, but she hoped they would hold long enough to find her balance.

"Fuck," Elizabeth said while falling forward.

Had there been witnesses, this scene might have retained some of its comedic value. Elizabeth fell straight down, mimicking a falling tree, and deployed her arms to cushion the impact.

"Fuck me!" Elizabeth yelled.

In anger, she slammed her fist against the ground, causing a cloud of dust to spread out. This sent her into another coughing fit, and that did *nothing* to help her mood.

After regaining the ability to breathe again, she grabbed the workbench and forced herself up for her second attempt. This time, her legs felt steady, although she could not see very far with her eyes tearing up. Funny, the feeling in her legs had returned, causing that fresh bruise to throb. Life had a way of pushing someone down, thus forcing them to fight through it.

With a grunt, she took a step away from the workbench and paused. Her sense of balance was still off, probably the result of that blow to her head. Still, she was able to take several small steps towards the door.

In the dim light, she saw that this door was heavy and made of steel. Even with the sliding mechanism out of the way, this door would require a lot of strength to push open. Fortunately, there was no lock fitted.

"So how can I disengage the mechanism?" Elizabeth asked.

The door had been designed to keep people out, not in. From this side, she could see where the handle used to slide the bar into a locking position had been. Now there was only a threaded hole to mark the spot. *Not very helpful.*

On a hunch, she reached through an opening in the door. The other side of the mechanism was exposed, and given her range of motion, she did not have enough leverage to move the bar.

"*Perhaps*—" The voice said.

"Perhaps I could find something to wedge in there," Elizabeth asked.

It was no surprise that there was nothing nearby. She returned to the workbench and grabbed onto parts of the frame used to cut her way to freedom. Most of the pieces had no give, except for that broken piping from earlier. Given her options, she flexed the piece back and forth until it snapped.

This piece was a couple of feet long; one side was sharp. At first glance, the piping looked like it might fit that opening. Alas, it turned out that the hollow side was too big to fit, and her attempt to use the sharp end did nothing more than scrape off some of the rust.

Disappointed, she roamed her cage and found a few more items with potential, namely more piping, some copper wiring, and a long strip of steel that she might be able to fashion into a machete if given the time.

"Time like that is something I don't have," Elizabeth said.

"*No kidding,*" her internal voice quipped.

"Not helping," Elizabeth snapped.

She tossed her latest finds on the workbench, except for the copper wiring. All of this humidity had turned the metal green, but the high gauge wiring was still flexible enough to be wrapped around her ankle, just in case.

"Whenever that is," Elizabeth said.

On little more than hope, Elizabeth did another search of the area. When operational, this place would have been overflowing with scrap metal and tools. What was left was either bolted down or left behind because it had no intrinsic value.

"Bolted down…" Elizabeth said.

Everything bolted down was large and heavy. Still, the workbench was not level. Odd, since the heavy equipment secured to it must have needed a stable surface.

Elizabeth hissed and ran a hand through her hair in frustration. Because her hair was dirty, oily, and matted, she winced in pain while working out the knots.

Without anything left to lose, she moved to the workbench to confirm her theory. There were holes for the anchors, but so far none were in place. She checked the corners and noted that one was still there. Unfortunately, the rust was so pervasive that it looked to be nothing more than a bump on the metal surface.

"Well that's disappointing," Elizabeth said.

*"Are you afraid of monsters?" The voice asked.*

"Yeah. That's why I'm here," Elizabeth said and rolled her eyes at such a dumbassed question. "What does that have to do with anything?"

*"Did you ever look under the bed as a child?" The voice asked.*

Elizabeth groaned before saying, "Bed?"

How could such an idea have spawned from the depths of her mind? There was no bed to be found here. If Elizabeth had any doubt about being tired and concussed, that question certainly drove the point home. At least, that had been the prevalent thought, until her eyes focused on the inky darkness below the workbench.

"You have got to be kidding me," Elizabeth whined.

Elizabeth dropped to her knees and slid into the prone position. This angle offered the same great view of nothing that she had when standing. Still, there might be something there, but given her limited eyesight, there was no way to be certain.

She hesitated, wondering if there was a rat's nest under there. After getting bitten by a vampire, she was not interested in getting nibbled on by plague carrying animals. Her hand hovered just at the edge of the shadow, oscillating as she worked through her anxiety.

*"Quit being a ninny,"* the voice said.

"Great. Now I'm the bully and the victim," Elizabeth replied.

Tired of this bizarre exchange, Elizabeth plunged her hand deep under the workbench and found nothing.

"Hah," Elizabeth exclaimed.

Unfortunately, she had been a bit premature in making that call. She brushed up against something the moment her hand moved to the right; there was something long, metallic, and coarse.

"What the—" Elizabeth said before she grabbed and retrieved the object from under the bench. "How did a pry bar get under here?"

Of course, the explanation was irrelevant. When this place was decommissioned, a lot of items must have gone missing.

*"Also, these guys are not the smartest bunch," the voice said.*

With the bar in hand, she ventured to the door. While it was too big to fit into the threaded hole, she was able to slip the pry between the frame and a riveted sheet that covered the mechanism. All it took was a bit of leverage to pop the first few rivets. With a new pivot point, the rest followed suit, and the steel plate dropped to the floor with a loud clang.

Elizabeth flinched and even held her breath, but no one came to investigate. Although, she did hear some howling in the distance, and by the sound of it, there were a *lot* of them out there.

"I hope Clara knows what she's doing," Elizabeth said while looking over the exposed mechanism. "Well… now I have a way out of my cage."

# CHAPTER 16

## *THE OTHERS*

Evelyn's deep green eyes were locked on the dancing fire ahead. She watched as the flames licked the logs, mingling with one another in an elaborate dance. This was a spectacle that never failed to leave her entranced.

Her kind had an aversion to an open flame, and some were driven into a blind panic at the sight of it. Those unlucky few were often discovered and destroyed by hunters. After all, a Victorian-era home in the winter with clear windows and no smoke coming from the chimneys was a dead giveaway.

Marc entered the room and paused long enough to get a feel for the situation. He then walked silently towards the corner bar and filled two glasses with cognac. His meticulous nature shone through his every action, which highlighted the stiff and regimented movements of this old soldier.

"*Merci, mon cher,*" Evelyn said absentmindedly.

Marc did not respond. Instead, he took exactly fifteen steps to reach his chair and sat down. Evelyn had no need nor desire to count the steps. They never varied, not as long as it was routine.

Evelyn picked up her glass the moment Marc's hands left the surface. As the flames from the fire lit up her face, she knocked back the contents in one hit. The alcohol left her with a warm feeling in her stomach, and that was the most she would get. Their kind were immune to all intoxicating substances, a reality that had driven more than a few junkies crazy, cursed to seek out a high they would never find.

She giggled before slamming the glass against the table. She was well aware that Marc abhorred such unladylike behaviour. In her opinion, a couple of centuries spent living under his ideals of a lady was more than enough.

"I know," Evelyn said flatly.

Marc did not reply; he rarely did. Instead, he reached for his own glass and let the liquid moisten his lips. Unlike his partner, he could not partake. Attempting to do so would invariably leave a mess, an expansive mass of chewed food and curdled blood that haunted those unfortunate enough to witness.

"For a man who never puts out," Evelyn said lightly. "You sure have a thing for getting teased."

Evelyn turned to face her sire and smiled. This was her *trademark* smile, the one that hinted of all the pleasures she would deliver if he surrendered to her. As expected, he did not react, and that remained a constant in their relationship.

"You think she has a chance?" Evelyn asked to change the subject.

The memory of the exhausted Clara cuddled next to her was still vivid. Evelyn had experienced a great many women in similar situations, but this one struck her as particularly memorable. Namely, Clara was forbidden fruit, a woman who might literally set her aflame.

There was more to it than the thrill of flirting with fire. It also went beyond appearances. After all, beauty was only skin deep. Evelyn, of all people, knew this was the truth. Only a fool would look over her history and think she was anything but a monster.

"She's on your mind?" Marc asked and those words boomed throughout the room as though he were unaccustomed to speaking.

Evelyn's eyes widened. They had a bond that few mortals would ever know. Even then, such connections lasted at most a lifetime, whereas their bond had endured centuries. Marc rarely needed to speak at all, because they had insight into each other's soul.

"Are you feeling left out?" Evelyn giggled

"It's rare to see you so focused on someone else," Marc said bluntly, now with a voice appropriate for the venue.

"Oh, you wound me so," Evelyn said with a wink.

Evelyn knew better. Breaking the wall of silence between them was proof of it. Still, there were expectations to their exchanges, and this was one of them.

"Why her?" Marc asked. "Everything has gone according—"

"Until those psychotic-shag-carpet-wearing mongrels kidnapped Elizabeth," Evelyn interrupted.

"To our benefit," Marc reminded her.

Those three words were said without emotion, and would have normally slid off her back like silk sheets against soft skin. This time, the effect was much more acute than expected.

"She's not a chew toy!" Evelyn snapped with such vigour that she literally spit out with every word.

"Since when?" Marc asked, using that same cold voice. It was the metronome-like cadence that tended to drive her batty when she was in one of these moods.

The inferno burning within the hearth was reflected in the depths of her eyes. Someone with a pulse would have suffered through rapid breathing and an elevated heart rate. Instead, Evelyn's vital signs went flat; that thin veneer of humanity had given way to something darker.

Before Evelyn could react, Marc grabbed her arms and buried them into the back of the soft chair. No matter how hard she struggled, she could not break free.

"Focus," Marc said.

"*Laisse-moi!*" Evelyn said in desperation.

Water swelled up around her eyes which turned into a steady stream of tears. A whole slew of complex emotions had intermingled to make this tempest possible. Despite their years together, her sire was ill equipped to deal with it. Without the ability to empathise, there was little he could do to relate.

Still, a logical mind could draw from experience. That in turn could lead to a long and drawn out process where they tried to resolve the problem. However, emotions were not a mathematical equation. In Evelyn's mind, they were like magical incantations or art, things that could not be readily qualified and quantified.

So, he let go of her hands and was immediately rewarded by having this fiery beauty slam her fists against his chest. He just stood there, stoic and unmoving, serving as a conduit for all of that fury.

"*Bâtard!*" Evelyn screeched as her desire to fight waned.

Marc looked on, and just as her last fist struck his chest, she collapsed into his arms. Instead of just letting her hang there, he wrapped his arms around her. The strength of this embrace had been precisely calculated, just enough to allow his partner to melt into his arms.

"She will pull through," Marc said softly.

Evelyn looked up, her eyes red and puffy. In many ways, Evelyn had surpassed her sire. Emotions enabled her to see the world differently and live in an environment filled with them. However, every so often, they clouded her judgement.

"You could have told me that earlier," Evelyn said in a nasal tone; she sniffled to clear her nose.

"I needed you focused," Marc said.

Like a gentleman, he reached into his front pocket and pulled out a monogrammed handkerchief. Evelyn looked down at the thoughtful gesture, smiled, and grabbed it.

"Why?" Evelyn asked before dabbing the water from her eyes.

"Her plan, as expected, is creative," Marc said. "However, there are several moving parts, many that are out of her control."

"And that's where I come in?" Evelyn asked.

Marc nodded, sensing that his partner was ready to carry on. He reached down for a remote and turned off the flow of gas to the fire, plunging the room in near darkness.

"Oh," Marc said. "I got word that Grace drove that ambulance over a pier. Since the vehicle quickly went under, authorities dispatched a team of divers to the scene."

"That's great news," Evelyn said. "I expect she buried herself into the mud?"

"Yes," Marc said, which was all she would get from him for now.

Evelyn stayed behind, her mind blessed with a renewed focus. When Marc closed the door behind him, she grabbed his glass of cognac and sipped it gently. To think, she had almost forgotten how much better sipping cognac was.

* * * *

Adrienne looked over the whole of the pack. Given the strength of the full moon, every member capable of change had done so. The largest in this group was William, his fur was dark and full, a sure sign of his youth. Still, no one here dared challenge him, at least not directly.

Those with the brains to orchestrate a coup had been weeded out early. William was the brawn, the symbol of strength that kept them together. She made sure that no one had the opportunity to get creative. What else could a good mother do?

William slammed his clawed fist against his chest, before howling at the moon. The pack joined their leader, and their howls were so loud that Adrienne needed to cover her ears.

She had witnessed these rallies before, typically before a hunt. Their howls roused their prey which made the event all the more sporting. Tonight, things were different. The fine feathered femme fatale would be sure to put up a fight.

"Drawing blood will drive them into a blind rage," Adrienne said, but even with a loudspeaker they would not have heard her.

A pack of werewolves was a terrifying sight to behold, and Adrienne would be safely within the confines of the mines before the big show. A pack driven into a frenzy was not picky about who they hunted.

Despite her familiar scent, Adrienne's human form was enough to put her in danger. Besides, who else could be trusted to look after the prisoner? Despite cradling her hunting rifle in her arms, Adrienne's hand reached for the large knife sheathed on her thigh. If things went sideways, she was certain that the harpy's rescue attempt would end with a funeral.

"She will not get her prize," Adrienne said.

William dropped on all fours and disappeared into the pitch-black treeline surrounding them. The rest of the pack followed, leaving her alone near the outskirts of the mine. It was only a matter of time before they caught the scent of something, and soon this place would be a hive of activity.

"William better make sure to leave enough of a presence nearby to deal with surprises," Adrienne said while heading towards the skip. "Or there'll be hell to pay."

# CHAPTER 17

## *THE VAN HELSING INCURSION*

Given the snow and moonlight, Clara had no trouble seeing through the barren trees. Still, she suspected that Julia's eyes were better suited for these conditions. That was the difference between creatures of the night and those who dutifully lived out their lives under the light of God.

"I think we are about to reach the dam," Julia said lightly, hesitant to make a statement that might turn out to be false.

Clara looked out further ahead and then, to the sides, but there was nothing that implied they were near large structures nor a body of water. Given the time of year, the lake's surface was likely frozen solid, so a lake or a clearing could look the same at a glance.

"How do you know?" Clara asked, while keeping an eye out for telltale signs.

"Just a feeling," Julia said. "I haven't been down this road in years, but this road is at risk of getting washed away every spring."

"That explains the brush we had to cut through," Clara said.

"Exactly," Julia said. "It's just easier to take the southern road in."

Clara had to admire the logic of it. An abandoned mine complex situated in a remote area of the state gave them privacy. The infrastructure that once served the mine would rot away with the passage of time. That dam would also eventually fail. Such structures could only take so much neglect and abuse. Without dedicated maintenance, a crack would eventually leak, erode further, and lead to a breach. *That could take decades...*

"See!" Julia said as the vehicle approached a large clearing.

Clara noticed that the surface beyond the shore was pristine and undisturbed. Animals here knew well enough to avoid the thin ice. Still, the crumbling concrete at the end of the black waters was more concerning. It would make an approach over the lake impossible.

Fortunately, she had options. Her only concern was to give Julia enough time to make some headway before having her fun.

"The dam is stable enough for me to get a solid footing and see what's going on?" Clara asked.

Julia nodded before saying, "Worried, are you?"

"No. I just like to confirm details before setting a plan in motion," Clara said. "Should I expect some company?"

"Not from the pack," Julia said. "But… they probably left the engineer up here."

As a hunter, Clara had sworn to protect human life. While she was free to destroy vampires, werewolves, and their ilk to her heart's content, it was not up to her to determine the guilt of a human. Ultimately, society had to judge the traitors and collaborators. In the absence of a readily available justice system, she had on occasion *guided* fate, but never directly took a human life.

"Just ducky," Clara said. "Stop here, while we still have some cover."

Julia stopped the truck and killed the engine. In the distance, a series of howls were carried by the wind. Julia's facial features went slack while blood flushed from those cheeks.

Clara did not need to ask about the source of those howls. Her partner's reaction was more than enough. What should a gal do in this situation? Let someone else suffer due to her actions?

"Are you sure that you are okay with this?" Clara asked.

Those words had no immediate effect. Clara chanced caressing Julia's clammy hand, hopeful that human contact would give her something to focus on.

"Yeah—sure," Julia said once the chorus of howls faded into the background. "Sorry. It's hard to ignore a summons."

"So, they know we are coming?" Clara asked.

"Well… expecting at least," Julia replied. "It also means you'll have about three dozen werewolves to deal with."

Clara smirked, opened the door, and walked around to the back. Done with hiding, she let her wings expand and experienced immediate relief when those stiff joints moved.

"Di mi!" Clara said before pushing off into the air for a quick jaunt and landed near the truck's tailgate.

This time, she unloaded the oversized bag which rattled and clanged when it hit the ground. Whatever Clara had in there, it was both heavy and metallic.

Lastly, she returned to the passenger side. This time, she stepped onto the running board and hovered there before loosening the shotgun between her shoulder blades.

"Here," Clara said after she cleared the weapon and handed it over, along with a belt of ammunition.

Clara could see the hesitation in Julia's eyes. She quickly realised that a weapon might come in handy, given the level of opposition they faced. Julia took the ammunition first, followed by a polite nod before grabbing the weapon.

"Thanks," Julia said with a meek smile.

"I should be thanking you," Clara said. "I'll start making some noise soon. I recommend you get some distance to avoid being in their path."

Julia nodded before saying, "It's about ten minutes to the old maintenance road that will take me down to the mine. I'll wait for some commotion before going downhill."

"Sounds like a plan," Clara said before considering her next words. "If you have any doubts, or don't hear from me—"

"Thanks for giving me an out," Julia said. "I'll get your friend out to safety."

"Thank—" Clara tried to say.

"You can thank me once this is all said and done," Julia said while turning the ignition.

Clara hopped off and closed the door. From this point forward, they were on their own.

"No matter," Clara said as she opened the bag. Inside, there was an assortment of weapons, explosive devices, and body armour. "On a night like this, a gal needs to accessorise."

\* \* \* \*

Clara's feet made contact with the dam, and she immediately dropped the bag to her side. Right behind her, the black water lapped up against the concrete. She ignored areas of the dam that had surrendered to the relentless force of the water behind her.

"Seems a bit high," Clara said, but busied herself by getting down to work.

The first thing she pulled out and slipped on was a vest fitted with ballistic plates. In combat, such a vest would help her avoid gunshot wounds and shrapnel. This evening, she hoped that it would slow down an enraged werewolf's claws. Fortunately, the vest had been modified to account for her wings at the cost of protecting her back.

The next thing that came out was a weapon fitted with an oversized barrel and simplistic iron sights. Clara popped the breech and looked up at the moon through the gaping hole. She smirked and grabbed something that looked like an oversized shotgun shell but fitted with a yellow cap rounded for ballistics. She smirked when the round was loaded and adorned a belt covered with similar ammunition.

"This should be fun," Clara said.

She then produced a pair of pistols, along with a pack of magazines that fit neatly in her vest pockets. These weapons had more of a kick than she was accustomed to, but given the size of her prey, she wanted to make sure those shots would sting.

Next, Clara pulled out a heavy case. When the lid flew open, she found a disassembled large calibre weapon inside. She had no problem putting the heavy weapon together, including the bipod and oversized muzzle break. Inside the case, she had three magazines fitted with black tipped rounds. As a precaution, she removed a round from the third magazine, chambering it.

"Good thing there's only a light breeze," Clara said.

A quick flick of her wrist revealed her watch and informed her that she had a few minutes left before Julia was in position. She pulled out a large item fitted within a canvas bag. She flipped open the top and quickly sealed it back up when satisfied that everything was set.

"I would have preferred a sea mine," Clara said with a chuckle. "Still, you can't find those at the neighbourhood corner store."

Before moving into a firing position, she looked across to the opposing bank, focusing on a tall concrete building. There was a door that led into the dam's powerhouse, one that might allow someone to sneak up on her. At least, that would be true if it had not been fitted with a heavy chain and lock.

"Seems like they really want to keep someone inside," Clara mused.

Now that everything was confirmed, Clara went up to the wall that overlooked the mine complex. Once settled into the prone position, she closed her eyes, focused, and dropped her heart rate to a low and steady level. When those steel-grey eyes opened, the world took on an eerie beauty, one that was interrupted by the sound of a deer carcass being torn apart.

She focused on that spot while slowing down time. Up ahead, some distance away, there was a small group of werewolves celebrating their kill. Their motions were slowed until they turned into a serial killer's rendition of *dogs playing poker.*

Through the weapon scope, she made out four separate targets, three of which were grouped around what looked to be a doe. The fourth was a distance away, and kept a lookout for competition.

"Smart," Clara said, but at this speed, it sounded more like a cricket's chirp to outsiders.

While remembering her marksmanship principles, she aligned herself with the weapon and the group. She then lined up the sights with the big werewolf at the centre, adjusted her scope for range, gauged windage, and took in a series of breaths.

When Clara was ready, she exhaled and, in between heart beats, squeezed the trigger. The weapon roared to life and sent a shockwave over her body that ruffled those feathers.

"Wow!" Clara said as the bullet passed through the disturbance towards her target.

Given the time, she would have watched the entire effect unfold, but there was a need to exploit this advantage. With a practised pull, she ejected a round and loaded another. She then selected the second largest werewolf and fired a round. At this speed, she could effectively fire off a second round before the unspent powder flashed.

Her third shot was even faster, shooting off another round in a fraction of a second. Clara sped up time just a smidge, enough to watch the red streaks from her projectiles fly out towards the targets. All that was left for her to do was wait.

"One, two, three—" Clara said.

The first shot missed the target but managed to hit the runt of the group just behind it. She watched with glee as the leg disappeared in a pink mist, severing the vital limb from its torso.

The second shot hit high, causing the werewolf's head to snap back. Despite the hit, that projectile continued on its trajectory and struck the carcass. The doe bounced from off of the ground, causing the one standing guard to investigate. This presented a larger target profile.

"Perfect," Clara said while slowing down time one more time.

As the third round impacted another werewolf in the centre of mass, she had already fired another two rounds. The first was aimed at the biggest werewolf, who stood there all confused. Since these bullets travelled faster than sound, the group had yet to hear the shots.

"Four, five—" Clara counted.

The big one took a round to the shoulder, severing his arm. She imagined the monstrous fur-covered stump making a loud thump. Even if it did, it was the screaming that got the pack's attention.

Unable to maintain an accelerated state for long, Clara returned to normal time, and let the carnage unfold. The fourth werewolf was hit in the heart, and the damage caused by an armour piercing round dropped him like a pile of bricks.

This time, when the pack howled, their individual voices came from every corner of the valley. In the distance, trees swayed violently despite an absence of wind.

"Come to mamma," Clara said with glee, while inserting a fresh magazine into the weapon.

As a precaution, Clara slid off the elevated platform. To her left, there was an open door that flooded the area with a dull red light. Framed in the door there was someone or something blocking the passage. *Huh? When did that door get opened?*

After her eyes adjusted to the change in lighting, she perceived a tall, skeletal man covered in bruises. His hair and beard were greasy, filthy, and riddled with parasites. It was long enough to block his eyesight, so he flicked it away constantly. Clara could see the fear in those eyes, like an abused animal that feared its master's disapproval.

Clara opened up her wings and blocked out the silvery moon. The way he looked at her made it clear that this was his first time seeing an angel, and yet he was not alarmed. Given the situation that Julia had described, she expected what was left of this man to cower and hide. *What is he waiting for?*

The man eyed the satchel bag and pondered its *raison d'être*. When she witnessed a flash of insight in his eyes, the man moved ahead to grab it. Clara was about to stop him, after all, this was not his fight, but someone else appeared between them. Despite not being able to make out her face, the raven black hair, olive skin, and white dress were a dead giveaway. It seemed that the angel of death had returned. *Who is she going to interfere with now?*

"Let him have it," Eleanor said softly as the world around them came to a pause.

Clara whistled at this impressive control over time. Still, based on their last couple of encounters, Eleanor's goals did not align with hers. *Should I even trust her?*

"Why?" Clara asked.

"You and I both know that we really don't have time to get into this," Eleanor said.

"You can pause time to your heart's content?" Clara asked.

"Not *globally*," Eleanor replied and let those words sink in.

"Right..." Clara said. "So, time is ticking away outside your bubble while we have a chat?"

"Let him have that bag," Eleanor said. "Let me have *this* soul."

There was something in those words that rang true, specifically that Eleanor's interests were solely focused on this man. Clara threw a quick glance at the man which was more than enough to tell her what she needed to know. This one was broken and would never be able to reintegrate into society. In reality, he died years ago, a soul trapped in his body that served as the prison.

"Fine," Clara said. "You'll owe me an explanation later."

And with that, Eleanor was gone and the world turned crisp and clear. She watched the Engineer grab the bag and sling it over his shoulder. The weight caused him to wince, but he was determined to go through with it.

"Good luck," Clara said while scanning the area for advancing threats.

\* \* \* \*

"What the fuck?" Julia said after hearing what sounded like machine gun bursts.

When she looked out past the brush concealing the truck, a second burst of flashes were seen. While too far away to make out any details of the shooter, it was a pretty safe guess as to the cause.

This time, Julia was better able to ignore the call to action when the pack howled collectively. Besides, she knew they would not hesitate to tear into her. Clearly, blood no longer had any meaning for them, only the wishes of the alpha and the one who pulled his strings.

"Bastards," Julia said before spitting out of the rolled down window.

She initially questioned why Clara would have chosen the dam to announce her arrival. But those shots had been a proverbial knock on the door, a clear sign that they had an enemy in their midst.

It would be sure to lure them in, and that standoff distance was an advantage. Werewolves were mostly renowned for their devastating attacks at close range not over the horizon.

After a quick diversion up on the dam, Julia spotted a dark figure climbing straight up the concrete cliff. Unbeknownst to either of them, a werewolf had been near when the first shots rang out. When motivated, werewolves were more than capable of climbing sheer cliffs of ice or rock.

"Oh right!" Julia said after realising that this diversion had been for her benefit.

Julia turned the ignition to the second to last position. The dashboard came to life, which also unlocked the steering wheel. Ready to go, she dropped the transmission from *Park* to *Neutral* and released the parking brake.

"Remember," Julia said to herself, "keep a constant pressure on the breaks."

Turning this ride into a speeding bullet would not be a smart move. If that happened, any hard turns left or right would risk a rollover.

"And draw attention away from Clara," Julia murmured as she banished her anxiety to the pit of her stomach.

\* \* \* \*

Clara was back into her firing position when she spotted a set of eyes peeking from the other side of the dam. The imagery reminded her of an alligator lying in wait in calm waters, waiting for its prey to lower their guard before going for the kill.

Without a second glance, Clara headed towards her discarded bag as time slowed down. Her senses sharpened, but she maintained comparatively slow movements, enough to conceal her enhanced reaction times.

Once she reached the bag, she knelt beside it, and with one hand, lifted it off of the ground. She then looked underneath where the bag had been, as though something should be there.

"Now," Clara said in corrected speech, the kind that never failed to drive her nuts because every syllable was long and sustained. "I could have sworn that I had one more—"

As expected, the werewolf used his tremendous strength to propel himself from behind the wall and up into the air. Clara was impressed. In a single bound, he would have landed directly on top of her. Even with armour and her unnatural strength, Clara would have been hard pressed to fend off this type of attack.

Instead, she spun around and swatted the werewolf with one of her wings. While she felt the hit, the effect on him was much more pronounced. The power in that strike was enough to reverse its course, sending the werewolf over the dam and into the void below.

Surprise was reflected in those eyes, more so once it clued in that gravity still had a role to play. The last thing she observed was the werewolf clawing at the gap between it and the dam. Without any divine intervention, it was a long way down.

"Odd. Why chance an attack without—" Clara said before the ground trembled.

Either that was an earthquake, or something big was moving nearby. She further slowed down time until the falling werewolf's howl's pitch shifted from an operatic soprano to a baritone.

That gave her just enough time to make sure her flanks were clear. For now, it appeared to be the case, but if this had been her fight, the bulk of her forces would attempt to outflank her. Once surrounded, chances for survival would be severely reduced.

"Clearly, I'm not dealing with a bunch of dumb doras," Clara said before grabbing her rifle.

Despite time being on hold, she grabbed the rifle with one hand and put away the bipod with the other. If she was right, there would be no need for stability.

Clara then leaned over the side, looking at a rotting concrete structure that ran straight down. Since the dam was curved inwards, it gave her a great view of seven werewolves… making their way up the wall. She committed their position to memory, shouldered the weapon, took aim for the biggest threat, and squeezed the trigger.

"One," Clara muttered.

With her ability to manipulate time nearing an end, Clara returned to actual speed as the weapon roared to life. The recoil nearly caused her to fall on her ass. Still, the werewolf quivered, paused, and fell from whence it came.

"Two," Clara said while she chambered another round.

Based on the speed of their movements, Clara had no choice but to start moving. After all, changing positions would prevent them from getting a bead on her. She backed away over the curved wall as the first two werewolves neared the platform.

Given the urgency, Clara took a knee and fired a shot. The round missed, but the bullets ricocheted, giving the werewolves a moment's pause. Without hesitation, Clara fired another round and pierced a lung. Alas, a third werewolf was over the lip by now, which forced her to give up ground.

"Three," Clara counted.

From behind, she caught the sound of concrete crumbling. Clara simply pivoted, aligned the barrel with the exposed head, and fired a round. Based on the range, there was no time to admire her handiwork. Instead, she relied on the sounds of arterial spray that followed the impact.

"Horsefeathers!" Clara exclaimed. "These things are fast!"

A lot faster than she had been led to believe, Clara made a note to one day pass on this useful tidbit to the instructors at the Tower. It was no wonder a pack of these things decimated an entire Roman Legion.

There were two rounds left, and Clara had every intention of making them count. In truth, she had known this position could never be held for long. Still, a bit more time would have been appreciated.

"Fuck it," Clara said as the first one to reach the top was joined by two others.

That meant there were another two behind her. She let her senses fill in the blanks; the thumps became sharper as they approached. She kept her eyes on the pack near the powerhouse door and raised her barrel to line up an attack.

Sensing an opportunity, the werewolf directly aft of her fell into a dead run. This time, the vibrations caused by those steps were strong enough to sour her aim. It was time to up the ante. She closed her eyes, trusted her senses, and in a blink, was gone. Clara used this opportunity to slow time just enough to get out of the way which sent the werewolf straight off the dam.

Alas, this particular specimen had been gifted with enough brains and dexterity to reach back in time. It dug those claws into the concrete, but slowing down a beast that size came at a cost. The werewolf's body weight caused his ligaments to stretch and tear, which marooned it in the middle of the dam.

Clara was not about to lose the initiative. She turned around, found her latest target and squeezed off a round. At this range, the muzzle flash illuminated its eyes along with five more pairs hiding in the woods.

"Five," Clara counted, but did not wait to fire off the last round. "Six," she added and tossed the weapon.

With time working against her, Clara pulled out the large bore weapon. She turned away from those in the forest and ran towards the powerhouse. Those near the structure had not been idle and had already closed the distance between them by half.

Clara lifted the iron sights, lined up the barrel, and squeezed the trigger. All she heard was a thump followed by a large object that went over the heads of the two nearest werewolves. Surprised, those two actually stopped to follow the trajectory.

When they turned back to look at Clara, their eyes said it all. The gal had missed, and their laugh reminded her of a hyena. *Is that how a werewolf laughs?*

The round, however was not meant for them. The projectile impacted an area above the doorway and exploded. While the shock was not enough to send the nearest werewolf to the ground, it did collapse the doorway onto itself, which stopped their hysterics.

"Who's laughing now?" Clara said with a smirk, while loading a fresh round.

The effect demonstrated from this weapon made them hesitate. That left her with enough time to confirm the doorway was buried in rubble, slowing their ingress into the powerhouse.

These creatures were not exactly known for being timid. From the corner of her eye, she spotted one running over the ice towards her. Clara's reaction was both quick and precise, firing a shot from her thumper. This time, the round bounced off harmlessly and left a ripple in the water.

"Too close," Clara said before letting herself fall backwards off the dam.

The werewolves converged on her, so eager that one was pushed right off the edge. The scene reminded her of a buffalo jump, how hunters exploited herd-mentality to their advantage. In this instance, their pack-mentality could be similarly used against them.

Not like that mattered. Once up to speed, Clara looked up, guessed the trajectory, and squeezed the trigger. Once more, a thump rang out as the projectile disappeared into the night sky.

Again, she would not look back to admire her handiwork. Instead, her wings spread open to provide her with lift. Now that she had lost the beachhead, it was time to venture deeper into enemy territory.

Those left behind were confused. However, the grenade slowed its ascent, hovered in mid-air near eye level, and fell onto the concrete. The group observed as the metal canister bounced, once, twice, and—

# CHAPTER 18

## *KHAN'S FOLLY*

All of the howling was beginning to wear on Elizabeth, although not as much as all the scurrying going on in the shadows. At night, the shaft was the perfect conduit for sounds, which created the illusion that she was sharing this place with tens of thousands of rats.

"*Or is that actually true?*" The voice inside her head asked.

Elizabeth cringed before saying, "I'd rather not think about it, if that's alright with you?"

The voice did not reply, so Elizabeth smiled. Sure, there was no one to see it, but that would not stop her from basking in the glow of the moment. That part of her mind was at odds with her conscious thoughts, and based on her professional judgement, that should worry her.

"Hardly a sign of sanity," Elizabeth said. "Still, given the situation, I should be happy that I'm not speaking in tongues while rocking myself to sleep."

Elizabeth's first confrontation with vampires had been an eye opener. Despite being a tall and imposing woman, she chose not to confront her threat, nor did she run away for that matter. Either of these options were preferable to dropping to her knees, closing her eyes, and covering her ears while Clara cleaned up the mess. In a way, that woman was still cleaning up for her, and it was high-time that changed.

To spice things up, a series of loud bangs rang out, very much like firecrackers set off during the Chinese New Year. If those were pyrotechnics, then why were some of the howls filled with pain? Elizabeth could not be certain, but she felt the pack was mourning their fallen. That meant someone was stirring up trouble topside.

"Clara?" Elizabeth wondered.

*"Who else would be foolhardy enough to venture into their territory?" The voice asked. "During a full moon?"*

Elizabeth nodded, and her smile grew tenfold. Her friend was risking life and limb for her. While Clara never once said 'I love you' or pushed her against the wall with hunger-filled eyes prior to moving in for a passionate kiss, this act of heroism spoke volumes.

"Figures. I stopped dating men in college," Elizabeth said, "but end up with the strong, silent type anyway."

Elizabeth sighed softly, but before she finished exhaling, the skip at the far end came to life. There were a lot of reasons why that thing was returning to the surface, and most of them were bad. A shame that the mechanical whirring effectively cancelled out all sounds from the surface.

"So why did they leave the elevator on this level?" Elizabeth asked herself.

*"To force someone to wait while it comes to them," the voice replied.*

That was true. Anyone waiting for that skip would be left exposed long enough for the werewolves to surround and move in for the kill. Elizabeth had to admit that this particular revelation did not sit well with her.

*"Clara would never take the main way in or out," the voice said.*

Well, not without confirming there was nothing left moving… those howls were a clear sign there was opposition topside, so Clara would not risk committing herself to the rescue just yet.

*"Besides," the voice added, "Clara probably has help."*

That was also true. It would be far easier to rescue someone when an elaborate distraction was enacted to conceal the intrusion. Again, a reasoned response. So why was she experiencing a growing sense of dread? It felt like she was in the shadow of a great monster, and the humid breeze she felt was actually its breath. While it was probably nothing more than her imagination grappling with the unknown, she knew that Clara was in danger.

When the skip stopped at what she assumed to be the surface, everything went still. For a moment she hoped to hear a familiar voice or anything that would shake this feeling from her soul. Unfortunately, a shot rang out into the night, one that was much closer in proximity.

"*That's not birdshot*," the voice said.

"No." Elizabeth said softly. "No, it isn't."

\* \* \* \*

"What the—" Clara said as flight control was lost.

Her wings shifted out of position to defend against an external threat which, in turn, sacrificed stability. Clara went from a straight course above the tree line to spiralling towards one of the nearby buildings. A shame that she had not been flying at an accelerated state. That might have enabled her to adjust and overcome the instability.

Alas, Fate had other plans for her. As the brick wall gained clarity, her eyes bulged while she held out her arms to absorb the impact. She might be tougher than the average gal, but a head-on impact at this speed would still hurt.

It was fortunate that she noticed a way to lessen the crash. Clara focused on a window just above the impact point. She timed her rotation, loosened up, and flapped her wings at what she hoped was the right moment.

As expected, the intervention helped her gain some altitude. That in itself was helpful, but she was slightly off the mark. Instead of crashing cleanly through the window, Clara felt a hard hit to her left shoulder. The force of that shock sent her weapon flying out ahead into the unknown. Meanwhile, her body pivoted sideways and her knees took the brunt of it.

Disoriented and winded, Clara hesitated until gravity asserted itself with a vengeance. Her legs dropped off the ledge, which required her to hold on. Had the window been opened before the incident, she would have been fine. Instead, shattered glass shredded her jacket.

"Horsefeathers," Clara swore while probing with her feet for something—anything to push up against. "Fuck. Nothing."

Unfortunately, it was clear that she was not there to make friends. During this moment of hesitation, another shot rang out, which was deflected by her wings. The present threat made continued exposure problematic. Despite the glass cutting into her palms, she pulled herself up against the window frame and dropped safely on the other side.

"Awww nertz," Clara said while looking over her surroundings.

Since the lights were out, targeting her would be difficult. As a precaution, she kept her head down and crawled to the other end of the room to find her weapon. She cracked the breech, confirmed that it was operational, and turned her attention to the next most pressing matter.

With a moment of peace, Clara looked at her hands. As golden liquid oozed from several wounds, she did not have the time to be dainty and would deal with infection later. So, she dug out the glass with her bare fingers, all without betraying that she felt anything at all.

Still, things were bound to get worse. The pack had managed to converge on her pretty fast, and she had no doubt they had the place surrounded. Unfortunately, leaving the way she came in left her exposed to the sniper. Either way, werewolves were probably able to jump that high, especially when properly motivated.

"I'm sure they are," Clara said as she pulled out a flattened roll of black duct tape from a pouch, "very motivated."

She pulled on the tab and wrapped her hand several times in the sticky tape to cover the wounds. When done, Clara tore the tape with her teeth and repeated the process for her dominant hand.

"Not pretty," Clara said. "Still, it beats bleeding everywhere."

Clara's mind focused on the situation, one where she was both surrounded and outnumbered. So, what was keeping them from storming the building? Or was it this room? Either they were fearful of this area, which was unlikely, or they had a newfound respect for her little thumper.

The thought of the latter made her grin. However, she glanced out the window and saw nothing within her line of sight. That meant the sniper had no direct line of fire either.

Lastly, she looked towards the door, then above at the ceiling. Over the years of neglect, a part of the ceiling had caved in to reveal a series of steel rafters high above. Clara quickly formed an image in her mind as to where she was.

Windows on two levels. Plenty of top cover. From aerial photos, she guessed that this building had a series of bay doors lining the far side of this building. This would have been the maintenance building, and this room was part of the second level office complex. It also meant there was a clear line of sight with the main mine entrance from the roof.

To help confirm her hunch, she scooted over to the door and felt a draught of fresh air originating from the other side. The doors were open, which meant they were free to waltz right in. Clara looked up, slowed down time, and flapped her massive wings.

The thick accumulation of dust was sent airborne, creating an opaque cloud of filth. Normally that would have been annoying, but it might just come in handy as a distraction if they decided to burst in. Fortunately, she only needed a few good flaps to reach the nearest rafter, which she grabbed on and winced from the pain.

There were times when Clara loved nothing more than to be proven right. This time, she would have loved to be dead wrong. The expansive maintenance floor was crawling with werewolves. Given their proximity, she was tempted to fire a few rounds and let the chaos unfold.

"Not yet," Clara whispered.

Clara scanned the rafters, figuring there were access hatches located at regular intervals. Sure enough, there was a hatch located near every fifth rafter, which meant there were several potential escape routes. *That's the first bit of good news so far.*

For now, she needed to get away from this office. That was the only way to make sure those grenades had enough distance to arm, especially if things got nasty.

* * * *

Julia adjusted the straps on her backpack and shifted some of the weight to her hips. That relieved tension on her shoulders, a valuable trait for someone about to do a lot of upper body work. The choice would pay dividends, especially if she slipped on a rung.

Up ahead, behind all of that dead vegetation, there was the rusted heap that once made up the skip's power and control mechanism. This particular skip had been used to bring up ore from the mine.

The ore skip was both larger and slower than the manned variant. If it were not for the warped rails further up the line, they might have been able to make use of it. Alas, even the strongest of the bunch could not straighten the large steel rails. Besides, werewolves were better known for breaking things.

Fortunately, the ladders fitted on either side of the rails were *serviceable*. Or at least they had been the last time she used them. *When was that again?*

"Shit," Julia swore under her breath. "That was almost three years ago."

She did have a mild advantage, given that the system worked on a sixty-degree incline. While steep, the act of slipping on a rung would not translate directly into freefall. But given the height of each level and how far it was to the bottom…

Julia paused and closed her eyes. Clara had been busy creating a distraction, which worked in her favour. But things had gone quiet, so Julia wanted to make sure there were no threats in the immediate area.

In the distance, she heard machinery whirring. As judged by the source, it was the man-skip.

"I need to get my ass in gear," Julia said after opening her eyes.

The snow compressed with Julia's every step. Since this site was remote, she had to be careful about breaking through the top layer, and not end up buried waist deep. Tonight, getting bogged down could mean death.

When she neared the edge of the shaft, she gave it a wide berth beyond what was visible. Snow and ice would have built-up around the ledge by now, which would not support her weight. One false step and—

"There," Julia said with a smile once she sighted the metal rails and the accompanying access ladders. Those had been anchored directly into the rock, which created a series of rungs that appeared to go on forever.

Of course, the first group of rungs were iced up, but she did not have the luxury of being choosy. It was either go in through the back way or slather her naked body up in barbecue sauce and embrace her fate…

"Here goes," Julia said.

On the fourth rung, her foot slipped when a gunshot rang out into the valley. The noise dredged up all of the emotions that *dream* had churned. *That's Adrienne's weapon.*

"Oh fuck," Julia said. "I can't be wasting my time like this."

Julia decided to skip the precautionary kick to confirm the rung was secure. After all, there were worse things in life than a sudden drop and stop. Unsurprisingly, Adrienne featured prominently on her list.

\* \* \* \*

"Come on," Adrienne said, giving the building a once over while waiting for the man-skip to arrive.

The place was surrounded by the pack, and many were slowly working their way through the bay doors. William stood guard outside the maintenance building, and his presence alone was why they had not charged in.

For all she knew, this show of force had been nothing more than a smokescreen, a way for someone to break in and get out undetected. Still, that line of thinking made no sense, since they needed someone who knew the layout inside out. It could not be an old timer who worked at the site; they were either dead or had one foot in the grave. It was not a vampire; the smell of death would have been impossible to ignore. That left people who were part of the inner circle—

"Julia," Adrienne hissed, as the man-skip ran home.

That realisation left her torn. Either head below and leave her ox of a son alone to deal with the threat, or stay above ground and chance losing everything. Without any leverage, how dangerous could this harpy be? How long could William hold the rest of this pack together if they committed all these resources and came up empty.

"Fuck!" Adrienne swore before withdrawing from the scene.

Without even thinking, she stowed her weapon, boarded the man-skip, and pressed down on the lever at her side. While going up was a slow and steady process, going down was a different matter. She pressed on the hand clamp to loosen the brake.

"Every time," Adrienne said as the insides of her stomach shifted. "Every fucking time."

They could get down in a hurry, assuming she did not mind arriving before her stomach contents. For now, a balance was called for, and that meant the brakes would squeal.

* * * *

"What was that?" Clara wondered.

The bulk of the werewolves were formed up near the office. Clara considered all of her options and knew they would spread out and widen their search if the office was empty. *That will spoil the fun*!

"Is that a bird cage?" Clara asked herself, and realising that the situation outside was changing, potentially for the better.

Without the sniper, she was free to roam and wreak havoc. To keep the game going, all she needed was a way to take that sniper out of the game, and she had the perfect solution to make that happen.

Clara slowed down time until the *tiptoeing* werewolves were no longer moving. She then aimed her weapon and pulled the trigger. At this speed, the grenade took a few seconds to clear the barrel. Another two rounds were fired in this fashion at those congregating on the maintenance floor.

With three grenades leisurely following their arcs, she used her wings to reach a hatch and launch herself through to the other side. Now, this was the tricky part. She landed on the roof of the maintenance building and scooted over to the edge facing the mine entrance. With a clear path to her target, Clara fired two more rounds. These projectiles were aimed at the mine shaft.

"That should do some damage," Clara chirped while looking over her last round.

# CHAPTER 19

## *FOUR HENS WITH ONE STONE*

J ulia caught the sound of three muffled explosions coming from the surface. She looked up, and saw nothing but the night sky. That was good news, otherwise, her goose would have been cooked.

The fact that Clara was once again wreaking havoc reinforced the idea that she needed to get her ass in gear. Now she dropped one rung every time, giving up entirely on the idea of confirming they were safe before placing all of her weight on them.

"Fuck!" Julia yelled when she heard another two blasts.

Those were a lot closer, since the sound reached her from below. Wait! Why would Clara block off an exit?

"Oh shit!" Julia swore. "Company!"

\* \* \* \*

Adrienne let go of the breaks when the three blasts went off. As the skip accelerated, she reached for the lever, but a second set of explosions went off overhead.

Because of the angle of the shaft, she could not see the blast, only an orange hue. Rubble would be following her lead, and she was the proverbial speed bump.

"That bitch!" Adrienne said before contemplating why the blast sounded like something from a Saturday morning cartoon skit.

Despite the reference, if any of that rubble hit her or the skip, she was done for. Her only chance was to reach the flooded levels before all that shit did. That would at least slow down the debris. *Wouldn't it?*

"This is going to—" Adrienne whined.

\* \* \* \*

Julia was moving from one rung to another as fast as she could. Her mind was on autopilot, since overthinking at this juncture would not only slow her down, but would increase her chances for a fall.

That likelihood jumped when the skip slammed into the water at high speed, an impact violent enough to cause the water to ripple below.

"What the—" Julia exclaimed after realising that both her hands had been jerked free of the ladder.

Her loaded backpack shifted her centre of balance backwards. With no ability to regain equilibrium, she launched herself clear of the rails using her legs. *I hope there's a clear path to the water.*

"This is going to—" Julia said.

\* \* \* \*

Clara watched as the grenades struck the mine shaft. Unlike a Hollywood explosion, there was no powerful fireball, only a brief flash of orange light, smoke, and flying debris.

It was hard not to grin at the sheer destructive power of military munitions. The skip's control mechanism had been shredded, and a part of the rock face was gone. Presumably, that debris was taking the express down.

She rarely had the opportunity to examine her handiwork. Clara heard several whines and whimpers from below that were normally associated with wounded prey. Perhaps this pack believed they would make short work of her, but that turned out to be a pipedream.

Or so she believed, right up until a blur appeared at eye level. Clara focused on those eyes, a predator's which were focused exclusively on her. This was not a small specimen either. In fact, it dwarfed those she engaged earlier.

Having temporarily expended her ability to manipulate time, all she could do was watch as its clawed hand rose above its torso. Ready to strike, she knew exactly what the next few steps would be.

"This is going to—" Clara said.

\* \* \* \*

Elizabeth had no idea what was going on. The shaft near her position had been the source of odd noises for several minutes now.

*"You know that's the one Clara sent to help you?" her internal voice asked.*

While she desperately wanted to believe that, her mind chose to dismiss it as false hope. She figured that anyone foolhardy enough to make such an attempt was certifiable. Although, less than six months ago, she would have just as easily dismissed the idea of vampires.

The only thing she was certain of was that the intervals between sounds were getting shorter. The progression lent to the theory of this being part of a rescue attempt, and if that were true, they must have been on a tight schedule, which begged the question, why?

"*Who knows?*" The voice said.

"Oh, like that's fucking helpful," Elizabeth huffed.

Before the voice had a chance to giggle, three distant blasts filtered down to her level. The reverberations from a multitude of blasts were disorientating. However, the last two blasts were near enough to feel the air displacement. Alas, Elizabeth had been too deep in thought to realise what happened.

"What the—" Elizabeth said.

The addition of splashes originating from both shafts was worrisome. Although the one nearest to her was delayed and clean, which made sense considering the blasts had been focused on the far end shaft.

"*I told you*," the voice said.

Elizabeth ignored that taunt as best she could. She had no appetite for making a formal apology to what was essentially herself. Although, she was tempted to reconsider that when something slipped out from the water.

"Sure," Julia said. "Swim to the ledge with a big assed backpack, but drop Clara's shotgun…"

In response to a new voice and the mention of that familiar name, Elizabeth bit her lower lip in anticipation. Still, she could not afford to be the fool who showed up at the gate only to confirm her warden's suspicions.

Instead, she stayed in place, right where they left her. Of course, as though by rotten luck, her nose began to itch. Elizabeth rolled her eyes in protest, but unsurprisingly, that proved ineffectual.

A series of waterlogged steps came to Elizabeth's ear that differed greatly from the previous visits. Was it nothing more than water being pushed out of the soles with every step taken? No, there was something else, something less tangible.

Her last visitor had a determined pace, with short iterations that were heavy on the heel. These were far more relaxed and casual. More importantly, the steps did not show hesitation, so they were familiar with this place.

"*An insider?*" The voice teased.

Despite being filled with an overwhelming desire to tell herself to shut up, she bit the inside of her cheek. The pain was sure to distract her long enough to stay focused…

Alas the voice giggled, which forced Elizabeth to utter, "Shut up."

"Elizabeth?" Julia asked.

No one here had used her name before, nor asked for it. Hearing her given name spoken out loud filled her heart with hope… or at least it had until a gunshot rang out.

"*Oh dear,*" the voice said, just after the dull thud of a body hitting the floor echoed throughout the cell.

\* \* \* \*

To counter the attack as best she could, Clara fell back and let gravity take over. As the claws swooped down, they missed her face and neck but dug into her left shoulder before running over the steel plate.

While the armour had been effective, the material holding in the plates had been shredded. It would not take much to lose the plates and leave her defenceless.

"Horsefeathers," Clara said.

She continued to curl her back in such a way as to give her arms some spring against the maintenance building's rooftop. For an additional push, she flicked her legs forward, which sent her into a controlled roll.

While not elegant, it permitted her to avoid the brunt of the attack. Right where she would have been standing, William landed with enough force to crack the surface. While hardier than the average gal, her bones could still shatter.

Now she had a problem. The alpha was far too close for an effective attack with the thumper. While she did have pistols, she was fairly certain that they too would be ineffective. Even in that calibre, she needed to target vulnerable spots, save shoving the barrel down its throat and force feeding it a whole clip. *Even then…*

For now, she needed to play a defensive game to drag this out. She figured that as long as the alpha was directly in this fight, the others would stay out of the way, an assumption based on her last engagement. *After all, my intelligence has been bang on so far…*

William rushed towards her, and she had little time to react. Fortunately, she stepped aside before he could strike and watched him sail by. For good measure, she whacked him on the ass with one of her wings.

An impact from a wing that size could have devastating effects. In this case, the hit forced his groin forward, while he cupped his ass cheeks. The spectacle made Clara giggle, and while she normally preferred to chuckle, the overt humiliation played in her favour.

"My, my," Clara said. "You must spend a lot of time at the gym to have an ass like that."

William did not stop, opting to make a long and deliberate circle to face her. With Clara in his sights, the alpha built up some speed. From Clara's point of view, this was a freight train, and he would not be fooled by a quick dodge this time.

That left her with two choices: pull back or confront. With a smirk, she chose to charge her opponent. That's when William hesitated. The pace between his steps slowed down by a fraction of a second. Clara smiled, knowing this was the right course of action.

One on one, she did not stand a chance. Werewolves were not the slow, lumbering beasts they had been taught to believe. They simply had a preference for brute strength over agility. So, she drew her pistols, dropped into a slide, and used her momentum to glide through William's legs.

For good measure, she popped a few rounds focused on his groin. Given the sensitive nature of the target area, she hoped that it would slow him down a smidge.

What she did not count on was the introduction of a new player. Where this one came from, she never knew, but the werewolf's presence was confirmed when it landed right on her chest. The impact left her winded and forced her wings into an unnatural position.

Broken? Only time would tell. In that moment, her most pressing concern was the roof collapsing all around her. This gave her a one-way ticket straight down into the blood-soaked carnage unleashed on the maintenance floor. What a shame. There were still several werewolves itching for a fight down there.

"Just ducky," Clara wheezed.

\* \* \* \*

Elizabeth was not sure what to make of it. On one hand, Clara did send someone to help her escape. This was an act of great courage itself, even when compared to the sacrifice Clara must be making to keep her captors busy. Still, the fact her saviour ended up getting shot put a kink in the plan.

For now, Elizabeth dared not move, but would not let go of that pry bar. Despite the chill from the cold steel, it left her feeling empowered. This potential weapon comforted her like being hugged by a loved one after a particularly bad day. Sadly, this day had yet to begin.

"Fuck," Adrienne said in frustration. "You choose now to jam on me?"

She picked up the sound of something splashing into the water. While she assumed it was the weapon, it could have just as easily been more falling debris. Still, she prayed that it was the rifle.

*"One cannot plan on hopes and prayers," her internal voice said.*

Those words rang true, pointing out that continued optimism might forever leave her in need of a saviour. Sure, Clara had been there once, and was here again, but an angel was not omnipotent nor omniscient. There would come a time when no one would ride to her rescue. What then? Wait until Death greeted her?

"How *dare* you!" Adrienne yelled.

While the words echoed throughout every part of this mine, no answer came. The gunshot victim appeared to be, for lack of a more sensitive term, dead quiet. Elizabeth was doing her best to do the same but found it difficult to keep her anxiety in check. The idea that this cold-blooded individual was so near, worsened her state of mind. Although, not many were able to keep their cool in this situation.

*"Stay calm," the voice said. "She doesn't know that you're awake, or that you have a weapon."*

"You just *had* to come down here and fuck with me!" Adrienne shouted.

Elizabeth listened as those footsteps approached. Every step added to the stress she was under, but to remain calm, she had to remember that she held the element of surprise.

* * * *

Clara crashed down hard on the concrete slab that made up the surface of the maintenance floor. The impact was hard enough to make her bounce a couple of times before settling. However, despite being surrounded by werewolves, the place was eerily quiet.

"Wait!" Clara said. "Shouldn't I be flat as a pancake?"

Clara opened her eyes and stared straight into another set a couple of feet above. These were not William's eyes, since they were smaller and more delicate. A shame that she could not infer what was going on inside its head, although surprise was probably the correct answer.

"Still," Clara said while sliding out from under the werewolf.

All told, there were five werewolves that should have been itching for a fight. Despite the threat, her mind soon focused on the sharp pains that shot through both of her wings. That meant she had bruising, sprains, fractures, or a combination of the above. Her right wing even dragged on the ground, the equivalent of pouring blood into shark-infested waters.

"Just ducky," Clara said.

These werewolves were twitching, their muscles begging to be pushed to exertion. She had seen this behaviour in dogs, and it rarely ended well for the prey.

William howled in rage. She peeked up through the fresh hole in the ceiling, but could not spot him or his silhouette. He knew well enough to avoid ending up in her line of sight. That explained his behaviour. So, what were the rest of these dogs waiting for?

"*Fear*?" Clara whispered.

A gal with a big gun was one thing, but one that could fly was another. However, a dame that could freeze a werewolf in mid-air? That upped the ante significantly and left witnesses of that spectacle... fearful. *Let them believe... or am I the one who should believe?*

Still, this battle could not be won within the confines of this building. There were far too many blind spots, and she was outnumbered. So, if this *hiccup* caused them to hesitate, then Clara would make sure to play the part.

"What?" Clara yelled. "Do any of you have the balls to take me on?"

The last part was purely theatrical splendour. Clara channelled all of the accumulated frustration built up since falling to Earth. The words boomed out over this unlikely battlefield, but no one answered her challenge. Although, they had also witnessed the change in her eye colour, from a cold steel-grey, to the dim blue light of a blowtorch.

"*Now there's an idea,*" Clara thought before she adopted a sickly smile.

She turned around in a full circle with her arms apart to challenge the werewolves. Again, not one dared to take her up on the offer. Still, the alpha would not back down, so it was time to meet him out in the open.

"Pussies," Clara said before walking out through the largest door and away from that damned building.

* * * *

Julia remained perfectly still and kept her breathing under control. She was hurting, but now was not the time for action, since the risk was too high. Instead, she needed to wait for an opportunity, if one ever came.

"You know," Adrienne said in a strangely calm tone. "You're a lot like your mother, and that's why I killed her."

From Elizabeth's point of view, the young woman's lack of response for such a grievous statement confirmed that she was dead. It would take a tremendous amount of self-control to stay quiet. Even she wanted to rush in to choke the life out her attacker.

"I slit her throat," Adrienne said before licking her lips, "with this very knife, in fact. I honed it until it could slice through meat like a hot knife through butter."

Again, no reply came, but Elizabeth's own sense of empathy was beginning to take over. She was not a fan of bullies at the best of times, but this one certainly deserved a special place in hell. Unfortunately, when she tightened her grip, it caused the pry bar to shift. The sound may have been faint, but it was enough to be heard.

"Well… Well…" Adrienne said. "What do we have—"

Julia used this distraction to launch an attack. With her right arm, she pushed herself up from the floor and sprinted towards Adrienne. Meanwhile, her left arm hung limply to her side, a sure sign the bullet had done damage.

Despite the injury, Julia covered the distance between them in the blink of an eye. However, Adrienne had been expecting the Lazarus effect and simply shifted out of the way. Out of spite, she also left a foot in the way to serve as a stumbling block for her weakened foe.

The plan was effective, sending Julia into a lurch. However, Adrienne was also thrown off balance, which left both of them precariously positioned. Adrienne was not wounded though, which gave her ample time to recover.

"Really?" Adrienne asked. "You thought that I'd fall for that?"

Julia fell to her knees once those words sunk in. She closed her eyes and clenched her jaw, all in an attempt to block from her mind that she was bleeding out. Adrienne always had a way of pushing her buttons, but this revelation demanded revenge. How could emotions not be involved?

With a bit of determination, Julia managed to get up, turn around, and casually walked over to the source of all her frustrations. This time she was confronting her demons in her kick-ass leather boots. While these boots were not made for walking, they would certainly be used to walk right the fuck over her.

Adrienne cocked a brow, but held her position. The smile on Julia's face should have worried her, but she was certain there was nothing more to this than putting on a show of force. Besides, she could take care of herself, and this was not her first kill, nor would this be her last.

This time, when Julia opened the attack with a jab, Adrienne responded with her knife, stabbing downwards, burying the blade deep in the bone of the immobilised upper arm.

For a moment, they seemed to be at a standstill. While Adrienne did land a blow, Julia was numb to it, unaffected. That is, until she violently sent her forehead forward and smashed it against Adrienne's. The impact of the head-butt was enough to send both women recoiling, but Adrienne's knife remained in play.

Adrienne grabbed the handle and pulled, but given the angle, snapped the blade. Despite the damage, the remaining portion was sharp and would serve her well. With a smile, she approached and swung the knife in a wide arc.

The jagged edge of the knife cut through Julia's clothing and left a thin red slice on her back. Julia curved her back in response and turned her gimp arm towards her aggressor, using it like a shield. Alas, it was too late to catch the blade slicing through her jeans, which left a gash in her thigh.

Adrienne looked for another opportunity to strike unopposed, but something brought a smile to her face. Julia was confused by the change, or was until the world began to spin out of control. Julia took a knee, then fell flat on the floor.

"Figures," Adrienne hissed. "You were always weak and pathetic."

* * * *

Clara's hunch was right, despite the hesitation shown by the rest of the pack, the Alpha jumped off the roof ready for battle. In fact, he skipped foreplay and moved in for the kill.

"In my day," Clara quipped before backing away from a handful of claws, "men would at least tell me that I was beautiful before trying to fuck with me."

William was not interested in her smart assed remarks, nor any other attempts at humour. He was determined, even comforted, by the knowledge that Clara could not parry, block, or evade him forever. When it came to strength and endurance werewolves were near the apex in both categories, and this one knew it.

Fortunately, he was not a creative fighter, and she suspected that this was the norm. After all, the Alpha she killed last year had been far older and more experienced. Simply put, werewolves were like wild animals, not world class fencing champions. None stood a chance against a grandmaster in chess... unless winning involved dismembering their opponents.

All she needed was time, and mercifully by the position of the moon, that wait would soon be over. Either way, hunters always assumed they would not make it out alive. Sacrifice was expected, and putting mission ahead of self was the reason she got her wings.

"Hey Willy!" Clara yelled. When he failed to answer back, she added, "So, you think your mother survived that fall?"

Those words, in addition to the grin, got the desired effect. William looked right up at the moon and howled, a primal voice that boomed throughout these lands. Clara used this opportunity to back away and ready herself for an attack. She even risked slowing things down a bit, just enough to keep it fun.

When William attacked, Clara did nothing more than sail effortlessly around his attacks. The fact that every attack ended up in a miss infuriated the beast further. Clara appeared to be nonplussed by the fight, even going so far as to leave her hands behind her back. Despite exposing the bulk of her upper body, the alpha sliced and punched the air. Clara was always somewhere else the moment he committed to an attack.

Clara giggled before saying, "Really? That's all you got?"

Words that had rolled off his back earlier were now actively contributing to his rage. Clara continued to dodge, back away, dodge, back away until there was nowhere left to go. She had managed to back herself straight into a rusted chain link barrier. Behind, there were banks of electrical equipment that hummed away loudly.

The werewolf paused, and Clara saw that twinkle in its eyes. What good was a manoeuvrable ship when out of sea room? His tongue ran over its razor-sharp teeth, and when certain of this victory, swung an arm over his head and came down hard. A move like that could slice a full-grown man in half, but it was stopped mid-way.

Clara had used her slight advantage in speed to grab the paw mid-motion and slowed it down until it came to a halt. Until that point, momentum made up the bulk of this attack, and Clara was far stronger than she appeared to be.

"I've been hit harder by girls," Clara teased. "Are you going to quit pussyfooting—"

William did not wait for her to finish and punched Clara with enough force to deform those ballistic plates. She went flying through the fencing and straight into a transformer bank. The effect was spectacular, with bolts of electricity arcing through the air. Everyone nearby ended up being showered in sparks.

Just as the sparks began to dissipate, a loud thump was heard throughout the compound. The werewolf from the maintenance building, the one suspended in time, was reunited with Mother Earth... face first.

# CHAPTER 20

## *LET IT GO*

A drienne grabbed what was left of the knife. While the blade had snapped, there was enough left to do damage. This harlot was the reminder of her lover's conquests, and nothing would stop her from skinning this traitor alive. This way, she could ensure that it was slow and painful.

In anticipation, she licked her lips then knelt by Julia. She paused and smirked while considering where to make her first incision. With one hand, she grabbed Julia's head by the hair and lifted it just enough to get a clear view of the scalp.

"I've always envied your hair," Adrienne said. "Now I guess I'll have it as a keepsake."

Adrienne laughed and positioned the jagged edge of the blade against the edge of her scalp. While Julia did not wake, that would surely change with a bit of coaxing.

"Get away from her," Elizabeth said faintly.

Those words only served to amuse the aggressor. Statements delivered as such had no weight, no conviction, and were easily dismissed. Would anyone listen to a quivering child making such threats?

"Get back in your cage," Adrienne said without looking back.

"N-No," Elizabeth said.

Again, this child-like exchange did little to convince Adrienne to comply. Nor was there any reason to believe she was at risk. That pain in her ass might have been taller, younger, and arguably stronger, but she lacked in cruelty, which Adrienne had in excess.

"Girl," Adrienne said in a stern voice that implied there would be hell to pay if her directives were not followed. "Get back to your cage."

"I said—" Elizabeth said.

"You what?" Adrienne said while pushing her blade into Julia's skin just below the hairline. As blood pooled around the blade she added, "You planning to bore me to death with talk?"

Adrienne's smile grew when Julia started to squirm. She revelled in the fact she was going to deprive this woman of a peaceful death. Heck, she could make good use of that soft skin—

"I *said* to leave her the *fuck* alone," Elizabeth said as the pry bar came into contact with Adrienne's head.

The hit was solid and to the side, fracturing the skull and knocking Adrienne out before hitting the floor. However, Elizabeth was not done just yet.

"What..." Elizabeth yelled as she struck Adrienne across the back of the head. "Kind... of... sick... fuck... tries... to... scalp... someone?"

With every word, Elizabeth struck as hard as she could even though that face ended up looking like raw hamburger. She did not care. This was warranted because it meant this vile woman would not be bullying anyone else ever again.

"*What are you doing, Elizabeth?*" The voice in her head asked.

"What have I done?" Elizabeth asked after a long pause, but before dropping the bloody pry bar.

Every piece of exposed skin was covered in blood splatter. Although, the fact that it was someone else's blood made it worse. Her hands were shaking and her eyes were beginning to well up.

*"Calm down," her internal voice said, but those words were not reaching her. "That girl is dying. If you don't tend to her wounds, she will not make it, and it will be your fault."*

"What?" Elizabeth questioned.

Her mind paused long enough to process what had been said. She then turned towards Julia and realised that there was a lot of work to do.

"Oh shit," Elizabeth said while dropping to her knees.

The first thing she would have to do was slow the bleeding. Hopefully all of that mandatory first aid training would pay off. Still, practice and reality were rarely one and, the same.

\* \* \* \*

Clara was not one for getting worked up over someone's bad habits. After all, she had yet to meet anyone who was perfect, and given her previous address, that was telling. However, that poor-man's imitation of a hyena's laugh was ruffling her feathers. This worsened when the others joined in, laughing at the funny way she *died*, a coping mechanism really, because they would soon have to deal with their fallen.

"God," Clara mumbled once her extremities stopped tingling. "I feel great."

She had experienced a transference of energy before. The first time it happened, the source had been magical in nature, but she guessed there was little difference, and that gamble paid off. When she opened her eyes, the world before her was bathed in a blue hue, and like Sparky, this was a sign that her batteries were charged.

Clara shifted slightly, enough to sense that in addition to her wing, she now had several broken or sprained ribs. She slipped out of her plate armoured jacket and felt immediate relief once the pressure was lifted from her breasts. As an additional measure, she briefly massaged them to get the tingling sensation out. Meanwhile, the werewolves continued to laugh, unaware of the dangers nearby.

"Oh boys!" Clara yelled before dropping the vest onto the metal wreckage. When they settled, she added, "I'm so going to enjoy giving you guys the electric cure."

Once those words reached their ears, the pack went quiet, and a few even went slack jawed. Still, it was the devilish blue hue reflected back in their eyes that sold the effect. So much so that they collectively could not break away from Clara's stare.

"Really, William?" Clara said. "What would your mother say about not confirming a kill?"

William shook his head and growled. Clara shifted from giggling to a mocking laugh, even going so far as to point at him while doing so. She wanted him to attack. No, she *needed* him to attack.

"Mommy's little boy can't beat up a girl?" Clara taunted.

This time he reacted exactly as expected. He buried a clawed foot through the ice and snow and pushed off towards her. They were right back to mimicking a bull and a matador. Although, Clara was going to go off script.

Before William was able to take his fifth step, Clara pointed a finger straight at the werewolf. That's when all of that negativity was channelled into a coherent bolt of blue energy that struck William directly in his chest.

The blast had been devastating. Not only did it stop him dead in his tracks, but it subsequently sent him barrelling into the rest of his pack. However, Clara was not done. Oh no! She was going to have fun before the night was out.

* * * *

"What was that?" Elizabeth said, feeling a dull and deep rumble that reminded her of an earthquake.

Elizabeth had just finished rummaging through the contents of Julia's backpack. Inside, she found a treasure trove of clothing and supplies needed to escape.

She had to admit it, Clara certainly knew her measurements. Everything fit exactly as prescribed, although some things were a bit looser around her midsection to make up for her generous bust.

"Elizabeth," her internal voice said. "*You just ran out of time.*"

255

Despite the voice emanating from the inside of her head, she searched the area. There was no one else on this level, and Julia's chest rose and contracted with regularity. Eventually, the young woman would need proper medical intervention, but she was stable for now. As for the body, she was pretty sure that it was not in a talkative mood.

*"Get Julia to that elevator,"* the voice said.

"What? Why?" Elizabeth asked, while wondering how her subconscious had more insight into their situation than she did.

*"Clara blew the dam,"* Evelyn said, her voice echoing throughout Elizabeth's mind.

For the first time, Elizabeth became aware that mannerisms and intonations in those words were not her own. The very idea left a chill, one that ran down to the depths of her soul.

"What the fuck!" Elizabeth yelled.

*"Elizabeth—"* Evelyn said calmly.

"Why the fuck—" Elizabeth continued.

*"Elizabeth—"* Evelyn said sternly.

"You fucking—" Elizabeth added.

The lights above fizzled in and out before going out completely. That forced Elizabeth to use the headlamp strapped to her forehead.

*"We don't have the—"* Evelyn said.

"We?" Elizabeth asked.

*"If you don't get moving… fast… you'll drown along with your friend,"* Evelyn said softly.

Her mind was torn between trusting someone who helped to get her out of that subway car, and railing against this most grievous of betrayals. While one was essentially indistinguishable from the other, it was hard to hold a grudge when dead.

So, Elizabeth chose survival and grabbed Julia under her arms. The young woman moaned in pain, but given the threat, there was little that could be done to minimise the trauma. Without much thought, she dragged Julia's legs along the ground until they reached the elevator. It came in two parts: one for the driver and the other suitable for whatever else.

"*The top part*," Evelyn said, although there was a hint of uncertainty in that voice.

Elizabeth struggled with Julia's body. The young woman may have been a lot smaller than Elizabeth, but she was essentially dead weight. Besides, she had to be careful, because dropping Julia into the top bucket might exacerbate her injuries.

In the distance, they heard water rushing into the tunnels. While the complex was huge, giving them time, that water would soon cover the distance between the shaft lines.

"I better—" Elizabeth said.

"*Hurry!*" Evelyn yelled.

The water from the level below was rising already. Even now, the skip was nearly buoyant, but something was scraping metal on metal. Either there was something ceased, or some sort of braking mechanism was engaged.

"Fuck," Elizabeth said while thinking over her options.

The last thing either needed was to remain tethered to those rails. She had no clue if the rails were safe, nor how the elevator would react when slammed by rolling waves. *So, what choices do I have?*

"Think," Elizabeth said. "Think."

Something came to mind, but she hesitated. While the idea was sound, it would mean getting near…

"*Go on!*" *Evelyn said. "It's her fault this is happening anyway.*"

It may not have been her fault for dying, but they were all here because of her. Why anyone would think that they stood a chance against a determined and battle-hardened foe like Clara was beyond her.

Elizabeth grabbed the bar and rushed back to the skip. This time, the water was high enough that her boots were getting wet. Based on how the skip was shifting with the current, Elizabeth could tell that the blockage was nearest to her.

She shifted into a better position and saw the metal structure surrounding the top part of the wheel. Those parts were so old and rusted that they had fused. Elizabeth slammed the top portion several times with the bar, which reflected the vibrations right back into her hands with every impact. *Fuck*!

Despite the pain, she continued to strike until enough material flaked off to create a gap. That gave her somewhere to wedge the pry bar, and with some leverage she broke the wheel free.

Just in time too. The rising water levels sent air rushing through the tunnel towards her. It would not be long until this level was submerged. She paused, thought it over, and took the pry bar with her.

"Just in case," Elizabeth said.

* * * *

The first sign of trouble came in the form of a dull rumble, sounding like a distant thunder over the mountains. That got everyone's attention, including Clara who stopped making the werewolves writhe in agony. While the pack looked to each other for answers, Clara adopted a big shit-eating grin.

The second omen came when the lights went out. Without the generator running, there was not enough juice to power the lights, so they dimmed before burning out. That meant little to nocturnal creatures normally, but it spelled trouble when one put two and two together.

The third sign was a tremendous cracking sound, one that reminded Clara of ice breaking free from a glacier. The sound was deafening and caused the werewolves to howl. So why was Clara not bothered?

"Time for a little swim, boys," Clara said with a laugh.

In the distance, there was a dull roar. As it got closer, a few realised what was going on. William, despite the charred flesh covering his chest, made another run for Clara. This time, she did not even bother to move. She was, as Elizabeth would say, 'fresh out of fucks.'

When William swung his massive clawed hand at her face, the angel did not move. Instead, she turned translucent, a pale imitation of herself, and his claws simply passed through. William looked at his hand, then her, refusing to admit that this was even possible. Instead, he continued to slash, punch, and bite Clara, but every attempt was for naught.

"William," Clara said in a disembodied voice. "You may want to look behind you."

William refused and opted for greater intensity in his attacks. Clara continued to smile, even when the wall of water slammed into them. She was submerged, surrounded by a vortex of chaos as all manner of creatures and flora were uprooted and given a one-way ticket downstream.

Clara stood there and observed the chaos unfold, showing no interest in William's fate. She had *nudged* this situation in her favour, but it would be up to the Fates to cut the thread.

With that in mind, Clara strolled off towards what was left of the dam, even as an uprooted tree passed right through her.

\* \* \* \*

Elizabeth had no idea if her plan would work. Water was now rushing in on all levels and flowed over the sides like a waterfall. As they floated up one full level, a powerful surge tossed them from side to side and derailed them. Despite bobbing around like a quark, they risked filling up the bucket and losing buoyancy. The only thing that prevented them from floating away was a rusty guide cable.

*"Best not dwell on that," Evelyn said.*

"No kidding," Elizabeth said.

Elizabeth could not complain. They were moving between levels, although slowly. Still, the angle of the shaft forced the flow of water to focus on the rails, which in turn kept them more or less centred. As a result, they were sheltered from the chaos all around her.

Meanwhile, Julia slept peacefully, comfortable in a world filled with dreams. Elizabeth was thankful for it, knowing that this one would have a lot of emotional scarring to deal with after waking up. With a little luck, those wounds would heal.

"*Look above*," Evelyn said.

Elizabeth did as the voice in her head commanded. Despite being a few levels from the surface, she made out some detail in the sky. Since the lights were out, that meant the sun was rising.

"The sun?" Elizabeth asked. "How did you know?"

*Evelyn giggled and said, "I always know when the sun rises or sets."*

"Makes sense," Elizabeth said absentmindedly.

This lull was causing her to lose some steam, which permitted all of that trauma to clamour for attention. Her kidnapping, being tied up and alone, witnessing something getting shot, and…

"I took a life…" Elizabeth said with a sigh.

*"And you saved two in the process," Evelyn said.*

"So why does that not make me feel any better?" Elizabeth asked.

*"It won't," Evelyn said. "You've just committed a cardinal sin in your mind."*

Those words resonated truth. Elizabeth never condoned the taking of a human life, to do so was unforgivable. And yet, she killed someone in the defence of another. Plenty would brand her a hero, even Julia, but ultimately, she had failed herself.

"Do you think I'll get over this?" Elizabeth asked.

*"Of course*," Evelyn replied.

"How?" Elizabeth asked.

*"You're not the first human who had to re-evaluate their core values,"* Evelyn said. *"Nor will you be the last."*

Elizabeth decided to focus on what was happening up ahead. In order to get out of these tunnels, they had to rise up through an oversized sink vortex. That meant this bucket would fill up, and fast.

"Even if I had a pail, it would do fuck all to help me," Elizabeth said.

Still, buoyancy was sure to play a part, she assumed. The same concepts that kept her afloat would apply once they were submerged. The rubber ducky always found its way to the top, no matter how deep the water was.

"Great," Elizabeth said while imagining herself shooting out through the surface like a bathtub toy.

This time, she planned ahead. She rummaged through the backpack for something that would help and pulled out a length of rope. Elizabeth was a bit rusty with knots but knew well enough to tie lots.

She centred herself in the skip and brought Julia in close until she was nuzzled into her back with legs on either side. She then proceeded to loop lengths around their shoulders and repeated the process between their torsos. As a precaution, she made sure that Julia could breathe and that her own mobility was not sacrificed.

Lastly, she bound Julia's legs together around her waist, using that spare length of copper cabling. That permitted Elizabeth to swim if they became submerged without fear of getting tangled. It would also prevent Julia from floating away.

Finally, she grabbed onto two large rings, rusted to the point of having a pitted surface. While she wasn't sure of their particular function, she knew it would give her something to hold on to.

"Here we go," Elizabeth said before taking a deep breath.

The water rushed in so fast that her legs were immediately soaked. Still, the skip did not linger for long. The water quickly filled the gap and sent it shooting straight up. Elizabeth's stomach contents dropped to her toes and reversed direction once they broke the surface. Up top, the current was much more pronounced.

This was exactly what Elizabeth feared. She had Julia with her, and given the opportunity, might be able to do something. But what? It's not like she could jump onto a nearby structure, not with the current and the weight of another person tethered to her. Elizabeth was also not at her physical peak, especially after the ordeal endured over the past couple of days.

"Think," Elizabeth said.

Her mind was drawing a blank, blinded by overwhelming fear and stress. While the latter could motivate, she needed to keep her head on straight. On either side of the rails there were ladders that led higher. Where to? Who knew? But it was higher than the current water level, which meant they had a chance.

As the cable strained, Elizabeth paid attention to the motion. If the rungs had been vertical, she would have been done for, but the angle changed the narrative. The skip rammed the railings and nearly sent both of them overboard. Clearly, being on the surface was making the situation temporarily worse. Without a choice, she stood up slowly to adjust to Julia's weight.

By some miracle, Julia was still breathing, but they were not out of danger yet. The skip was once again headed towards the railings. This time, Elizabeth was ready and grabbed onto the highest railing she could reach just as they hit. The shock almost forced her to let go, but she managed to hold on. When the skip moved away, the girls slipped out of the doomed contraption and were sent crashing into the rungs.

"Fuck," Elizabeth said as the wind was knocked out of her.

Still, she held on and used her legs to stay in place. Now came the hard part, lifting their combined weight all the way up the ladder. It was slow and painful, but at least it was progress.

"Too slow!" Elizabeth yelped.

Fortunately, the cable snapped and sent their life raft further downstream, but not before smashing into the railings on the other side. A good thing she did not try to swim or they would have been crushed.

"And a one…" Elizabeth said, moving her arms higher, "and a two," she added after pushing up with her legs, "and a three!" She yelled as the rope dug into her joints and made her fingers go numb.

"*See,*" Evelyn said with a giggle. "*You have this well in hand.*"

* * * *

As the sun broke over the horizon, Clara felt herself heal. Despite the pain, she forced her wings to unfurl and experienced every bruised and broken bone mending. Soon she would be right as rain, and would be able to swoop down to assist Elizabeth and Julia.

It was safe to assume that something had gone wrong with the plan, since their truck had crashed into a building a couple of minutes ago. Since there were no passengers, Clara could only assume they never made it out before the dam broke.

She might have been able to double back and search for them on foot, but given the flooding and the size of the area, it would have taken days, if not weeks, to thoroughly search the complex. Her only option was to get to high ground, heal, and swoop down.

The devastation below was extensive. All of the structures were flooded, although not completely submerged. In the distance, she spotted a few survivors on the roof of the maintenance building. Clara furrowed her brow. Even from this distance, she could tell they were naked. With the full moon spent, they had all reverted to their human selves. *Gee, there are some mighty small specimens in that group.*

"Shame," Clara said, disappointed that she did not manage to drown them all like the vermin they were.

They were not a priority. Her eyes focused from one point to the next. Every time, she searched for movement or even for a floating body. If Elizabeth or Julia did not make it, Clara was not sure she would be able to forgive herself. After all, it was far easier to put her own life on the line than another's.

"There!" Clara shouted.

In the distance, she watched Elizabeth and Julia climb over some railing and onto an ore dump. It was not the highest point in the camp, but the water levels were steady, so that was good enough.

"That's my gal," Clara said proudly before the words dredged up thoughts from the depths of her mind.

This was confirmation that Elizabeth did not need to be saved, at least not directly. And that meant the final phase of her plan had come to fruition. After all, Clara had not planned to live past the night.

"A beautiful day it is too," Clara said

A new day and a fresh start, or at least it was for some. In the last two days, Clara had unleashed carnage on this place, and rid the world of a whole slew of monsters. That did not bother her. In fact, she would sleep better knowing that their base of operations was now submerged.

What did bother her was her moment of weakness, which led to her transgression. Clara may have been frustrated and in dire need of human contact, but she should have waited. After all, it would have taken no more than a bit of humility, patience, and honesty to be with the one she loved.

"Love..." Clara said.

If only she had been able to see the truth two days ago. Clara was certain of one thing: she would not be able to face Elizabeth just yet.

"Confession is good for the soul, I'm told," a man said.

Clara turned around so fast that the scene before her eyes changed in the blink of an eye. Just ahead of her, there was a man whose details were marred completely by the sun. Because of this, she was not able to make out how the speaker looked.

"Wow! Really?" Clara said before whistling. "That's going to be a doozie."

Whoever it was never replied. Instead, Clara blinked and he was gone. All that remained were the blinding rays of this glorious sun.

"Curiouser and curiouser," Clara said.

Left with her original thoughts, Clara was certain that she should keep a healthy distance. With that certainty in her mind, she flapped her wings and flew through the massive tear in the dam.

\* \* \* \*

Elizabeth was exhausted by the time she reached the top and collapsed onto the flat surface. She had no clue where she was, nor the purpose of this particular structure, and did not care. Instead, she just let her body rest.

After cutting Julia free, she cuddled into her wounded companion while confirming a strong pulse and steady breathing. After what they went through, Elizabeth was not sure how she would have reacted had this one died while making their escape attempt.

She closed her eyes and sighed contentedly. The water levels did not appear to be rising anymore, and this structure was solid. She was certain that other buildings had either collapsed or were severely compromised.

"Good," Elizabeth said softly, comforted by the idea that this place would no longer serve a dark purpose.

If Elizabeth was unsure if she was dreaming or not, there came a sound, faint and distant at first, reminding her of those late-night action movies her father invariably fell asleep to.

The sound grew louder and louder. It eventually forced her to open her eyes, and she realised that this was not part of a dream.

"Could it be?" Elizabeth asked and rose up just enough to see over the lip of the structure.

There was a helicopter in the distance. While she did not know why it was here, she guessed that it was not here by chance. How could anyone know? She also doubted that the water had reached a large settlement by now, since their drive had been a *long* one.

Once more, hope welled up inside of her. She carefully extracted herself from Julia and began to jump and wave to flag down the helicopter. She prayed they would spot her and send help, but given their distance, they could just as easily turn back without spotting her.

Just then, red and blue lights appeared up over the ridge and a series of law enforcement vehicles lined up, the sight of which was enough for a bunch of naked men to launch themselves into the cold water below to avoid justice.

There was something to be said about people who would rather meet Death than face the consequences. *Wait… I'm part of that group…*

Elizabeth's enthusiasm waned for a moment, but she realised they had no way of knowing. There had not been enough time, and right now, Julia needed help.

As the helicopter moved closer to her position, she waved even harder. Eventually, it hovered nearby, long enough to get a good look at the both of them.

Elizabeth was not sure what to do, other than stop waving like a cheerleader. Instead, she walked with a limp, coughed, and pointed towards Julia. Would they get her clues?

"We radioed in for search and rescue," a voice boomed out from the helicopter's loudspeaker. "Stay where you are and a unit will be dispatched to your location."

Elizabeth's eyes teared up and she blew them a kiss. As the helicopter moved off to search these flooded lands, Elizabeth went back to spooning Julia and promptly fell asleep.

# CHAPTER 21

## *LIKE SANDS THROUGH THE HOURGLASS*

**One week after the incident at the dam...**

A repetitive beep was the first thing that surfaced through Julia's clouded mind. This chime was distant at first, distorted, but remained persistent and annoying.

"Where am I?" Julia mumbled, which was enough to make her lips bleed.

When she tasted the iron in her blood, she knew for certain that she made it. Surely wherever she ended up in the afterlife would either be far more painful or much more pleasant. Cracked lips would not concern her in either locales.

"Julia," Elizabeth said.

The words warbled in her mind, since whatever they had her on was really throwing her for a loop. In an effort to reconnect with reality, Julia tried to open her eyes but felt nothing but resistance.

"Julia," Elizabeth said softly, and this time she felt a warm hand take hers.

With some coaxing, Julia forced her eyes open. The world before her was all a blur, as though she were suffering from a migraine. Still, there was an absence of pain, and those blobs of colour eventually broke down into defined shapes, faces, and smiles.

At first, she focused on Elizabeth, the one holding her hand, and tried to smile but her lips hurt. She then turned to face a young woman dressed in an expensive suit. Despite the smile, she pegged this one as being a high-priced lawyer, which led her to wonder about the kind of trouble she was in.

Her eyes then drifted to the background and settled onto a uniformed cop. Unlike the women at her side, this one was not smiling, which gave her a legitimate reason to worry. Incidentally, the beeping from earlier shortened its interval.

On instinct, Julia tried to back away but realised that her other hand was handcuffed to the bed. That attempt to move caused the two women to rush forward, as though she were about to tear some stitches.

"Miss Black," the lawyer said, "I'm Vivian Thompson of..."

The sound of her voice fell off into the distance as her mind drifted back into a drug induced sleep. She fought it as best she could, but the drug's hold was too strong to ignore.

"I advise you to say nothing unless..." Vivian said, which were the last words that filtered through before Morpheus reclaimed his prize.

* * * *

**Four weeks later...**

"You have fifteen minutes," the uniformed officer said. "Also note that the bathroom area is not structurally sound."

Elizabeth took in a deep breath to centre herself. She did not have a lot of time, but that was the best her lawyer could manage. Sure, paying for a lawyer was burning a hole in her life savings, but she had no intention of owing anyone.

"I understand," Elizabeth said after nodding.

The officer broke the seal around the makeshift door and walked inside first. After he had a good view of the area, she was allowed to walk into the place she once called home. For now, she was cooped up in a hotel, living off of a small insurance stipend, with little to no clothing to her name. She needed some of her things, especially outfits suitable for work.

Elizabeth's eyes welled up the minute she walked in. The path of destruction that led from the door and continued on until the outside wall of the bathroom caught her eye. It was hard to imagine anyone showing that much disrespect. Although, she also noted how their neighbour's door also had a police seal.

While the damage was hard enough to take in, it was the smell that alerted her to one important detail. On the island counter, there were a bunch of dishes neatly laid out. Given the passage of time and the warming weather, the carefully prepared food had taken on a life of its own.

Nevertheless, that meant Clara had prepared a meal in anticipation for her early morning arrival. There was also something that looked to be a note facing down on the counter. Unfortunately, she was not able to take a closer look.

Anyone could rise to the occasion and play the part of the hero. In the end, that did not mean they were in love with, or even knew the one saved. Clara would have waged war against Hell itself to save an innocent soul, and would do so without question.

It was the little things, the amount of attention and detail that really mattered. Clara had not done this for glory, for fame, or even to win her heart. Clara just happened to care enough about Elizabeth, as a person, to give a shit.

"Ma'am," the officer said.

Elizabeth looked away, took a deep breath, and wiped a few tears from her eyes. She had known this was going to be hard but never realised how profound the reaction would actually be. Alas, time was against her, so she bit her lower lip and walked calmly into the bedroom.

That's when things got a bit weird. For one, her bed was neatly made, something she almost always neglected to do herself. Besides, who else made their beds with hospital corners in this day in age? Right between the two decorative pillows, there was a stuffed bear waiting for her, one with a black-metal feather dangling from the collar. *Odd, since I don't own any.*

Still, she had to get packing, so she went to Clara's closet to pull out a suitcase. At first, she thought it was wedged in tight, but when it popped out, the suitcase slammed onto the floor. If not for the throw rug muffling the impact, the officer would have come in to investigate.

After a few deep breaths to calm down, Elizabeth opened her closet door and found it to be mostly empty, except for a few dresses she would never wear. All of Clara's outfits, however, were still neatly in place. *Wait! What?*

Elizabeth rolled the suitcase over to the bed and plopped it on the comforter. She then unzipped it and flipped open the covers. All of her clothes were already packed, neatly folded, and crammed into the suitcase. Her eyes widened in response. Given the allotted time, she would have been lucky to pack away a quarter of this.

Again, it was about the little things. In truth, she would have preferred to learn that Clara was okay some other way. *Why did she leave?*

"Ma'am" The office said. "Ten minutes."

"Thank you," Elizabeth said while shifting items from Clara's closet to her own, ensuring that every movement was accompanied by steps to the bed, along with a whole lot of noise. When she was down to a couple of minutes, she zipped up the suitcase and dropped it off the bed.

As she heard footsteps approach the bedroom, Elizabeth closed her closet door, grabbed the bear, and then pulled out the travel handle from the top. The officer appeared to be surprised that she was ready but asked no questions.

"Here," the officer said as he reached for the suitcase. "I can deal with that."

All the while, he stared at the bear. Given the room's decor, he may have pegged her as someone who would not be caught dead with such things. Elizabeth beamed a smile, while her cheeks turned red from embarrassment.

"What? She won it for me at the fair," Elizabeth lied.

If the officer suspected anything, he was not going to let her know.

\* \* \* \*

**Three months later...**

William walked down some desolate street. To keep a low profile, he kept his hood draped over the eyes. He did not really need to look up. This neighbourhood was an old haunt, a place they once called home. All of that was gone now: the den, their clubhouse, his mother... everything.

Every second step was stiff due to the healing skin on that side of his body. While he was visibly pained on that side, in truth, every step hurt. Heck, even breathing caused him a great deal of discomfort. He had to admit it the dark angel sure managed to fuck him up.

He initially wondered why she spared him but realised that she simply did not care. No, what mattered was that friend, and the harpy would have scorched the earth to find her. He was just in the way, and based on their final confrontation, was nothing more than a pleasant distraction. Knowing that, how could they stand a chance?

"Mother was wrong," William said, and even now, feared the repercussions of uttering those words.

While he did not know for certain, he suspected that his mother never left that mine. The harpy's friend had been on the news recently to talk about her miraculous escape. They never mentioned his mother nor any other survivors, except for his half-sister who was arrested for aiding and abetting.

He supposed that his own escape had been nothing short of a miracle, although, he remembered nothing after that wall of water enveloped him and sent him downstream. His first memories were from hours later, when he woke up cold, naked, and confined to a body bag. Search parties must have assumed he was dead, based on his low body temperature and nearly non-existent pulse.

"Bitch," William swore while thinking of the harpy.

A series of bikes approached him from behind. As a precaution, he turned his head to the side, as they passed by. Initially, it appeared that his ruse had worked since they continued driving off into the night. Unfortunately, they hit a red light, and the group collectively stopped.

William recognised them as being from that rival pack that had taken over their clubhouse. Since one of his own had been accused of killing some of their boys, the last thing he needed was for one to catch his scent.

That might have worked if he had not been downwind of them. A light breeze ran up the street towards the gang. He kept wishing that the traffic light would change in time.

"Come on come on come on," William said while the light remained stubbornly red.

That's when one of the bikers raised his nose into the air. That in itself was not a sign. There were thousands of scents carried by the wind, any of which could get their attention.

"Shit," William swore as the three collectively turned around and stared directly at him.

With no obvious avenue of escape, he simply looked down and continued to move forward. If he acted like nothing was wrong, then they might ignore their senses. If he ran, they were sure to run him down, even if that meant calling in reinforcements. He should know. That's what he would have done.

"Fucking hell," William said as the light turned green, but the bikes doubled back.

Just ahead, there was an alley. While narrow, it would not slow down someone on a motorcycle. Besides, he knew they could intercept him on the other side. To each side there were warehouses. Again, he might lose them initially, but they would not lose his scent once they were on his trail.

"Well mother," William said. "Guess it's time to man up."

The bikers converged on his position and began to loop around him. He pulled back his hood and stood up tall. While it hurt, the act of doing so made him feel more like himself again. He would not cower, nor beg for his life. Doing so was beneath him.

With a whistle, the bikers stopped, and everyone drew out their weapons. The man before him had a sawed-off shotgun. It looked to be a nasty piece of work, and he had no doubt that he would use it.

"William," the lead man said. "What a pleasant surprise."

William never said a word. Instead, his eyes narrowed in on that man, imagining his hands wrapped around that throat while squeezing the life out of him.

"Not talking, eh?" the lead man said.

With a nod, two shots were directed at William from either side. Given the proximity and impact point, he never heard a thing.

\* \* \* \*

**Two months later...**

Clara passed through the heavy oak doors and was immediately greeted by a dry heat. The smell of incense, wood, and cleaning products hung in the air. While it had been nearly a century since she last visited a house of worship, those odours immediately set her mind at ease.

She crossed the vestibule and moved past another set of doors. These were lighter in build and style, but the door creaked with every inch of travel. She subconsciously cringed. Not for fear of what people would think, but for announcing her presence.

"May as well wave a flag," Clara muttered.

Before venturing down the middle aisle, Clara dipped her fingers into the pool of holy water and made the sign of the cross while invoking the holy trinity in Latin. Even now, her mind worked on auto pilot. These rituals and norms were seared into her brain.

Her eyes floated along the walls, noticing the stained-glass windows bearing scenes from the twelve stages of crucifixion. She also noted how the altar was curiously facing the wrong way, a dramatic change from her last attendance. Lastly, she noticed a confessional booth in the distance.

With a wry smile, Clara made her way there, passing a series of burning candles near the altar. In her time, a church of this size would have been full of parishioners, but tonight, this place was deserted. Clara knew that religion had lost a great deal of its lustre over the years, but experiencing it first-hand served to make her feel a tinge of sadness.

"You'd have known, if you bothered to come to church before now," Clara whispered.

While true, Clara seriously questioned her own presence here. As a hunter, faith had been one of her most potent weapons. While her time in Heaven had only served to reinforce her beliefs, discovering certain truths had done much to destroy those foundations.

"What else are you going to do?" Clara asked quietly. "Post on Bealzabook?"

Without more to go on, she confirmed that the confessional was available before opening the door. The sight of that lonely wooden bench brought back a lot of memories of her past confessions. For a gal that loved nothing more than a good bit of mischief, her sessions tended to be long and arduous.

Once the panel separating the two sections of the confessional was opened and the priest uttered a few words, Clara reacted on instinct. The first thing she did was make another sign of the cross.

*"Tantum benedictionem habes pater, quia peccavi. Hoc mihi ex quo ultimum saeculum fuerit confessionem,"* Clara said in flawless Latin.

There was a long pause on the other side. Clara waited patiently, using the time to focus her thoughts. Clearly, they did not have time to go over all of her sins, which forced her to focus on the *highlights*.

"Apologies, my child," Father Lilliman said through the screen mesh. "My Latin is not what it used to be."

"Oh," Clara said before pausing. "Oh right! That changed with Pius XIII."

"You know your history?" Father Lilliman said.

The non-committal nature of that question implied that the priest was not sure of it himself. Clara did not sound old, nor did she behave like someone who lived through that era.

"Something like that, Father," Clara evaded. "Confessions were always done in Latin in my order."

"Your order?" Father Lilliman asked, while confusion dripped off every syllable. "My child."

"Of course," Clara said. "A very select order, one composed of priests and nuns, Father."

That statement did not appear to have an effect on the conversation. Still, Clara decided to dispense with the cleansing of her soul and focused instead on the real reason for being here.

"How odd," Father Lilliman stated.

Again, his words sounded non-committal, as though he was fishing for details. Clara recognised the tactic, although she had never seen it so poorly executed

"No Father," Clara said. "My order is open to those willing to serve our cause."

"Really, child?" Father Lilliman said. "Charity? Education?"

"Oh, I think you know full well what order I'm talking about, Father," Clara said softly.

Those words were accompanied by another intermission. Clara's words, although cryptic, appeared to be having an effect on the man who occupied the opposite side of the confessional.

"I'm sorry, child," Father Lilliman said. "I don't quite follow."

"An order of holy soldiers who hunt creatures that hide from the light of God, Father," Clara said bluntly.

"...there is no such order," Father Lilliman said, "my child."

Clara heard something shift on the other side, while the man fiddled with the locking mechanism to his door. It seemed like an odd thing for a man of the cloth to be doing during a confession. Of course, the confessor rarely sensed that they were being judged.

She slowed down time just enough to get the jump on the priest. She opened her own door while pulling out a long thin blade from her boot. Without hesitation, she pushed the weapon until it was buried deep into the frame and passed right through into his door. That effectively kept the Father locked in and placed him entirely at her mercy. To prevent anyone from getting suspicious, she snapped the handle and closed her door before returning to normal.

"Now, Father," Clara said, "how can you be certain that there is no such order?"

The man tried to push open the door, but it did not budge. He even tried to throw his shoulder into it, but given the limited space, he succeeded only in bruising it.

"Let me out," Father Lilliman pleaded.

"Not yet," Clara said softly.

"How dare you defy a man—" Father Lilliman threatened.

"Did you threaten Isabella like that?" Clara asked, referring to the name of the victim.

The other side was eerily quiet, and if it were not for the rapid heart rate, she might have wondered if he died. That name had been banished to his subconscious long ago, along with many other dark secrets. Still, such sins were never truly absolved, not if one kept the truth hidden away from the light of God.

"How do you know that name?" Father Lilliman said.

"The same way I know of Joshua's name," Clara said, referring to the patsy in this sordid tale.

This time the priest choked, as though the air around him were thick as molasses. While he violently cleared his lungs, Clara waited, knowing what line would soon be proclaimed.

"That's impossible. They are both—" Father Lilliman said.

"Dead?" Clara answered, confirming the worst of his fears. "Tell me, *Father*. Was it in this very confessional that you robbed Isabella of her virtue?"

"Lies," Father Lilliman replied.

"Is this where you came?" Clara asked.

"Lies," Father Lilliman hissed.

"Impregnated her?" Clara declared.

"Lies!" Father Lilliman snapped.

"Then choked the life out of her three months later when she confessed to you that she was with child," Clara said.

"That never happened—" Father Lilliman said.

"Oh, that's right," Clara said. "That happened in the rectory. You even called her a filthy whore for temping you in the first place."

The silence was deafening, a sign that those words hit home. Had he been wise, this man could have thrown himself at her mercy and accepted that confession was good for the soul. However, she suspected that killing a girl and framing a socially awkward altar boy for the crime were indicative of his true nature.

"Lies!" Father Lilliman yelled as his hands tore through the screen.

Clara never flinched. Expecting his attack, Clara turned pale and translucent, to the point of resembling a disembodied soul. She hated this particular form, because it left her feeling like death, but it sure did come in handy.

When those murderous hands passed right through her, they immediately turned his skin to gooseflesh. Clara smiled, a sickly sort that implied that getting out of this situation would require more than a simple case of murder. Heck, he was not even able to talk his way out of it.

"How?" Father Lilliman asked.

Clara was not about to have this discussion with him. Besides, a man so heavily indoctrinated into his version of the *one truth* was ill prepared to accept any other. His mind would simply reject the truth and replace it with a lie that was easier to deal with, namely that she was some sort of witch, one they would need to purge, just like so many women before her.

"So why did you keep them?" Clara asked.

"Keep?" The priest asked.

"You kept her bloodied panties," Clara said bluntly, "in that little jewellery chest, you have. Beneath the silk pillow, the one you use to prop up your rosary…"

His breathing became shallow and fast, while his heart raced with fear. Clara was not particularly bothered; she was not going to break her vows as a hunter. While she would never take a human life, no matter how guilty, the potential to nudge Fate in her favour was still in play.

"Not going to confess your sins?" Clara said. "Fair enough."

With those words, the temperature in the confessional plummeted. Soon, his breath condensed in the air, and the outer walls became covered in frost. Clara did not seem bothered by it. In fact, that had all been part of the plan.

"I think it's time for you two to get reacquainted," Clara said before opening the door and slipping outside.

On the other side, there was an unearthly glow, one that reminded her vaguely of a moon glade's glow with a tinge of green. Clara maintained her ethereal form and allowed her wings to expand to their full size.

"God that feels good," Clara said.

She then buried all of those feelings associated with this form, especially the cold. As-is, she not only appeared to be a disembodied soul, she was also able to communicate with them.

"He's all yours," Clara said to Isabella, the youthful looking soul with a crushed larynx, and bloodshot eyes.

The spirit smiled, a sadistic little smile that hinted at the horrors that would soon be wrought on the guilty. Silently, it glided into the confessional, and the door slammed shut behind it. This time, the frost crept over Clara's side of the confessional until it looked to be nothing more than an elaborate ice structure.

The priest was sure to scream in horror, but alas there was no one here that would sympathise. Isabella needed closure, and that man was in dire need of a reckoning. Clara was happy to put those new found talents to good use.

In the background, the lit candles dulled in intensity and stopped flickering. Freezing time for an entire location was still a bit beyond her ability, nevertheless, she sensed that there was nothing to worry about.

"We keep running into one another," Clara said, seemingly to no one in particular.

"Death tends to follow you," Eleanor said.

Eleanor slipped out of thin air as though she had stepped through a curtain. Once more, the raven-haired beauty wore a long white gown, whereas Clara was more appropriately dressed for a funeral.

"So, you've been following me a while?" Clara asked on a hunch.

"I was present when your mother died," Eleanor said casually.

The idea of being so close to an angel of death at such a young age left her cold and numb. The veil between life and death was thin. Still, this truth forced her to wonder if those early exposures created a link between both worlds. *Is that why I've never feared death?*

"So..." Clara said. "Why couldn't I see you?"

"We are normally invisible to the living. Very few people are capable of even sensing our presence," Eleanor replied before smiling.

"That is, until we are about to die?" Clara asked.

"Precisely," Eleanor replied. "That is when the barrier between life and death is thinnest."

"So why are we having these pleasant chats?" Clara asked, even though the answer was fairly obvious in hindsight. "I doubt I'm on your list."

"No," Eleanor said with a chuckle. "I think you know why."

Clara furrowed her brow before adopting a shit-eating grin. If there was one thing she enjoyed, it was a challenge.

"You were there when Victoria died?" Clara asked.

"Of course," Eleanor said.

"And yet, I could not see you," Clara said.

"You were not ready," Eleanor said.

That implied something had changed since then, but she had to be careful. It was a snap to dismiss any single event as inconsequential. Still, she thought back to something Eleanor had said back at the club.

"I had yet to embrace that aspect of myself?" Clara guessed.

"Somewhat," Eleanor said. "Have you known other angels to possess these newfound abilities of yours?"

"Well... no," Clara said. "Not even the natural born who are always functioning in an accelerated state."

Clara shivered, certain that living in a world perpetually in slow motion would be her idea of Hell. Doing so selectively was hard enough at times, especially if there was a need to conceal the fact.

"Hecate exhibited these traits," Clara said.

"Did she?" Eleanor asked, although her tone implied that this was an answer more than a question.

"That's why you warned me about attacking you?" Clara asked.

Eleanor nodded before saying, "You would most likely have felt compelled to guide souls."

"I tend to be more on the soul releasing side of the equation," Clara said with a smirk.

"You don't say?" Eleanor said before falling into a deep chuckle.

"So, what brings you here?" Clara asked.

Eleanor turned to face the confessional before returning her gaze to Clara. Unsurprisingly, it seemed that her meddling ended up with real-life repercussions.

"Thanks to you, two souls are now at peace," Eleanor said.

"Glad I could help," Clara replied. "What about the priest?"

"Oh, I expect he will need my guidance soon," Eleanor said. "I've rarely seen souls call out to me so long after their death."

Clara guessed that souls who were not ready shortly after death were often trapped in the mortal realm. That meant that those like Eleanor were witnesses and could not interfere, forced to keep an eye on souls, so tortured and twisted, they became a blight on this world.

"Again," Clara said with a smile, "I'm just glad to be of help."

"I feel like I owe you one," Eleanor said.

"Surely not," Clara said. "I owe you for getting that man to pick up the satchel charge."

"Actually," Eleanor said. "He was looking for release, and you gave him the opportunity to leave this world on his own terms."

Clara had seen it in the man's eyes. Years of being beaten, tortured, starved, and nearly driven to the brink of death. Many would have begged for the sweet release.

"He recognised you," Clara stated.

Eleanor nodded before replying, "Yes. One of my lost souls that I have been keeping an eye on for some time."

That explained why the dam had blown so effectively. Clara had planned to drop the charge into the water. Her hope had been that it would not be sucked into a water intake, be destroyed prior to detonation nor travel harmlessly past the system. It seemed that this man, with Eleanor's help, had delivered the charge to the structure's weakest point.

"Still. Why would you owe me anything? To me, it looks like I owe you," Clara asked.

"The why is not particularly important," Eleanor said while ignoring the second part of Clara's statement. "Feelings rarely need reasons to be; they just are."

"True," Clara said, even though she had spent so much time ignoring hers that she questioned the validity of that statement.

"You should retrace your steps," Eleanor said.

"Pardon?" Clara asked.

"Retrace the steps you took in life," Eleanor said. "You may find what you are looking for."

Clara cocked her head to the side as those words sunk in. How in the world did Eleanor manage to know what Clara sought? She doubted that this angel of death had Evelyn on speed dial.

"What do—" Clara said.

As those words rang out into the church, Clara realised she was alone. Not only was Eleanor gone, but there were no other heartbeats within this sanctum. Isabella must have had a pretty compelling chat with the *good* Father.

"Looks like Eleanor is going to be working overtime tonight," Clara said as she walked out of the church.

\* \* \* \*

**Four months later...**

The blinding light forced Julia to squint. While the sunlight warmed her face, she was reminded of how long it had been since she basked in the sun.

"Get a move on," a guard barked.

Julia complied, fearful they would drag her back inside. The call of the wild was growing by the hour, and being locked up in a fortress of concrete and steel would complicate matters.

The doors slammed shut behind her, but she dared not look back, let alone give them the finger like she wanted. To calm down, she closed her eyes and basked in the sun's glory.

"Miss Black," a feminine voice said.

Julia waited for her eyes to adjust. At first, there was an elongated silhouette shimmering in the heat. However, the shape and colour gained fidelity over time until she made out a well-dressed woman standing beside a black car with tinted windows.

"Oh great, the high-priced lawyer," Julia muttered.

Even in blistering summer heat, Vivian was dressed smartly in an expensive wool suit. She appeared to be immune from the sun's unwavering onslaught. In contrast, a bead of sweat was already rolling down Julia's forehead.

"Yes?" Julia said while squinting to avoid using her name.

The lawyer's demeanour did not change. She approached, those high heels kicking up dust. There was a black backpack in her hand that appeared to be new. *It's like she just bought it at the store.*

"I apologise for taking so long to secure your release," Vivian said.

"I told you to leave me alone," Julia hissed.

The lawyer bit her lower lip while checking out Julia's attire. Every item in her outfit was *new* to her. These were the only things that fit her from the donation box. She wore a pair of faded jeans that were rolled up because they were too long, a plain grey t-shirt, and a dark-green windbreaker that was two sizes too big. *I'm wearing everything I own.*

"I don't follow directions from you, Miss Black," Vivian said. "My client wished to see you released, and *we* went through a great deal of trouble to make it happen."

Julia furrowed her brows and huffed. This whole situation reeked of freshly exuded cow patties. No one ever gave a fuck about her. *So, why start now?*

"You still can't tell me who your client is?" Julia asked. "Can you?"

"I am not—" Vivian said.

"—at liberty to say," Julia finished.

"However, they wanted you to have this," Vivian said and brought the bag forward.

Julia looked over the backpack as though it were brimming with explosives. It was not in her nature to trust the system, and this lawyer was little more than an interchangeable cog. Just like the police officers who arrested her, the judge who sent her here, and the guards who gleefully spread their misery and jeer to the inmates within.

"What's in it?" Julia asked.

"If I had to *guess*?" Vivian said. "Passport, driver's licence, money in various currencies—"

"Wait! What?" Julia sputtered.

"—credit cards, burner phones, and a sealed letter addressed to you," Vivian rhymed off mechanically.

Julia grabbed the backpack and was taken aback by the quality of it. Whoever bought the pack and its contents knew that Julia would not be loitering by the pool at a five-star hotel. The red waterproof liner crammed into the bottom-most pocket meant it would go anywhere she went. *Red? Someone is fucking with me?*

"Can we interest you for a ride in the city?" Vivian asked. "It's quite the drive to get here."

Julia focused on the treeline shimmering out in the distance. There was no wind, and the heat was oppressive, but she ached to heed the call. She felt it in her bones that this was the time to surrender to her instincts.

"No," Julia said. "Thank you."

"Very well," Vivian said. "Oh. One last thing…"

"Yes?" Julia asked.

"My client wished me to pass on a message," Vivian said. "*When you feel strong enough, read the letter and join me.*"

"What?" Julia said. "Find whom? How?"

As judged by the smirk on the lawyer's face, this would be their last encounter. Vivian shrugged, turned around, and went back to the waiting car.

Julia shouldered the backpack, adjusted the straps, and set her eyes on the forest. The moon was full tonight, and Julia hoped she would turn for the first time in over a year.

Upon reaching the encroaching forest, Julia said, "I'm home."

# CHAPTER 22

## *BURNING BRIDGES*

**Two weeks after the incident at the church...**

Elizabeth sat at a booth with her nose pointed straight toward her phone. Since she was waiting for an order, she appreciated the ability to kill time without catching the eye of some drunk looking to check off an Asian chick from their bucket list. Alas, her timelines on Bealzabook and Twitcher were mostly static.

"How did I manage before?" Elizabeth muttered while looking at the endless stream of pictures and memes from friends and family.

Everyone was smiling, happy, living without a care in the world. She supposed it was easy to feel that way when the truth remained hidden. With a bit of effort, Elizabeth could find similar pictures on her own profile, but those were from another lifetime.

In frustration, she put her phone down and reached for her cup of coffee. After the first sip, she cringed and added sugar to taper off the bitterness before trying again.

"Better," Elizabeth said before letting out a long sigh.

Just then, her phone vibrated, so she pressed on the lock button and noticed a new icon. Since the icon was unfamiliar, Elizabeth unlocked the phone and tapped on the notification. The photo app came up, and presented her with a shot taken last year.

"On this day... a year already?" Elizabeth asked, knowing the answer, but still needing the time to process the truth.

It was a picture of Clara in the tub, one taken from the bathroom door. Elizabeth had caught her at just the right moment. Those dark wings were off to the side, granting her a glimpse of her sharp facial features.

There was nothing *risqué* to see, considering the sheer amount of bubbles. The scene was reminiscent of a Hollywood movie, but the reason for that layer of bubbles was not for modesty. If anything, Clara was not shy about her body. *Heck, she even flaunts it.*

"She did it to have fun," Elizabeth whispered while her mind played back the ditty Clara hummed at the time.

"Pretty hot for a grandma," the waitress said while refilling the coffee cup.

"What?" Elizabeth asked, sounding all confused.

"I said she's pretty hot for a grandma," the waitress repeated before a smirk broke out on her face.

Elizabeth knew full well what the waitress had said. To have this breach of trust confirmed pissed her off. Still, Elizabeth had to wonder why that line sounded so familiar.

"Why were you looking at my phone?" Elizabeth asked as a way of voicing her displeasure, while opening the door for a potential apology.

"Truth is," the waitress said, "I've been keeping an eye on you for a while now. But I've never been much of a dingle dangler so…"

"Dingle dangler?" Elizabeth asked before her mind was able to delve further into that vocabulary.

The only reason Elizabeth even knew that expression, or what it meant, was through her interactions with Clara. These days, people were not generally known for insisting on using a phone to talk to others. On the other hand, texting…

Elizabeth put her phone down and turned to face the waitress. Sure, she had been looking at the woman when placing her order, but those had been mere glances. Now it was time for her to get a good look.

To put it mildly, there was nothing noteworthy about her. She was the very definition of average in hips, bust, weight, height, and facial features. This was someone who could melt into crowds, unseen and unheard. The only memorable detail was those steel-grey…

"Clara?" Elizabeth asked.

The waitress smiled, moving a lone finger to her lips to signal Elizabeth to keep quiet. She then snapped her fingers, and the world around them faded and blurred. Everything near the booth took on a sepia tone, as though she were looking at a photo taken with some retro filter.

Beyond the invisible barrier, people carried on, oblivious to what was going on inside. The motions were blurred, lacked detail, and appeared disconnected from reality. It was a bit like looking at an old black and white movie on fast forward.

"Sorry," Clara said as she sat down opposite Elizabeth. "I wanted to make sure we were not overheard."

"You mean Evelyn?" Elizabeth asked.

Clara closed her eyes and two buds grew out of her back. Within seconds, the buds expanded and gained detail until they morphed into her wings. All the while, her defining features asserted themselves, a metamorphosis that replaced the mundane with the spectacular.

"How did you find out?" Clara asked.

"The truth sort of came out during my final moments in the mine," Elizabeth said.

"Still—" Clara began.

"Stop it," Elizabeth interrupted.

Elizabeth leaned back into the booth and crossed her arms. The narrowed eyes and non-existent smile were clues the time for idle chit-chat was over.

"I… was keeping my distance," Clara said softly.

Upon hearing those words, Elizabeth cocked a brow. That much was obvious. What she wanted were the reasons, and that turned out to be the hardest part for Clara to deal with.

"Well... for one," Clara said. "I figured the constabulary would be on the lookout for me. Especially after that fight outside your place and the altercation at the dam."

The reference to the apartment being *hers* bothered Elizabeth. Sure, she had been living there well before Clara showed up, but over the short time they were together, Clara managed to introduce several personal touches... mainly in the kitchen.

"Go on," Elizabeth said calmly.

"You know," Clara said, "I saw that you pulled Julia out of the water."

"Really?" Elizabeth asked. "You didn't think to swoop in and lend a hand?"

"I did," Clara said, "but you didn't *need* my help."

"What exactly is your definition of help?" Elizabeth said. "Because it sure as *fuck* didn't feel like I had everything under control."

Clara was not biting. She replied, "Had I swept down to save you, we would have been right back at square one... except—"

"Except?" Elizabeth asked.

Elizabeth's mind ran over the scenario. She wanted to be mad at Clara for bailing out on her, but the first couple of reasons made sense. Their relationship had been defined by their initial encounter, one that imposed an imbalance of power that proved difficult to overcome.

"This time, I'm certain that I love you," Clara said. "Sadly, I realised this after I betrayed you."

Elizabeth stopped breathing for a moment as those three magical words sunk in. She might have leapt for joy, had Clara not followed through with that bludgeon of a statement. *How have you betrayed me?*

Why would she betray her? Especially when they were not actually a couple. Normally, she would have found this line of questioning preposterous. Then again, how often did one feel betrayed by their moral compass? *Like I did...*

"Evelyn?" Elizabeth guessed.

Clara nodded and replied, "She was there to fulfil a need, one that she likely engineered. Still, it was ultimately my call, my sin, and the real reason I've been staying away."

So, Evelyn had played them both. To what end? Elizabeth suspected that neither grasped the scope of such a colossal mind fuck. Well... other than just because it could be done.

"I forgive you," Elizabeth said.

"You have a big heart," Clara said.

"And an empty bed," Elizabeth said, although the delivery fell flat.

Clara chuckled and smiled meekly, an indication that she was not buying Elizabeth's saint-like ability to forgive. Not a Herculean feat mind you, not when the one who forgave was not entirely convinced of it.

"I'd like to believe that," Clara said. "Take you in my arms and forget for a moment that the world is as fucked up as it is."

"So that means you are leaving?" Elizabeth confirmed.

Once again, Clara nodded but her eyes were shimmering in the light. Elizabeth was getting a glimpse of her true self, more than was normally permitted. Then it all changed in a snap. The eyes dried up, and her quivering lips were replaced with a warm smile that made her face glow.

"I miss you," Clara said just as she reverted to that stone wall of a persona. "I really do, but you need some time to think about how you want to move forward."

Clara raised her hand in the air to stop Elizabeth from interrupting. There was a desire to let those words have an impact, although, it would take weeks to really come to terms with tonight's bombshell.

"Meanwhile, I've been given the most obscure clue to follow," Clara said. "Who knows where it will lead? Still, a general direction is better than nothing at all."

Elizabeth suspected that Clara was putting on a mask to ease this part of their *chat*. There was a lot to say, and betrayal only complicated matters, especially, when the puppeteer was factored into the equation.

"How will I be able to reach you?" Elizabeth asked.

Clara smirked before answering, "You already have all you need to reach me."

"Talk about cryptic," Elizabeth said.

"I know," Clara repeated with a snicker. "It must be a trait that I inherited from my inner goddess."

"Not *helping*," Elizabeth said.

"I know," Clara said before sticking out her tongue. "Do you think Evelyn is still listening?"

It took a while for Elizabeth to realise what was being asked. Clara's mind could veer suddenly onto another subject with little to no notice. That trait was often associated with a brilliant or overactive mind.

Once Elizabeth clued in, she answered, "How can I tell?"

"You probably can't if they are just eavesdropping," Clara said. "At least, if I remember my lectures correctly."

"So, what do I do?" Elizabeth asked.

"Do you still trust me?" Clara asked honestly.

"Yes," Elizabeth said without hesitation.

Clara got up from behind the booth and walked over to Elizabeth. This was one of the rare situations where her friend towered over her. Somehow it never failed to put a smile on her lips.

"I have to warn you," Clara said. "You'll have a nasty headache, and after you recover, I'll be gone."

"I can live with a headache," Elizabeth said while attempting to hide her disappointment for the latter.

"Thanks," Clara said.

Clara then placed a hand against Elizabeth's forehead. While her hand did not feel warm to the touch, there was a current that flowed through the contact points.

Without waiting, Clara began to recite something in Latin. At first, Elizabeth did not feel a thing, but as they progressed, a headache built up in the dead centre of her forehead. Eventually, it grew so powerful that she closed her eyes, all in an attempt to shut out the light.

"Ouch!" Elizabeth yelled.

That's when she realised that she was surrounded by the hustle and bustle of the diner. After a bit of controlled breathing, she opened her eyes to let in a sliver of light. While the headache lingered, the light no longer aggravated the pain. She opened her eyes to get a view of her surroundings.

"There you are," the waitress from earlier said. "I'll go fetch your order. I thought you went to the bathroom and didn't want your meal to get cold."

"T-Thank you," Elizabeth said. "How long was I out?"

The waitress did not seem to be particularly bothered by the question. She looked up at the clock and towards the ceiling before returning those pale-blue eyes towards Elizabeth.

"About five minutes, give or take a couple," the waitress said. Once she noticed that Elizabeth was rubbing her forehead, she asked, "Want anything for that?"

"Yes," Elizabeth replied. "Thank you."

"Coming right up!" The waitress said before making her way to the kitchen.

When the waitress disappeared through those double-hinged doors, Elizabeth said, "It sure as hell felt longer than five minutes…"

\* \* \* \*

Evelyn sat comfortably in her chair, the one with padded leather that long ago formed to the curves of her body. Like most of her wardrobe, this chair fit her like a glove, although fashion had not played a part in her choice of furniture.

Marc was at her side, staring intently into the fire. He was tight lipped on most subjects, more so when it came to the subject of his life before they met.

Evelyn knew full-well that he had seen war, personally experienced the devastation that accompanied those who served as the king's gauntlet. She even suspected that he preferred the blood-soaked battlefields and the company of common soldiers over being in his father's shadow.

That was a trait they both shared: a complex relationship with their fathers. She often wondered if Marc had also taken an active interest in ensuring that his father met a gruesome death?

She reached for the glass of wine at her side. With the glass firmly in her hands, she swirled around the contents. The act of doing so kept her grounded in the land of the living. It was easy for their kind to forget where they came from, even easier to conclude that humans were either vermin or the enemy. Evelyn drew parallels with their kind, since they were all flawed creatures who struggled daily to avoid leaving this world alone. Humans simply lived it out on a significantly reduced timescale.

When she moved the glass to her lips, a flash of pain enveloped her. Despite closing her eyes, Evelyn saw bright flashes of white in her eyes. The effect went out like a flash bulb but left behind hundreds of little bolts of lightning that ran throughout her vision. The muscles in her jaw bulged, and she tightened her grip around the glass until it shattered.

"*Merde!*" Evelyn yelled.

After the pain subsided, Evelyn opened her eyes and found Marc beside her. She smiled meekly and opened her hand enough to get a good view of the injury. A large piece of lead crystal was lodged in her palm. Without much thought, she slowed down the bleeding before removing the shard. Once gone, Evelyn focused further until the wound was healed.

Sensing that Marc was not going to go away, she looked up and said, "I'm fine, *mon cher.*"

Despite there being no exchange of words, she knew that he was sceptical. The man had seen her walk out a bloodbath no worse for wear. After all, their kind had spent centuries developing her ability to disconnect mind from body.

"I'm fine… really," Evelyn said. "I think our winged friend found out that I've been snooping."

"I've never heard of such a bond being broken," Marc said to break the silence.

His words were cold and emotionless. Still, speaking at all left her to believe that he really cared for her well-being.

"I thought so too," Evelyn said. "Still, I can't feel Elizabeth's presence anymore."

"You are fortunate that breaking the bond didn't shatter your mind," Marc said.

"I'm pretty sure that part was intentional," Evelyn said.

"Oh?" Marc asked.

Evelyn nodded before replying, "*Mon cher*, had Clara been inclined, she could have severed the link directly from the source… by freeing me of my head."

"So, this was a message?" Marc confirmed.

"Of sorts," Evelyn guessed. "Stop meddling, but you'll be held to account if anything happens to Elizabeth."

"So, Clara is leaving?" Marc asked.

"I think so," Evelyn said. "About time, too."

Evelyn had devoted a lot of her time to reaching this point. Clara was a loose cannon, and while a powerful ally, it was important to keep her pointed in a safe direction.

Despite external interference, it seemed that her overall plan had borne fruit. She would have preferred that they remained unaware of the interference, but one did not always get all they wanted.

"You think Clara got her attention?" Marc asked.

The question was telling in several ways. For one, it implied that Marc was no longer concerned about Evelyn's well-being. The clarity in her words managed to convince him to shift his focus on to business. Besides, Marc was not known for worrying over minor details that would resolve themselves.

"Her influence over this city has been significantly weakened," Evelyn said. "I'm pretty sure that was the equivalent of sending a shot across the bow."

"More like slapping her across the jaw with a gauntlet," Marc said.

The attempt at humour led Evelyn to question what she heard. The delivery had failed utterly, but there was something about those words that implied a degree of levity. *That sounded just like something Clara would say.*

"Either way," Evelyn said, "she won't let this stand."

"Do you think she will try to come after us?" Marc asked.

"*Mon cher*," Evelyn said, "you were the strategist. So, what would you do?"

Marc did not immediately answer, leaving her to wonder if he regressed to his normal quiet state or was busy considering his options. While she suspected it was the latter, Evelyn used this opportunity to review how her plan played out.

"I'd meet my enemy on the battlefield," Marc said. "However, I'd also dispatch a small team to distract and demoralise the opponent."

"So, being hard to find would be advantageous?" Evelyn said.

"I'd say so," Marc said.

"Well then," Evelyn said before a smile formed upon her lips. "I think it's time we revisit some of our old haunts."

Marc nodded and silently walked out of the room. His silence was proof that he agreed and would get things started. There was a lot to do, including laying traps for any would be trespassers.

Evelyn was not worried about the move. While they had been here a few centuries, the city would function without them. What bothered her was that Clara was still very much on her mind. Normally, she haunted the minds of friends and foes alike, not the other way around.

"Damn you," Evelyn muttered, while wishing Clara a long and successful life.

What a shame that the angel could no longer be tracked. Things had worked beautifully in the beginning; cell phones and credit purchases were invaluable to keep an eye on the situation. Those tools had been used extensively to confirm they were not being double crossed.

Ever since the incident at the dam, Clara had gone silent. Evidently, she must have learned a great deal in her short time here and tapped into residual Tower resources to gain financial independence.

"Smart," Evelyn said. "Sexy, too," she added before that trademark smile fell upon her lips.

# LEXICON

| | |
|---|---|
| **A Snap** | Something which is quick or easy. |
| **Ab-so-lute-ly** | Agreement in the affirmative. |
| **Absent Treatment** | Dancing with bashful partner. |
| **Airtight** | Someone who is extremely desirable or attractive. |
| **Attaboy** | A congratulatory statement. |
| **Balled Up** | Confused and/or messed up. |
| **Baloney** | Complete nonsense. |
| **Baby** | Another word for sweetheart. Can also be used to denote something of high value or respect. |
| **Baby Vamp** | A woman considered attractive or popular. |
| **Bank's Closed** | Not interested in kissing or fooling around. |
| **Barneymugging** | Euphemism for sex. |
| **Beat It** | Another word to go away. |
| **Batty** | Driving someone crazy. |
| **Bee's Knees** | Excellent or very high quality. |
| **Berries** | Someone attractive or pleasing, or another word for great. |

| | |
|---|---|
| **Berry Path** | Euphemism for a woman's genital area. |
| **Betty** | An attractive woman. |
| **Billboard** | A flashy man or woman. |
| **Bimbo** | Slang for a tough guy. |
| **Bingo** | Used to express satisfaction at a sudden positive outcome. |
| **Bird** | A term for odd or strange which applies to either gender. |
| **Bird Cage** | Elevator car. |
| **Biscuit** | A pettable flapper. |
| **Black Tuesday** | Also known as the Great Crash of 1929. |
| **Blower** | Slang for the telephone. |
| **Blowhard** | A braggart and/or a bully. |
| **Bootleg** | Alcohol that has been illegally produced. |
| **Bronx Cheer** | Loud sputtering noise to show disapproval. Also known as a raspberry. |
| **Bub** | Often used as an insolent term of address. |
| **Bull** | Slang referring to a police officer or another branch of law enforcement. |

| | |
|---|---|
| **Bump in the Night** | Unexplained and frightening noises at night, purportedly caused by ghosts. |
| **Bumped Off** | To have someone killed. |
| **Bum's Rush** | To be forcibly removed from an establishment or locale. |
| **Cable** | Message sent by telegraph. |
| **Cash** | Euphemism for a kiss. |
| **Caper** | A criminal act which normally involves an elaborate plan. |
| **Cat's Meow** | An excellent person or thing. |
| **Chassis** | Slang referring to the female form. |
| **Cheque** | Euphemism for saving a kiss for later. |
| **Chippy** | A woman who is the polar opposite of frigid. |
| **Clip-Joint** | A dance club filled with rich or sophisticated patrons. |
| **Coffin Varnish** | Moonshine. |
| **Cool His Heels** | Forced to wait. |
| **Copacetic** | That which is wonderful, fine or alright. |
| **Cupid's Bow** | The way a flapper uses lipstick to make the bow more prominent, while their lips appear smaller. |
| **Crashing the Party** | The act of getting into a party in which one was not invited. |

| | |
|---|---|
| **Daddy** | A young woman's boyfriend or lover, especially if he's rich. |
| **Dame** | A lady. |
| **Dapper** | A flapper's father. |
| **Dead Hoofer** | A lousy dancer. |
| **Declaration of Independence** | A divorce. |
| **Di Mi** | Dear me. |
| **Dimbox** | Slang for a taxi cab. |
| **Dingle Dangler** | Someone who insists on calling. |
| **Doll** | An attractive woman. |
| **Doozie** | Something that is hard to comprehend. |
| **Dough** | Slang for money. |
| **Drugstore Cowboy** | A man who tries to pick up women on a street corner. |
| **Dumb Dora** | A woman who is considered lacking in intellectual prowess. |
| **Ducky** | Great or wonderful. Can be used sarcastically to imply the opposite. |
| **Edge** | A term applied to the feeling of intoxication. |
| **Electric Cure** | As in, electric chair; a way to end a problem for good. |

| | |
|---|---|
| **Face Stretcher** | An older woman who adopts youth fashions or wears heavy makeup to conceal her age. |
| **Fancy Smancy** | A derogatory way to refer to something high-class. |
| **Finale Hopper** | Someone who arrives after everything has been paid for. |
| **Fire Extinguisher** | A chaperone. |
| **Flapper** | A stylish, brash, hedonistic young woman with short skirts & shorter hair. |
| **Flat Tyre** | A dull witted, insipid, and disappointing date. |
| **Flivver** | A Ford Model-T or any old car after 1928. |
| **Flour Lover** | Girl who is too liberal with the face powder. |
| **Four-Flusher** | A term applied to cheats, swindlers, and liars. |
| **Gams** | A woman's legs. |
| **Getaway sticks** | A woman's legs. |
| **Giggle Water** | An alcoholic drink. |
| **Goofy** | To be in love. |
| **Hayburner** | A vehicle that uses a lot of fuel. |
| **Heater** | Slang that is applied to firearms. |

| | |
|---|---|
| **Heebie-Jeebies** | Nervous or anxious. |
| **Helluva** | Alternate pronunciation for hell of a. |
| **Hen Coop** | A term referring to a beauty salon. |
| **High-Hat** | A snub. |
| **Hit on All Sixes** | Going full throttle or all out. |
| **Hoity-Toity** | Marked by an air of assumed importance. |
| **Hole** | Slang for solitary confinement in prison. |
| **Hooch** | Another term for bootleg alcohol. |
| **Hoofer** | Slang for a dancer. |
| **Hoofing** | The act of dancing. |
| **Hoosegow** | Slang for prison. |
| **Horsefeathers** | The equivalent of a modern swear word. |
| **Indoor Aviator** | Also known as an elevator operator. This is a play on the fact that their lives are composed of a series of ups and downs. |
| **It** | Slang for someone with sex appeal. |
| **Jalopy** | An old car or a beater. |
| **Jane** | A term applied to any female. |
| **Juice Joint** | Another name for a speakeasy. |
| **Keen** | Attractive or appealing |

| | |
|---|---|
| **Kick the Gong Around** | Smoking opium. |
| **Killjoy** | A person who spoils other people's fun or enjoyment. |
| **Knee-Duster** | Slang for a skirt. |
| **Kodak Moment** | A memorable moment that one would wish to capture on film. |
| **Mad Money** | Cab fare home if she gets in a fight with her escort. |
| **Make Do** | Working with what one has. |
| **Malarkey** | Talk that is nonsensical. |
| **Middle-Aisle** | The act of getting married; walking down the middle-aisle at church. |
| **Moll** | A gangster's girl. |
| **Mistress Grundy** | A priggish or extremely tight-laced person. |
| **Munitions** | Face powder and rouge. |
| **Mustard Plaster** | Someone who is not wanted and will not leave. |
| **Neck** | The act of kissing with passion. |
| **Nobody Home** | Describes someone who is dumb or dumbfounded. |
| **Nertz** | Used to express disgust, defiance, disapproval or despair. |
| **Nervous Nellie** | Timid or worrisome. |

| | |
|---|---|
| **Off-Time Jive** | To be inappropriate, impolite; to have bad manners. |
| **On the Lam** | Someone who is fleeing from the authorities. |
| **On the Up and Up** | Legitimate and above board. |
| **Ossified** | Someone who is intoxicated. |
| **Palooka** | An average or below average boxer. |
| **Peashooter** | The term for a firearm, normally of smaller calibres. |
| **Petting** | To make out or foreplay. |
| **Petting Party** | A party where young couples make out. |
| **Piece of the Action** | Share of the profits or advantages generated by an activity |
| **Pill** | A person who is generally unlikable. |
| **Poufter** | An effeminate male. |
| **Pushover** | Individuals who are easily convinced or seduced. |
| **Quiff** | A term applied to sexually active females. |
| **Racketeering** | Service offered for a problem that does not actually exist. |
| **Real McCoy** | A term applied to an item that is genuine. |

| | |
|---|---|
| **Ritzy** | Based on the Hotel Ritz; implies elegance. |
| **Rock of Ages** | A middle-aged woman, usually over thirty. |
| **Sap** | Someone who is easily fooled. |
| **Sapphic** | Slang for a lesbian. |
| **Says You** | A reaction of disbelief. |
| **Shell-Shocked** | The term employed during the Great War referring to Post-Traumatic Stress Disorder (PTSD). |
| **Speakeasy** | An illicit drinking establishment dealing in bootleg alcohol. |
| **Spifflicated** | Someone who is intoxicated. |
| **Spiffy** | Something that is elegant or opulent. |
| **Stewbum** | Someone from the dredges or an old drunken hobo. |
| **Sure-Fire** | Will not fail. |
| **Swanky** | A term similar to ritzy. |
| **Talkie** | Original term for movies where actors speak. |
| **Take for a Ride** | The final drive someone will take before they are murdered. |
| **Tapped Out** | Slang used to imply that one has no money. |
| **Tarte** | Slang for a prostitute. |

| | |
|---|---|
| **Tits** | Slang for breasts. |
| **To a Tee** | Something which is made properly or to exact specifications. |
| **Toe-to-Toe** | Being in direct confrontation or opposition. |
| **Torpedo** | A hired gun or enforcer. |
| **Tough** | Too bad. |
| **Townie** | Someone from the city. |
| **On the Up and Up** | Open and honest. |
| **Upchuck** | Slang for the act of vomiting. |
| **Wallflower** | A person who stands apart from others during a dance or party. |
| **Waterworks** | Crying. |
| **What am I, Chopped Liver?** | Frustration or anger at being ignored on a social level. |

# ABOUT EVELYN CHARTRES

Evelyn Chartres is the *nom de plume* for a self-published Canadian author. The writer of five Gothic fantasy novels, Evelyn released her debut novel, *The Portrait*, in 2016, and her latest, *Dark Hearts*, in 2022.

A fan of the phrase live to eat, Evelyn shares her recipes on evelynchartres.com. These recipes have a loose focus on French-Canadian cuisine, which feature deep-dish meat pies, seafood and desserts that are rarely seen outside of *La Belle Province*.

Evelyn is currently living in Halifax, Nova Scotia, and is busy laying the foundations for her next project.

**Follow Evelyn on Facebook**
http://www.facebook.com/theportraitofawoman

**Follow Evelyn on Instagram**
https://www.instagram.com/authorevelynchartres/

**Follow Evelyn on Twitter**
http://twitter.com/EvelynChartres

**Visit Evelyn's Website**
http://evelynchartres.com

# ALSO FROM EVELYN CHARTRES

## THE PORTRAIT

*"A vision from the past becomes a writer's deadly obsession."*

Available below:
http://bit.ly/2PtXvWO

The Portrait is a Gothic fantasy about Victoria Frost, an author who develops an unhealthy obsession for her character. As events unfold, her infatuation sours, forcing Victoria to question her sanity. Is she simply slipping into madness, or is there something else at play?

The Portrait features a mixture of contemporary and historical scenes brought forward as Victoria explores the world of her muse. Using both prose and art, every scene yields a new piece of the puzzle, providing insights on the origins of her character's portrait and its featured model.

Discover how a vision from the past becomes a writer's deadly obsession.

# THE GRAND

*"Even things that go bump in the night need a place to unwind."*

Available below:
http://bit.ly/2DzPqgE

You will find the Grand nestled atop a cliff that overlooks a cursed valley. Surrounded by foreboding mountains, this ritzy French palatial-style hotel is a place where a roaring party's success is measured by its body count. This hotel does not cater to the rich or famous. Instead, its staff and facilities serve a clientele with a more *discerning* palate.

The Grand is a collection of Gothic fantasy stories with an overarching storyline that incorporates supernatural themes. The Roaring Twenties serves as a rich historical, linguistic, and cultural backdrop.

Centred on the victims, each story brings a unique perspective to the hotel, the staff, and their esteemed guests. At the Grand, it is best to remember: even things that go bump in the night need a place to unwind.

# THE VAN HELSING PARADOX

*"A gal has to look out for herself after all."*

Available below:
http://bit.ly/3inTKyT

Clara Grey's parents once said that the world was a dark and dangerous place. There was more truth than fiction in those words. There were things that lurked in the shadows which defied the laws of nature: perversions that fed on the dead, terrorised the living, or escaped the chill touch of the grave.

Clara is a member of the Tower, a religious order of hunters who work outside the confines of the Church. As keepers of the arcane, her order takes an active role in countering such threats. Alas, the life of a hunter can be short, and many go missing before they are ready to serve. So, what does it take to succeed against all odds?

Explore Clara's origin, a child born before the dawn of the twentieth century. Witness her rigorous education, how she faces adversity, and fights in the Great War to become the derringer-wielding flapper she is.

Throughout her tale, keep in mind that no matter the threat, a gal has to look out for herself after all.

# THE VAN HELSING RESURGENCE

*"While the Roaring Twenties are long gone, a heroine's work is never done."*

Available below:
http://bit.ly/2XvgFQF

For ninety years, Clara yearned to take an active role in the mortal realm.

In an attempt to alter the course of history, scientists trigger an experiment with devastating results. The effects are felt not only on Earth, but in other realms as well.

Clara and an echo from her past are sent to Earth to investigate the case of a stolen soul. For this transgression, Heaven could go to war, but they choose to send Clara—and Edith. They fall to Earth, focused on their mission.

Both had been isolated from the mortal realm for generations. In their lifetimes, monsters were on the decline, but learn how much the modern world has changed. While navigating this alien land, will they adapt to their surroundings to fulfil their mission? Or be swallowed up by the evil that lurks in the shadows?

Before reading on, be sure to remember: While the Roaring Twenties are long gone, a heroine's work is never done.

# HIGH WATER MARK

*"When humanity has been driven into the sea, what lurks above the waves?"*

Available below:
http://bit.ly/3CxZXlh

Anna is a humanoid mermaid that spends her days with the local timekeeper until a podmate comes to her with a proposal. They hatch a plan to head out into the watery ruins of humanity in search of lost technology and materials. For a young mermaid living in the dredges of society, the promise of riches from such a find is just too good to pass up.

Armed with nothing more than an old map and some rusty road signs to follow, they are soon reminded that adventure often brings forth more than its fair share of rough waters. Her friend gets captured, leaving Anna alone in a world where mermaids are nowhere near the top of the food chain.

Follow Anna as she makes landfall and learns why her ancestors abandoned the surface. Lost in a world that is perpetually covered in a thick fog, Anna must navigate through what remains above the high-water mark. What will she find? An ally? A foe? Or will she find nothing but death and destruction?

Before reading on, be sure to consider: With humanity driven into the sea, what lurks above the waves?

# DARK HEARTS

*"She may look like the Little Red Riding Hood, but she really is the wolf."*

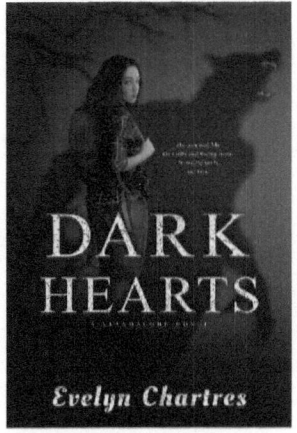

Available below:
http://bit.ly/3pZ211H

Julia is a werewolf who turned against her pack and saved an innocent life. As a reward for her good deed, she ends up in prison, but thrives while others like her waste away.

On the eve of a full moon, an unknown benefactor arranges for Julia's release. Faced with the prospect of returning to the city that nearly killed her, she opts to disappear into the surrounding woods.

This is the opportunity she needs to find herself and reconnect with the wild. As her past resurfaces, the supernatural and dark elements within humanity take notice of her.

Before reading on, be sure to consider: She may look like the Little Red Riding Hood, but she really is the wolf.